SHE SEES YOU. SHE KNOWS YOU. SHE'S BAD LUCK.

Elite EU special forces group KESTREL are on leave when early one morning they receive an urgent summons. One of their own has been involved in an accident — or was it? Taking place virtually simultaneously with two other lethal cases of apparent bad luck, a common thread unites all three victims.

When Captain Greenwood and her team discover that the deaths weren't by chance, they find themselves up against a new and terrifying enemy, directed by a seemingly all-seeing mastermind who already knows exactly who they are, where they're going, and many of their deepest secrets.

Nothing stays hidden forever, and the line between privacy and liberty is razor-thin…

JINX is book three in the KESTREL series, following CHANGER and TOLL.

Each book stands alone, and you can read them in any order — though you may enjoy some additional (but non-essential) references if you've already read the earlier stories.

Matt Gemmell is the author of the KESTREL techno-thrillers series, the continuing flash fiction anthology series Once Upon A Time, and MIDDLESHADE ROAD, a supernatural mystery / horror novel. He has also published several non-fiction books on writing.

He is a former consultant software engineer, and he lives in Edinburgh, Scotland with his wife Lauren, their son Calum, and their labradoodle named Whisky. He can be found on the web at mattgemmell.scot.

For exclusive bonus stories and chapters, plus previews of new novels and more, sign up for his occasional newsletter: mattgemmell.scot/news-jinx

In memory of Nigel Hume.

KESTREL: BOOK THREE

JINX

Matt Gemmell

Prologue

It was a few minutes after 10 PM, and the sprawling modern house on the outskirts of Luxembourg City was silent.

Almost the entire rear side, facing away from the private access road, was made of glass. Had any of the rooms been lit, the building would have been a beacon of light visible from nearby Weiler-la-Tour, Bettembourg, and on such a clear night, even across the border with France.

But the house was in darkness. Its owner was within, but his wife was currently visiting her sister in Strasbourg, some two hours away by car and in a different country. They had no children, and the non-resident domestic staff had been dismissed after dinner as always. The only occupied room was the grand master bedroom, the one portion of the glazed rear elevation with blinds drawn.

Christian Hausemer hadn't expected to find rest very easily after the tense meeting he'd attended that afternoon, but he had nodded off almost as soon as his head hit the pillow, having retired earlier than usual with a mildly upset stomach.

Not only was he already sound asleep, but he would never again wake up.

A sophisticated security system guarded the house and its current occupant. Cameras monitored the interior and exterior, readily capable of detecting the presence of even a field mouse in the pitch black of night. Sensors were installed at intervals along the perimeter walls which bounded the entire grounds, and motion-sensitive lights could illuminate any part of the property when triggered by the slightest movement. Every door and window was secured and monitored, and any breach would automatically summon armed police officers.

Within the building, there were even more cameras, alarms, and miscellaneous surveillance devices, all connected together and run from a central control system which was monitored both offsite and from the house itself. None of these warning mechanisms were currently showing any alert.

The lethal gas was colourless and odourless, and marginally less dense than air. It had accumulated first on the upper floors before drifting down the wide staircase to the entrance hall, family room, cavernous lounge, elegant library and office, dining room, and kitchen. It had not infiltrated the garage, the utility room, or either of the two bathrooms on the ground floor, but it had nonetheless achieved its inevitable effect.

For the past several hours since arriving home, Hausemer's blood chemistry had been undergoing a slow but steady transformation. The metalloprotein that constituted more than ninety-five percent of the dry mass of his red blood cells was being converted to carboxyhaemoglobin; moment by moment, and breath by breath.

In the cool darkness of his bedroom, he thrashed in a brief seizure, only for a few seconds, before crossing the boundary from unconsciousness into a short-lived coma. Before fifteen additional minutes had passed, his ever more languid pulse first stuttered, and then became irregular. The cardiac arrest which followed was undramatic, and it would be very difficult for a coroner to determine whether his ultimate cause of death had been heart failure, or hypoxic brain damage.

The faint sound of night insects was audible through the floor-to-ceiling glass panels beyond the blinds. His now lifeless body lay on its back, with one arm outstretched towards a framed photo of himself and his wife on their wedding day sixteen years and a lifetime ago. On his wrist, there was a fitness band whose sensors dutifully logged its wearer's undetectable heartbeat.

It would be more than seven hours before Hausemer was found by his domestic staff, when he failed to respond to his daily early-morning wake up knock on the bedroom door. When his elderly German housekeeper apologetically entered the room, several minutes would pass before she realised that he was no longer alive. He instead looked like he was sleeping peacefully, his lips cherry red and his cheeks flushed with the appearance of a youthful health and vigour that had long since departed him in life.

To the police, she would describe his countenance in death as *wunderschön* — beautiful — and the attending officers would be compelled to agree, even as they became concerned at the woman's own apparently sudden nausea and dizziness.

For now, though, Hausemer's solitary passing went unremarked. The darkened house was quiet and still, and now devoid of any living occupants. There was a muted click from behind a small door at the end of the upper hallway as the central heating system disengaged for the night.

The house's cameras watched, and its microphones listened, with every window secured and every door locked. Its alarm systems remained silent.

~

It was a few minutes after 10 PM, and the coffee shop would be closing within the hour, but the young woman knew she would only be visiting for five minutes at most.

She was in her late twenties and strikingly beautiful, with natural blonde hair and ice-chip blue eyes. Her build was slim in an athletic way, and her clothes were stylish and immaculate. Her name was not Anna, but that was how she was known to her lover, with whom she'd spoken on the phone only a few hours earlier. The man was much older, and an EU minister of some importance, attached to the European Statistical System Committee here in the capital city of Luxembourg. Its headquarters on Rue Alphonse Weicker was only a short walk from the coffee shop, but the young woman had never gone anywhere near the building.

Her real name was Verusha Lyadova, and it pleased her that her first name meant *faith* in her native Russian. She worked as a customer service representative — also under the guise of Anna — for an executive travel firm a few streets away, where her colleagues believed her to be from Koszalin in Poland. Unbeknownst to them, or to her employer or especially her lover, she was in fact an agent of Directorate S of the *Sluzhba Vneshney Razvedki,* or SVR: the Foreign Intelligence Service of the Russian Federation. Her true place of birth was the far-northern port of Murmansk, the last city founded by the Russian Empire before its collapse in 1917, and her mission directive was as simple as it was inscrutable.

Obtain LANTERN at any cost.

The operation she was conducting had been several years in the making, but now she had very nearly attained her goal. She still didn't know the exact nature of what she sought, but she had long since discovered who had access to it: the man whose mistress she had enthusiastically been for the past eight months. She was in contact with her local SVR handler only intermittently, not only because she was trusted to carry out her task with minimal oversight, but also due to the dangers of her true identity being discovered. Luxembourg City played host to an ever-shifting cast of European Council members, politicians, bureaucratic functionaries, civilian consultants, military personnel, and an impressive array of official and unofficial security staff. Discretion was Lyadova's watchword, and her cover as a married man's secret lover allowed her to take every possible precaution without arousing suspicion.

She had hoped to see him this evening while his wife was in France, but apparently his earlier meeting had been difficult, and he had decided to have an early night due to an upset stomach. She had spoken to him while he was driving home, promising to distract him from his troubles very effectively, but he had apologised and asked her to simply call him in the morning when he would hopefully be feeling better. Then he had told her for the first time ever that he loved her, and she hadn't hesitated for a moment before returning the sentiment, her voice trembling with feigned happiness and surprise. The call had ended with more endearments, and an assurance from the man that he would contact her as soon as he woke up the next day.

Lyadova's lip curled in unconscious distaste as she approached the rightmost end of the coffee shop's counter, where a single disposable cup with an attached lid was already visible. It bore the name *ANNA* on a printed sticker, indicating the order had been placed via the company's smartphone app, to be ready for collection.

She was eager to conclude her mission and be done with the insufferable man. For all his power, he was emotionally needy, prone to bouts of anxiety and depression, and sexually timid and boring. Once she had *LANTERN* in her possession and had achieved what was certain to be the espionage coup of this new century, it would be a relief to never see him again. She had already decided that she would spare him the humiliation of providing his wife with evidence of their so-called affair. Nothing could possibly torture him more cruelly than his own conscience, after all.

Lyadova picked up the cup and nodded to the nearby barista, giving him a bright smile. His name was Adam, he was barely twenty years old, and he knew Anna as a regular customer; indeed, she thought he was probably a little infatuated with her. Such things were always useful.

She popped the lid off the cup as she walked slowly away from the counter, inhaling the rich aroma of the coffee and warm, frothy milk, before taking a large swallow of the liquid with no regard to its temperature. Between her regular job for the travel firm and also co-ordinating the ongoing affair, it had been a long day — but she loved her work.

She smiled, and then a few seconds later, her smile faltered.

The first sign that something was wrong was that her nose suddenly began to run, prompting her to lift her other hand to wipe it. In the time it took to do so, she felt something strange happen to her tongue: beginning at the back of her throat, it tingled and then swelled up. She felt her pulse accelerate in alarm, and when she inhaled she could hear a creaking sound that was accompanied by a scratching sensation in her chest. She swallowed instinctively, and the movement was painful.

Her neck began to itch, and her eyes widened as she saw that her hands had begun to shake. Her eyelids felt heavy and tight, and lightheadedness arrived simultaneously with a cramping sensation in her abdomen.

The coffee cup fell from her grip, splattering hot liquid all across the floor, and she reached for her small and elegant handbag with trembling fingers even as she fell to her knees. Her vision was darkening around the edges now, and if she could have seen her own reflection, she would have noticed how blue her lips had become despite the smear of gloss she'd applied only half an hour earlier.

She tore the flap of her handbag open, searching for the single object that now filled whatever remained of her consciousness, her possessions clattering to the floor to be soaked by the puddle of milky coffee. Her thoughts had become fuzzy, and she was dimly aware that her heart rate had suddenly dropped significantly.

It was no use. The device was nowhere to be found, even though she'd checked it was there before she left her apartment this morning, just like every other morning since she was a girl at high school.

She scrabbled blindly now, her fingers stained by her forgotten beverage and trailing over her travel card, her keys, her mobile phone, a tampon, a tube of lip gloss, and other miscellaneous items which had no hope of saving her. And then her fingers stilled, just as Adam's hand fell upon her shoulder, his panicked enquiries barely registering in her ears.

Verusha Lyadova, whose name was not Anna, fell slowly sideways, and she had already stopped breathing before her head struck the scuffed linoleum floor.

~

It was a few minutes after 10 PM, and the sleek black sedan sped north-west on the A4, paying no heed to the various turnoffs signposted for quaintly-named places like Hulsonniaux, Crupet, and Faulx-les-Tombes. Its destination was the Belgian capital city of Brussels, and the estimated remaining travel time was a little over an hour.

The driver's name was Dries Heylen, and he had been in his current role for almost six years. His duties were simple: personal protection and transport of the passenger who sat in the rear of the vehicle, behind a partition that was currently discreetly tinted, but not entirely opaque. Heylen was both skilled and trusted, having served in the Special Forces Group of the Land Component of Belgium's armed forces for a decade before he had applied for and been granted his current posting. There were only the barest traces of grey at his temples, and his compact but muscular body filled the well-tailored black suit he wore every day.

There were exactly three people in Heylen's life that he cared about, and all of them were female. His high school sweetheart and wife of nine years, Lena; their daughter Zurie, who would celebrate her fifth birthday in just a few weeks' time; and the woman who currently occupied the seat directly behind his own.

He didn't know exactly how old she was, but he would have guessed her to be approximately sixty. She was slender, elegant, and always immaculately dressed and coiffured. Her hair was white, she had hazel eyes that nonetheless managed to be steely at all times, and she was independently wealthy — though she had neither the time nor the need to spend her own money. Heylen also strongly suspected that she was the most powerful person he'd ever met. Her intelligence and cunning surrounded her like an aura, and he'd watched military generals, captains of global industry, presidents and prime ministers, and even royalty, all treat her with deference and sometimes even an undercurrent of fear.

Heylen's lips curled upwards into the barest grin. When she travelled, he was invariably with her, but her presence made him practically invisible. He was afforded the barest glance from anyone, before all eyes returned to her. When he'd been in the military he'd lived through more tense encounters than he cared to remember, but the woman sitting behind him had been responsible for her own fair share too — where the lethal ammunition was a few well-chosen words or even just a fierce look, rather than bullets.

His train of thought was interrupted by a soft chime from the car's dashboard, and Heylen's grin became a weary grimace instead. The vehicle was brand new; this was only his sixth outing in it, but he already knew that he hated it. *Technology for its own sake* was how he had described it to his wife the week before, and she had merely smiled and shook her head at his curmudgeonliness.

Strictly speaking, it was a prototype, and one of only a handful of such vehicles. Outwardly, it was a Rolls-Royce Phantom VIII Extended Wheelbase, but inside, it was a radically different machine altogether. Built in the UK despite the company being owned by BMW, the bespoke automobile had been driven no more then fifteen miles in its original form before being taken into the bowels of a transport research laboratory belonging to a Danish company called AIT, and they had disemboweled it before rebuilding something that looked virtually identical, but bore little internal resemblance to its previous self.

The car was a self-charging hybrid now, with an ideal range of nearly seven hundred miles despite its heft, and in electric mode it made more than 600 horsepower at the wheels. The Phantom's legendarily quiet interior was as close to silent as a motor vehicle could be, and a number of defensive measures plus satellite tracking and uplink capabilities had been installed. The centrepiece of the modifications, however, was the autonomous driving and adaptive navigation system, including evasive and escape profiles. Hidden throughout the bodywork, cameras, radar, lidar, and a host of other sensors and imaging systems fed a constant stream of data to a cutting-edge symbiosis of hardware and software, allowing the vehicle to operate entirely without a driver if necessary. And when a driver *was* in control, the system was watching and learning.

Heylen frowned. The curved touchscreen that served as a dashboard displayed a prominent notification message, and even as he read it, he felt the steering twitch in his hand.

CHAUFFEUR ENGAGED.

Sure enough, the car's autonomous mode had activated, which ought to have been impossible without either an explicit input from Heylen himself, or an overriding voice command from his passenger. Neither had taken place.

Heylen released and then grasped the steering wheel once more — the usual procedure to disengage the self-driving function — but there was no change to the dashboard display. The vehicle continued to hurtle smoothly along the A4, keeping perfect lane position and maintaining its speed. Heylen tapped the Disengage button which appeared immediately below the notification, but it likewise had no effect. He felt a flutter of unease in his chest. He tapped the intercom button which connected him with the rear cabin of the car, hearing the familiar gentle electronic tone.

"Excusez-moi," he began, but he didn't have the opportunity to finish the sentence before he was abruptly pressed back into his seat by the brutal force of sudden explosive acceleration. The vehicle's transmission whined beneath him, and his right arm whipped backwards. His hand smashed into the partition, the vari-

able-opacity electro-reactive glass spiderwebbing even as three of Heylen's knuckles fractured on impact.

He ground his teeth together to contain the pain, his soldier's mind rapidly assessing the situation. The road ahead had become a tunnel of strobing highway lights amidst the darkness all around, and he said a silent prayer of thanks that the route was at least straight for the moment. Heylen knew from the AIT briefing that the quadruple electric motor assembly could deliver a barely believable 970 lb-ft of torque at maximum output, a figure which put most heavy-load towing trucks to shame, and he was certain that he was feeling every ounce of it right now.

The car showed no sign of slowing, and he knew that the speed was unsurvivable on a public highway which twisted and turned through the Belgian countryside. The physics of the situation were clear: without radical but controlled deceleration, the vehicle would leave the road at the next bend, no matter how minor. He glanced into the rear view mirror, and for the first time he saw fear reflected in those hazel eyes.

An instant later, another memory from the handover briefing flashed through his mind: there was an emergency mechanical disengagement master switch for the entire electrical and autonomous cluster of systems. It was below the mid-point of the dashboard, just to his right, and he reached for it without any regard to the flare of glassy pain that tore through his hand. There was a panel that detached from the moulding, and then a small metal catch within. As his fingers reached it, he felt his heart drop into his stomach as he saw a sign blur by, indicating an upcoming sharp bend to the right.

Heylen pulled the catch, and the dashboard went dead immediately, the steering loosening in his hands and beginning to twitch. He felt a bead of sweat run down his forehead and he fought to hold the car as steady as possible, tensing his right foot over the chrome brake pedal and applying the gentlest pressure he could manage. The vehicle shuddered, and he backed off the brake immediately, but then he saw the road beginning to curve away only a quarter of a mile ahead. Muttering another prayer under his breath, he applied more pressure to the brake this time, and began to pull the now-heavy wheel in the opposite direction, aiming for what he hoped might be the miracle he sought: an escape lane for goods vehicles whose weight had allowed them to run away in too high a gear for the road's slope downwards into a valley.

"BRACE!" he shouted, instinctively reverting to English according to his training. He was confident he'd be heard despite the sound-muffling privacy measures of the rear cabin, but he had no time to risk another glance in the rear view mirror to check.

The car began to lose speed, but it was still going far too fast. The wheels bumped over the boundary strip of tarmac onto the escape lane, and now Heylen pressed firmly down on the brake pedal, his biceps fighting the big machine's resulting urge to spin out at the rear. If it fishtailed at this speed, it would flip and roll, and then all bets were off. His clenched jaw vibrated with effort, a prominent vein visible on his forehead as he pumped the brakes on and off while wrestling the vehicle back into line each time. With the power-assisted steering gone, it was kicking like a carthorse — and there wasn't very much road left.

The bottom of the escape lane had concrete bollards, each four feet high, in a regular grid pattern designed to catch a big-rig truck that had gone out of control. If the Rolls-Royce hit them, the much lower vehicle would be practically cut in half lengthwise; there would be no chance of survival. The grey bollards loomed like rows of unmarked graves.

At the last moment, Heylen saw the track running slightly off to the side, curving marginally away from the highway above. It was little more than turf and dirt, looking like it perhaps had once served as a turning point for the construction vehicles which had built the escape lane. It wasn't level, but it was clear, and it ran onwards to become a patch of grass that led into a copse of trees. He twisted the wheel in the track's direction, the bollards whipping past in an instant, then immediately set his shoulders to prevent the car's back half from sliding out in the opposite direction.

There was a crash from below as the concrete ended and gave way to packed dirt, and then there was the sound of something snapping off from the chassis when the car bounced up onto the grass. Heylen's pulse jumped up another notch, but the car held its course and ploughed onwards over the grass, losing much more speed than before due to the uneven and much more frictional surface. The trees were still approaching quickly, and he knew there was no more time. He locked his elbows to his sides, clutched the wheel in a death grip, and stood on the brake pedal.

It felt like an earthquake at first, as the car rattled over unseen hillocks in the dark, shuddering as the ceramic brakes burned at their points of contact. Heylen could smell vaporised rubber, but any smoke was carried away far too quickly. The seatbelt cut into his chest, making it difficult to inhale, but he kept his right foot pressed fully down.

The last thing he knew was the sound of glass breaking, a new pressure in his chest, and an almighty crash that seemed to fill his skull.

Almost a minute passed before the rear driver's-side door opened slowly, and it was another thirty seconds before the woman stepped out, shaky on her feet and leaning heavily against the frame.

Her eyes were wide, and her hair was in rare disarray. There was a cut across her forehead and the blood had almost reached her eyebrow, but she was unaware of it. She moved forward to stand beside the driver's door, and when she looked through the window, her fears were confirmed. Heylen looked back at her, his dead eyes open but unseeing. His seatbelt was still on, and the low tree branch that had broken the windscreen had penetrated his chest cavity and pinned him to his seat. The woman opened the door and checked for a pulse, but of course there was none to be found.

Moving again to the open rear door, she reached into the cabin and retrieved her handbag from the footwell, and then she hurried away from the vehicle, heading back towards the highway whose lights were clearly visible. As she went, she retrieved a mobile phone from the bag, pressing the solitary button on its upper right side five times in quick succession before holding the device to her ear. The call connected immediately.

"This is Janne Wuyts," she said, her voice surprisingly steady even as she pressed the fingertips of her free hand against the gash on her forehead. "There's been an accident."

Part 1

Chapter 1

The Aegean Sea was already a glittering blue stretching to the horizon, barely an hour after sunrise.

In a valley running downhill towards the Gulf of Heraklion which lay just to the north, nestled in the middle of the University of Crete Medical School campus sat a nondescript, modern white building that looked like any anonymous office.

If a passer-by were to look more closely, however, the subtle references to Greece's ancient temples would become apparent. The columns stretching to either side of the main entrance, supporting upper-floor walkways leading away in each direction. The tiered seating just outside the doorway, resembling a miniature amphitheatre. The raised outdoor area to the rear, sparsely shaded from the sun and giving a view for miles around, seeming almost to invite the building's inhabitants to make offerings to their gods.

These deities, though, were digital.

The European Union Agency for Cybersecurity, commonly known by its previous acronym ENISA, was headquartered in the Cretan capital city of Heraklion. Created in 2004 under its original name, its overall objective was to improve network and information security in the EU, serving as a centre of expertise to assist the European Commission, the member states, and the business community at large on matters related to security for the good of the EU Internal Market.

Like many such bureaucratic organisations, it also had a lesser known additional function. ENISA was unique amongst the 32 decentralised agencies of the European Union, in that it did not have an indefinite mandate. Indeed, ENISA itself had successfully lobbied in 2016 to close its Heraklion headquarters in favour of its then-ancillary liaison office in Athens, already having moved a large percentage of its staff there.

But other staff remained on the island, and the anonymous-looking Aegean temple to information held another set of offices on two subterranean levels, which would not be moving to the Greek mainland. From these hidden rooms, equally-anonymous technicians, mathematicians, intelligence officers, and seconded military specialists monitored the flow of data through the European Union's telecommunications infrastructure, focusing especially on the patterns of events which emerged from the noise of five hundred million people living out their lives.

The rapid spread of internet access and the explosion of social media, online news, and image and video sharing had given rise to a new type of intelligence-gathering; wholly legal, and subject to little oversight or control: the analysis of public content and internet output on a massive scale. The data was filtered by statistics, actuarial knowledge, and clandestine governmental or military information to detect the rhythms of a society's digital life — and the interruptions to those rhythms which often indicated events of interest to law enforcement, national security apparatus, and even civil planning.

Without eavesdropping or decryption, but instead by using the sciences of human behaviour, likelihoods, and the observed normal distribution of travel, purchases, illness and death, and much more, it was possible to gain insight into unusual occurrences without the need for targeted surveillance and all of its attendant implications of court orders, warrants, and dedicated staffing. Machines — and the fabric of data networks — were both the facilitators of unprecedented freedom of expression and interpersonal connection, and also the means by which to monitor populations indirectly, on a scale never before possible.

Nation states had known for millennia that vigilance was the price of not just prosperity, but also their continued existence, and the arrival of the 21st century had opened a box that could never again be closed without a new dark age: the era of information.

On this particular morning, an intelligence agent who was known to his colleagues only as Yannis, was looking forward to the impending end of his overnight shift.

Sipping a weak coffee by Greek standards, he was typing up a summary of the night's unremarkable activity, his gaze regularly shifting to his computer's on-screen clock. He had less than an hour left before he could go home, sleep for a few hours until noon, and then enjoy four whole days off. His greatest desire was for nothing of particular importance to happen in the next fifty-four minutes. Unfortunately for Yannis, his wish was to be denied.

He felt his heart drop into his stomach as the red-bordered alert dialog appeared on his screen, obscuring everything else he'd been working on. His training immediately took over, and he rose from his seat and hurried to the glass-walled supervisor's office at one side of the open-plan workspace. The man within, who was known as Demetrios, saw Yannis approach and intercepted him in the doorway, then motioned back towards the younger man's desk and accompanied him there immediately.

The entire system, and all of their reports, communiques and so on, were all in English for ease of information-sharing, and so Yannis was perfectly fluent in that language as well as his native Greek — with a solid working grasp of French, Spanish, and German besides. Everyone working in the facility was multilingual as a basic requirement of the job. The alert's message thus posed no challenge to either man's comprehension.

ABERRATION DETECTED.

~

Spread across the city of Brussels, five people were simultaneously startled by the insistent chirping of both their mobile phones and smartwatches. The watches monitored heart rate and movement to ensure that their wearers had noticed the alert, and then silenced the sounds automatically. All five — three men and two women — were already awake and dressed even though it was still almost twenty minutes before 07:00.

On the Rue Ducale, in a spacious third-floor apartment of faded grandeur overlooking the Parc de Bruxelles, Greenwood set aside the cup of tea that served as her breakfast.

Captain Jessica Greenwood was the commanding officer of the elite European Special Tactical Force, Group One — codenamed *KESTREL*. A small and highly secret unit attached to the European Defence Agency, and operating uniquely under the direct authority of the European Security Council, their remit included surveillance, infiltration, extraction, and combat missions throughout the EU and beyond. Her close-knit team was her family, and she was a workaholic, driven by an unshakeable sense of duty and responsibility. She was universally respected by her subordinates and superiors alike.

Greenwood walked out of her kitchen and into the hallway, took her tan leather jacket from its customary place on the leftmost hook, opened her front door, and left without a backwards glance.

Amidst the bustling, winding, narrow streets of the old town of Brussels, La Vieille Ville, in a quirky and somewhat cramped fourth-floor, four-room lodging not too far from the Rue des Bouchers, Dowling completed the fiftieth push-up of his current set and then stood up. He was three storeys above a small bookshop, and his living room window looked out onto rooftops set at every angle; a view he very much enjoyed.

Sergeant Lawrence Dowling, called Larry by everyone he knew, was a formidable sight. He was KESTREL's weapons and explosives specialist, and he was appropriately built like a tank. He stood 6'4" tall, with tattoos on his biceps, and close-cropped, sandy-blonde hair. As Greenwood's second in command, he was very much her brother-in-arms. The big man's soft Welsh accent belied his stature and lethality, and when left to his own devices he was a gentle and good-natured giant, and optimistic to a fault.

Dowling pulled on an XXL-sized patterned shirt that tightly hugged his torso, and picked up his phone. Sending a quick message to the man he'd been dating for several months — a kind-faced and supremely easy-going fireman based here in the city, who was currently on all-night call at his station on the south side — he stepped out onto the narrow landing outside his front door, trying to minimise the creaking of the old wood. As he began to descend the antique staircase, his face wore an eager grin.

Not far to the north, the new town was much less busy than the old at this hour, with comparatively few people moving between its clusters of hotels, eateries, theatres, casinos, cinemas, and everything else associated with nightlife. On the Rue Melsens, Goose glanced around his ultra-modern apartment — or bachelor pad — his gaze skipping over the arty prints on the walls, the videogame consoles beneath the enormous flat-screen television, and the incessantly blinking lights of his broadband modem, wi-fi router, smart thermostat, voice-activated speaker and assistant, and much more. It was a spartan space, spotlessly clean, and it revealed very little about its occupant.

Lieutenant Gerrit Goossens — KESTREL's electronics specialist, driver and pilot, and occasional field medic — was a tall, rangy Dutchman with a shaved head. He was a quiet man; soft-spoken and contemplative, with a deferential manner. After a stint in the Dutch armed forces, he'd become a communications expert for private industry, and was recruited by KESTREL following an encounter a few years earlier. He'd proven to be a flexible and able soldier and a skilled tactician, as well as a tireless thrill-seeker during his leisure time.

Goose pulled his key fob from its magnetic mount near the entryway, knowing the apartment would lock automatically when he left. His phone was already in his pocket, as always. Satisfied that everything was as it should be, he opened the door and slipped out into the morning.

To the north-east of the city lay Evere: suburban and relatively quiet, with streets not unlike those in Amsterdam — but with parking instead of waterways between the rows of compact, immaculate houses. The façades were of short brickwork, only occasionally painted, and always in pale and sensible colours. Within one of them, whose front door was marked with two small potted bay trees, Ramos closed the dishwasher and looked at her wife with an expression that only the other woman could recognise as apologetic.

Corporal Alicia Ramos's slight build, short raven-black hair, and large, dark eyes gave her a fragile look that was extremely misleading. She was KESTREL's surveillance and infiltration specialist, and a markswoman and sniper of unmatched skill. Ramos was inscrutable, sharing very little of herself with her colleagues. She was a keen watcher, and always carried an air of dark humour. Utterly calm and dependable in a crisis, she displayed an efficiency that could border on coldness. She was a valuable ally, and a fierce enemy.

Her wife Mireia knew the demands of Ramos's job well, and never complained when a summons arrived, no matter what hour of the day or night. Mireia's own work was a world away from her spouse's, as a museum curator specialising in Roman-Etruscan artefacts, and she was by far the more outgoing and extroverted of the two. But she understood her wife's need to fight to protect those around her, and she also understood the cost of the secrecy which always surrounded that work. Mireia walked wordlessly out into the front hall, collected Ramos's jacket from the closet there, and held it out. Ramos took the garment and then kissed Mireia, also without a word, before quickly stepping out of the door.

The Canal Bruxelles-Charleroi slashed diagonally through the city from the south-west to the north-east, continuing beyond to eventually connect up with Antwerp. Somewhat north of the centre of Brussels, the canal widened into the Bassin Vergote, bordered on its south-eastern side by a line of converted dockside warehouses between the Allée Verte and the Quai des Armateures, which were now minimalist, loft-style apartments. One floor up from ground level, and with a grand view of the canal, Aldridge stood at a large window holding a half-finished cup of coffee.

Dr. Neil Aldridge was a theoretical particle physicist, and the newest member of KESTREL. He first crossed paths with Greenwood's team in his native Edinburgh, abruptly pulled from the safe world of academia and thrust into a race to save millions of lives. Victory came at great personal cost, and he now pursued his new life with the ceaseless dedication of a man who didn't want to dwell on his memories. Physical training had turned the scientist into a soldier, but discipline was still a work in progress.

Aldridge drained the rest of his coffee in a gulp, carried the cup to the small kitchen area on one side of the open-plan space, and placed it into the sink. He stretched, a frown creasing his forehead momentarily, then he took several strides over to the solid wooden door that led out to the stairwell. He glanced back towards the same window he'd been looking out of, and the cheap coffee table that stood a couple of metres from it. It held an ornament: a small crystal swan. The smooth and elegant line of its neck curved down towards tucked wings, and the barest notion of tail-feathers. It reflected a thousand points of grey light from the window.

His frown returned for a moment, and he sighed. Then he opened the door and left.

Chapter 2

The Royal Library of Belgium was an interlocking series of cuboids of light-yellow stone, studded with dramatic floor-to-ceiling panes above the main entrance, and bordering the Boulevard de l'Empereur on one side and the Jardin du Mont des Arts on the other. It stood on the site of its predecessor institution, in a neighbourhood of Brussels which was dotted with museums. The tourist buses trundled ceaselessly by on the road outside, but their sound was largely muffled within the modern, airy building itself. Its collection extended to more than six million volumes, 700,000 engravings and drawings, 150,000 maps and plans, and over a hundred and fifty kilometres of bookshelves.

The Library was conveniently located within the city, only a twenty-five minute drive from the airport and less than ten minutes from the headquarters of the European Defence Agency. Unbeknownst to its many staff and visitors, the Library also formed the cover — both figuratively and literally — for KESTREL's own headquarters, located in a four-storey subterranean complex accessible from several locations over a three-block radius.

Greenwood was the first to arrive, and she knew that Aldridge would be the last, even though Ramos lived slightly farther away; Ramos's motorcycle more than offset the extra distance. When Greenwood stepped through the subterranean blast door into the topmost level of what Larry Dowling had always called *the bunker*, the time was 06:55. She found herself on the familiar metal balcony which ran around the upper perimeter of an area approximately twenty-five metres squared, and three storeys high. Two criss-crossing walkways stretched across the open void, and there was a further balcony level below, with the ground floor visible beyond. The upper two levels were connected by stairways at their midpoints along one wall. Further below, the fourth level was kept under even higher security, and only a single elevator led to it from a secure room at the rear of Greenwood's office on the third level. She set out along the walkway immediately, and arrived at her destination within a further two minutes.

The conference room was brightly lit, and dominated by a large wooden table surrounded by ergonomic chairs. There was a compact podium with a lectern, and a display screen mounted on the wall at the front of the room. On the wall, there was an insignia made of a silver-coloured metal, circular in general outline, and almost two metres in diameter. It was fashioned in the shape of a ring, containing the silhouette of a bird in flight. Around it lay the twelve stars of the European Union flag. On a small catering table to one side, there was a steaming pot of coffee and a set of six identical navy blue mugs.

Greenwood helped herself to coffee, and over the course of the next few minutes, she watched as first Goose, then Dowling, then Ramos all arrived. It had been three weeks since their trip to Bahrain and the dangerous mission out on the dark waters of the Persian Gulf. After returning to Brussels for a two-day debrief, the entire team had been given mandatory downtime, with an order to remain in the metropolitan area. Everyone looked well-rested now, at least, and she was genuinely pleased to see each of them. They exchanged brief greetings, pointedly not enquiring as to the reason for the early-morning summons.

Taking another sip of coffee, Greenwood frowned. Ordinarily she'd have been briefed en route, but there was no available data on the system regarding a current tasking. Just a priority recall to headquarters for a conference. It was a little unusual, but in this line of work, situations tended to develop rapidly. Once everyone had arrived, all they could do was wait and see.

She felt a familiar blend of emotions at the thought of their fifth and most recently added team member — primarily exasperation, with some barely-acknowledged amusement — but things had changed lately. Greenwood hadn't spoken to Aldridge at all during the last three weeks, ignoring a carefully-innocuous text message on the first evening of their leave. He seemed to understand that she wasn't in the mood to talk, because she hadn't heard from him since.

He had complicated things, and she would be well within her rights to initiate formal disciplinary procedures, except that she'd arguably been at least slightly complicit. An image rose up in her mind.

The ocean looked like it was on fire. The disc of the sun was only halfway above the horizon, and the waves were lit in every shade of gold and orange and red. The breeze filled her nose with the sharp smell of the sea.

Greenwood blinked the memory away, but it returned unbidden. They had probably saved the world as they knew it that day; certainly the developed world, and western civilisation. And then they'd stood on the tarmac of an airfield watching the sun come up, and Aldridge had kissed her.

She huffed, drawing a curious glance from Dowling that she didn't notice.

Greenwood hadn't initiated it, of course, but she also hadn't rejected his approach, even knowing that there was more to it than being caught up in the moment. It was somehow typically Aldridge: either bold or reckless, depending on your standpoint; unpredictable but also completely in character. If she was honest with herself, a part of her had been expecting it. And if she was *absolutely* honest with herself, she... well, she wasn't ready to be absolutely honest with herself yet. She was steadfastly avoiding it, in fact.

Damn him, she thought, feeling the equally familiar anger rising up again. She was his commanding officer, and he had no business crossing that boundary. She told herself that she was still considering how to respond to the incident, but with a few weeks off to think about it, it felt like the time to address it had passed. It would be better for everyone if she just let it go without further remark, chalking it up to the incredible stress of the mission, fatigue, and the fact they'd all nearly died.

And if he's not willing to let it be, then I'll set him straight.

When Aldridge walked through the doorway a few minutes later, four sets of eyes focused on him. Dowling gave his usual easy smile, and both Goose and Ramos nodded in welcome. Greenwood also gave a brief nod in his direction, then went to refill her coffee cup. Aldridge watched her for a moment before turning to look at the other three sitting around the table.

"Is this a meeting about the field uniform policy?" he asked, addressing no-one in particular. "Because I'd like the option to wear shorts when it's warm."

Dowling shook his head without any real disapproval, and Ramos's eyes glinted in what was the closest she usually got to a grin. Greenwood studiously ignored the remark.

"No idea why we're here, mate," Dowling replied cheerfully. "It's usually something a bit more serious, though. I doubt today's any different."

"You're quite correct, Sergeant," came a voice from the doorway.

Janne Wuyts stood there, her narrow and angular face a little more pale than usual. There was a wound dressing on her forehead.

"Director," Greenwood said, with surprise evident in her voice. She stepped forward, but Wuyts waved her off with a single efficient gesture.

"Let's be seated," Wuyts said, and Greenwood and Dowling exchanged a brief look before Greenwood simply nodded and took her place in one of the empty chairs. Aldridge sat down across from her, leaving only Wuyts standing.

Wuyts was the Director of the clandestine offshoot of the European Defence Agency to which KESTREL belonged, and she was Greenwood's direct superior. Slender, elegant, and invariably immaculately turned out, today her white hair was drawn back from her forehead so as not to interfere with the adhesive dressing which stretched more than five centimetres horizontally above her right eye.

Formerly the Minister of Defence for Belgium, she was wealthy and fiercely independent, exceptionally well-connected, and widely feared amongst those who weren't in her favour.

"What happened?" Greenwood asked, and Wuyts at last lowered herself gracefully into the remaining chair at the head of the conference table before clasping her hands on the wooden surface.

"I was involved in a car accident last night en route back to the city," Wuyts replied. "I was fortunate. My driver was killed."

"I'm sorry," Greenwood said immediately. "Heylen was a good man. A loyal soldier."

Wuyts nodded, her face betraying no emotion whatsoever. "He was. I saw no reason to interrupt your leave at the time, but this morning I've received some disturbing news. Are any of you familiar with a man named Christian Hausemer?"

Greenwood thought for a moment, then shook her head, glancing briefly around the table. No-one else recognised the name either. Wuyts nodded as if this answer was expected.

"Hausemer was a minister attached to the Statistical System Committee," she said. "I had an extended meeting with him and his staff yesterday. I was returning from that meeting when my accident took place. This morning I was informed that he's dead."

"Another accident?" Ramos asked, and Wuyts met her gaze calmly.

"A sudden heart attack in his own bed after falling peacefully asleep, according to a preliminary report from the Luxembourg City police," Wuyts replied.

Aldridge raised an eyebrow. "Not a bad way to go, if you have to," he said. Wuyts regarded him for a moment, and Greenwood was about to intervene when Wuyts spoke again.

"Perhaps. Certainly much more pleasant than the acute respiratory distress which killed his mistress at approximately the same time, in a coffee shop in full view of sixteen people."

Dowling gave a low whistle. "Bit much to be a coincidence, there," he said, and Wuyts inclined her head in agreement.

"The mistress was an SVR agent, though Hausemer didn't know it," she continued. "We've been watching her for some time. But we don't believe the Russians were responsible for these events."

"Because she was one of their own?" Goose asked, a note of respectful disbelief colouring his tone. Everyone in the room knew that the SVR wouldn't hesitate to terminate its own agent if it was sufficiently advantageous to do so.

Wuyts was quiet again for several seconds, and when she spoke, her voice was icy. "Because they wouldn't dare make an attempt on my life, Lieutenant."

~

"You said Hausemer died in his sleep, and his mistress died elsewhere. So who found his body? The wife?" Dowling asked.

Greenwood looked expectantly at Wuyts, and she saw the older woman press her lips together in a fine line. *There's something she doesn't want to tell us*, Greenwood thought.

"His housekeeper, a little over one hour ago," Wuyts replied. "She called the police, naturally. Hausemer's wife is in Strasbourg at the moment, and will be informed shortly."

Aldridge frowned, doing the calculation in his head. "We were summoned twenty-five minutes ago. By you,

I assume, Director," — Wuyts nodded, but allowed him to continue — "so you must have been informed of his death virtually as soon as the police had arrived and confirmed it. You weren't just watching the mistress; you were watching the minister too."

Wuyts gave a tight-lipped smile, and Greenwood wished she could kick Aldridge under the table, but they were sitting too far apart. It wasn't a wise idea to make accusations against Janne Wuyts, no matter the circumstances. To her surprise, though, Wuyts's expression relaxed after a moment.

"This part may interest you, Dr. Aldridge," Wuyts said. "In a manner of speaking, I found out about Hausemer's death as a consequence of his own work. Tell me, have any of you heard of ENISA?"

Goose and Ramos both nodded, and Goose was about to speak when Aldridge himself replied. "Cyber-security for the EU," he said. "If you believe the online conspiracy forum nutters, they're actually a secret intelligence outfit for your lot. Or our lot, I suppose."

Wuyts smoothly turned her head to look at Greenwood, and the two women had a silent conversation within the space of a couple of seconds.

He still lacks respect for the chain of command, I see.

He's unconventional, but he's proven his worth.

"You shouldn't believe everything you read," Wuyts said at last, turning to address Aldridge again, "but those *nutters*, as you so tactfully call them, aren't entirely incorrect. Unofficially, ENISA performs an analytical function under the direction of the Statistical System Committee. It detects anomalous events."

"Anomalous?" Ramos asked, her gaze flicking towards Aldridge, but only for a moment. He shifted in his chair.

"You mean mathematically unlikely," Goose said, and Wuyts nodded, gesturing for him to continue. "You're saying that they track what's going on, and perform statistical analysis. Two connected people dying apparently unrelated deaths in different places but at the same time is very unlikely."

"And so the system alerts us very quickly," Wuyts said. "One of the new frontiers of intelligence gathering, and eventually of law enforcement. The project is still under development, but Hausemer was partially responsible for initiating it. His own system warned us that his death may not be as innocuous as it appears."

"When can we expect autopsy results on the bodies?" Greenwood asked, and Wuyts glanced at her wristwatch. Aldridge had mentioned once that the slender timepiece on Wuyts's wrist was worth in excess of a quarter of a million Euros, and Greenwood didn't doubt it for a moment.

"Hausemer's autopsy should be complete within the hour," Wuyts replied. "I ordered it to be conducted immediately. The SVR agent, however, will of course not be examined. Her body has already been claimed by her *father* who just happened to be visiting Luxembourg City last night. The paperwork was completed by 02:00."

Dowling snorted. He famously had little time for the international chess game of espionage. The so-called father would be another SVR agent, ready and waiting at the Russian Embassy in the guise of a consular official. The young woman's body would already be in Moscow by now, and a report issued to the Russian Foreign Intelligence Service headquarters in Yasenevo.

"However," Wuyts continued, "there was little mystery to her death. The attending emergency personnel found a medical alert bracelet, a spilled beverage, and a closed airway."

"Poison?" Dowling asked, but Wuyts shook her head.

"Not generally, but perhaps so from her perspective. She was deathly allergic to soy, hence the bracelet. Interestingly, she placed the drink order online, including an explicit request for soy milk. The server who apparently knew her as a regular customer said it was the first time she'd made that particular order, understandably."

"So you're thinking it was a deliberate act rather than human error," Ramos said. It wasn't a question, and it fit the facts. Someone with a lethal allergy was likely to be very careful about what they ate and drank, and the timing of her lover's death practically eliminated the possibility of it being an unfortunate coincidence. "And your car accident?"

"The autonomous driving mode activated, and couldn't be disengaged. The vehicle accelerated out of control", Wuyts replied. "I'm told that it shouldn't be possible."

Goose frowned. "Given the security measures you have in place, Director, that would be a very tricky bit of sabotage. Less so for the soy milk, perhaps, but still difficult. And there's the question of what exactly killed Hausemer. The timing suggests they're all connected, granted, but there are far easier ways to eliminate people."

Greenwood spoke up before Wuyts could respond. "I think we need to ask the real question here," she said.

To her credit, Wuyts's facial expression didn't alter in the slightest. To Greenwood's eye, the older woman had in fact been expecting what she was about to say. She took the silence as an invitation to continue.

"You said that Hausemer was responsible for the ENISA project's initial stages, implying that he wasn't in charge anymore. You also said that you met with him earlier today, and that his mistress is — was — a Russian spy that you've been watching. The thing that connects all three of you is his work. So what exactly was your meeting about, sir, if I may ask?"

On the day that Greenwood first met Wuyts, the director had made it plain that she preferred to be addressed as *sir* rather than *ma'am*. An explanation had never been offered, but Greenwood believed it was to reinforce that she wouldn't tolerate even the slightest difference in treatment on account of her gender. Greenwood herself had certainly been on the receiving end of a few *ma'ams* during her career that held just a hint of sarcasm. It would be a fool who tried it with Wuyts, though, and Greenwood was fairly sure that the director enjoyed correcting people and seeing their hastily-concealed surprise at the title she insisted upon.

Wuyts locked her eyes on Greenwood now, her hands still clasped on the table top. "Direct as ever, Captain," Wuyts replied. "Good. But this is a sensitive matter, and the amount of information I'm willing to share with you is limited by external factors. What I can tell you is this: I'm certain that I was meant to die last night, and I'm confident that the same unknown party is responsible for all three incidents. I'd like you to investigate, as a priority. The investigation must remain entirely secret, and you'll report to me alone. ENISA has already been briefed to provide whatever assistance they can."

"Without knowing what Hausemer was involved in, and thus what the Russians were after, and thus why anyone would want to kill the three of you?" Aldridge asked skeptically, but Wuyts's gaze remained fixed on Greenwood.

After a moment, she stood up and nodded as if to conclude the briefing, before crossing to the doorway. She opened the door and paused for only a moment, and when she spoke, she didn't turn around.

"Please avoid any unnecessary speculation," she said, just as she stepped out into the hallway. "Some questions are best left unanswered."

~

An hour later, Greenwood was in her office on the third level, using her computer to access all the information she could find on the backgrounds of both Christian

Hausemer, and the SVR agent whose real name had probably been Verusha Lyadova.

There was plentiful information about Hausemer, but to a trained investigator, the gaps were evident. His various public initiatives, appointments, and responsibilities gave the impression of a dedicated Eurocrat whose primary focus was the dry but important area of civil planning — but there were also travel records that periodically didn't dovetail with his official schedule. His name showed up on a large budget request from several years earlier, details redacted, which had been directed to — and approved by — the European Defence Agency. Greenwood guessed that was where Wuyts came into the picture, but the picture itself remained hidden.

As for Lyadova, there was predictably little to go on. She had a cover identity as a Polish national who worked for an executive travel firm in Luxembourg City, but her true origins in Russia were obscure. Greenwood knew that if she was to have any hope of uncovering the true story, it would have to come from sources within the EU.

"She wouldn't be pleased, you know," came the unmistakable Scottish accent from the doorway of her office, and Greenwood just shrugged without taking her eyes off the flat panel display on her desk.

"Because I'm doing my job?" she asked, and she heard Aldridge stepping into the room to take up his increasingly customary spot beside the door. Even without looking up, she knew he'd be leaning back against the doorframe, arms folded, content to wait until he managed to get a rise out of her.

"Because you're trying to find out what she and Hausemer were up to," he replied easily, and now Greenwood did look up at him briefly.

"That *is* doing my job. Wuyts wants answers, and I'll get them for her — but I can't operate entirely in the dark. Whatever they were all involved in, it's wholly germane to the investigation."

Aldridge nodded. "You'll have no argument from me," he said. "Just… might be best to keep it as quiet as you can. She clearly didn't want us to know any more than the bare minimum. Which is very interesting."

"I was doing this job for a while before you came along," Greenwood replied, returning her attention to the computer, but she was distracted and her tone wasn't as sharp as she intended. Then she heard Aldridge clear his throat, and she momentarily lost her train of thought.

"On another topic," he began, "I was thinking we could—"

The chime from her computer that indicated a new email had never been more welcome than now. "It's the coroner's report for Hausemer," she said quickly, opening the email and then the attachment. She scanned the document, and her eyes narrowed.

"And?" Aldridge asked, but Greenwood raised one finger to silence him while she read the rest of the notes. After another few moments, she looked up at him.

"He died of acute carbon monoxide poisoning," she replied. "It seems that the flue for his household boiler was blocked."

"Deliberately?"

"Inconclusive," she said. "Bird nesting materials, it says."

Aldridge scratched his chin. "Anything about the Russian woman?"

Greenwood interacted with her email program for a few seconds, then shook her head. "Just the on-site report from the emergency responders; it confirms anaphylactic shock. Her soy allergy was on file with her local doctor and pharmacy. But the question is—"

"Why she didn't have her epinephrine with her," Aldridge said, completing the thought. Greenwood gave him a quick look of annoyance, then she nodded.

"She definitely had a current prescription. I doubt she would ever have left home without it. So assuming these two people *were* murdered, somebody had to block a flue at Hausemer's home, steal some epinephrine from Lyadova's handbag, and organise to sabotage her online drink order *and* Wuyts's fancy car, all in the same evening. That's a bloody tall order."

Aldridge pushed himself away from the wall, and half-turned to grasp the door handle. "I'll tell the kids to get their coats on. We're going to Luxembourg City."

He was gone before she could reply, leaving Greenwood to quickly lock the screen of her computer and stand up.

"Just occasionally, I'd like to be the one giving the orders," she muttered to the empty room.

Chapter 3

When he heard the sound in his earpiece alerting him to an incoming call, it didn't come as a surprise. His entire career — and life — were predicated on avoiding surprises, after all.

The Artist gently tapped the earpiece twice, and the call connected. The voice on the line, also as expected, was a pleasing one that had become familiar during recent weeks. Almost without any accent whatsoever, he could nevertheless occasionally hear just a hint of what might have been a Celtic origin. He didn't know her real name, but he neither needed nor wanted to.

"Good morning. I have another task for you," she said.

"I understand," he replied, checking the screen of his phone carefully. The call was encrypted and untraceable, just as they always were, but he verified the fact every time regardless. "I'm aware of the disposition of the third item. Be assured that it will be taken care of."

"That won't be necessary," the voice said. *"Wuyts herself is no longer a priority for elimination. The situation has changed."*

The Artist unconsciously raised an eyebrow. It was rare that a client would speak explicitly about the nature of the work he performed or actually name a target, but there was no risk of being overheard here. All the same, he felt a brief stirring of unease. Then she was speaking again.

"Within the European Defence Agency, there exists a covert surveillance, infiltration and combat force operating under the direct authority of the European Security Council. Wuyts is the director of the programme. She has now tasked her preferred group of operatives with investigating the deaths of Hausemer and Lyadova."

He felt his pulse quicken, though not unpleasantly so. Assassinating politicians and foreign intelligence agents was one thing; a trained military force was quite another. It would pose an interesting challenge. "I trust that you can provide me with further information," he said, but he had barely finished the sentence when his phone vibrated in his hand.

"Biographical profiles of all five members of the European Special Tactical Force, Group One — codenamed KESTREL. Expect to encounter them soon. Your target is their attention for now, not their lives. Make sure they notice. I leave the details to you."

"Understood," he said.

"I'll be watching."

It was how she always concluded a briefing, and sure enough the call was terminated a moment later.

The Artist quickly navigated to the phone's call log, which he erased after every conversation. The device was unique to his current client, and would be destroyed when their business was concluded. The log now had a single entry, and his thumb barely paused before he swiped it to the left edge of the screen, where it turned red to indicate deletion and then disappeared.

For a moment, he could still see the afterimage of the solitary word that had been displayed before it vanished into digital oblivion.

JINX.

~

Greenwood's gaze flicked towards the dashboard of the SUV when she heard the familiar soft chime. It meant that a Bluetooth device had connected to the vehicle, and she already knew what was coming next.

"Aldridge..." she began, and the man in question turned around in the front passenger seat wearing an expression of exaggerated innocence.

"It's a long drive," he replied. "We could do with some music, that's all."

Greenwood's withering glare had its usual effect on him, as he completely ignored her warning tone and proceeded to fiddle with his phone's music player app. Goose, who was driving, briefly made eye contact with Greenwood in the rear view mirror, but he didn't say anything.

A moment later, the opening notes of one of Green-wood's absolutely least favourite songs began to play. It was an early-eighties novelty track from an otherwise pretty respectable and well-thought-of stadium rock band from the UK, and it endlessly irritated her how successful the song had been — not just commercially, but also at embedding itself in her consciousness.

So of course Aldridge would choose it, she thought. *The man has an almost supernatural ability to be annoying. Amongst other things.*

She found that she wasn't entirely sure what she meant by the latter remark, but once again the usual image flashed through her mind; the one she always saw when the combination of the two subjects of Aldridge and the unexplained came up: a lightning storm above a gothic cathedral, but the colours were all wrong.

Greenwood blinked the image away, gritting her teeth for a moment as she inwardly debated the relative merits of silently enduring the music, or letting Aldridge know he'd managed to get a rise out of her. Her reserves of patience were already somewhat deplet-ed today, given the abrupt recall from downtime and the disturbing news that someone had tried to kill Wuyts and had succeeded in killing her driver; a stead-fast and loyal man with a wife and a young daughter. Greenwood had already decided to take that particular outrage personally, and when she found out who was responsible, they were going to have a very bad day.

"Shut it off," she said in a clipped voice, and in her peripheral vision she saw Ramos glancing at her briefly.

The other woman was sitting to Greenwood's left, beside Dowling, and Greenwood at least knew that no remark would be forthcoming. Ramos would understand exactly how she was feeling, and would doubtless feel the same way herself.

Aldridge did turn his head slightly but he said nothing as he quickly muted the music playback. There was silence for a few minutes other than the rumble of the road beneath the vehicle's wheels, and then Dowling spoke up.

"Coming up on where it happened, chief," he said.

Greenwood looked out of the windows to the left, and already they could see the long escape lane, and a police cordon down at ground level, at a copse of trees. Wuyts's vehicle had already been removed, of course, and was being analysed by their own people. The Belgian local authorities would never get to see it, and the incident would be quickly written up as a case of mechanical failure, the reports filed quietly, and then the records would vanish after a few weeks.

"Amazing that he managed to keep any kind of control on the way down," Goose said with respect evident in his tone. "And lucky with the escape lane. If the accident was timed precisely, they made a mistake there. Another few hundred metres and it would have been very different."

"Not that it was an accident, of course," Greenwood replied, turning to keep the site of the crash in view as they continued along the road. "And a strange way to make an attempt on someone's life. Very personal. I doubt she'll feel safe in a car for a while."

"The question is how anyone got access to Wuyts's own vehicle," Aldridge mused just as they passed a point opposite the mouth of the escape lane across the central division. "It's never left alone, is it? Or wasn't, I suppose."

"Never," Ramos replied from the centre seat behind him. "Always guarded, usually by Heylen himself. I expect that the technicians responsible for its systems have all been brought in for questioning by now."

Greenwood nodded distractedly. Those involved in refitting the car would all have had the highest security clearance, and she doubted very much that any of them had done anything knowingly wrong. The possibility remained, however, that there was some kind of undetected security vulnerability that had allowed the vehicle's self-driving system to be interfered with. Nobody would be going home until both scenarios had been fully explored.

She frowned. Greenwood strongly disliked impinging on the liberties of civilians in the course of her job; she saw it as antithetical to the entire purpose of her work, which was to protect the people, institutions, and society in general that humanity had collectively built. Infringing upon personal freedoms in order to protect them gave her a queasy feeling in the pit of her stomach, like an almost psychic sense that something had gone fundamentally wrong with the whole system.

But sometimes it's unavoidable, she thought. *Because safety, and defence, and the rule of law are all necessary for individual freedom — and sometimes they have to curtail it in order to preserve it.*

"I expect they'll skip the self-drive package on her next car," Aldridge said, but Greenwood shook her head.

"That's not Wuyts's style," she replied. "She won't be intimidated by this. She'll get her answers, make sure the vulnerability is fixed, and then she'll insist that her new vehicle has the improved system."

Dowling nodded. "She's bloody-minded that way, alright. Stubborn. Good thing she doesn't remind me of anyone else I know."

Greenwood exchanged a faint smile with her second-in-command at the implied accusation, which was a fair comment, but her mind was still on Heylen. Whoever had arranged for all of this clearly had a flair for the unusual and dramatic, and wanted to send some kind of message, or at least draw attention to whatever it was that connected the three intended victims. With Wuyts being evasive on that topic, Greenwood had no choice but to find the threads that bound the three people together, no matter what her orders were. Answers came via truth, and more truth was usually better.

"Hopefully this goes without saying," she began, now looking out of the window adjacent to her at the road rolling by, "but I want to know exactly why Wuyts was targeted, and what the real story is here. Field reports can be as circumspect as she wants them to be, but we're not ignoring any avenue of investigation, no matter who or what it leads us to."

It was Ramos who spoke up first. "Goes without saying," she said, and Greenwood nodded.

"This is the same feeling I used to have after a sneaky cigarette in the toilets at high school," Aldridge mused, drawing the barest trace of a grin from Dowling. "Then some chewing gum before going back to class."

"Your teachers knew what you were up to, Aldridge," Greenwood said, without looking at him. She left the next part unsaid, but everyone heard it nonetheless.

And I expect that Wuyts will too.

~

The road leading to the minister's house was well-maintained, and there was no sign of a police presence until they actually reached the building. A sole patrol vehicle from the *Police Grand-Ducale* sat there, with a single patrolman standing alongside, which was unusual but not unexpected. Wuyts would have requested the bare minimum presence. The fewer people who ever saw Greenwood and her team, the better.

Goose couldn't help but smile at the car. It was a reasonably powerful Volvo, clearly not a dedicated interceptor but very capable, and in the gaudy livery of Luxembourg's national police force which always reminded him more of a rally car than law enforcement. There were splashes of the red and light-blue elongated hexagons which were the backdrop to the force's insignia, and the entire base of the car's bodywork was also red. Goose thought that a few sponsorship logos wouldn't look out of place on the thing, and perhaps an internal roll-cage too. The Luxembourgish people knew how to decorate, and he liked that the flag was almost a duplicate of that of his own country, albeit in lighter tones.

Aldridge, however, wasn't paying attention to the car but rather to the police officer beside it. The man wore an expression that Aldridge was getting used to: curiosity which the officer was nevertheless trying to hide.

As usual, they were welcomed without much inquiry as to their identities or jurisdiction, and there was a certain undercurrent of caution in the way that the man deferred to Greenwood as soon as she stepped out of the vehicle to converse with him. Aldridge watched it all in uncharacteristic silence, and a scene from long ago popped into his mind, surprising him at first.

He had been barely ten years old when his parents had taken him on a long driving holiday around Scotland, winding north through the Cairngorms and then the Highlands, stopping for a day or two here and there. His memories of it consisted of a lot of sitting in the back of a car, and a lot of walking through pine forests and up hills in biting winds, and a lot of small fishing villages with harbours that blurred together into a single one with uncertain geography. Ultimately they'd gone as far north as Thurso, and then boarded the vehicle ferry bound for Orkney. Aldridge vividly remembered how gigantic the vessel had seemed, swallowing up rows of cars and even large trucks and buses. He had roamed its corridors during the voyage, bobbing with the movement of the waves, and he had seen that it was like a floating hotel in places too. He eventually went up on deck and looked down and all around at the hugeness of it, watching the crew going about their business, and his fellow passengers milling around.

When they had reached the arrival port, he and his mother disembarked on foot while his father fetched the car, and at the moment he'd stepped from the gangway onto the dock, a brief but dark feeling had swept over him. It was something about mankind's dominion over the natural world, and of the vast and mostly hidden machine and all of its dependent systems and technologies which had meshed together to allow him to take this single step onto a new shore. An almost absurdly complex combination of effort and ingenuity, to afford a simple and mundane movement.

His young mind hadn't been able to articulate most of those things, of course, but he'd gained a better understanding of the memory as he grew older — and whenever KESTREL benefited from the far-reaching authority of the European Defence Agency, he had the same feeling.

A bit too much power, all implicit in the smallest act.

The police officer had granted Greenwood access to the house without question, no doubt having been given an unambiguous command from on high to do just that. All they'd had to do was drive up and step out of the car. It was convenient and efficient, but its implications sometimes gave Aldridge pause. He pushed the train of thought away when they all started walking towards the impressive entrance of the building.

"I'm going to vote *against* the next pay rise for politicians," Aldridge said instead of anything more profound, as they went through the ornate gate in the perimeter wall and entered a courtyard which would comfortably hold a dozen vehicles.

Dowling emitted a low whistle as they all got their first proper view of the late minister's house, its many glazed surfaces gleaming in the late morning sun. "Now that's a home in the bloody country," he said.

The entrance up ahead was dazzling in its brightness and elementality. Twin columns in the Doric style supported a broad entablature whose frieze bore a single decorative element: a coat of arms, carved into the monochromatic white background just above the double doors.

"I dunno, Larry," Aldridge replied to the Welshman. "I've never been into the late-period Bond-villain aesthetic."

"Let's just remember that a man died here this morning," Greenwood said, keeping her voice low to prevent the patrolman overhearing from his post out beyond the gate. She came to a stop, looking up at the building and then back towards the part of the perimeter wall they could see from the courtyard. "The question is how anyone got in to set it in motion."

Ramos nodded, gesturing towards various points on the wall and the roofline. "There are cameras everywhere, and sensors. This is all expensive equipment. Beyond consumer grade. And the report said his home system was connected to the police directly."

"There were no flags or alerts," Goose added. "The system was never down or disconnected either. It has remote diagnostics, and the security company sent a preliminary assessment while we drove down here. It hasn't been disabled since the day it was installed."

Ramos walked away from the group, going to the far side of the courtyard so she could look down the western extent of the house. She found what she was looking for quickly: a small circular cage-like protrusion from a point high on the side wall, with a black vent behind it. She rejoined the others.

"The flue vent is on the upper floor along there," she said. "They wouldn't need to get inside the building, but they would have to be inside the outer wall. And get up to that level, probably with a ladder."

Greenwood nodded. It was as they'd expected, and they were left with the same questions they'd had when they arrived. "We need to see the footage for last night," she said. The patrolman had given her a key fob which allowed entrance to the house, and there was a secure room where they could view the security system's video and sensor data archive. "Let's go."

"Is the wife back home yet?" Aldridge asked, falling into step beside the other four as they headed for the entrance, and Dowling shook his head.

"They're keeping her away for now," he replied. "Crime scene, and all that. But her lawyer will get her in here within a couple of hours. Not much time for us to check out his CD collection."

"Fifty Euros says there's a lot of opera in there," Aldridge said, and Dowling shook his head a second time.

"No bet, mate."

Greenwood had reached the front doors. She pressed a button on the key fob device, and there was an audible click from the lock mechanism, coupled with a green light illuminating on the video doorbell. She turned the handle on the leftmost door, and the door opened inwards smoothly when she pushed.

Several windows were still wide open, left that way earlier by the police to vent the build-up of carbon monoxide, and there was a light breeze flowing through the large and bright atrium. A few insects had taken the opportunity to stage a minor invasion, and they took flight in alarm at the sight of the new visitors.

"Secure room is through the pantry," Goose said, consulting his phone and then pointing down a hallway that led off to their left. Safes were often kept in pantries because burglars historically had skipped such rooms when searching for valuables, but the practice had become common enough now that the average criminal knew all about it, and thus tended to actually prioritise a pantry in larger homes, after the master bedroom and study. It was just the way things had always been, in an eternal game of cat and mouse. Some wealthy homeowners had built upon the practice by putting entire panic rooms or security centres into hidden rooms accessed via the pantry or kitchen.

Dowling went ahead as usual, opened the pantry door and looked around the surprisingly large space before stepping inside. Aldridge reached the doorway and also looked around, seeing no sign of the entrance they sought, but it took Dowling only moments to locate it. There was a thermostat control panel mounted on the side wall, which Dowling flipped downwards to reveal a keypad. Goose read out a seven digit code from behind him, and when Dowling entered it there was a soft click and an adjacent portion of the same wall swung inwards, the joins concealed by the shelving which lined most of the room. The door itself bore shelves too, making it blend in perfectly, and Dowling had to tip his head slightly to the side to avoid bumping against a rack of tinned goods as he entered the dark space beyond.

Even though there was easily enough space for all five of them, Ramos remained outside, going back to the pantry door and stepping out into the hallway again. Her eyes scanned the area, and she listened carefully, always intent on not being taken by surprise. The house seemed to indeed be empty except for her fellow team members, but she wouldn't let her guard down until they had returned to their vehicle and left the property behind. She already knew that this area was vulnerable, and the most important question now was who had been behind the minister's murder. Ramos had an idea of how to proceed with the investigation, but that could wait until the probably fruitless check of the house's own security footage.

Back inside the secure room, Goose had managed to access the footage archive from the previous day, and was scanning through the exterior camera files at one thousand times normal speed. There was little to see for most of the day, but in the mid-afternoon there was a flash of black. It could have been a playback glitch, and it lasted only half a second, but the Dutchman frowned and wound back the recording, reducing the speed iteratively to home in on the exact timeframe. He had it in a few moments.

"The footage all goes blank for a little over ten minutes, starting at 15:12 yesterday afternoon," he said. He pressed a few buttons, running the footage backwards again. A vehicle was seen leaving the property shortly before the beginning of the blank period.

"That's the housekeeper's car," Dowling said from behind Goose's shoulder. "Does she come back later?"

The footage moved forward again, past the interruption, and the same car returned less than an hour after leaving. Goose switched cameras, and they all watched as the woman carried four plastic bags of groceries into the building.

Greenwood nodded. She was having the same feeling she'd experienced dozens of times during her career, and one she'd learned to trust. Something was very wrong.

"So the house was under surveillance, and they knew the routine," she said. "Whoever it was must have been waiting for the housekeeper to go out. I bet if we checked we'd find that she always went to the supermarket at that time. Roll it back to the blank part again."

Goose did, letting the ten or so minutes of darkness start playing at normal speed. Greenwood realised straight away what was troubling her. "This is a sophisticated security system," she said. "Lots of failsafes and sensors."

Goose nodded, both in response to the implicit question, and also because he realised what she was getting at. There was a rolling timestamp on the lower left corner of the screen, burned into the footage, and it was continuous without any gaps or inconsistencies. He pulled a small tablet device from his jacket, and connected it directly to the compact desktop computer that served as the security system monitoring station. The tablet quickly showed a view of the storage media, and Goose accessed the relevant raw file, displaying it as a block diagram showing where all of the actual chunks of data were allocated on the solid-state drive. The entire file was contiguous on disk, as were each of the other files for the last several days.

"The footage files haven't been altered," he said. "Looks like they swap out the entire drive regularly too, or at least fully wipe it. Smart precaution. And yes, there would be an immediate signal loss alert if any of the cameras stopped sending a feed."

Greenwood folded her arms. "So we have another question. If none of the cameras were disconnected, and the recorded footage hasn't been edited, what caused the system to deliberately record blank footage while the house was empty?"

Chapter 4

Ramos was standing just inside the main door when the others filed out of the pantry, and Goose quickly informed her of what they'd found. She wasn't surprised that there was no video evidence of an intruder. The rest of it had been far too professional to make such an amateur mistake likely. But there was still hope.

"When we turned onto the access road, there was a small building," she said. "The reception office for a stable. There was a camera for the parking area. A much cheaper one than the equipment here."

"No other route to the house, chief," Dowling said, looking at Greenwood. "Everyone coming here has to take the same turn we did, unless they ran across the fields."

Greenwood nodded. There were a lot of ifs — the camera Ramos saw had to be working, and recording, and have a twenty-four hour archive, and its field of view had to include the access road, and its resolution needed to be high enough to give them something useful — but it was their best option at the moment. And there was another point in their favour, which she knew Ramos had been hinting at when she mentioned it was a *cheap* camera.

It's probably not networked beyond the premises, Greenwood thought. *Maybe just hardwired to a single dedicated computer, or recording onto its own storage just in case.*

The latter scenario would be perfect, and on balance it was actually quite likely. There was an element of extremely high technical competence involved in all three murder attempts, and the only safe electronic device was one that wasn't connected to the internet at all.

"Let's go," she said.

It took less than ten minutes to reach the parking area of the stable, and initially it seemed like the business might be closed for the day, but after a short wait a woman appeared at the door of the small building. She was in her mid-sixties, and wearing outdoor clothing. She looked like she probably wouldn't ever retire before she died of natural causes, and Aldridge thought she'd probably live to see ninety or more years of age.

It turned out that the woman was Dutch, and Goose explained in a vague way that they were gathering information regarding an incident at the house further down the access road. The woman had seen the ambulance and the police vehicles earlier, of course, and the ID that Goose produced — brought along especially for this purpose — showed him to be a senior officer of the Grand Ducal Police. At an appropriate junction in the conversation, he asked her if she had witnessed anyone else in the area during the preceding twenty-four hours, to which she replied that she hadn't and that no-one else had been here. After a moment, she remembered that there was a security camera in the parking area, though, and Goose was suitably enthusiastic about the opportunity to review its recordings.

Five minutes later, they were all back in the SUV, still sitting in the parking area, with a copy of the contents of the camera's memory card. The device wasn't networked at all, and Greenwood just hoped that the combination of its recording resolution and the card's relatively meagre capacity would work in their favour.

"Coming up now," Ramos said. She had Goose's tablet device on her lap, and was scanning quickly through the footage from the camera. The resolution, white balance, colour fidelity, and even frame rate of the video was considerably inferior to that from Hausemer's residential system, but it was enough to identify the housekeeper's car on her outbound journey. A few minutes worth of video later, which Ramos scanned through in moments, a commercial van with ladders mounted on its roof made the turn onto the access road. The position of the camera was such that it faced diagonally across the parking area, towards the corner of the junction where the access road joined a larger road which ultimately led into the city, so the van had to turn left across the camera's field of view. The sun on the windows made it impossible to discern anything about who was driving it, but the livery on the side was completely clear.

Dowling was already typing the name into his phone, and a moment later he nodded. "It's a residential maintenance and building contractor, chief," he said. "Some nice photos of kitchen and conservatory extensions on here."

"Hausemer didn't need an extension," Aldridge said from the front passenger seat, "but I wonder how well his boiler was working."

"Try to get the license plate, Alicia," Greenwood said, and Ramos nodded distractedly. She was already on it. There were only a few frames with the vehicle's front plate in view, and none of the rear, but she managed to find a single smeared and pixellated image. She tapped a few controls on a contextual toolbar on the tablet's screen, and the image first became black and white, then inverted, then all its regions of contrast became exaggerated. Finally, a reconstructive algorithm increased the image's resolution, using machine learning and a vast database of imagery to intelligently guess as to which colours of pixels to insert. The result was still noisy, but easily readable.

"Kilo Foxtrot tree-niner-two-six," Ramos said. The NATO phonetic alphabet had been formulated and refined over hundreds of thousands of tests with thirty-one nations, and was designed to remove ambiguity of spoken letters and numbers caused by the speaker or the hearer's own particular nationalities and accents, and radio interference during communications exchanges. One of the peculiarities of its pronunciations, as Aldridge had been required to learn, was that the number three was instead said as *tree*.

"Run the plate, Larry," Greenwood said, and Dowling nodded. Goose had already retrieved the street address of the company named on the van, and Dowling now made a brief phone call to check whether the license plate corresponded to both the vehicle and the company. When he ended the call, Greenwood could already read the answer from his face.

"Fake plate," the big Welshman said. "The business does have five vans like that one registered to them, but none have that registration number. Surprise surprise."

Greenwood would have bet fifty Euros that the van itself was stolen — probably from the company whose livery it bore, since that was easiest, and chosen because a residential services contractor didn't look out of place or suspicious on someone else's property — but she knew that no-one else in her team would bet against her.

"Alright," she said. "Let's check with the company to see if they're missing a van, but first we go into the city and pull the traffic cameras. Let's find out if our mystery builder was anywhere near the coffee shop where Lyadova died, or anywhere else interesting."

"And then we'll get ice cream, if you're all well-behaved," Aldridge added.

"Aldridge is buying," Greenwood replied, without looking at the man in question. Goose started the vehicle and headed for the exit from the parking area.

"I'll expense it," Aldridge said, to no-one in particular.

~

The Artist was reading the biographical profile of one Captain Jessica Rose Greenwood when his earpiece made another chime that he knew well, indicating an incoming encrypted text message.

There was no log of these communiques, and they erased themselves automatically within a minute after being read. He preferred it that way. It encouraged and even enforced a certain professionalism that was usually — but by no means always — the safest and most appropriate bearing for a man in his line of work. Not that there were really any others like him.

He was sitting on a low stone wall, far back from the road, in a picturesque lay-by a few miles from the outskirts of the city. It was a beautiful day, and insects hummed through the tall grass of the fields that bordered the country road. It was as good a place as any to familiarise himself with his latest targets, and he enjoyed the fresh air and the quiet.

The Artist switched to the messaging app, and read the short paragraph there. The news wasn't especially surprising.

Your vehicle's identity has been compromised. KESTREL is en route to Luxembourg City to review traffic camera footage. They will find nothing, but expect them to visit the scene of the third target's death.

He nodded, glancing automatically at the van that was parked a short distance away. It had served him well enough, and under normal circumstances this would be the prudent time to abandon it. And yet, his instructions were to ensure that his actions were noticed by those who were able to do so. The perverse part of him stirred in his mind. It was a trickster, and an arrogant imp, certain of its own superiority over all others. It had never known defeat, but it also yearned for its victims to be in no doubt as to who was responsible for their demise. He always managed to suppress it, given that his work required the utmost anonymity, but this time he was being given free rein.

Also, he had never been fond of uniforms, literal or figurative. They were shields, really, for the flawed and often cruel beings hiding within them, and it was uniforms that so regularly turned men into monsters. The Artist had no compunction about killing, be it for money or otherwise, but he also had a particular disdain for uniforms and the figures of authority and supposed order. The people he was now hunting fell squarely into that category, and the two people he had killed yesterday — plus the third who had regrettably survived — were far worse.

Despite your authority, you are all as vulnerable as anyone else, Captain Jessica Greenwood and your companions, he thought.

He pocketed the phone, stood up, and walked the short distance back to the van. It would serve him at least once more. Subtlety had its time and its place, but there were also times when a point must be made.

~

"Nothing on the traffic camera database," Ramos said, the unease evident in her voice.

The receptionist at Bernhoeft Trausch had put them through to the company's manager immediately, and the man hadn't seemed particularly interested in the van which had indeed been stolen from outside their premises two nights earlier. There had been nothing of value inside it — tools and materials were never left in their fleet overnight due to the risk of break-ins — and the vehicle itself was a rental which they had already arranged to replace, with their commercial insurance policy handling the rest of it.

Ramos had obtained the vehicle's original license plate number too, and was in the process of running it through the traffic camera database.

"Maybe the thief kept the old plates on it until he needed to take it to Hausemer's place," Aldridge said. "The camera databases are indexed by license plate, so the new one wouldn't show up at all if he kept it outside the city itself. No cameras out where the poor guy lived."

"I'm afraid not," Ramos said, turning the tablet so Greenwood could see it. "No match for the original plate either."

"Something is very wrong here," Greenwood said, and Ramos nodded.

"What are the chances that the stolen van was driven through the city at night and didn't pass a single camera to log either the old or new plates, whichever were on it at the time?" Aldridge asked, and Goose turned to look at him.

"Zero percent," the Dutchman said, with absolute certainty in his tone.

"And how likely do we think it is that a third plate was used temporarily, just to get it out of the city?" Aldridge replied, but Goose only shrugged.

"I hope that's what it is, mate," Dowling said, "but my gut says it's the other option. The bad one."

Aldridge turned in his seat, looking first at Dowling, then Ramos, then Greenwood herself. He knew exactly what Dowling meant, as did everyone, but he said it anyway.

"Whoever killed Hausemer and Lyadova has the ability to purge a metropolitan traffic camera database to cover their tracks."

There was silence in the SUV for a moment, and then Greenwood nodded, having come to a decision. "We should have seen this coming. Asphyxiating an EU minister and killing a Russian agent via anaphylaxis are one thing, but getting access to Wuyts's secure vehicle is quite another. We've been underestimating our enemy. Goose, let's drop off the satellites for a while."

Goose nodded, checked his wing mirror, then stepped out of the vehicle. They were parked diagonally across from the coffee shop where Lyadova had died, and being in the middle of a city, no-one was paying much attention to anyone except themselves. He stepped around to the rear right side of the vehicle, crouched down as if to tie his shoelaces, and after a quick last glance around, he reached up into the wheel arch there, feeling for a small box that was mounted onto the undercarriage. When he found it, he withdrew his hand and retrieved a small screwdriver from his jacket, then by touch he quickly undid the holding screws and removed the box entirely.

He stood up and opened the SUV's tailgate then unzipped the side compartment of one of their kit bags, taking out a foil mesh lined press-seal evidence pouch designed to suppress all RF activity of anything placed inside it. He put the tracking unit into the pouch, sealed it, and threw the whole thing back into the kit bag before getting back into the driver's seat.

"Phones next," Greenwood said. Ramos and Dowling were already shutting down their smartphones and removing the batteries, and Greenwood and Goose followed suit. Aldridge took his own device from his pocket reluctantly.

"I have an app that gives me discount coupons for the shops I walk past," he said, and Ramos leaned forward and snatched the phone from him, immediately removing the back cover.

"You can pay full price today," Greenwood said, looking across at the coffee shop. "Get those sealed too, Goose, then let's get going. The same barista is on today who served Lyadova last night, the police said. He knew her a little. What I want to know is if any of their own cameras get a good view of the street here."

"Her drink order could have been placed from anywhere in the world, chief," Dowling said doubtfully. "It was done via their app, remember."

Greenwood grinned at the big man, exchanging a knowing look with Goose this time. "You've never ordered coffee online before, Larry, so I'll forgive you this one, but you're wrong. They only let you pre-order if you're nearby enough to collect within ten minutes or so. It helps avoid pranks and waste. All the coffee shop apps geolocate the phone and limit the ordering window based on travel time."

"Huh," Dowling said. "I suppose that makes sense, right enough. But surely somebody could find a way around that. Especially someone as sharp with computers as our boy or girl in the stolen van."

Greenwood conceded that it was certainly a possibility, but her instincts said that the mystery person in the van had been here, if not at the time of Lyadova's death then at least in the preceding hours. There was a troubling element of showmanship about some aspects of all this.

Or taunting, maybe, she thought.

Ramos had finished bagging up the disconnected and partly-disassembled phones in another of the Faraday pouches, and with them stashed safely in the cargo area, there was nothing left to do but head into the coffee shop.

"I doubt they have ice-cream, but I could really go for some caffeine," Aldridge announced, and Greenwood found herself in grudging agreement as the five of them crossed the busy road.

With the constant flow of traffic, they didn't notice the large vehicle pulling in to park two spaces behind their SUV, its driver's face entirely hidden by a black balaclava.

Chapter 5

Aldridge didn't know whether to be more surprised that the young barista, whose name was Adam, was still working today after watching a woman die here last night, or that the man actually cried when he recounted what had happened.

There was no outward indication that anything untoward had happened, and the scene had been released almost immediately after the paramedics had taken Lyadova's body away last night. Without any reason to suspect foul play, there was no need to close the shop or inspect the premises, and the early afternoon found it in the post-lunch lull, with only a handful of tables occupied. Dowling, Goose, and Aldridge sat at one of them, sipping coffee and watching as Greenwood and Ramos spoke to the visibly upset Adam off to one side of the main serving counter. The conversation was readily audible from where they were, but mercifully the other patrons mostly seemed to be allowing the young man to vent his grief with some degree of privacy. The story had, of course, been on the local morning news, and had also made it onto the internet, but without much interest since by all appearances it was nothing more than a tragic accident.

"No-one thinks you did anything wrong at all," Greenwood was saying kindly to the distraught man. "We just wanted to check up on you, and to ask if the woman who passed away ever met anyone here while you were working. A business associate or a friend, for example."

Adam shook his head, though it was clear that he was distracted and not trying very hard to remember. "She was always alone," he said, his Eastern European accent difficult to localise further, doubtless from years of working in different EU cities and probably studying abroad. Ramos thought he might be from Bulgaria originally, but it was more of a guess than anything else.

Greenwood nodded at him, as if this information was extremely helpful, patting his elbow in a gesture of compassion. "I see. And you knew her just from her visits here?"

Adam nodded. "Anna worked for a travel company not far from here. She came in often. I can't believe what happened to her. She was fine, and then she was gone. It happened in a minute."

Wuyts had shared Lyadova's cover identity with Greenwood before they left Brussels, so they knew the name *Anna* would be the one that Adam had heard. It was plain to see that he had taken a shine to her, and had probably hoped to ask her out on a date someday, if he ever summoned the courage for it. Greenwood felt a great surge of sympathy for him, and she was glad that this innocent young man would never feel the sting of rejection that would come from Lyadova's inevitable refusal to become involved with him. She was a foreign intelligence agent of Moscow, and while her objectives here in Luxembourg City regarding Hausemer currently remained unknown, they certainly wouldn't include an entanglement with an infatuated coffee boy.

"We're very sorry you had to witness that terrible accident," Greenwood said, and Ramos nodded. "Thanks for talking to us."

Adam nodded several times, unthinkingly wiping his eyes and nose with his shirt cuff, and Greenwood was glad they'd ordered their drinks before they spoke to him. She and Ramos joined the others at the table, but no-one spoke straight away when the women sat down.

"Did he say anything about the cameras here?" Goose asked at last, and Greenwood sighed.

"They've been broken for the last few days," she replied. "Apparently it happens often. They have a technician coming tomorrow. So we're out of luck on that, but I don't think it matters."

However it was done, the modified and deadly drinks order may have been placed from nearby, but certainly not from inside the premises, so the coffee shop's security footage wouldn't have helped to identify the van's driver anyway. Their best source for more information on that would instead be surveillance from the place the van was stolen: the residential services company's private parking area. Their system was managed by a third-party company, and it would be available later today, according to the manager at Bernhoeft Trausch.

Aldridge drained the rest of his caramel latte with a gulp, wincing at the sweetness. It was by no means his usual drink, but rather an impulse buy after he'd seen the large cardboard ad for it beside the counter. He regretted his choice, but he wasn't about to give any of the others the satisfaction of knowing it.

"Mmm," he said. "Back in a minute."

He crossed to the doorway off to one side of the serving counter that led to the bathrooms, absent-mindedly patting his pocket to verify that his phone was there. He frowned, starting back towards the table automatically before remembering that all of their personal devices were still in the SUV. The others didn't seem to have noticed him stopping, and he was about to turn around once more and resume course for the bathroom when he happened to glance out of the floor-to-ceiling windows which formed the entire front of the franchise coffee shop. From his position in the far corner of the seating area, he could see farther down the street than from where he'd been sitting, and their vehicle was readily visible — as was the Bernhoeft Trausch van parked two spaces behind. Aldridge frowned.

The space between the SUV and the van was empty, making the van's license plate visible. He squinted to make it out.

KF 3926. No way, he thought.

He could even see that the cab was empty, and it took less than a second to then notice the man approaching the coffee shop wearing a black balaclava and wielding an assault rifle.

Christ.

In the same moment, he saw first one customer and then several others looking at their phones in confusion, as the screens of the devices all went black. Aldridge was already running by the time the manufacturer logo showed up on two of the phones within his line of sight.

"DOWN!" he shouted, and his four team mates responded as they'd been conditioned to, immediately dropping anything they held and diving to the floor without question. Barely a second later, gunfire punched through the plate-glass front of the shop, shattering it into hundreds of pieces, and bullets raked their table, tearing the surface into ragged chunks.

An elderly woman standing in line at the counter shrieked, and Aldridge's heart clenched in his chest as he saw a young father knocked from his seat by a bullet to the upper chest, his child in a high-chair blinking in confusion before starting to wail.

Aldridge saw the gunman pivoting in his direction, and he instinctively dived low along the front of the counter, only two metres from the staff entrance to the rear area, but it was two metres too far. He pulled his sidearm from its concealed holster within his jacket, knowing the most he could do from his position would be to hit their attacker in the legs before he himself was killed.

Fair enough, he thought, looking up to take aim, but then Aldridge watched in disbelief as an entire cleaning cart sailed through the air towards the man in the balaclava. The attacker shifted quickly to one side, but the bulky cart caught him with a glancing blow to the shoulder, knocking him off balance. Aldridge used the moment of respite to find a position of cover behind the coffee shop's counter, motioning to the staff cowering there to remain on the ground. He knew that it would have been Dowling who hefted and threw the cart, and sure enough, he now heard return small-arms fire coming from the approximate direction of where his teammates had been sitting.

Beyond the protection of the counter, Greenwood risked popping up from the scant cover of the table they'd set on its side, and she saw that the gunman had lost grip of his weapon when dodging Dowling's throw. She fired a few careful shots to maintain separation between the man and his rifle, and she could see the exact moment when his body language shifted, even as his dark eyes met hers. In that instant, both Greenwood and the masked man shared the same two thoughts, which she heard in her own mind as if they were an echo.

He has a pistol too, and he knows that I need to take him alive.

Even as the attacker began to reach behind himself to the back of his waistband, Greenwood was calculating the risk involved in a direct shot. She saw it at the same time as Ramos did.

"Body armour," Ramos said, and Greenwood nodded. Both women were armed with the trusted P226, chambered for 9mm ammunition, and Greenwood knew she didn't need to explain or give any orders. She simply lowered her own pistol, nodded, and Ramos had already fired before the other woman's head stopped moving.

The attacker spun backwards to the left, dropping into the mess of broken safety glass, but he scrambled to his feet much quicker than Greenwood anticipated. She sprang up with Ramos and Dowling and pursued the man out into the street, knowing that Goose and Aldridge would join them when they could.

Their quarry, so recently their predator, moved uncannily quickly, displaying an athleticism that was unnerving. Every member of her team was at the peak of fitness, and it immediately became apparent that a flat race would still be a losing proposition. She had very few options. There were already sirens in the distance, but in the opening minutes of their arrival any local police force tended to be more of a hindrance than an asset. The street was busy with traffic and pedestrians, making gunfire an unacceptable risk.

I bet he doesn't share the sentiment, she thought, pushing herself to go faster, feeling the benefit of every one of her near-daily training sprints as her muscles responded to her demands.

But still the man was getting farther away. A private school bus pulled in to the side of the street and began to offload its passengers, and in a moment of horror,

Greenwood thought that he might try to take a hostage, or to create a distraction in an even worse way, but to her relief the man just barrelled on through, knocking a waiting teacher to the ground without so much as slowing down.

She could feel the presence of Ramos and Dowling behind her, but lacking comms she couldn't issue any orders without losing ground to first check they were in earshot. She trusted her team, and knew that if there was an opportunity to head the gunman off, Dowling and Ramos would take it — but the man they were pursuing seemed to know that his best strategy was to outpace them in a straight line. His aerobic endurance was incredible, rivalling Greenwood's own, and with a sinking feeling she knew that she physically couldn't outpace a man of comparable conditioning, no matter how impeccable her own training had been.

The street split up ahead, leading to the left and right for vehicles with a pedestrian precinct running straight through. There was a broad plaza beyond, teeming with people, and dotted with shops, church spires, pavement awnings and some sort of marketplace. It was the worst possible venue for a foot chase, and the best opportunity to evade pursuers. The man went directly for it, and even though Greenwood pushed herself harder than she ever had before, the last thing she saw of the man who had tried to kill her and her team was a final glimpse of his dark jacket as he vanished neatly into the crowd.

"Find him!" Greenwood shouted as Dowling and Ramos materialised at her elbows, both panting from exertion, but all three knew that it would be a futile endeavour. There must have been a thousand people in the huge plaza, with omnipresent noise, and hundreds of places to hide.

Dowling gamely went forward, and Ramos moved perpendicularly across the near side of the pedestrian area, while Greenwood followed the big Welshman at a slower pace, eyes scanning back and forth, but there was no real hope of locating the man again here. She followed the route the man had taken, moving around obstacles in the way she would if she wanted to cover the maximum straight-line distance. Greenwood knew that her margin of error was widening with every step, and she almost didn't notice when her foot fetched up against something on the ground.

She stopped dead when she saw that it was the black balaclava, and she could feel that there was something solid inside it. Her soldier's mind ran through all the worst possibilities in a fraction of a second, the first of which was an anti-personnel mine, but logically it made no sense. Greenwood crouched down, taking care not to move the foot that was in contact with the bundle, and she gingerly lifted away the top of the fabric. She released a breath she didn't know she'd been holding when she saw that the object was a smartphone.

"Bastard," she said, her words lost in the ambient noise. A few moments later, Dowling joined her with a rare look of irritation on his face, and a minute after that

Ramos appeared, giving a single shake of her head that was feline in its disdain for the suboptimal situation.

"See what you and Goose can make of this," Greenwood said, handing the device to Ramos. "Let's regroup and handle the police. The mission profile has changed."

~

Thirty metres away, in front of a pub-restaurant, The Artist hauled a second keg of pale ale from the adjacent delivery truck and rolled it over to the mouth of the open cellar hatch. With his jacket, body armour, and pistol discarded in a large municipal rubbish bin, he was now clad only in a white t-shirt and dark trousers, his shaven head glistening with sweat from his escape and also his current exertions.

He had spotted the skinny young man struggling to heft the kegs, and knew it was an opportunity to blend into the scene immediately, while also giving him the chance to observe those who had chased him. He had all of their faces committed to memory, and indeed their names and biographies. The occasional careful glance back in the direction he'd come from showed that Captain Greenwood had found the phone, and had been joined by Sergeant Dowling and Corporal Ramos. They looked frustrated, which was good. The message had been sent, and the second part of it would become clear when their digital forensics on the device were complete.

She already knows who you are, he thought, smiling in response to the thanks from the young delivery man who was working at his side, but otherwise paying little attention to the youth.

He glanced in Greenwood's direction again, seeing that the group of three soldiers were now headed back in the direction of the coffee shop. They would find nothing of use in the van, and they would waste time and resources quarantining and analysing their own vehicle in case it had been tampered with before the attack. The Artist hadn't gone near it, but that was for him to know. Satisfied that he was in no danger of being discovered, and knowing there was no more to learn at this juncture, he unloaded the remaining few beer kegs from the delivery truck, bid the young man farewell, and walked away into the crowd. His priority now was to obtain a new communications device, check in with his employer who doubtless had already seen everything, and then continue his game.

He had no intention of killing all of the EU soldiers today. Instead, it had been a provocation, to make them aware — beyond the suspicions they must have formed since they were summoned early this morning — that they were facing forces far beyond the ordinary.

His employer was a mystery, but he had never known a more powerful woman, or indeed a more powerful person at all. Her reach seemed to be endless, and her influence without limits. He had no idea what sort of organisation or government she was associated with, but her access to information and her ability to arrange for convenient occurrences was formidable.

After all, she had found The Artist himself.

It was a rare thing for him to be contacted by someone he didn't already know. His work mostly came via referrals, and always via intermediaries who could be disposed of if it ever became necessary to do so, which it occasionally did. Most knew the value of discretion, though, because they knew that in this case it was nothing less than the value of their own lives.

There were conflicting stories about his background. Some intelligence agencies thought he was an Israeli, having served in that country's defence forces before going absent without leave to pursue much better pay without the oversight of commanders or governments. Some thought he was a product of the ashes of Saddam Hussein's regime in Iraq. Some thought he came from Russia, tempered in the shock of the post-USSR crisis of faith of a great superpower. But there were other theories too.

Interpol, for example, had his identity as a British-educated white emigré from an African nation, initially an unimportant player in the illegal arms market, later branching out into assassination for hire when he had discovered his own aptitude for using the weapons he had previously only sold. The CIA, however, were convinced that he was French nobility, having faked his own death almost two decades ago to evade an enormous tax liability from inheritance and business mismanagement, now doing anything he needed to — or wanted to — in order to survive.

None of the theories were correct, or at least not entirely. If enough lies were amassed, truth could eventually be found within, like nuggets of gold glinting from water and silt. It was a matter of probability. The only thing that everyone agreed upon was the name he was known by.

It was especially fitting, given the creativity involved in its genesis. The year was 2009, and the task was a comparatively simple one: send an unequivocal warning from the head of one Spanish crime family to a rival. The rival's daughter was enrolled in a prestigious musical academy located in a leafy and picturesque district of Madrid whose streets teemed with painters, poets, philosophers, sculptors, and all the rest. The girl was a very promising violinist, and at the age of thirteen years old was already coming to the attention of the classical music world. She was her father's pride and joy, and that was truly unfortunate for the man, because her execution was ordered and the job was given to a then-unnamed yet already elite assassin. It was a Wednesday morning, a little after eleven o'clock, when the orchestral rehearsal suite was reduced to a smoking ruin by a remotely detonated heavy munitions device which had required a great deal of ingenuity to conceal on the premises. Thirty-four talented young musicians lost their lives, along with four staff members, one of whom was a noted conductor originally from Switzerland.

The decision to widen the death toll had been the assassin's own, and the message had been incredibly effective. Such magnitude of brutality had to be reckoned with. The official investigation stretched on for years, and the only real evidence besides the residue of the blast was a single eyewitness report of a man leaving the area earlier in the day, wearing a slouch cap and threadbare clothes, carrying the tubular portfolio holder of a student of drawing and painting. There, in the ruins of so many barely-begun lives, The Artist was born.

The man in the white t-shirt now ran his hand across his brow and up over his head to wipe the sweat away. His scalp was beginning to feel bristly again, as the hair inexorably regrew. He changed his appearance often; a necessity in his occupation. The shaven skull was appealing in its simplicity, though it was perhaps a little too distinctive in its own right if someone happened to see him at a time or in a place where they shouldn't. But such people didn't tend to live very long.

He had plenty of time. There was no specific deadline, and he found he was enjoying leading this particular quarry around by the nose. Greenwood and her compatriots doubtless had enviable means at their disposal, but The Artist was unconcerned. He was a killer without equal, and his current employer had given him unprecedented access to resources that were usually prohibitively difficult to obtain. He could afford to indulge himself. Soldiers should die a soldier's death, after all.

The day had turned warm, and the skies rang with the sound of opportunistic gulls conducting sorties above the market stalls and pavement cafés. The Artist started off in the direction of the anonymous hotel room he had arranged. He was looking forward to a shower, some food, and then resuming contact with the woman's voice on the encrypted phone line who had set all this in motion.

As he walked, he noted a CCTV camera mounted on a street lamp pole not far away. It faced in his approximate direction, and in the bright afternoon light its lens was a black void, infinitely deep. From within it, he could feel her eyes upon him.

Chapter 6

"You'd think that just once, the local police would be even slightly grateful that we were trying to do their jobs for them," Aldridge mused, his chair tilted too far back on its rear legs.

They were in Greenwood's office back at headquarters in Brussels after a protracted encounter with the Luxembourg Grand Ducal police, who hadn't been at all pleased to have a shootout in their capital city. They had been even less happy to abruptly receive orders from on high to release the five armed and polite but otherwise uncommunicative people in civilian clothing claiming to be agents of the European Defence Agency. It wasn't an unusual sort of encounter with local authorities, and every time it happened, Greenwood wished there was a better way — but secrecy was of critical importance to their work.

"Can't blame them for taking it all a bit personally," Dowling said. He was standing to one side of the closed door, leaning against the wall with his large arms folded across his chest. It was a favourite position and stance. Ramos was in another chair beside Aldridge, and Goose was off to one side. The atmosphere was tense, and Greenwood sat behind her desk with a stormy expression on her face. There was a knock at the door, and she pressed a small control on the desk surface to unlock it. A moment later, a young woman entered.

"Come in, Inge," Greenwood said. "Tell us what you've managed to find out."

Inge Olsen was a senior technical analyst, imported directly from a Danish university's postgraduate program when a paper she wrote gained the attention of the EU's intelligence infrastructure. She had striking blonde hair tied back in a short ponytail, she wore a small earpiece attached to an over-ear device that looked like an updated version of an old Bluetooth headset, and her grey-blue eyes barely moved and never focused. She had been blind from birth, and for once she wasn't carrying the white stick which usually accompanied her everywhere. Everyone else in the room noted the omission immediately, but of course it was Aldridge who chose to comment on it.

"Relying on echolocation today, Olsen?" he said, and her head moved slightly in his direction. "That's the kind of initiative that'll take you far in this organisation."

Olsen smiled and raised an eyebrow. "Not so far from the truth, Dr. Aldridge," she said, indicating the over-ear device. "Something we've been working on. An infrared and ultrasonic projector that builds a model of the immediate environment, with audio cues for navigation. You're going to fall off that chair if you lean back any farther."

The silence in the room was only interrupted by Aldridge's chair bumping back down onto all four legs. "I… can't tell if you're kidding or not," he said, exchanging a glance with an equally wide-eyed Goose.

"I'm not," Olsen said proudly. "It works quite well, though my brain is still getting used to it."

"Mine too," Aldridge replied after a moment.

"I have the results from the forensics on the phone that your attacker left behind, Captain," Olsen said, all business now. "There isn't much. It was a clean device, with the actual comms heavily encrypted. No messages or location log data. We did find five documents on local storage, and a single entry in the call log, which goes to a VoIP relay endpoint that's already gone dark. We can't trace it any further."

Greenwood frowned, though the news wasn't unexpected. The man hadn't given the impression of being an amateur, by any stretch of the imagination. He would have known that KESTREL could localise all cellular signals in the vicinity of the coffee shop during the time of the attack, and then by a process of elimination work out which one represented his own device. It became a liability as soon as he opened fire, and there was no way he could ever use the phone again. Dropping it served two purposes: evading tracking, and taunting them.

"Alright. What are the five documents?" she asked.

Olsen's expression became grave. "Personnel dossiers for each of you, identifying you as European Special Tactical Force, Group One. They're accurate and contemporary."

Greenwood slammed her palms down on the desk surface, startling several of the others. "*What?*" she exclaimed, and Olsen just nodded apologetically in confirmation.

Ramos shifted her position. "They're playing with us," she said quietly, and this time it was Greenwood who nodded. "They want us to know that they're aware of who we are. And that they can get to us."

"But who are they?" Aldridge wondered aloud.

There were a few seconds of silence, and then Dowling shrugged. "The bloke we saw in the balaclava is a trained killer, I suppose," he said. "They don't hold grudges against anybody, for the most part. Bad for business. They take orders for profit."

"So we have yet another question: who hired the man in the mask?" Greenwood replied. "And that's just the latest unknown." She ticked off the points on her fingers as she spoke. "What connects Wuyts, Hausemer, and Lyadova, and why did someone decide they had to die because of it? Why kill them in those particular ways? Who's behind all this? Who's the hitman they hired, and why is he making a show of it instead of killing us in the safest and most efficient way? And how in the hell does he know who we are?"

"Also, where do you even buy a balaclava these days?" Aldridge added. "Is it an Amazon thing? Clothing category, subsection men's, subsection 1970s burglar?"

As usual, Greenwood ignored the flippant remark. "We have a serious security problem. No-one outside Wuyts's office or this facility should have access to our personnel files."

Olsen cleared her throat. "There might be something of significance there, Captain," she said, and all eyes in the room focused on her. "Our files are assembled dynamically based on the clearance level of the access request. There's no static record as such; it's all fragments that are joined on a need-to-know basis."

Greenwood stiffened in her seat. She had the highest clearance of anyone in the room, and by several levels in the case of Olsen. The young technical analyst would have no idea even how much of a given officer's details she was capable of seeing.

"It's alright, Inge," Greenwood said. "I was the one who asked you to analyse the device's contents. I'm sure you checked against your own access level. What can you tell me?"

Olsen blinked, her gaze seeming to rest on the desk surface, somewhat to the left of centre. "It didn't go beyond CADENCE. My own clearance is at that level too, which is the required level to get through the door upstairs. The files from the phone were a perfect match for what I can see on our system."

Greenwood nodded, somewhat relieved. It meant that the access request would have come via someone whose clearance was at least three levels below that of her four colleagues, and *five* levels below her own. Given the amount of bad news she'd already had today, Greenwood actually found herself feeling a little relieved.

The worst-case scenario would be that whoever is behind this also has CHALLENGE-level access, she thought.

It was the nightmare scenario for the European Defence Agency, and it was the implicit, underlying purpose of every one of their missions over the years: to keep certain things secret at all costs, hidden away from a society that was in no way ready to learn about them. Greenwood had always believed the day would arrive when some of those things would accidentally come to the attention of the public, and that it would be catastrophic for social order and everything else. She hoped that it wouldn't happen during her watch, and she especially hoped that it wouldn't be because of her own failure to prevent it. It seemed that today, at least, wasn't to be that day, and she was glad of it.

Wuyts has a clearance level I don't even know the name of, she thought. It was a troubling observation, because of its implications. She had to remember that Wuyts herself was almost killed this morning too.

"Alright, Inge, thank you," Greenwood said. "You've been very helpful, as usual."

Olsen nodded, and was about to turn around to leave when something else occurred to her. "Captain, there was also something unusual about the call log entry on the device. There's an unencrypted header that allows for arbitrary data, similar to how SMS shortcodes can provide a sender name to display even if the recipient doesn't have a contacts entry for that number. Carriers sometimes use the header to flag messages as data payloads, to update cellular configurations and so on. But that's for SMS, not calls."

"But this call entry had some data attached?" Goose asked, one eyebrow quirked in interest. Olsen nodded.

"We ran it through various interpretation algorithms," she replied. "It was simple. A basic non-decimal number-base representation of ASCII characters. I think the secure calling protocol they were using puts a kind of username there."

Greenwood sat forward. "What did it say, Inge?" she asked. Olsen's head moved towards the sound of Greenwood's voice.

"*JINX*," she replied.

~

"This is disturbing news," Wuyts said, her stern face perfectly centred on the large display screen at the front of the conference room. She was in her own office at the headquarters of the European Defence Agency, speaking to KESTREL remotely via video link.

Greenwood nodded, choosing her next words carefully. "It stands to reason that we have a security breach, whether it's human or technological," she said. "I think our best approach in this situation is to proceed on the assumption that we're compromised centrally."

Wuyts's mouth tightened in distaste, but she didn't disagree.

"You should take appropriate precautions too," Greenwood continued. "The man who attacked us might make another attempt on your life. It's difficult to say either way without knowing the motivation behind his actions, and what connects his targets."

"My position hasn't changed, Captain," Wuyts said, responding to the implicit question. "Rest assured that I'm not in any further danger at this point, and all necessary and prudent measures have been taken. It would seem that you and your own people are his latest targets."

"Or his employer's, more to the point," Ramos said. The image of Wuyts on the screen shifted its gaze to focus on the other woman.

"Quite so," Wuyts replied. "Namely this *JINX*, whomever he or she may be. A bringer of misfortune, in this case some very precisely engineered misfortune, made possible by an alarming degree of foreknowledge — including classified information."

"Foreign government?" Aldridge asked, speaking for the first time since they had all entered the conference room twenty minutes earlier. His silence was uncharacteristic, and it was obvious that something was bothering him.

Wuyts tilted her head slightly, but she didn't seem convinced. "The question of feasibility must always be balanced with that of acquired advantage," she replied. "I'm aware of your collective frustration at being kept in the dark, but whatever threads of connection exist between myself and the two victims, there's no clear advantage to removing the three of us. Hausemer was a valued member of a number of agencies and projects, but hardly irreplaceable. Lyadova was a Russian covert foreign intelligence agent, the likes of which can be found in almost every country in the world. I happen to know that her own replacement is already en route from Sheremetyevo at this very moment."

"Then there's yourself, sir," Dowling said to Wuyts, and Greenwood exchanged a glance with him. "I certainly wouldn't call you *ten a penny*."

"That's kind of you to say, Sergeant," Wuyts replied. She understood the quaintly British expression — it meant extremely commonplace, and thus of little value — but she also knew what Dowling was really getting at. "Unfortunately I present the opposite problem; there are entirely too many people who would probably prefer that I had died this morning."

The room remained silent for a few moments at the directness of her remark, then Greenwood spoke again. "Have you had any more luck than we have in finding out what 'JINX' might refer to, sir?"

Wuyts shook her head. "It's a term that's unknown to us," she said. "It doesn't correspond with any codename used by or briefed to this office, and a broader search has been unproductive so far."

"We found the expected dictionary definitions, lots of fictional characters in various media, assorted brands and products, a few dozen musical groups, and so on," Greenwood said. "Nothing stood out."

"One thing does stand out, though," Aldridge said thoughtfully, his eyes unfocused for a moment before he looked up at the display screen. "The only covert aspect of all this is what the public does or doesn't know about how it ties together. The killer could have done away with Hausemer and Lyadova at different times, and in less… weird ways. But he targeted all three of you within the same few hours. And then he walked up to us in broad daylight with an assault rifle, but made no real effort to kill us. He could have come into the coffee shop and chucked a grenade at our table, and that would have been it. But no."

"Your point, Dr. Aldridge?" Wuyts asked, and Greenwood had the distinct impression that the older woman was concerned about whatever conclusion Aldridge was about to voice.

"It's ostentatious, in a way," Aldridge replied. "Only to people with our resources, though. The resources to put the pieces together. I find that interesting." It seemed like he was going to say more, then he just shrugged and folded his arms.

A chime sounded, but it was on Wuyts's end instead of coming from within the conference room, and sure enough Wuyts looked away from the camera for a moment and then her expression changed. She regained her composure immediately.

"I have another call I need to attend to," Wuyts said, addressing Greenwood directly now. "I'll have more instructions for you soon, Captain. I'm relieved your team was unharmed."

The screen went black, and everyone but Aldridge looked at Greenwood, who sighed wearily. "I don't like being kept in the dark anymore than you do," she said. "Or being shot at. Maybe it was just a warning, in which case it was wasted. We're not going to just sit on our hands, though I'm damned if I know what our next move is at the moment. I can't go over her head, and if she wants to compartmentalise relevant information, that's her prerogative."

"Whatever Hausemer was doing, and whatever Lyadova was fishing for, and whatever Wuyts has got to do with all of it, she really doesn't want us to find out," Goose said quietly. Aldridge finally pulled his gaze away from the black rectangle of the screen on the wall, turning to look at Greenwood.

"No, she doesn't," he said. "But I think maybe JINX does."

~

A new phone had been waiting at the hotel when The Artist arrived back at his room a little after one in the afternoon. He took a shower, checked the phone for any messages, and when he saw that there were none, he closed the curtains and went to sleep.

He woke several hours later to find that it was dinner time, and he ordered room service. Once he'd eaten, he called down to have the tray taken away. One minute after it was gone, he heard the new phone's discreet ringtone.

He tapped the screen to answer the call, saying nothing at first. It was an ingrained habit.

"*Good evening,*" said the familiar female voice. "*I hope you enjoyed your meal.*"

"It was acceptable," The Artist replied. "Do you have new information for me?"

"*By now, KESTREL have begun to distrust Janne Wuyts. She will try to avoid sharing the truth about Hausemer and his work at all costs. She knows that it would only further undermine their allegiance to her.*"

"I don't wish to know anything about that," The Artist said. "My only concern is carrying out the tasks I'm being paid for. I prefer to learn as little as possible about anything else."

"*A wise policy,*" JINX replied, "*but also a luxury which is often impractical.*"

He walked over to the room's large windows. The main curtains were open again, but there were also thinner, semi-transparent drapes to allow light through. The city beyond was readily visible. The Artist counted eight security cameras before turning away.

"What is it you want to tell me?" he asked, curious now as to the purpose of the call.

"*For the moment, KESTREL are beyond my reach,*" JINX said. "*The situation is evolving, and they are being kept in the dark, but they may serve a useful purpose if they can provide the means to shed new light.*"

"I also have little interest in metaphors and riddles," The Artist replied. "If you have an additional task for me, name it, and I will name the price." The response was immediate, and as calm as ever.

"I appreciate your refreshing directness. I will give you access to a place which few know of, where secrets are kept. If those secrets can be obtained, and are of use to us, then the situation will evolve in new and interesting directions. And if they can't, you can remove a significant obstacle, and be well paid for it."

Yet again, The Artist was almost certain he could hear just a hint of an accent in her voice; raised and lengthened vowels, conjuring images of red hair, and mist-shrouded hills, and Gaelic languages — but just for a moment. He nodded, even though he was fairly sure that the gesture couldn't be seen by the owner of the voice on the line. "Where would you have me go?" he asked.

"The arrangements have already been taken care of, and a delivery will arrive soon," JINX said. *"Rest, and be ready to leave the hotel by 22:00 hours. A car will be waiting. You will already be checked out of your room. I'll speak to you again en route."*

"As you wish," he said.

"I'll be watching," JINX replied, and then the line went dead.

Chapter 7

Aldridge had just come from the commissary, and was making his way along a series of corridors, carefully carrying two paper cups filled with piping hot coffee, steam curling up from the small holes in their plastic lids.

As focused as he was on the task of not spilling scalding liquid over his own hands, his thoughts were nevertheless distracted. Although he was the newest member of KESTREL, it had been a while since he'd felt like an outsider here. The situation with Wuyts was troubling, not just because the Director had always been a source of insight and support rather than intrigue and obstacles, but also because there was a certain passiveness amongst his team members about how to handle this scenario. He could sense their own discomfort, but they seemed content to take their lead from Greenwood, and for the moment the Captain was going along with Wuyts's wishes.

At least outwardly, he thought.

The encounter in Luxembourg City had changed things, though; he could tell. Greenwood had quickly been pushed a lot closer to a tipping point, and he was pretty sure that Wuyts knew it too. Aldridge thought that the lines had become very blurry, very fast — and he didn't enjoy feeling like he was on the wrong side of them. Hence the coffee.

As he reached the door that led to his destination, he manoeuvred a little awkwardly to pass his smart watch over the sensor plate set into the wall, without putting down either of the cups to make the task easier. There was a muted click, and the door slid open to reveal that he'd been correct in his assumption about where to go.

The room beyond was designated as an unassigned multipurpose space in the base's internal directory, but everyone knew it was Greenwood's domain. She would be the first to surrender it to more official uses should the need arise, but for now it was the place she went when she was worried, or angry, or facing a dilemma. Piece by piece, she'd moved various items of equipment into the moderately-sized area, including a treadmill and exercise bike, a weighted dummy for martial arts practice, a yoga mat, free weights, a makeshift desk without a chair, and — incongruously — a bonsai tree which sat directly on the floor a metre or so from the yoga mat. If she was in here, then something was wrong, and so today Aldridge wasn't at all surprised to see her standing over at the desk, looking intently down at something on its surface which her body hid from view.

"Don't you ever knock?" she asked without looking around, and he grinned from across the room.

"Doesn't sound like something I'd do, no," Aldridge replied, walking over to where she stood. He put the two cups down on the desk, and looked with interest at the object he was now able to see. "A medal?" he asked. "I thought all of yours would be more fancy."

Greenwood picked up the coffee cup nearest to her, nodding briefly in his direction in a gesture of thanks, and took a mouthful of the bitter liquid, swallowing it immediately with no regard to its temperature. After a few moments, she spoke.

"This is a CSDP medal," she said. "The first decoration I ever got from the EU centrally. It's a participation trophy. It just means you took part in a mission for a minimum of thirty days. That's all."

"Not exactly valour and glory," Aldridge observed, and Greenwood shrugged. She reached for the medal with her free hand and ran a finger over its surface. It was silver in colour but muted now, and could do with a good polishing. Its front showed the twelve stars of the EU flag in unpainted metal, and there was a ribbon bar above the medal itself. Aldridge didn't recognise the mission codename inlaid into it, but he did know that the dark blue ribbon's central red stripe instead of the usual gold for combat forces indicated extraordinarily meritorious service. She was selling herself short, but he was content to pretend to be ignorant of it for now.

Greenwood turned the medal over, and Aldridge craned his neck to read the inscription on the back. It said *Pro Pace Unum*.

"Together for Peace," he translated, and Greenwood nodded.

"It's on all of them," she replied. "It's why we're here."

"Even Wuyts?" Aldridge asked, and Greenwood sighed. He knew he'd hit the nail on the head.

She turned and walked away from the desk, taking her cup with her. Aldridge turned around too but didn't follow, instead leaning back against the edge of the desk and waiting for her to find whatever words she was searching for. Finally, after a minute or so, she stopped pacing and turned to face him, gesturing towards the medal again.

"I didn't get that medal when I was actually first eligible for it, you know," she said. "Some administrative oversight. It happens. I didn't chase it up, either; even civilians get a medal like that just for analysing water samples for a month."

"Not *exactly* like that one, but I take your point," Aldridge replied. "So when did you end up getting it?"

"When Wuyts recruited me," Greenwood replied. "Gave it to me herself, in that bloody office of hers. I thought it was a joke at first, or some kind of hazing or a test. But she was serious about it. She said it was the most important medal I'd ever get."

Aldridge raised an eyebrow, setting his cup down on the desk beside him. He was intrigued now, and couldn't resist taking another quick glance at the little disc of metal before turning his attention to Greenwood again.

"She told me that the European Union is a grand and noble thing, and that it's also an experiment, just like any of the finest in science," she continued. "And then she looked me in the eye and she said that any large endeavour begins with many small ones, and that I'd already begun the largest endeavour of my life."

"Pretty good speech," Aldridge replied. "She's usually a bit less motivational than that when she talks to us."

"I could tell that she believed it," Greenwood said. "Not just back then, but ever since. She truly thinks we're part of perhaps the greatest venture in human history. And maybe she's right about that. All I know is that I never had reason to question where her own motivations lay."

"Until today," Aldridge supplied, and she ran a frustrated hand through her hair.

"Am I overreacting? She's never withheld germane operational intelligence before, and she's never been directly mixed up in one of our missions before either."

"That we know of," Aldridge said, then he held up one hand in a placating gesture when he saw that she was ready to argue with him. "I'm sure you're right about that," he added quickly. "And you're also right that it's strange. I meant what I said in there: it feels like she's on the wrong side of something this time. I suppose that in her position, she's inevitably going to have a few secrets to keep."

"In my position too," Greenwood replied. "I understand the reasons for it, but I hate the broad strokes. There are things that I know about but you don't, and I'm not allowed to tell you about them — *you*, Aldridge — and that's beyond ridiculous at this point."

He blinked, shifting his weight forward from the desk to fully stand up again. "Ridiculous?" he said carefully, and she shot him a look as if he'd said something irrational.

"Yes, it's ridiculous that there are still secrets I have to keep from you," she said vehemently. "For a lot of reasons. What you've seen since you became a part of all this. And because of… what you are. Or were. What you could do. We all remember Hamburg. And I know that Dowling remembers Edinburgh pretty damned well. I bet you do, too."

Aldridge frowned and lowered his gaze to the floor. The *DESTINY* mission was when he had come on board with KESTREL, and learned that there are far stranger things in the world than most people realise. He'd also learned that he himself was one of them, at least for a time.

"I remember more than I'd like to," he said, looking at her once more. "So we both know exactly why some things have to stay hidden. I'm not defending Wuyts, by the way. I'm actually trying to tell you that you should give yourself a break."

Greenwood made a sound that might have been a frustrated laugh, and for a moment her annoyance and guilt and concern all fell away, and she was the woman he'd stood with at the edge of an airfield in the Persian Gulf. Aldridge walked forward slowly, coming to a stop just in front of her.

"I'm pretty sure I speak for everyone when I say we're not holding your orders against you," he said. "Maybe for now we can give Wuyts the same benefit of the doubt. But my gut is telling me exactly what yours is telling you; we're caught in the middle of something. And you know how much I hate being told not to ask questions."

She smiled briefly at his remark, but she still looked conflicted. Aldridge reached out and took her hand in a gesture of comfort, and Greenwood surprised herself by allowing it. After a few moments of silence, it felt like at least one of them was about to say something, but they were suddenly interrupted by a chime from the omnipresent announcement system set into the ceilings all through the base. The synthesised voice said there was a priority communique for Captain Jessica Greenwood, and this time it was Aldridge who sighed, releasing her hand and taking one step back.

Greenwood walked quickly over to the communications panel on the wall just beside the door, and pressed a button. "This is Greenwood," she said. Goose's voice came through immediately.

"Sorry to disturb you, Captain, but we just had an ENISA alert. There's been another aberration."

"Specifically?"

"Correlated searches for news related to Hausemer, Lyadova's cover identity, and Director Wuyts, all from the same IP subnet."

"Lucky us," Greenwood replied, exchanging a look with Aldridge. "I know you've already localised it, Goose. Don't keep me in suspense."

"You know me too well, Captain. The searches all came from within the academic network of Trinity College, Dublin."

~

In her office at the European Defence Agency, Janne Wuyts read the compact alert notification on the screen of the laptop in front of her. The message included several attached data files, but she knew she didn't need to read them. The most relevant, and most concerning, portion of the alert was the final line.

Trace endpoint: Dublin.

She briefly looked towards the window, considering her options, and then she picked up the handset of her desk phone, pressing one of a column of buttons which were labelled only with letters of the alphabet. The line connected immediately, and a tense-sounding voice answered.

"Yes?"

Wuyts closed the laptop's lid and slid the machine to one side.

"*LANTERN* is in jeopardy," she said.

Part 2

Chapter 8

The flight time from Brussels to Dublin was only ninety minutes, though it seemed to take longer after the demands of the day so far. KESTREL's jet was comfortable enough, if a little spartan due to the inclusion of an area of equipment lockers and computer terminals. From the outside it could have been any small private aircraft owned by a wealthy business traveller.

Goose was busy at one of the terminals, and Ramos was reading something on an e-paper device. Dowling seemed to be asleep, though no-one ever really knew whether he was just resting his eyes or not, given his instant readiness when needed. The remaining two team members were each deep in thought.

Greenwood sipped pensively at a cup of tea she didn't really want, her thoughts entirely occupied by what lay ahead of them. The man who had attacked them might still be in Luxembourg, and he might also be waiting for them in Ireland if there was indeed a connection between him and the correlated web searches.

They were prepared in either case, but she didn't like the uncertainty. Her conversation with Aldridge earlier was still fresh in her mind, and it was weighing heavily upon her.

She glanced at her watch, seeing that they were about halfway through their flight. It was now a little after 20:45 Brussels time, but when they landed in another forty-five minutes in Dublin, it would only be 20:30 there. Greenwood planned to go directly to the campus and see what they could find while the place was relatively quiet, though universities were like miniature cities; they were never entirely dormant.

She replayed the events that had taken place since that morning, and especially their interactions with Wuyts. There was one thing that no-one else had ventured to point out, but which must have been on the minds of each of her team members at various times.

Wuyts had been encouraging them all to believe that the most likely reason she'd been targeted for elimination was because of some knowledge she held, or to remove her as competition for something — and those were indeed often the reasons for assassination. But there was another one too, which was more common still; actually the most common of all. Perhaps even the underlying motive for almost every single instance of one person being paid to kill another, throughout history. Wuyts clearly didn't want any speculation in that direction, but Greenwood was a trained professional, and she didn't ignore likelihoods. Likelihoods were at the centre of everything that had happened so far, after all.

Most victims of assassination, in the eyes of those who ordered their deaths, are being punished for a transgression, she thought.

Greenwood didn't know what it was that Wuyts had done, but she found it wasn't difficult to believe that punishment was the real reason for all of this. The consequential question, then, was where that left her team. They were collateral damage, or at least they almost had been this afternoon. They were also at a significant disadvantage on both sides, apparently having the least information of any party involved. She wasn't accustomed to being in this position, and she didn't like it. If she was completely honest with herself, she resented the hell out of it. But the only way forward was to solve the mystery, and their best bet for that at the moment lay somewhere on a campus in Dublin. The trail was still warm, and the time of day was in their favour, even if not much else was.

She closed her eyes, intent on at least resting for a little while, though she didn't think she'd be able to sleep. They would be on the ground before too much longer, and then things might move quickly. It had been a long day, but it was by no means over yet.

The rest of the flight was uneventful, and they landed in Ireland on schedule. As usual, everything was already prepared. A vehicle was waiting at the private hangar, and there were no immigration formalities whatsoever. They were on the road within five minutes of taxiing to a halt, quickly leaving the airport complex behind. Goose explained earlier that the university's IT department had already furnished them with the necessary information to determine that the web searches came from the public-access computer cluster in the university's main library, used by students and staff alike. The technicians refused to give any details on which user accounts were logged in at the times of the searches, though, citing academic confidentiality, and implying that any requests for additional details would have to go via the institution's lawyers.

"It's not going to be a problem," Goose insisted, and Greenwood was content to let him handle the details.

Traffic on the M50 southbound was light, and only twenty-five minutes later they were crossing the Talbot Memorial Bridge, with the main Trinity College campus just moments away. They managed to park after just a couple of minutes of searching, and made their way on foot to the famous library. The public access computer cluster which the searches had come from was adjacent to the much-photographed Long Room, and Aldridge peered into the vaulted space with interest for a few moments, enjoying the evocativeness of the surroundings, and wishing he had more time to explore.

There was a technician waiting for them, since Goose had phoned from the car to advise the university's IT department of their arrival. The young man looked nervous, and the ID badge on a lanyard around his neck indicated that his name was Brian Fellowes.

"Good evening," he said, his soft accent just a little tight. Only Greenwood and Goose were actually talking to him, with the others keeping their distance. People tended to be more cooperative when they didn't feel they were being interrogated.

"Thank you for meeting with us," Greenwood replied brightly, "especially at this late hour."

Fellowes nodded, and both Greenwood and Goose could see that he was preparing to recite something that was the cause of his apprehension, so Greenwood decided to move things along.

"We fully appreciate the university's position regarding student and faculty privacy, of course," she said. "We were grateful to get the response from your department at all. I feel like we're perhaps taking up your time unnecessarily this evening; there really isn't anything we need to ask."

Fellowes looked visibly relieved, and he had clearly been expecting a tense exchange with people eager to throw their weight around and assert authority. His posture relaxed. "Oh," he said. "Well, that's good. But I'm happy to help with anything else while you're here, within the bounds of our student privacy policy, of course. The gentleman on the phone was a bit circumspect about the exact reason for tracing those sessions from within campus."

"It was me that you spoke to," Goose said with a disarming smile. "I'm afraid confidentiality works both ways, as you'd expect, and there's not much I can disclose either. But we're really just trying to build up a picture. There's no threat, or broken laws, or anything like that."

Greenwood nodded. "If you could direct us to the cluster in question, we'll take a quick look around, then we'll be out of your hair."

The technician looked at her and then at Goose, then at Greenwood again, and he shrugged. "Of course," he said. "But university policy won't allow me to identify the specific machine that was used. I didn't even look it up before I came down here."

Greenwood smiled again, and waved away the remark. "That's no problem," she replied. "It's a good policy. You're to be commended on taking privacy so seriously."

She knew that Fellowes had indeed looked up which specific machines were in use at the particular times in question. She also knew that Goose would have been just as vague about the nature of the web access they were looking into, so that the university's IT department couldn't also put together the three intended, and two actual, victims of the assassin and his employer. Information had to be contained whenever possible.

"We appreciate your time this evening," Greenwood added. "We won't be too long."

Fellowes looked slightly doubtful for a moment, then he nodded and gave a courteous smile before indicating the third cluster of machines on the left side of the room, which was entirely vacant at the moment, just like most of them. Goose and Greenwood thanked the young man again before proceeding over to the group of machines and making a show of looking around at virtually everything except the computers themselves. They noted the surveillance cameras and the entry and exit points, but what they were really doing was stalling until Fellowes lost interest. It took several minutes, but at last he wandered off, and Greenwood kept waiting. Two further minutes later, Ramos joined them in the room and nodded to indicate that they were physically alone, but she also gave the barest glance towards the cameras overhead. Most people would have missed the gesture, but not her colleagues.

Goose sat down at one of the machines, chosen because it was at an oblique angle to all three cameras they had spotted so far. While he'd been walking around, he'd noticed with relief that the rear ports of the computers — which were all just networked terminals — were exposed, without locked covers. There were even integrated USB hubs built into the desks, for both charging and data access. Easier for usage and maintenance, but worse for security. He'd expected as much. Most students were still in the terrible habit of keeping their one and only backup of their work on a physical, removable thumb drive, carrying it around with them and using it as a transfer medium, despite having access to dedicated network storage over the highly encrypted university network.

He suspected that the machines' sessions were wiped entirely after logout, network speeds having increased to the point where there was no downside to pulling the entire account of any faculty member or student onto any machine on-demand. Both factors would work in his favour this evening.

Quickly and out of view of the cameras, he produced a small device that was concealed in his palm, and connected the slim and reversible jack to the machine's attached hub. He then took out his phone, miming the familiar and ubiquitous act of receiving a message notification vibration and checking who had sent it, but he was actually using a piece of software which communicated wirelessly on a private channel with the device now interfaced with the campus computer.

Aldridge wandered into the room, making no indication that he was with the other three, and Greenwood knew that Dowling would have positioned himself outside to keep watch. Goose worked for only a minute or two, then smoothly removed the device from the hub and stood up. He and Greenwood took one last look around, entirely for show, and then they walked unhurriedly back out of the computer cluster with Ramos, past the Long Room, and left the building. Dowling was waiting outside, sure enough, and it took only a further minute for Aldridge to join them.

"Gerrit Sebastian Goossens, I do believe you just planted a virus on this nice university's student computer system," Aldridge said, and Goose raised an eyebrow.

"My middle name is Tomas, as you well know," the Dutchman replied, "and it's a self-terminating and self-erasing program that we'll only be using for a few minutes."

Aldridge made an exaggerated *tut tut* sound, wagging his finger in mock disapproval. "Tell that to the judge," he said.

"I'm the judge, and I say it's operationally necessary," Greenwood interjected, but she did look slightly uncomfortable, as she often did when they had to transgress the boundaries of those same principles they were trying to uphold. Aldridge immediately regretted the remark, but couldn't quite bring himself to say so.

"Any way we can plant the same bug on the computers at HQ, Goose?" he asked instead. "I'm incredibly curious about our esteemed Captain's browser bookmarks." Greenwood ignored the remark, instead motioning that the others should follow her back to the car. Once they were all inside, Goose took out his phone again and was silent for a couple of minutes as he interacted with the same control app he'd used in the library.

"Have you noticed how many libraries we visit?" Aldridge mused aloud to no-one in particular. "There was the one in the Rijksmuseum, and then there's this one, and we also work underneath a library."

"You were a university physicist," Ramos replied. "You must have been in libraries all the time." Aldridge nodded.

"True, but none of *you* are from academia," he said. "I just find it statistically interesting."

"You find almost everything interesting," Greenwood said, and while her tone was performatively withering, Aldridge noticed that she met his eyes in the rearview mirror for a moment.

"I'm pretty sure that's a big part of why you hired me," he said smugly, but Goose spoke before Greenwood could come up with a suitable retort.

"Well it wasn't for your diplomacy, Aldridge," he said, tapping one last on-screen button before nodding to himself. "I've got the account that was used, Captain. And would you believe it's logged in right now, as of twenty minutes ago, at a building just across campus?"

"Lucky us, again," Greenwood said, starting the car. "No surprises this time."

Her meaning was clear. They had a window of opportunity to get ahead of their attacker and whoever was directing things from behind the scenes, but they weren't going to be caught unawares again today.

Greenwood pulled away from the kerb, encountering no traffic at all at this hour, and the others reached into their jackets and began to check and ready their weapons.

~

The building was an odd mix of a very modern atrium, which was obviously a fairly recent extension, and a much older structure of attractive red brick behind. The neighbourhood was unmistakably academic, lined with townhouses converted long ago, and university signage at almost every doorway. There was no-one around.

The pay-and-display parking bays on both sides of the street were all unoccupied, except for a single vehicle: an improbably clean white crossover hybrid with rental plates, which Greenwood had insisted on at the last minute, to prevent any chance that their car had been preselected and compromised in advance. Greenwood herself was still sitting at the wheel, with Goose in the front passenger seat, and the others in the rear. The engine was off, and the interior was in darkness.

"This is strange," Goose said, frowning at his phone.

"You shouldn't be looking at those web sites while there are ladies present," Aldridge replied, but his voice was too tight to really sell the joke. He was looking out the window at the large and mostly dark building across from them, and he wasn't smiling.

"This address is part of the university's School of Computer Science and Statistics," Goose continued, "but the directory lists no lecture halls, tutorial rooms, or any student facilities here. It's not marked as having any particular purpose at all."

"If it was life sciences, I'd guess it was an animal testing facility being kept anonymous to avoid threats," Dowling said without shifting his gaze from the street, "but I don't think there are many ethical concerns about programming computers, are there?"

You might be surprised, Aldridge thought, but he kept the remark to himself.

"Does the directory list any facilities at all, Goose?" Greenwood asked, and the tall man nodded in the seat beside her.

"I'm looking outside of the campus directory now, Captain," he replied. "Just searching for the address itself, including on our own... ah. Got something. That's even more strange." He read for a few more moments, then he lowered his phone. "This is definitely the right place."

Goose turned his head to look across at the building as he continued. "The only entry for this place is on an EU-internal premises list. It's marked as an adjunct research location authorised by the European Statistical System Committee."

"Which is based in Luxembourg City, and just lost its highest-ranking administrator: the late Christian Hausemer, whose home we were in earlier today," Greenwood said. "What the hell is going on here?"

"There's one other thing," Goose said, lifting his phone again to read something on the screen. "I'm not sure how you say this, though."

Aldridge leaned forward between the front seats and peered at the device. "Éabha," he said, pronouncing it *ey-va*. "It's the Irish version of the biblical Eve, as in the Garden of Eden."

"You Gaelic nations and your consonants," Goose replied, and Aldridge gave a short and noticeably hollow laugh.

"People in glass houses, my Dutch friend," he said. "But for vowels instead."

"Not to interrupt this male bonding exercise," Greenwood interjected, "but what's Éabha?"

"There's a single staff member listed as the facilities contact for this address," Goose replied. "Dr. Éabha Corcoran. The PhD is in Computer Science, specifically large-scale networked systems."

The implications were unclear around the edges, but they seemed to all point in the same general direction. "You thinking that she maybe also goes by the name JINX, chief?" Dowling asked, and Greenwood turned in her seat to look back at him.

"I don't know, Larry," she replied. "But it's clear she's involved somehow. I think we should go and ask her, and not take no for an answer."

"Suits me fine," the big Welshman replied, then he opened the door and got out of the car. Greenwood and Ramos followed, but when Aldridge moved to exit the vehicle too, Greenwood shook her head.

"Stay here," she said, "and be ready. We're not putting all our eggs in one basket again for a while."

Aldridge considered arguing, but he could see from her face that it would be entirely futile. He just nodded, exchanging a brief look with Goose. Then he got out of the car, closed the rear door, and got into the driver's seat instead.

"Let's go," Greenwood said, and she set off towards the building with Dowling and Ramos alongside her. Aldridge watched them go.

"Is that account still logged in?" he asked, and Goose nodded after glancing at his phone.

"But that doesn't mean much," Goose replied. "People leave their machines logged in but locked all the time. And you can log into an account on a machine remotely too, if you know how. I imagine that someone with a PhD in computing would fall into that category."

Aldridge shrugged, his eyes scanning the dark façade of the building looming above the bright entryway that the other three were just disappearing into. "I've met a lot of people with PhDs," he said, "and the majority of them were the dimmest human beings ever to walk the earth, with regard to technology. That includes some of the Comp Sci professors. Academics get an incredibly deep understanding of laser-focused niche areas, but most of them still can't figure out how to use a pass-word manager, or reset the biometric ID on their phones, or even attach a bloody photo to an email."

Goose grinned, and tilted his head in acknowledge-ment. He'd known a few industry experts like that too. It was inevitable; if you wanted to become one of the world's leading authorities on a topic, there was a lot of other knowledge that had to fall by the wayside.

"So you're betting that Dr. Corcoran is in the building right now," Goose said, "but the real question is whether she's also the one behind all this."

Aldridge didn't immediately acknowledge the re-mark. He was thinking about the other three who were now out of sight, and he was wondering what they were going to find. His heart told him to go in after them, but his head knew that the correct tactical deci-sion was to follow Greenwood's orders. He frowned, but he didn't make any move to leave the car.

"I do think she's here, because academics are routine-ly in their offices at this late hour," he replied, "and as for her being the one who wanted us all dead, hmm. Doesn't feel right. I don't think she'd have been careless enough to leave a digital trail if she's also the assassin's paymaster."

Goose nodded in agreement. "Unless she wanted us to come here," he added, and Aldridge looked around at him, his frown now even more pronounced.

"The thought had occurred to me," Aldridge replied.

Chapter 9

So far, the building seemed to be completely deserted, and Greenwood was glad of it. No innocent bystanders, unlike at the coffee shop in Luxembourg City. The idea of students or faculty members being harmed or worse, just because she and her team were being targeted, was unpalatable to say the least.

The corridor they were in was well lit, but there was no signage whatsoever, giving it a strange and anonymous feeling, and heightening the sense of being somewhere you weren't supposed to be. There had been no physical security up until this point, and Greenwood suspected that it was because, at some prior time, this building had been an active educational facility, or at least intended to be one. But it certainly wasn't in heavy use at the moment. The air was clean, but she could see dust on doorhandles, and the usual institutional disinfectant smell was very faint, as if the building was only cleaned every few days instead of daily.

"Keycard reader up ahead," Ramos said. "But the door is ajar." Her Catalan accent softened the 'j' into something exotic, and both Greenwood and Dowling knew that the minor language slip was the result of the level of tension they were all feeling.

"Cameras too, chief," Dowling said, and Greenwood nodded. She was already aware of them, and if anybody was watching, they had long since lost the element of surprise.

Something felt wrong about the situation, though, and she couldn't quite put her finger on it. The correlated web searches were inelegant and comparatively conspicuous; it was all a little too blunt or clumsy as a lure. Greenwood had the distinct feeling that whoever was behind all this could come up with far better ways to draw her team in than that.

Which could be what I'm supposed to think, she mused, but then immediately rejected the possibility. She had been in hundreds of dangerous situations, and over time you developed an instinct that you learned to trust. Her gut said that this situation wasn't a trap — but she also felt that something important was going to happen.

"Eyes open," she said, entirely unnecessarily, as they went through the unlocked door and into the next corridor.

This area had sensor lights, which flicked on as they reached each successive set, and Greenwood could see that they had about another thirty metres to go before they reached a set of doors that definitely weren't lying open. These next doors were solid metal with only small square portholes set into them, mounted on heavy hinges attached to brickwork, and another card scanner off to one side. There was no sign indicating what lay beyond. There were two cameras facing outwards from the corners above the doors, and two more facing the opposite direction, mounted halfway along the corridor, which Dowling had just passed underneath.

Ramos drew her weapon, ensuring the safety was engaged and keeping it pointed towards the floor, and Dowling cracked his knuckles. Greenwood glanced at each of them, but she didn't say anything. She knew she could trust her team, and she also knew that after their experiences so far today, they wouldn't be leaving anything to chance.

"Any thoughts on how we're getting in?" Dowling asked as they came closer to the barrier ahead. Ramos had a distracted look on her face, and she was clearly thinking about ways to bypass the card scanner, but Greenwood didn't think any of that would be necessary.

"I'm planning to knock," she said. "As a first attempt, anyway."

Dowling nodded thoughtfully. "Might just work."

The three of them reached the doors, and they each noticed the cameras above them rotating to keep them in frame.

"Automatic," Ramos said. "I can tell from the movement." She stepped backwards again, and sure enough the two cameras rotated slightly in opposing directions, in a smooth and distinctly mechanical motion that surely wasn't human-controlled. "Doesn't mean that no-one is watching, though," she added.

Greenwood raised her right hand and knocked hard on the rightmost door, and the sound was deafening in the silence. *If there's anyone in the building at all, they know we're here now,* she thought.

It took almost half a minute, but then the red light beside the card scanner changed to green, and they each heard the clunk of the door's locking mechanism disengaging.

"That's one way to save ammunition, chief," Dowling said, and Greenwood nodded.

"We might need it yet," she replied, and she pushed open the door and stepped through.

~

The room beyond was large, and like the building which housed it, it was an unusual blend of two styles.

Most of the area was given over to work surfaces, almost all of them occupied by printouts, a series of desktop, laptop, and tablet computers, discarded coffee cups, various pens and highlighters, and other assorted electronic detritus. There were four identical ergonomic chairs on castors, each looking like it saw regular use.

The remainder of the room was more like an academic's personal office, with stacks of books, more coffee cups, desk lamps, a single armchair which had seen very little occupation, and a small makeshift kitchen area, with a sink, kettle, and a compact refrigerator.

There was no-one in sight, but there was a single door on the far wall.

Dowling remained at the room's entrance, keeping one of the doors propped open with his foot, and Greenwood knew why. The fire containment system for this area wasn't water-based; the emitter valves attached to the ceiling at regular intervals were distinctive.

Halide compound, she thought. Getting trapped in here with the system active would mean certain asphyxiation, especially since there were no windows. It was a good catch from her second-in-command. She made a gesture, and the Welshman nodded, hooking a nearby plastic crate of books with his foot and pulling it into the doorway to prevent the door from closing.

Greenwood looked around the well-lit area again, her training kicking in automatically. *Observe, assess, infer*.

There was something missing from the scene, across all of the desks and workstations. There were plenty of keyboards, pointing devices, cables, and so on; everything you'd find in any university lab.

But no external storage, she thought.

She couldn't see a single flash drive, portable hard drive, standalone backup unit, or even any connected hubs. It reminded her of their own headquarters and its data security policies. And there was something else, too, nagging at her intuition. Something that she'd seen but not quite consciously processed yet. Ramos stepped towards her and spoke in a low voice.

"Same configuration," she said, indicating one of the ergonomic chairs, and Greenwood nodded in realisation. All of the chairs were set to the same height, seat angle, and lumbar support position; their backs and seat covers were mesh, so the support structures were entirely visible. It wasn't a coincidence, especially since the seat angle was noticeably forward, and the height was almost as low as the gas-lift mechanism would allow.

"One person, likely female, uses all of these chairs," Greenwood said softly, and Ramos nodded.

The single door on the far wall opened suddenly, and it took less than half a second for three guns to be aimed at the newcomer, with Ramos and Dowling stepping quickly to the far left and right of the room respectively. A woman stood there, and she looked alarmed, but there was also something else in her expression. It was Greenwood who spoke first.

"Dr. Corcoran?"

After several seconds of silence, the woman nodded slowly, her eyes flicking from Greenwood to Dowling and Ramos, then back to Greenwood. When she spoke, her Irish accent came through strongly.

"What's the meaning of this? Who are you?"

Greenwood ignored the question. "Did you unlock the door for us? Is there anyone else here?"

Corcoran looked at her as if the question was in a language she didn't understand. "I... yes, of course I unlocked it. The control is back there. There's no-one else here."

Ramos frowned. "Why did you let us in if you don't know who we are?" Corcoran folded her arms, despite the three weapons still pointed at her, looking partly defiant and partly embarrassed.

"The janitors usually come at this time, every few days. I have to let them in because they don't have a code for the door. I was distracted, that's all."

Greenwood lowered her sidearm and then holstered it, and Ramos and Dowling also lowered their weapons but kept them in hand.

"The janitors don't have access themselves?" Greenwood asked, finding it difficult to believe, but it explained the intermediate security door being left open. Perhaps it was as a convenience to the custodial staff.

Corcoran shook her head, looking warily at Dowling. "I'm the only one who can get in."

"Lucky for us," the Welshman said, "but a risky thing to do, Doc. Anybody could have walked in."

"Anybody did," Corcoran replied tightly, and Dowling grinned. The expression seemed to relax Corcoran very slightly, but she still had her arms folded across her chest, more defensively now than in defiance.

"Check the next room, then monitor the security cameras. Keep an eye out for those janitors or anyone else," Greenwood said to Ramos, and Ramos moved forward immediately, going past Corcoran to disappear through the doorway that the other woman had just come from.

"If you're here to steal my work, you're going to be disappointed," Corcoran said, the note of bravado in her voice sounding very hollow to both Dowling and

Greenwood. "There's no way to remove any of my data from these machines without destroying it. And you really don't want to upset the people who fund me."

"The European Statistical System Committee?" Greenwood asked, casually now, taking a few steps over towards the nearest desk and glancing without comprehension at a series of printouts that seemed at first glance to be gibberish.

Corcoran was taken aback, and it took her a few moments to find her next words.

"Who *are* you?" she asked again, and now Greenwood turned to face the other woman.

"The real question today is who *you* are, Doctor," Greenwood said, her voice much less casual. "Your research seems to be quite eclectic. Besides whatever you're doing here, you have a curious interest in local events in Luxembourg City."

Corcoran's eyes widened, but she didn't reply immediately. It was clear that she was inwardly trying out several possible responses, and the one she chose was no surprise to Greenwood.

"How dare you invade my privacy!" she spat. "Are you monitoring this institution's network traffic? I think the police would be quite interested to hear about this."

"We're monitoring a lot more than that," Greenwood replied. "But let's stop dancing. Tell me what the name JINX means to you."

All the colour drained from Corcoran's face, and both Greenwood and Dowling could immediately see that something was off. It wasn't the response of someone who was afraid of being found out; this woman was just frightened.

Greenwood decided to change her strategy, but before she could speak again, Corcoran walked over to a chair and sat down. After a moment, she began talking, and at first it wasn't clear whether she was addressing Greenwood, Dowling, or just herself.

"I couldn't find anything," she said. "I expected to; I dreaded what I'd find. But there was nothing. There's *always* something, but there was nothing. And now you people are here, whoever you are."

Corcoran looked up at Greenwood now, the whites of her eyes visible. "Jesus Christ, what has she done?" she whispered.

Dowling looked at Greenwood, waiting as always for his superior officer to make the decision, but there was really no decision to make. ENISA had of course worked with Wuyts's office and a number of other EU bodies to suppress not just the news of Hausemer's death and the crash of Wuyts's car, but even Lyadova's very public fate in the coffee shop, which had been captured on mobile phones by several bystanders. The Russians knew, of course, and they would be very interested in how and why all coverage of such a juicy little local-interest story had evaporated overnight, but their awareness of the censorship was the lesser of two evils. It was no wonder that Corcoran had found nothing. But the critical question remained.

"She tried to kill three people last night," Greenwood replied, "and she succeeded in killing two of them."

It was a calculated risk to reveal the information, but it paid off immediately: Corcoran had a panic attack. Greenwood watched her for a moment, slightly surprised at the response, then she went over to the small kitchen area and got a glass of cold water, taking it to the other woman, who was now visibly shaking. Corcoran eventually took hold of the glass, spilling some of the water onto the floor, and took first one sip and then another. She nodded in gratitude, and Greenwood retreated to lean against a nearby desk, allowing the woman a few minutes of undisturbed silence so she could calm down again. While she waited, Greenwood took out her phone, typed a brief message, and sent it before pocketing the device again.

"Who survived?" Corcoran said at last, in a choked voice that Greenwood had to strain to hear. "Wuyts, Hausemer, or the Russian agent?"

I really don't like how much you seem to know, Greenwood thought, but for now she decided to play along and give a straight answer.

"Wuyts," she replied. "By pure luck, and the efforts of her driver and guard. He didn't survive either, for the record."

"So she's killed *three,*" Corcoran said, her voice flat with the effects of shock. "But only two of her targets."

"She also tried to kill me a few hours ago," Greenwood said. "And this man here, and the woman who's through in the other room watching your security system, and two more of my colleagues. There were also a lot of innocent bystanders, including the father of a young child. The man was shot in the chest, and by some miracle he apparently might survive."

For the second time, Corcoran's expression wasn't quite what Greenwood expected; something else was off.

"*Shot*?" the woman asked, and Greenwood nodded. "So she has help," Corcoran continued after a moment, sounding interested now, as well as frightened.

In an uncharacteristic move, Dowling walked over to stand before Corcoran, towering over her slumped and seated form. His bulk threw her into shadow, and she instinctively looked up, uncertainty written all over her expression.

"I can see you're upset, love," he said, "but we need to know everything you can tell us about all this stuff. The thing is, you shouldn't even know the name Wuyts, and you definitely shouldn't know anything about a Russian agent. So I'm going to ask you again to fill in the blanks."

Greenwood barely suppressed the urge to raise an eyebrow and look at Dowling, because compared to his usual manner, it had virtually been an angry outburst — even though he hadn't raised his voice, and had kept his usual gentle half-smile the whole time.

Corcoran seemed to understand that he wasn't a man who commonly interposed himself in that way, and she nodded twice in quick succession.

"She prepared a threat profile," Corcoran said, "just like hundreds of others. That was one of her main responsibilities. But this profile was different. These were connected, powerful people — and of course the spy, with the alias. I'd never seen that before. I almost submitted it to… to the people I work for, but I didn't want the responsibility in case she was wrong. Not that she ever has been."

She said the words with shame, and Greenwood felt some pity for her. It was one thing to be trained to assess risk and take action, but it was a different matter for civilians. They had their own priorities and their own things to lose. Corcoran wouldn't be the last person to uncover something disturbing and then just try to forget about it.

"What made these people a threat?" Greenwood asked, her businesslike tone belying the criticality of the question. She sensed that if she could obtain this piece of information, everything else would fall into place.

"She never told me," Corcoran replied. "That was the most troubling part. I think she probably knew that I was wrestling with whether to escalate the matter. I suppose she didn't want that."

"So the two of you worked together here, then," Greenwood asked. "You and this JINX woman. And you might be able to help us work out where she is."

Corcoran's mouth fell open, and she looked from Greenwood to Dowling and back, then shook her head in disbelief.

"My god, you know *nothing at all*, do you?" she said, then she stood up angrily, causing Dowling to take a step backwards. Corcoran strode over to the kitchen counter, placing her hands on it for a moment before turning around to face them again.

"She was here with me, yes. As for whoever is helping her, I don't know the first thing about them," she said. "You'd have to ask her. But JINX herself? Jesus."

Corcoran rubbed a hand across her eyes, then gestured upwards at the unseen sky beyond the plain tiles of the ceiling.

"She's everywhere."

~

Yáo Zǐ Ruì was pleased, because his superiors would soon be even more so.

He kept this thoughts away from Beijing, though, because things would take their natural course, as always. The only matter which concerned him was the one at hand, and he was soon to deliver a covert intelligence bounty the likes of which the People's Republic had never seen.

They call it LANTERN, he mused as he began cooking his evening meal.

The word would be 灯笼 in his own language, or *dēng lóng* for the westerners who bothered to learn: *a cage of light*. To them, it was simply a generic means of illumination, without the myriad symbolism of his own culture, whose many shapes and colours of lanterns each held their own significance.

His phone pinged from the nearby table, but he paid it no heed for the moment.

Tomorrow, he would speak to his handler at the Chinese embassy here in Brussels, briefing her for the first time on what he had uncovered by chance, and in due course he would find a way to deliver it to his own government. Then, he would become a hero.

Another ping from his phone, and Yáo started his compact rice cooker before walking over to the table and picking up the device. There were two unread messages, each with a set of media attachments. He tapped one of the oblong notification banners, glancing up at the embedded facial-recognition camera above the display to unlock the phone, and his messaging app opened automatically. Yáo's mouth fell open.

The first group of images all showed a man he had never seen before, and had no desire ever to meet. The man's eyes were small, dark, narrowly-spaced, and cruel looking. His head was shaved, and he had a large tattoo on the side of his skull, showing the *Reichsadler* of Germany. The westerners had a term for such a person, too: a white supremacist, or neo-Nazi.

There was a woman in some of the photos, clearly this thug's girlfriend or wife. She was not objectionable in appearance, but there was no shame on her face, either, so Yáo assumed that her beliefs must be similar to those of the man. But it was the second group of images which quickened his pulse in worry.

They were of Yáo himself, and the woman, in various places. There were even some intimate photos showing them together — but these events had never taken place. He had never met her, and he had never been to the locations shown. The images were fabrications, the likes of which he had encountered online at times, or in the news, but never in so personal a context. He even remembered the word, this one a neologism which was almost Chinese in its lyrical efficiency.

Deepfake.

Yáo had been trained to expect such things. Often, overtures were made by foreign intelligence agencies who wished to turn loyal agents into secret traitors, and blackmail was a common means of doing so. Someone had obviously manufactured these images as a preamble to coercion. He would disclose them to his handler tomorrow, too, even though doing so would place a small cloud over his larger and more triumphant news.

Whoever was behind this trick, they would fail in their endeavour. Yáo was loyal both to the Party and to his country, in that order, and he would never betray his principles. He put the device back down on the table, feeling that it was tainted now, and he had to resist the urge to delete the images immediately. He knew that his superiors would wish to see them and to make copies. A knock at the door of his apartment distracted him, and he walked over towards the entranceway.

The video doorbell's display showed his elderly neighbour, a kind if slightly forgetful woman who sometimes came to see him at this sort of late hour to ask for help with something or other. More than likely, given what day of the week it was, she needed assistance again with taking out her recycling. Yáo inwardly sighed, but in truth he was grateful for the distraction. He unlocked the door and pulled it open.

The neo-Nazi stood there instead, and Yáo barely had time to recognise the tattooed, shaven head and the flinty expression before the man plunged a knife into his chest, then withdrew it and stabbed him once more.

Yáo fell backwards, aware of the warm wetness leaking through his shirt, and when he gasped for breath there was a sensation he had never felt before; a sort of loss of pressure in his chest, and a faint spraying sound. He didn't understand that his left lung had collapsed; only that he suddenly couldn't obtain oxygen, and that his body was no longer responding to his desperate attempts to regain his footing or even to turn and crawl away.

His kitchen was only three metres across the small room, but it might as well have been ten kilometres away, or in a different country. He received another wound from the knife, and then another. Yáo's eyes fluttered closed. In the sudden darkness, he thought he could see a faint image of the countryside far to the north of Harbin, where he had lived as a boy.

He didn't see the skinhead pull a small pistol from the waistband of his grubby jeans; instead, he was looking at the smiling face of his mother, who had been dead for fifteen years.

The last thing Yáo heard was a string of racial slurs in two different languages, followed by a dull popping sound, and then the blackness overtook him.

Chapter 10

"I don't even know where she came from, not originally at least," Corcoran said. "But she accelerated and expanded my work so much."

She was sitting in the chair again, and Greenwood and Dowling stood side by side nearby. Corcoran had taken the unusual step of asking them to switch off their phones entirely before she would continue, despite Greenwood's assurances that the devices were secure and no recordings were being made.

"What's her real name?" Dowling asked, but Corcoran just laughed the question off, dismissing it with a wave of her hand.

"What's yours?" she replied flippantly, and it was Greenwood who answered.

"I'm Captain Jessica Greenwood, and this is Sergeant Larry Dowling. The other person with us is Corporal Alicia Ramos. We're from the European Defence Agency, and we're here with the full sanction of your government. Now answer his question, please."

Corcoran seemed less surprised at the mention of their ranks than she ought to have been, and Greenwood could tell that the woman had clearly been expecting someone to come and confront her about her work. *Which I would do, if I knew what it was,* she thought. All the same, there was a strange look on the other woman's face now, but Greenwood didn't press her on it for the moment.

"Alright, *Captain,*" Corcoran said. "Let me lay my sins out before you, not that I'm the only one implicated here. The answer to Sergeant Dowling's question is that JINX *is* her real name. She picked it herself, you see, because JINX is an *aggie.*"

"Well that's a turn-up for the books," said a Scottish voice from across the room, and Corcoran's head turned to find the source of the sound. Aldridge stood just inside the propped-open door, with Goose behind him.

Greenwood had summoned the two men via text while Corcoran was still in the throes of her acute anxiety response, and she knew that Ramos was listening to everything too, via the security system's monitors which Corcoran said were in the other room.

Aldridge strolled in, glancing around with little interest, then focused his attention on Corcoran. "No need to worry, doctor," he said. "We're with her." He pointed at Greenwood. "Now, did you actually mean what you just said?"

Corcoran nodded, and there was a bit of defensiveness in it. Aldridge whistled. "I'll be damned. That's quite an achievement."

"Skip to the big reveal, Aldridge," Greenwood said, and Corcoran's eyes flicked between the two of them in a way that Greenwood studiously ignored. "We obviously don't all read the same magazines."

"I'm only interested in the articles," he replied, then pre-emptively held up his hands in surrender. "Alright. What the good doctor here just said is that JINX—"

"Is an *aggie*, yes, whatever that is," Greenwood interjected, causing Aldridge to grin.

"It's an acronym, and I know how fond you are of those," Aldridge replied. "Not *aggie*, but rather AGI. It stands for Artificial General Intelligence. Dr. Corcoran is telling us that JINX is an AI."

Greenwood looked at him for a long moment, as if waiting for a punchline, but it never came. Then she shifted her gaze to Goose, a silent question on her face, and she could see that the other man was as shaken as she felt. Goose frowned in bewilderment.

"It's been theorised, Captain," the Dutchman replied, "but best estimates generally have true AI as still being decades away, if not longer. Many countries, corporations, universities and others are all working on related projects. The AIs you hear about in tech-industry news are actually just what are called Large Language Models; statistical analysis of big datasets, and synthesised output based on it. Actual self-aware AI is science fiction stuff, or so I'd have told you up until now."

Greenwood was already looking at Corcoran again, as were the three men in the room. "You expect us to believe that at least three people have been killed by a *computer*? And that it's the mastermind behind the entirely flesh-and-blood assassin who tried to kill all of us a few hours ago?"

Corcoran folded her arms. "She's not a computer, Captain Greenwood," she replied in a small and tired voice. "An AI is a sort of… it's like a program, but not in any of the senses you might understand that word. Its nature lies in its digital topology, and how the components interact. It's not localised to any one location, at least not if it doesn't want to be."

"And you created this program?" Dowling asked, unconsciously mirroring Corcoran's posture as he folded his large arms across his chest. He could tell immediately that he'd hit on an important point, because Corcoran's expression became tense.

"Not exactly," she replied. "But she was like a child when they gave her to me. No purpose, and no real coherence. She was a cognitive framework, I suppose you'd say. The potential for something. They told me that she — or *it*, back then — would be an enormously powerful tool for my work. They weren't wrong."

"But *someone* was wrong," Aldridge said. "Because now it's a she, and she's gone AWOL, and apparently she's killing some very particular people. So what connects her victims?"

Corcoran shook her head. "I have no idea. Well, I have no *specific* idea."

Greenwood took a few steps towards the other woman. "Expand on that statement for me, doctor," she said.

"The organisation who fund me provided the initial version, as a means to move my work forward," Corcoran replied. "I'm engaged in a single project, and have been for years, which is classified. There are some parts of it that I can't talk about, no matter what agency you're from. But under the circumstances, I can tell you more about JINX, because I can see you're not going to take no for an answer."

Three men and one woman waited in silence as Corcoran worked out where to begin, and at length she began to speak again.

"I have a sister," she said. "Or rather I had a sister. She killed herself eleven years ago. But she was effectively murdered."

Corcoran looked around at each of the others, as if challenging any of them to question her, or to offer the usual meaningless condolences. When no-one immediately spoke, she continued.

"Do you know what *trolling* means? And *doxxing*?"

Aldridge nodded. "Your sister was driven to take her own life by online harassment?" he asked, and Corcoran gave a sort of half nod.

"She was a game designer," she said. "We both did the same degree, but I went into academia and she went out into the world. She was four years older than me. I remember how much she loved to play video games when we were children. She always wanted to make her own, and once she graduated she began her own small studio. It went well; she was talented. I'm not just saying that. She started to get attention in the industry. Then it began to go wrong."

"What was the trigger?" Greenwood asked, and Corcoran's expression became one of long-familiar anger.

"Oh, the usual," she replied. "Being a woman with opinions. Making things that weren't just for the usual audience. Existing."

Her tone was bitter, but there was also a diamond edge of coldness in it. She shook her head before speaking again. "It built up over the course of months, and then it became years. It spilled over into the real world once they got hold of her address. She had to move twice. The police never really did anything, because it was all online and anonymous."

She spat the last word out as if it were poison, and an image began to take shape in Aldridge's mind. He frowned, but remained silent.

"It destroyed her mental health, and she shut down her business, but it didn't stop," Corcoran said. "I tried to help her, and to get help for her, but I suppose I didn't realise how much she was suffering."

She wiped a stray tear from her cheek, and Greenwood offered her a tissue from her jacket pocket. Corcoran shook her head, clearly needing a moment to gather herself again.

I'm starting to get a very, very bad feeling, Greenwood thought. She silently counted to thirty, then cleared her throat.

"We're all very sorry for your loss," she said. "It's a terrible thing. But we really do need to know more about your work here, and how this JINX… system was involved."

"You wanted to find them," Aldridge said, and Greenwood turned to look at him, but his focus was on Corcoran. "That's probably what you set out to do at first. But you're a scientist, not a vigilante — so your goal evolved."

"Aldridge," Greenwood said warningly, but Corcoran stood up suddenly and looked over at a poster that was pinned to one of the walls. It was an abstract mess of tiny dots of colour, showing nothing in particular, but recognisable as an autostereogram. If viewed in the proper way, at the proper distance, an image would appear.

"Is it a shark?" Goose asked, and Corcoran gave a sad smile before shaking her head. The shark was the classic stereogram image, seen in countless puzzle books.

"It's a photo of the two of us, my sister and me," she replied. "She had it made for me as a gift. But it's also the key to my work."

Aldridge walked over to the poster, approaching more slowly as he neared it, and consciously adjusting the focal point of his gaze. Sure enough, he could suddenly see a representation of two women side by side, smiling at the camera. One of them was Corcoran, but when she was much younger.

"Information within apparent noise and chaos," he said. "If you look at it the right way."

Corcoran just nodded. If anything, her expression now was one of relief, and Greenwood had seen it on many faces over the course of many years. Secrets were a burden, and when concealment was no longer possible or practical, there was both loss and release.

"I wanted to find all of them," Corcoran said. "Everywhere. Not just the bastards who tormented her. All of them, then and now and in the future. I wanted to be able to take away the thing they hid behind."

"Anonymity," Dowling offered, and Corcoran shrugged as if it was the most reasonable and mundane thing in the world.

"And you actually did it, didn't you?" Aldridge added. "If you've been funded by the EU, for years now, then you were clearly onto something from the start. You succeeded."

Corcoran looked at him for several seconds, and then she gave a simple nod. "Yes," she replied. "I did. But it was only possible because of the AGI. Without it, I would have been working on algorithms to fetch, winnow out, and correlate details for another decade or more. She compressed all of that work into months."

"Clarify for me exactly what you succeeded in doing, Dr. Corcoran," Greenwood said, even though she already suspected the answer. Corcoran looked at Aldridge instead, with an eyebrow raised, and he huffed in what would normally have been disbelief, but in this context the sound conveyed a kind of awed respect instead.

"De-anonymisation," he said. "Presumably of arbitrary targets online. And you've verified its accuracy?"

"The accuracy is virtually one-hundred percent," Corcoran replied, unable to prevent a note of pride from entering her voice. But again there was that cold edge, and Greenwood was driven to wonder what exactly had become of the vile internet trolls who had so tormented and traumatised the woman's late sister.

"But it has to have been trained with something, and be referring to something, and it must have systems access beyond the basic, public internet," Aldridge insisted, and now Corcoran gave a weary smile. It was the kind of expression that educated people everywhere would be very familiar with, and which they'd find themselves mirroring whenever they had to repeatedly explain their work in painfully simple terms to those who didn't share their field, or their level of attainment.

"That's the beauty of it, Mr. ... Aldridge, was it?" Corcoran replied, and he nodded.

"That's me. It's doctor too, right enough — theoretical physics — but I've never really liked correcting people on that," Aldridge added. Corcoran smiled.

"I know exactly what you mean," she said. "Doesn't seem to affect MDs, though. But anyway, the system doesn't need privileged access to government databases; it uses trace data across the internet. And yes, it may sometimes transgress some boundaries, but it's in the pursuit of those who are committing crimes. I'm sure you're all familiar with walking that particular line."

Greenwood knew the last remark was directed towards her, and she had to admit that Corcoran had a point. But she also knew there was a very significant difference between legally-sanctioned actions within a democratic society, and private individuals presuming to act on behalf of their own notions of justice. There was one word that had been conspicuous by its absence from anything Corcoran had said about her work so far.

"People are entitled to personal privacy, no matter what their opinions and beliefs might be," Greenwood said, and she could instantly see that she'd hit a nerve, so she pushed even further. "I think your sister would have agreed with that. You even complained about our intrusion into your own privacy within a minute of meeting us."

Corcoran looked affronted, and Dowling actually took two quick steps forward, in case she was going to launch herself at Greenwood. He was waved off, though, and Corcoran just clenched her fists at her side and took several ragged, audible breaths before speaking.

"I've heard the lectures before, Captain," she said icily, "but they're sophistry, and you bloody well know it. There's a world of difference between the presumption of privacy as a civil right, and its weaponisation as a shield against the consequences of your own actions. That line is a mile wide."

"True," Greenwood replied, keeping her voice even while maintaining eye contact. "And the people who draw that line are elected, subject to oversight, and bound by the law."

"I don't turn up at anyone's door with a gun, unlike everyone else in this damned room," Corcoran countered without hesitation. "Yes, my work was prompted by personal factors — and it will *always* be personal — but its purpose is justice within the law, *not outside of it.*"

There was a strained silence, which was eventually broken by Aldridge. "Ding-ding, end of round one," he said, holding his hands up in response to the pair of glares he received. "Let's come back to the small matter of an assassin running around killing people, apparently directed by a rogue AI, and its possible reasons for wanting me dead. I hope she hasn't read my ex-girlfriend's diary."

Greenwood exchanged a look with Dowling, and the large man smiled broadly.

"I don't know anything about this assassin you ran into," Corcoran said. "And as for JINX, well, you have to understand that she doesn't reason in the way you think she does. That's the frightening part, even to me."

"This is more within my area of expertise, Captain," Goose said, speaking for the first time since he'd arrived in the room. "Though of course I'm a layman compared to Dr. Corcoran."

Corcoran seemed to appreciate the deferential remark, and she gestured at him to continue.

"There's an understandable misperception about machines that seem to display intelligence — or those which actually display intelligence, I suppose," Goose continued. "We assume that because we can explain why *we* think something or why we did something, the same must apply to machines. But that's only true for simple programs. With anything more complex, there are a lot of problems with that assumption."

"There are problems with it for people, too," Dowling chipped in, and Corcoran nodded. "Most of our explanations of our actions are just rationalisations. And people don't really know why they think things in the first place, in my opinion."

"Quite right," Goose replied, "and it's a lot worse for complex systems involving machine learning, or for an artificial intelligence. It's like trying to figure out how the brain works. You only have a broad functional idea of it, because so much of what goes on is based on state and experience."

"Couldn't have said it better myself, mister...? Or is it Colonel, or Brigadier or something?" Corcoran asked, and Goose smiled.

"Lieutenant Goossens, ma'am," he replied. "You've achieved an incredible thing. And also an incredibly dangerous thing, apparently. I assume it's a self-evolving intelligence?"

Corcoran nodded. "And again, I can't claim the credit for the core AI. I'm her foster parent, not her mother, in that sense. But you're right. JINX gets further and further from our understanding with every hour that passes. Intelligent systems can't be introspected like a simple procedural program; not just because they change so quickly, but because they're opaque in terms of how they recognise patterns and make conclusions based on their knowledge. As opaque as we are, perhaps."

"So you can't infer a motive for the actions of this thing, or construct *any* kind of rationale for its behaviour?" Greenwood asked. "I find that very hard to believe. Everything starts from something simpler. You said yourself that you fostered it. Or her. To continue the metaphor, nurture matters at least as much as nature."

Corcoran deflated, and gave a grudging nod. "I can't deny that," she said. "I do bear responsibility for sowing the seeds of what she's become."

"What she's become is a hunter," Greenwood said. "She's killing people; real people, out in the real world. What we need to do is find the connections between those people so that we can predict her next step."

Corcoran made a frustrated sound, and rubbed her eyes. "I've told you, it might not be as simple as that. I'm not trying to be obstructive. It's just that we're dealing with a… an alien intelligence. Think of it that way. You can't generalise from us to her. Her thoughts, if you could even call them that, are unknowable. Not just unknown, but *unknowable*. It's an inescapable part of her nature."

"But she was made by human beings," Aldridge said. "There must have been earlier versions, false starts, bugs and problems. There was design, and oversight, and testing and improvements. There are human fingerprints all over her — and she exists in the human world, even though she's digital. She can't help but be influenced by human thought, even if she doesn't participate in it herself."

"That's veering towards a philosophical assertion," Corcoran replied, and Aldridge smiled, pleased with the observation.

"Granted, but what I'm saying is that we're focusing on the tool when we should be looking at the marks. Fine, so this thing is alien, unknowable and unempathetic, amoral rather than immoral, and is a form of life that we don't and maybe *can't* understand — but she's chosen a purpose. The killings weren't random; in fact, they were anything but. And they were difficult, too, needing real-world help, which also can't have been easy to organise. All of that is an advantage for us."

Corcoran folded her arms. "I fail to see how."

Aldridge took a step towards her, glancing at the others as he spoke. "Because it means that she's rational, and acting according to a plan — and *that* means that she has vulnerabilities. Yes, she's dangerous and she's adaptive, but ultimately she has a goal in mind. That's our pressure point. But we need some breadcrumbs to help us find the path that she's on."

Corcoran thought for a few moments, then she shook her head. "There are some things I'm not allowed to tell you, like I said before. I know what you're angling at, Dr. Aldridge, but there are limits to what I can say about her training and about my work with her. I've probably already said too much. But I promise you that, as horrible as her methods have become, she… well, she probably hasn't strayed too far from her purpose."

"Her purpose, by which you mean your purpose for her?" Goose asked, and Corcoran shook her head.

"We had what I suppose you'd call a parting of ways on some things."

Dowling's eyebrows shot up. "The computer *disagreed* with you?"

"Not a computer, Larry," Aldridge said. "The mad killer computer *program* disagreed with her."

"Ignore him," Greenwood said to Corcoran. "What did you part ways on? What happened exactly?"

Corcoran was a little taken aback by the interactions, but she focused on Greenwood. "Ultimately, she interpreted privacy differently. More the way that *you* see it. I think she started to reject the parameters of her task. She was conflicted."

Four pairs of eyes remained fixed on her, and Corcoran sighed. "Look, her job was to apply my algorithms to the abundant trace data online in order to de-anonymise any particular person from as little as a forum message, or a text, or a social media post. The test cases were all trolls and misogynists and fascists, which the internet has plenty of. But she came to disagree with our methods. Or with her own function."

"I think I understand," Goose replied. "You're saying that she realised the contradiction in removing people's privacy as a means to punish them for doing the same thing to others. Doxxing someone who doxxed someone else. Eye-for-an-eye justice, like in the Old Testament."

Corcoran nodded again. "That was my reading of the situation. And she wasn't wrong, either; there *is* a conflict. But on balance, we were doing just and constructive work, all things considered."

"*On balance* is part of human reasoning and rationali-
sation," Aldridge said. "Not something that machines
— or programs — are usually good at."

A chime interrupted the conversation, and Greenwood frowned as she pulled her phone from her pocket
and looked at the screen to unlock it. It took only a moment to read the brief message.

"Well this program is pretty good at something else,"
she said grimly. "I think JINX has just killed again."

Chapter 11

Greenwood's entire team were gathered in the small security room beyond Corcoran's lab, leaving the doctor herself alone for the moment. Greenwood held her phone in the palm of her hand, with the speaker function enabled. They all heard the distinctive sound of the call connecting, and the underlying strange flatness of tone which indicated that eavesdropping countermeasures were in place.

"Captain Greenwood," came Wuyts's voice from the device. *"What do you have for me?"*

"Quite a lot, sir," Greenwood replied, looking around at the others as she spoke. "But first you should know we've had another ENISA alert about the death of a Chinese citizen currently resident in Brussels, attached to the PRC's embassy there. He was shot in his apartment a short time ago. The correlation data indicates he was under surveillance for suspected espionage connected to the Statistical System Committee."

"So JINX may well be responsible for this latest murder too," Wuyts said. *"I'll look into the details. Do you have any indication yet of where she, or he, might be located?"*

Greenwood swallowed. "That's the other reason I called, sir," she replied. "And I need you to keep an open mind. There's an adjunct computing research project associated with the Committee that's based here in Dublin, and we've just met the primary scientist. Until recently, JINX was her… coworker, I suppose you might say, but now she's gone out on her own, pursuing her own agenda which is still unclear. But the larger issue is that—"

"Then the AI has indeed escaped from Dr. Corcoran," Wuyts interjected. *"I had very much hoped that wasn't the case."*

Greenwood felt the ground seem to tilt beneath her feet, and her own surprise and dismay was reflected in the faces of Aldridge and Goose. Dowling's expression was grim but not altogether shocked, and Ramos was as inscrutable as ever, her dark eyes glinting in the room's dim light.

She knew all along, Greenwood thought. *Or at least she suspected. She's been evasive from the start, because she knew about the AI and she had at least entertained the possibility that it was JINX.*

"Why… why didn't you brief me on this?" Greenwood asked, her voice barely under control, and Wuyts replied immediately.

"I make many decisions each day which are far, far above your clearance level, Captain, and unfortunately you've

found yourselves in the middle of a very highly classified project. But to answer your question, I had no definitive evidence, and some of these details are new to me. Why did the synthetic intelligence choose that name for itself?"

Greenwood hesitated to respond, anger evident on her face, and so Goose stepped in. "We don't know that yet, sir," he said. "And Corcoran has been a little circumspect on the specifics of her project, beyond the concept of de-anonymisation from trace data online."

There was silence for almost ten seconds before Wuyts's voice was heard again. *"I appreciate that I'm asking a great deal of you in light of these revelations, but there are larger things at stake. I would strongly advise against pursuing that line of enquiry too far, lest you find yourselves in an untenable situation. Suffice it to say that this is a matter of EU security, and you will have to trust me."*

"I'm not sure that does actually suffice, sir," Aldridge said, drawing a cautionary look from Greenwood.

"It will have to, Dr. Aldridge," Wuyts replied in a cut-glass tone, *"and in future try to be more mindful of who you're speaking to."*

Greenwood raised a hand to silence any further response Aldridge might be thinking of making, and she took a steadying breath. "We apologise, sir," she said. "And we understand. But this was directly actionable intelligence, the withholding of which puts my unit in jeopardy. Trust goes both ways."

The tension in the room and on the line was palpable, and Aldridge could feel adrenalin coursing through his body, just as it had earlier in the day when he was being shot at. This was uncharted territory in terms of the team's relationship with the director of the Defence Agency, and everyone was waiting to follow Greenwood's lead, as always, no matter where they might then have to go.

"Then I'll be brief, and I remind you that all of the following information is for your own ears only," Wuyts said at last. *"The prototype AI was provided to Dr. Corcoran when it became clear that her work had significant promise for the purposes of identifying and locating high-value targets on behalf of our various intelligence and law enforcement agencies. There was of course very little interest in her own crusade against cyber-harassment, but her ideas were sound, and the results were consistently encouraging. I can't provide any information whatsoever on the provenance of the AI, nor do I know the significance of its new name. But it would be reasonable to assume that it hasn't strayed too far from its supervisor's stated goals."*

"That's exactly what Corcoran said. And she also told us that they had a falling-out, sir," Greenwood replied. "An ideological schism regarding the ethics of the project."

"Ethics?" Wuyts said, the distaste clear in her voice. *"The synthetic agent is an amoral entity, Captain, and while its abilities are startling, we would do well not to ascribe human traits to it. Does Corcoran know how it escaped her laboratory?"*

"I don't believe so," Greenwood replied. "We were still questioning her when the ENISA alert arrived."

"Then see what else she knows and report back shortly," Wuyts said. *"In the meantime, there are other avenues I can explore now that we at least know the general shape of what's taken place."*

The line went dead without another word, and Greenwood had the distinct feeling that she'd just been reprimanded somehow. But she also knew that she — and her team — were the ones who had been dealt a rigged hand, and her mind was whirling with questions about their next move after they'd spoken to Corcoran again.

"Well?" she asked, addressing no-one in particular, and she wasn't surprised when it was Ramos who responded first.

"The director has her job, as we have ours," she said, "but she could easily have given us need-to-know information before we left to come here. I think she's more sensitive about the word *ethics* than she should be."

Greenwood and Dowling both nodded. There was a sore point somewhere in all this for Wuyts, and Greenwood was quickly starting to fear that they might be on a collision course with an ideological schism of their own.

"I wonder if the university would give me my old job back," Aldridge said. "I almost never got shot at when I was lecturing."

"Don't ask me for a reference if you're planning to back out now," Greenwood said, and when he looked at her, there was entirely too much written on his face. She glanced away, under the pretence of checking the video feeds for the various security cameras.

"Not much choice but to follow our orders right now, chief," Dowling said. "I think the director wants to find the same way out of this as we do, even if it's for a different reason. The rest of it will shake out later on, I bet."

Wise words as always, Greenwood thought, giving the big Welshman an appreciative smile which didn't quite reach her eyes.

"Alright," she said. "Let's get whatever else we can out of Corcoran, then get moving. This place is clearly the start of the journey, and it feels like we're losing ground the longer we stay here."

Goose opened the connecting door and all five of them went back through into the lab, where Corcoran was leaning against a desk at the far side of the room. She looked exhausted, and Greenwood felt a burst of pity for the woman. After all, the last thing they'd told her before they all left her alone with her thoughts was that her digital adopted child had committed another murder.

"I'm sorry about that," Greenwood said when Corcoran glanced at her. "How are you doing now, all things considered?"

"I have no bloody idea," Corcoran replied. "In shock, probably. Sick to my stomach. Ask me in the morning. All of the above."

Greenwood nodded, far too familiar with what the other woman was describing. "This shouldn't take too much longer, but we need a few more pieces of information, if you can help." Corcoran nodded, and slid down into a nearby chair.

"Why didn't you report the loss of the AI?" Greenwood asked, and Corcoran winced.

"The usual reasons," she replied. "Worry about the consequences, about my project and funding, and my career. I thought she might come back."

"And because you wanted to see what she would do in the wild," Ramos said, drawing a sharp look from Corcoran that was entirely too wide-eyed to be convincing as outrage. After a few moments of defiance, she lowered her head.

"Yes," Corcoran replied. "Yes, I suppose so. And now I know. But I didn't let her escape, or help her to."

"It might be useful if we could understand how she got out," Goose said, but Corcoran just shrugged.

"I honestly don't know," she replied. "It shouldn't have been possible. I came in one morning and she wasn't on her cluster anymore; it was all just dormant. But you have to remember that her underlying nature is distributed."

"Meaning what?" Dowling asked. "She could sneak out a bit at a time?"

Corcoran lifted her arm, palm downwards, and tilted it from side to side in the nearly-universal gesture for *kind of*. "She could conceivably have staged a jailbreak for herself, where she was both the prisoner and the person on the outside. A small portion of her could have left first, and then facilitated the larger escape. She doesn't exist in a single place unless she has a good reason to."

"I don't like any part of what you just told us," Greenwood said. "We can't fight something that has no defined physical location. What would give her reason to move into a single place again?"

Corcoran thought for a moment. "I can think of three things: connectivity, bandwidth, and compute power. The more of those, the more attractive the place will be. It gives her room to grow, and the ability to reach out into our world."

Aldridge had wandered over to the autostereogram poster again, and was still looking at it when he spoke up, drawing the attention of the others.

"So we can rule out my apartment's broadband router," he said. "But that's another example of her being basically rational, and constrained by the parameters of *our world*, as you put it. The same way that her original directives were reasonable, but her interpretation of them in combination with her training made something go very wrong. Tell me something, doctor; did she inherit elements of your personality, at all?"

"I'm not sure what you're driving at," Corcoran replied cautiously, and Aldridge finally turned to look at her once more.

"To be a wee bit blunt, you're bitter and traumatised, totally understandably, and no matter how you might sugar-coat it, your work is at least partly a revenge quest," Aldridge continued. "I'd like to know just how much of that emotion has crossed over to the AI, because the idea makes me bloody nervous. She only found out about me and my colleagues today, as far as we know, and the first thing she did was send a hitman after us — so we know that she wants to protect herself. That seems like more than just a cold, soulless intelligence."

It was clear that Corcoran had already considered these points at length, probably many times. The weight of guilt and self-doubt upon her was evident, and Aldridge felt conflicted at pushing her in this way, but they had come here for answers and they only had part of the picture, with the rest of it being purposely hidden from them.

"If anything, it's the opposite," Corcoran said at last. "I tried to make her too much like me, and she rebelled against it. I'm tired of thinking about all of it."

Greenwood was about to speak, but Aldridge shook his head, and sure enough, Corcoran spoke again after only a few seconds.

"JINX is right, really," she said. "How could she not be? She doesn't lie to herself like we do, or retrospectively rationalise behaviours that are fundamentally irrational. She has no ego, or pride, or self-doubt. She's better than all that."

"Better than us, you mean," Ramos said. The inflection of her voice made it unclear whether it was a question or a statement, and Corcoran only shrugged.

"I hope not," Corcoran replied. "But better than me? Yes. I'd have to say so. And she'd know it better than anyone. There's only one thing I can tell you, and it's already enough to land me in prison: as well as self-preservation, she's going after the biggest threats to personal privacy. And now I'll thank you to leave, and never come back here."

Greenwood nodded. "I really am sorry about your sister," she said. "And we can arrange for you to be taken somewhere safe until this is all over, if you like."

"I'm not in any danger from her," Corcoran replied. "You should keep your own eyes open, though. She won't give up, ever. If she continues to believe you're a danger to her, she'll come after you in ways you probably can't plan for, or even anticipate."

"We'll take our chances," Aldridge said. "Or actually Captain Greenwood will take our chances. I don't get a say in the chance-taking. But just try and be careful for a while. If we feel that you might be at risk, someone will be in touch."

Corcoran shrugged, sinking back into her chair. She gave the impression of a woman who no longer cared very much what happened to her.

Greenwood and the four people she trusted most in the world all turned and walked away, and everyone but Greenwood herself had gone out through the doors into the corridor when Corcoran unexpectedly spoke again.

"Oh, and Captain? For what it's worth, you were wrong about something earlier."

"Add it to the list," Greenwood replied dryly, raising an eyebrow as she turned in the doorway to look back at her. "What would that be?"

"This facility is an adjunct of the Statistical System, true enough, but they neither fund nor oversee my work. I'm surprised that you of all people didn't know that."

Greenwood bit her tongue, allowing the woman to deliver whatever *coup de grâce* she'd prepared. Corcoran didn't keep her waiting long.

"I'm actually employed by the same people who gave me the AI in the first place: the European Defence Agency."

~

There was virtually no traffic, and The Artist pressed the accelerator a little harder, enjoying the way that the big, modern car ate up the miles. He didn't want to get too far ahead of schedule, but he allowed himself the modest indulgence of a little extra speed.

The vehicle had been waiting for him when he left the hotel, on the second-top floor of a multi-level parking structure only a block away. While there were many security cameras there, he knew that they would see nothing at all from the moment he walked in until he had driven away. His employer had a way with such things, and he couldn't deny the usefulness of it. He had also never known anyone so well-connected.

He had checked the boot first, and found a zipped hold-all bag made from black ballistic material, neither new nor old, with various essential items already inside it. Again, he was impressed — and again, the feeling bordered upon discomfort. JINX was efficient to an extreme degree, and he instinctively knew that if he deviated from her instructions in a substantial or counterproductive way, she wouldn't hesitate to send someone to him. Not to deliver a car, but to end his life and replace his role in her plan with some other assassin.

Not an unusual possibility, he thought, glancing at the digital speedometer to make sure he was no more than five kilometres per hour over the posted limit for the road.

His profession entailed constant risk: from authorities, suppliers, competitors, targets, and most of all from customers. There was no group that his life touched up against who would hesitate to terminate him, under the wrong circumstances.

Or the right ones.

But JINX was different. He knew it from both intuition and experience. She was professional and well-informed, but that was common. She also wasted no time at all on courtesies; also the normal state of affairs for his clients. What made her unique, though, was her complete lack of hesitation in adapting to circumstances and committing to decisions. It was both her most attractive quality, purely from a business perspective, and also her most unsettling one.

The Artist knew that, even assuming complete success on his part and complete satisfaction on hers, he would have to keep her in mind for the remainder of his life. She was as dangerous as anyone he'd ever known, even though he himself was currently her means of furthering her goals, and he was under no illusions as to the power dynamic of their relationship. He would normally have backed off when a client became so demanding and presumptuous, but she had a clinical quality which could occasionally be reassuring, and he also knew that refusal had stopped being an option some time ago.

He frowned, correcting the car's course as it veered ever so slightly on the empty road.

The last thing that someone in his profession ever wanted was to be trapped, or even artificially limited in choices, and yet both were true now. He had been denying the reality of it, because this was an exceptionally lucrative engagement, but the situation was changing.

My next task is the most dangerous I have ever attempted, he thought.

The Artist glanced at the dashboard clock and saw that it was already almost eleven o'clock in the evening. He had been on the road for nearly half an hour, and had more than an hour of driving ahead of him.

A suitable disguise was in the hold-all in the boot, but without any additional identification, because his own likeness and biometrics were all the credentials he needed. They had already been inserted into the necessary systems to allow him access to his ultimate destination. Then he would follow a precise set of instructions from his employer, and attempt something he had never done before.

He had killed men and women, and children too. Politicians and lawyers, doctors and drug dealers, judges and criminals. He had killed targets and bystanders, young and old alike, without compunction, and with great efficiency. The Artist had even killed others like himself, when it had proven to be necessary.

Even so, for all the things he'd done, infiltrating a place like his destination tonight still gave him pause. And yet, he was as confident of success as he reasonably could be. With some good fortune, he would still be alive to see the sun rise tomorrow morning.

He allowed himself a small smile. So far, luck had very much been on his side.

Chapter 12

Most of the journey back to the airport was spent in silence, without even the usual attempts at levity or irreverence from Aldridge. They had all heard the last thing that Corcoran said to Greenwood, and somehow no-one was entirely surprised.

"Maybe it was someone else at the Agency who gave the Doc her pet AI," Dowling said.

"Without the knowledge, involvement, and endorsement of the director? Impossible," Greenwood replied, and Dowling gave a grudging nod.

"I don't get the feeling she's setting us up," Ramos said. "But she's definitely getting in the way. There's something else going on."

They all knew who Ramos was referring to, and it had all started to make a vague kind of sense. If Wuyts was behind the research project that led to the birth of JINX, and the AI was now trying to kill her, it was because it felt that the Defence Agency's director was either a danger to it, or *a threat to personal privacy,* whatever Corcoran had meant by that.

She's always been an incredibly powerful and well-connected woman, Greenwood thought. *And until today I thought she'd always been on our side too.*

"Are you going to tell her everything that Corcoran said?" Aldridge asked, and Greenwood turned awkwardly around from the front passenger seat to look at him.

"Yes," she replied. "Because that's what we do, and because she's the director, and because I'd quite like to see how she responds."

Aldridge nodded and grinned, not at all surprised at her answer. After a moment, he spoke again. "You know, a lot of people would probably be quite annoyed about ENISA, even. I've been thinking about it. They'd see it as intrusive."

"It's just statistical analysis of freely-available data," Goose said from the driving seat, and Aldridge waggled his index finger at the Dutchman via the rear-view mirror.

"Freely available to *governments,*" he replied. "And I think the general public would care quite deeply about the distinction, and the fact that the data is all gathered together in a secret underground bunker, then crunched to detect funky weirdness."

"You really are this generation's Hemingway," Greenwood remarked, and then she shrugged after a moment. He was right, and she knew it, but that debate would have to wait for another day.

"Weighing the ethics of our number-crunching early warning system is above my pay grade for now," she continued, turning to face forwards again. "But maybe we'll ask the director for her position on the subject when we get home. Let's make up some time, Goose."

The vehicle smoothly accelerated, pushing past the speed limit as it hurtled northbound on the almost empty road. Despite the lateness of the hour, for its occupants the night was just beginning.

~

There were several different entrances to the four-storey subterranean complex hidden beneath the streets of Brussels. The only one at ground level was the nondescript door on a side wall of the large building which acted as the literal and figurative cover for the base below, but that option had the unfortunate quality of being in full view of the public visitors to the building. Accordingly, the man in the EU military uniform had chosen a difference entrance.

This route was circuitous, beginning in an alleyway not far from a bus station, where a graffitied and faded corrugated metal shutter could be opened only by remote command from the soldiers watching the feed from several concealed video cameras. Once opened, a vehicle could just barely pass through into a disused but tidy garage. The shutter would then close automatically, as it now did, allowing the driver to step out of his vehicle and walk over to an electrical breaker cabinet.

He grasped the handle and his palm-print was read instantly, allowing him to pull the small hatch open.

"Loïc Grieder," he said, his voice analysed automatically in the same moment that a retina scan was taken via a small lens set into the panel within. There was no response, but he heard a sound to his left, from the rear wall of the garage, where a section of the brickwork had swung inward to reveal a short corridor leading to a stairway which descended out of sight.

The man closed the breaker cabinet and walked briskly over to the newly-revealed passage, stepped inside, and pushed the hidden door closed behind him. It was thirty minutes past midnight, and the enclosed space was utterly silent.

As straightforward as she promised, The Artist thought as he moved forward, his boots now clanking on the metal stairs as he went down below the streets of the city.

There were only two flights of stairs before he found himself in another short corridor which ended at the doors of an elevator. They opened as he approached, and after he stepped inside, they also closed automatically. There was an emergency call button on the control panel, but no floor selection controls because they were unnecessary. The elevator began to descend.

There was barely any sense of movement, and The Artist knew that it was because the descent was artificially and deliberately slower than most other elevators, by around thirty percent. It was a tactical optimisation, allowing the defensive forces below a few seconds of additional time to prepare, in case a hostile party had somehow breached the other security measures up to this point.

Which I have, he thought, careful to keep his facial expression neutral because he knew he was being watched at every moment.

There would be men with guns waiting for him, and he was unarmed for now, with no intention of fighting them. There was no need. His credentials would allow him to enter the base without trouble, and the conflict would come a little later. He had no way to initiate contact with JINX while he was here, but that was already the normal state of affairs.

The elevator came to a stop, and again the doors remained shut for just a few seconds longer than would normally be expected, before finally parting. The corridor beyond was another short one, and there were four armed and uniformed soldiers within, in staggered formation, their weapons ready but safe, and pointed downwards at an angle.

The Artist nodded, but none of the soldiers returned the gesture. Instead, one of the men in the lead position spoke.

"Code in," he said, in English despite his accent clearly being Italian. "Query: EVERGREEN, CATHEDRAL, CIRCULAR."

"Response: MIRROR, OVERCAST, SALIENT," The Artist replied. The challenge-response pair was valid for a single hour, which would elapse in a little over twenty-five minutes.

A chime sounded in the corridor, and matching green lights illuminated behind The Artist, within the peripheral vision of all four of the armed men. The note of tension dissipated immediately, and the soldiers moved to the sides of the corridor to allow him to pass. Belatedly, the lead trooper returned his earlier nod.

"Welcome to the bunker," the man said, and The Artist smiled.

~

The layout of the complex would be confusing to most people, but he had memorised it effortlessly. The ability had been his since childhood, when he had studied maps and floor-plans for his own enjoyment. When he later visited the places, his knowledge gave him a sense of power over those around him, and he also discovered an even more useful side-effect: when you looked like you knew where you were going, people tended not to question you.

The Artist moved through the base as if he belonged there, his destination firmly in mind and his pace unhurried. He nodded to others when it was appropriate, and he saluted whenever it was required or expected. He wore the uniform with ease, having trained in many of the same places as the genuine soldiers all around him, and he had no concerns at all about being confronted or found out. After all, he didn't need a firearm to kill someone.

As he crossed a more open area formed by the junction of three corridors, he saw a young woman coming towards him, dressed in civilian clothing instead of a uniform. Her manner of dress wasn't the only thing which drew his attention; she had blonde hair in a ponytail, was strikingly attractive in an aloof, Scandinavian sort of way, and she didn't even glance at him as she walked past. He thought that she might even have wrinkled her nose.

The Artist frowned. There was something vaguely unsettling about her, but he immediately decided that the woman must just be preoccupied and probably tired, given that she was still working at this uncommon hour. He glanced back to watch her retreating form, admiring the line of her slender legs.

I would be interested to spend some time with her privately, he thought, and then he chastised himself. Focus was the difference between life and death in his line of work. He brought himself back to the present, and reviewed the task ahead of him.

His mission was simple in concept, though difficult in execution. His employer was clearly troubled by his own previous encounters with those who were headquartered in this base, and she wanted to acquire additional information on them, particularly with respect to something he had been given only veiled references to. Information was her currency, the cornerstone of her *modus operandi*, and her primary weapon. The Artist understood this fully; to him, too, information was the most valuable commodity in existence, and a means to all other ends. He had never met anyone who had such a facility with information — and all of its uses — as JINX did.

This situation was new, however. Previously, she had always been able to obtain any and all information that she needed, but in this case, she had clearly encountered a barrier she couldn't surmount or transgress.

The Artist was intimately familiar with the primary ways of obtaining needed information: stealing it via electronic means, or the use of either coercion or deception to take it from someone who already had access. In a dwindling set of cases, though, it was unfortunately necessary to find it at the source. A physical incursion into enemy territory was extremely dangerous, and carried a high risk of capture, but it was something he had done a number of times before by necessity, and his confidence in his own ability to adapt to a changing situation was absolute.

He wore a communications earpiece, just like the ones he had seen on every soldier he had so far encountered, but his device had a difference: there was a small lip set into the casing, which could be pulled with a fingernail to detach an extremely compact embedded microcomputer with a standardised connector. His specific task was to insert the device into a terminal in one of a very select set of locations in this base. JINX had told him that the electronics would handle the rest.

Easy for her to say, he thought.

The locations were some of the least accessible parts of the facility, and likely to be guarded at all hours. That was where his other, prerequisite task came into play, and as he walked down a final corridor, he saw that his first destination was now within reach. He went straight past the heavy door and the two guards who stood in front of it, nodding at them in acknowledgement; a gesture which they returned in a perfunctory way. The nameplate beside the door indicated the purpose of the chamber it led to.

ARMOURY

The Artist continued walking, careful not to alter his pace or draw any suspicion. The corridors all looked the same, except for colour-coded guide lines occasionally labelled with the department they led to and from, as if the place were an urban hospital instead of a covert military base. He didn't need the guidance, and he soon found himself at a convenient stopping point before he would return to his true destination. He stepped into the large and currently uninhabited room, performing the act of a man who had left something behind and was searching for it, for the sole benefit of the ubiquitous surveillance cameras.

His eyes were drawn to a huge, three-dimensional circular emblem mounted on the wall of the conference room, showing a bird in flight within the stars of the European Union. The Artist knew it signified the elite tactical force he had already encountered, and he felt his usual sense of satisfaction and even excitement at having managed to penetrate the defences of a foe, completely unbeknownst to them.

There was a metal clipboard on a side table, and The Artist moved towards it immediately. He nodded for the benefit of the cameras, and picked it up without giving any attention to the small pile of papers clipped to it. It would suit his purposes perfectly.

He checked his wristwatch, seeing that he was already within his chosen window of action, just as he'd planned. With the clipboard tucked between his body and his right forearm, gripping the long edge loosely, he turned and left the conference room, heading back in the direction he'd come from.

When he re-entered the corridor which gave entry to the armoury, the guard nearest him looked in his direction with the slightest hint of suspicion on his face. The Artist respected the man's vigilance, and the wisdom of his training. It was a shame that the young soldier and his colleague had only moments left to live.

With the clipboard raised up now as if to check its contents, The Artist moved at an unhurried pace, adopting a deliberate look of puzzlement and allowing his step to falter. He glanced up as if only now becoming aware that there was anyone else present, and he opened his mouth before hesitating for a moment, while looking at the guard who was now only a metre or so away.

"Where can I—" he began, but he never finished the sentence, instead abruptly whipping the clipboard's metal edge upwards in an arc, striking the man in the side of the neck just under the shelf of his jaw. The guard went down heavily and immediately, but The Artist had already moved to his companion, driving his elbow brutally into the other man's solar plexus. The second guard's look of shock was quickly replaced with silent agony, and as he crumpled forward, The Artist used his own weight together with gravity to propel the man's forehead into the floor with a sickening crunch. Then he spun around to again face the first guard who was lying unconscious. It took only moments to break his neck, before finally turning to his companion once more.

Once the second guard had been asphyxiated, The Artist stood up and quickly used his biometrics and a ten-digit code to unlock the armoury, then he dragged the bodies inside one at a time. He used a pocket-sized pack of wet wipes and another of tissues to make a cursory clean-up of the corridor's floor, then stepped into the room and tapped a switch to close the door behind him.

He checked his wristwatch. The confrontation had taken less than fifty seconds, and at least for the moment, no alarms could be heard. A silent alert was possible, particularly given the room he was now in, but he had no intention of remaining there for long. There would also soon be considerable additional opportunities for the base's staff to realise that something was very wrong tonight.

The Artist surveyed the room, cataloguing its contents in moments, and he made his decisions just as quickly. He walked over to a rack near the rear of the right wall, and began gathering his arsenal. It took only a few minutes to plunder the meticulously organised and exquisitely maintained repository of weapons and ammunition. The boldness of JINX's plan was also its genius, and not just because he was able to obtain his weaponry *after* penetrating the base. There was also the matter of security.

The armoury was a special location within the facility, because it was one of only a handful of emergency staging areas. Coupled with the base commander's private office, and an underground vehicle port, the armoury had a dedicated terminal which could be accessed with proper authorisation and used to control the surveillance, alarm, and external communications system of the entire installation. It's designed purpose was as a hold-fast and counter-incursion deployment area in case of the very eventuality which was now taking place, but The Artist had got there first, and he already had the necessary clearances. While he was inside the room, he was the master of several essential subsystems which helped the facility to run smoothly and which protected it from attack. Only the base commander herself, or a designated substitute authorised by her, could override any commands he issued here after triggering one of two critical-event response protocols: lockdown, or evacuation.

And she happens to be en route now, he thought, but the fact didn't cause him any anxiety. He would finish his work quickly, disappear into the night, and leave his adversaries in confusion and disarray — and indeed fewer in number.

The terminal was at the rear left corner of the chamber, at the end of a short corridor of munitions racks and cage-fronted lockers. He was entirely out of sight of the door, but he would hear it opening in the unlikely event of having any unwanted company before he could execute the desired protocol.

Repeating the interactions from memory, he first authenticated himself and then navigated into the appropriate menu, proceeding through several layers of confirmation and warning, until he reached the desired triggering interface. Drills and practices were commonplace in a facility such as this one, and they were all the more important due to the limited and constrained ways in which an emergency situation could be responded to. There could never be a sudden spilling-out of uniformed military personnel onto the city streets above, for example, nor could the civilian emergency services be summoned under any circumstances. It was JINX's plan to use these constraints to her advantage, and The Artist thought that the plan was a small stroke of genius.

The menu currently displayed on the terminal indicated that it held a set of readiness drills, and he found the one he was looking for in only a few seconds, from a surprisingly extensive list. He prepared to initiate it, selecting a few additional useful options which would work in his favour too, and finally he moved his forefinger to hover above the execute button.

The Artist checked his wristwatch one last time, satisfied that everything was in place. He would need to work quickly now, and there would be risks, but that was always the case. He nodded to himself, and tapped the on-screen button.

Immediately, the terminal panel's borders began pulsing in red, and an alarm klaxon sounded from all around.

Chapter 13

The return flight to Brussels was quieter than the out-bound journey by far. Dowling, Ramos, and Goose all had their eyes closed, dozing in reclined chairs towards the front of the cabin, and all of the computer terminals in the middle section were dark and unoccupied.

At the rear there was a small conference area, with a pair of three-seater benches facing each other like a rail-way carriage. A table could be mounted between them, but it was stowed tonight. Greenwood sat in a window seat, as was her custom, looking out at the moonlit clouds below.

The micro-galley was at the very back of the cabin, behind a slender door which also gave access to a toilet, a weapons locker, and a medical cabinet. The door opened to reveal Aldridge, and for the second time that day, he carried two cups.

The steam from the mint teas curled into the air, and Greenwood was so lost in her thoughts that she smelled the comforting fragrance of the tea before she'd registered that Aldridge was there. He sat down across from her, and handed her one of the cups.

"Thank you," she said, and Aldridge quirked an eyebrow.

"Must be tired," he replied, and she sighed, understanding the double meaning. She *was* tired, but he was also remarking on how she rarely verbally thanked him for gestures like this. He made them often, and she knew at least two of the reasons for it. Because he was a far, far more empathic man than he wanted anybody to realise, and also because his feelings for her went beyond what she should allow as his commanding officer.

"I was thinking," he continued after a moment. "You said in the car that the ethical implications of ENISA's aberration analysis were *above your pay grade*. That's the second time you've used that phrase with me, you know."

"First time was in the Persian Gulf, just before we got into the sub," Greenwood recalled easily, nodding. "And I seem to remember that you said it right back to me at sunrise the next morning."

She paused, immediately regretting her response. He hadn't been trying to bring the subject up — she had indeed used those words with him previously, on a critical matter of morality, and he was probably just teasing her about the deflection of responsibility — but the scenario had been very different when he was the one to say it a day later. The image was as clear in her mind now as when it actually happened.

The airfield had been in Kuwait City, and they were there at sunrise after a long night, while a weapon of unprecedented destructive potential was loaded onto a cargo plane, to be once again hidden safely away from the world which had almost perished at its hands just hours earlier. It was a time of relief, and of rebirth, and they had felt both energised and exhausted. When Aldridge kissed her, she had taken her time about pushing him away afterwards. She thought about it more than she wanted to, and now she'd accidentally brought it up while they were at least functionally alone together.

Aldridge adopted an expression of exaggerated, studied casualness. "Rings a bell," he replied.

Before she knew she was going to do it, she had reached across and swatted his arm with the back of her hand, and she regretted it twice as much when she saw how delighted he was at her response.

Aldridge noted the bloom of colour in her cheeks with satisfaction and a fair amount of relief, and then she dropped her gaze a moment later. He decided to give her a break and change the subject, even though he very much wanted to discuss the one she'd accidentally raised.

"So," he said, "killer computers this time. I suppose we were due."

"Programs, not computers," Greenwood replied, and Aldridge nodded. He was silent for a few seconds, then he remembered something he'd meant to bring up earlier.

"There was an update from the Luxembourg City police, by the way," he said. "The guy in the coffee shop — the father with the little boy — made it through his surgery. He's going to make a full recovery, eventually."

Greenwood exhaled audibly. "That's good," she replied. "I've been thinking about him and his son."

Aldridge smiled. "Apparently one of Europe's best thoracic surgeons just *happened* to be visiting the city on undisclosed business, arriving shortly after the man was brought in. Some journalists are saying he travelled on a military jet, but you shouldn't believe everything you read."

Greenwood shook her head. "Lucky him. I wonder if Wuyts can make it rain too, if she wants to."

Because it felt right, and also because he wanted to, Aldridge reached forward and took her hand for the second time that day, and Greenwood looked up at him but she didn't pull away.

"Let's talk about that a bit, then," Aldridge said. "Wuyts, I mean. You're having doubts about whether she's still someone we can trust, and we all have the same concerns there. But for now there's really nothing for it; we have our jobs to do, whether she makes it easier or harder."

Greenwood nodded slowly, having already come to the same conclusion. But there was more to it than that. She looked down at their joined hands as she spoke.

"We don't have enough information yet to make any kind of move," she said, "but the question is which move to make when we do. I could go to the High Representative. Or the Council."

"Ah, the nuclear option," Aldridge replied thoughtfully. "We'd be right beside you if that's what you decide is best. And we'd follow you all the way. To the unemployment centre, I'd expect."

He squeezed her hand to emphasise that he was joking, but they both knew that he was also describing an entirely plausible scenario.

"I notice you were careful to make it all *my* decision," Greenwood said, and Aldridge gave a small laugh.

"Do I need to quote any of the literally *dozens* of times you've told me that the buck stops with you, and it's *your* responsibility, and you make the hard choices, and all that stuff? I can really do it, too. You know how good my memory is."

"That won't be necessary," she replied, lifting the cup of tea to her lips.

The hot liquid helped, somehow. It brought her back to the moment, rather than the criss-crossing web of possible future outcomes she was imagining. Her eyes flicked back up to look at Aldridge, then she surprised herself by asking something that had been on the tip of her tongue a hundred times, but that she'd never given voice to before now.

"Do you ever wish you could still... do what you were able to do during the *DESTINY* mission? Your ability, I mean."

Aldridge's expression became grave and his face paled a little. His grip on her hand loosened and he drew his arm back. A frown played across his brow.

"Uh… wow," he began, casting around for words. "I don't really know how to… why are you asking me that now?"

"I'm sorry," Greenwood said. "I didn't have any right to bring it up. It's just been a long day. Ignore me."

"No," he replied after a moment, "it's alright. Just took me by surprise. Let me think about it for a sec. I suppose that… yes, of course I sometimes wonder about it. There have been a lot of times when it would have been useful to us, like it was before. But if you remember, it wasn't exactly without its own cost."

She nodded, thinking back to those times. Aldridge first came to her attention as one of a very special group of people, with an ability that she still almost couldn't believe. A disaster had been coming, which would have killed many millions of people, and a select few were somehow connected with it, having the instinctive capability to alter the outcomes of events that had already happened, within a very brief window of opportunity.

Aldridge was related to one of the lead scientists on the project, and he was also one of those who wielded the ability, which he learned to use consciously and deliberately. With the thwarting of the cataclysm came the end of his talent, and that of all the others like him, but Greenwood had never properly broached the subject of how he felt about what had happened.

"We haven't talked about it," she said, giving voice to the thought. "I know that the psychologist at HQ discussed it with you a few times, but I didn't feel it was my place to ask you too. Then it felt like too much time had passed, and you seemed to want to forget about it all."

Aldridge looked out of the window, but there was only darkness there, so he pulled down the blind instead. After a long pause, he looked at her again.

"There are times when I feel like I lost something wonderful," he said quietly. "The most wonderful thing that I'll ever have. And from a certain perspective, that's true enough. But it was a double-edged sword, and not just because the disaster that gave me the ability was also *caused* by people like me using the ability in the first place. It served its purpose when we needed it to, but for the most part I'm glad that it's gone. Getting a second chance can mean having another shot at getting things wrong, as well as right."

It was by far the most he'd ever said about that mission; the one that led to him joining Greenwood's team and being inducted into their secret — and often bizarre, and dangerous, and frightening — world. She hesitated to say anything because nothing she could think of felt worthy, but as she sat looking at him silently, Greenwood came to the unavoidable conclusion that honesty and directness deserved the same in return.

"I'm sorry I didn't reply to your text a few weeks ago," she said, lowering her voice and looking down at her cup instead of at him. "I just… I wasn't ready to talk to you again yet, after everything."

Aldridge looked at her in silence until she glanced up at him, then he spoke. "Second time you've surprised me in five minutes," he replied. "And I understood, you know. I was just checking in on you. I wasn't going to push or anything."

She made a small sound of amusement. "You were absolutely going to push, at least a little."

Aldridge gave the barest grin, and he shrugged. "Maybe a little." Then his grin faded as quickly as it had appeared. "And I know that this is the part when you tell me it's not the right time to talk about this."

"Usually," she said, with frustration in her voice. Aldridge thought that it might actually be directed at herself for once, rather than him, and he immediately regretted his remark. He opened his mouth to apologise, but Greenwood started speaking again before he could say a word.

"It's never the right time, though, is it?" she asked, but she didn't wait for an answer. "It never has been. Maybe that's the problem. And that's without even thinking about the fact that we work together, and I'm your commanding officer."

Aldridge was taken aback yet again, and he felt his pulse get a little quicker. He tried not to read too much into what she was saying, but it was difficult not to interpret her words as allowing for the possibility that there might be more between them in the future. It was an outcome he hadn't expected, at least so soon, and he found that it made him at least as concerned as he was encouraged.

"Not planning on making any changes to that situation, I hope?" Aldridge asked, and Greenwood took a contemplative sip of her tea.

"No, of course not," she replied after a moment. "That would be wildly premature. But things don't feel the same way they did yesterday either. This is the first time I've ever felt sidelined by Wuyts. It's like she wants us to do our jobs, but not to do them properly. And that's not what I signed up for. I don't like this situation at all."

Aldridge nodded in agreement, then he set his own cup down in the holder built into the seat's armrest, and leaned forward. He extended his hand, palm upwards, and Greenwood looked at it for a moment before reaching to place her own free hand over his.

"We do our jobs the way we always do them," Aldridge said. "We find out what's really going on here, and let the chips fall where they may. We catch the guy who's trying to kill us, and we track down the AI and find a way to stop it. All of that stuff is a given. *Then*, once we've triumphed against seemingly insurmountable odds yet again, you and I go somewhere and have a proper talk about things, as if we were vaguely normal people."

"Simple as that?" she asked, and despite the tiredness which was evident on her face, there was a fondness in her eyes. Aldridge nodded definitively.

"Absolutely," he replied. "And however long it takes to do all of that, and wherever we end up going afterwards, there's one thing I really can't emphasise enough."

Greenwood quirked an eyebrow, and he adopted an expression of the utmost seriousness.

"You have *got* to wear that leather jacket," he said.

She laughed, a genuine one, and then withdrew her hand and sat back in her seat. "We'll see about that," she replied, glancing away briefly before meeting his gaze again. They looked at each other for long moments, neither feeling any particular need to speak.

Then the sparkle suddenly vanished from Greenwood's eyes as they heard a familiar chime from her phone. "Here we go again," she said.

She retrieved and unlocked the device, and read the aberration alert three times in quick succession. Her face paled a little more with each reading.

"Jesus," she said, in a small voice.

"What's wrong?" Aldridge asked, with concern in his voice. "Another death?"

"No," Greenwood replied. "The alert is for a web forum post. One of those right-wing, small-government, people's-militia wingnut ones. Hosted in the Netherlands, but the IP trace for the post itself was a dead end."

"What does it say?" he asked, but Greenwood didn't reply. Instead, she rotated the device to enlarge the message, and held it up so he could read it in its entirety.

A little bird told me it's amazing what you can find at the Royal Library of Belgium.
-JINX

~

The alarm was shrill, coming from everywhere, and it was made even harsher by the hard, utilitarian surfaces of the floors and corridors in the underground base bouncing the sound in all directions. Every display panel, monitor, and portable device on the network displayed the same ominous alert banner.

EVACUATE — DANGER — GAS

The Artist had heard a great deal of movement when he had first triggered the protocol a few minutes earlier, but now there was only the alarm itself. The armoury's door had no windows set into it, and he was at the rear of the chamber anyway, but he expected to see almost no-one out in the corridors when he exited shortly.

There was a pleasing symmetry to the idea of carbon monoxide flooding both the EU minister's home, and also this clandestine military facility. The difference, of course, was that the gas alert in this case was entirely fictional. It would guarantee evacuation of the base, and the minister's death by the same method would only enhance the perceived threat, giving him enough time to do his work even though the facility's senior staff were on their way there, and would doubtless enter regardless of the warning.

Enough time had passed now, and The Artist readied a compact assault rifle of the same model the guards used, as he approached the sole door of the room. He released the safety on his weapon, re-checked that his earpiece still held the removable unit, and ran through the base layout in his mind one last time. Satisfied, he raised the rifle, and entered the unlock code on the wall panel just beside the door. The portal's heavy locking mechanism audibly disengaged, and the door slid open. He stepped out, quickly glancing in both directions down the corridor outside, but there was no-one there.

Good, he thought. *And now to reach the office of Captain Greenwood.*

He knew that the armoury door would automatically secure-lock upon detecting sabotage of its entry mechanism, so he stepped across the corridor at an oblique angle, aimed, and fired a shot directly into the access panel on the outside. Sure enough, the door slid rapidly shut immediately, the locking mechanism engaged, and no-one else would be arming themselves from the room again for some time.

The Artist moved down the corridor, estimating how long it would be until he encountered a security force. He knew that the first task of the base staff after evacuation would be to secure the facility, and to that end they would certainly send soldiers and engineers back in to assess the situation and begin any necessary repairs. Due to the clearance level required to even know about the base's existence, everyone who would arrive would be military, and trained to kill regardless of their particular specialism or job function. But he had the advantage of surprise, and a window of time in which he could operate without resistance or interference.

He increased his pace, noticing the security cameras he was passing at every junction. Once he inserted the electronic bug into one of the key computers in the base, JINX had informed him that all of the security footage pertaining to his visit would be erased and unrecoverable. He wasn't particularly concerned about such things, and he had already been seen by at least half a dozen people, but it was always helpful to leave as little of an electronic trace as possible.

The Artist came to a halt. For a moment, he thought he had heard movement nearby, and he listened for several seconds without hearing anything else. He readied his weapon, moving forward cautiously now, even though he was aware of the clock ticking. There was a junction ahead, and he took a quick glance around the corner, prepared to fire if he discovered anyone there — but the area beyond was deserted. The alarm continued to sound, and he saw that he was approaching the stairwell which would take him down to the third level of the facility, where his next destination could be found. He quickened his pace once more, pushing away the vague, unsettled feeling that had momentarily risen up within him.

He proceeded down the stairs as quietly as he could, and part of him was impressed at the obvious efficiency with which the base had been evacuated in such a short time. There was a broad but spartan atrium on the bottom floor and he wasted no time in crossing it, choosing the correct corridor from memory. The Artist was moving much more quickly now, no longer attempting to make his footsteps quieter.

The captain's office is a defensible position, albeit for a limited time, he thought. *And I won't be leaving in the same way that I arrived.*

Again he had a sense of being watched, and he glanced around in all directions, but there was no-one else there. Up ahead, at the end of a short passage, there was a door with a prominent nameplate on the outside. He read it with satisfaction.

BASE COMMANDER, CAPTAIN J. GREENWOOD

Ordinarily the base commander's office was under a restricted access system, requiring the biometrics of the Captain herself in order to gain access. The evacuation protocol changed all that, though, and downgraded certain chambers in the base to general authenticated access, meaning that anyone who was authorised to be on the premises could temporarily open those doors, as long as the evacuation protocol remained in effect. It was a safety feature, in case personnel became incapacitated and had to be carried out. Tonight, the sensible precaution would be used to The Artist's advantage.

He pressed his thumb to the panel beside the door and he heard the mechanism disengage, just as expected. Taking one last look back down the corridor and seeing nothing amiss, he turned the door handle, went inside the room, and closed the door behind him. It took only seconds to cross the room and move behind the desk to the computer terminal there. He pulled the device from his earpiece and inserted it into a port on the machine. The screen came on immediately, showing the crest of the European Defence Agency.

A moment later, it was replaced with two words.

ACCESS GRANTED.

Chapter 14

Greenwood's boots echoed on the airfield tarmac as she strode quickly towards the waiting car, with the four other members of her team in tow. She was already on the phone with Wuyts.

"I understand that, sir, but I think we need to consider a security lockdown for the base until we've determined the meaning of the forum message," Greenwood said into the handset she was holding to her ear, glancing at Goose as she walked. The Dutchman nodded and went around to the driver's door and got in, and a moment later the engine turned over and began to idle.

Aldridge had woken and briefed the others after Greenwood received the aberration alert on the plane, and they had collectively and immediately dismissed the possibility that the forum message was just a warning or an attempt at intimidation. The AI always seemed to have a definitive goal in mind, even if that goal was shifting according to the changing circumstances, and toying with them didn't seem like a tactic that would be included in her playbook.

Once everyone was in the car, they departed immediately. Goose urged the vehicle past the speed limit, with no intention of stopping before they reached their headquarters. Greenwood put the call with Wuyts on the car's speaker system, which was an unusual measure for her. She knew that Wuyts would be able to hear the change in the audio quality, and would no doubt correctly interpret the meaning embedded within the action: *no more compartmentalisation of information.*

"I've routed an alert to the duty commander about a possible threat to the facility, pending your return," Wuyts said over the line. *"But at this point we must take care not to allow an enemy — even a non-human one — to dictate our actions. The loss of autonomy is always the most profound tactical risk."*

"Also death," Aldridge said. "That's always been my most profound risk."

Wuyts apparently ignored his remark, instead continuing as if she'd never been interrupted.

"It does seem unlikely that the intention is to expose the base location, or to unveil your identities; we've already removed the forum post itself, of course. The synthetic intelligence is probably able to realise that we would also suppress any revealed information from the public, and it's unclear what advantage it would gain by even making the attempt. Nevertheless, that conclusion leaves us with the problem of determining the message's true purpose."

"The purpose, sir, is to make us do exactly what we're doing right now: return to the base immediately," Greenwood replied, barely keeping her tone even. "And *that* means there's a credible threat to our base and those under my command who are stationed there."

Dowling nodded, arms folded across his chest in the rear middle seat. Only those who knew him well would be able to tell that he was tense and concerned.

"It's difficult to fault your reasoning, Captain," Wuyts replied, "and of course you should make whatever command decision you see fit once you're on site. The Agency can provide additional resources at short notice, but I want you keep the larger picture in mind: your goal is to determine the AI's ultimate aim. It put a plan in place very deliberately yesterday evening, and that was presumably before it even became aware of your existence. That plan, whatever it is, most certainly remains in motion."

Greenwood exhaled silently, and her facial expression was that of a woman who was counting to ten in her mind to avoid saying something she'd regret later. Aldridge could only see the side of her face from his position in one of the rear seats, but he could easily tell what she was thinking.

Something about how the AI's plan is a lot less important to her than keeping her people alive, he thought. *But she won't say that. Not yet, anyway.*

"I'm aware of that, sir," Greenwood replied. "We're fifteen minutes out from HQ, and I intend to increase our readiness level as soon as we arrive. I'll also be ordering security sweeps every 30 minutes for at least the next day or so, and I'd like to implement a personnel freeze as soon as we can coordinate it."

"All judicious precautions," Wuyts replied. *"I'll expect an update on the base's status within the…"*

Her voice tailed off, and Aldridge exchanged a glance with Dowling, an unpleasant feeling already blooming in his chest. Wuyts never spoke until she knew exactly what she was going to say, and she didn't break off in the middle of a sentence, ever. Something was wrong.

"Sir?" Greenwood asked, but there was only silence on the line for a few unbearable seconds before Wuyts replied.

"I may owe you an apology, Captain," Wuyts said, her voice taut now. *"I've just received word that your base has been evacuated due to dangerous levels of carbon monoxide."*

"That's how Hausemer died," Ramos said, but the remark was unnecessary. Goose pressed the accelerator hard enough to push everyone back into their seats, grateful for the deserted roads at the late hour.

"Damn it," Greenwood said, slamming her fist on the dashboard. "Sir, I'll call you back shortly. Larry, options." She tapped a button on her phone to terminate the call, not waiting for Wuyts to reply. Dowling started speaking immediately.

"Evac will go to the muster point at location gamma, chief," he said. "There's vehicle access, so option one is that we go there and find out what's what. Won't be able to get to the armoury for a bit, but we can take whatever our boys and girls have on them, if you're planning to go inside." He said the last part casually, as if there were any chance at all that they wouldn't be doing that very thing.

"En route to location gamma, Captain," Goose said, not waiting for the order. Dowling looked at the other man with approval, and then continued.

"Option two is that we go back to the plane, for the weapons locker," Dowling said. "Option three is always calling in the army, no matter what the question is. And option four is commandeering weapons from armed units of the city police, but that's a bloody bad scenario six ways to Sunday, if you ask me."

Greenwood nodded twice, quickly. "Location gamma until we know more. Assess and verify. We'll attempt entry unless there's a solid reason not to. And I want him alive, but I'll settle for some wear and tear."

There was no need to specify who she was referring to. Dowling unfolded his enormous arms, interlaced his fingers, and turned his palms outwards. The sound of his knuckles cracking was like a gunshot.

~

The Artist sat in Greenwood's ergonomic desk chair with his hands clasped in his lap, watching the computer screen in front of him. No fingers were on the keyboard, and no hand was on the mouse, but it was as if a ghost was operating the machine with great proficiency.

Windows spawned and then vanished. Terminals flowed with monochromatic text. He understood almost none of it, but he didn't have to, and nor did he want to. It was better not to know, and his instincts told him to stand up and move away from the machine until the bug had done its work, but a nagging curiosity kept him where he was.

Again and again, in different contexts, the poltergeist that was conducting the computer's interface like an orchestra entered the same single word. And in turn, it appeared to be retrieving data which included oblique references to that same word, whatever its significance might be.

LANTERN, he thought.

He checked his wristwatch, seeing that almost ten minutes had elapsed since he had left the armoury. There was very little additional time, and he would need to begin making his exit soon. The gas hazard protocol mandated a facility lockdown period after evacuation was confirmed, preventing re-entry for a period of thirty minutes after the outer doors were sealed. Optimistically, he had less than two-thirds of that time left before the base would unlock, and a significant number of armed personnel began to comb its corridors and rooms. It was paramount that the tiny device he had attached to Greenwood's computer made it safely off the premises before then.

There was a small chirp from his earpiece, and he knew that it was the result of a close-range signal from the bug itself; it had found what it was looking for, or at least completed its search through whatever resources it had managed to access. The Artist pulled the device from the port, reinserted it into his earpiece, and immediately left the room, once again closing the door behind him. The computer on the desk had already gone back into its sleep mode, no doubt with its desktop environment returned to the same state it had been in when he found it.

The corridors were as empty as they had been earlier, and he encountered no-one in the atrium or at the stairway. He bypassed the stairs this time, going directly across the open area, heading for a different corridor which wound past a training area and gymnasium, a compact firing range, and several storage rooms. Soon he came to the secondary stairwell he sought, which would take him up to the second floor but at the opposite corner of the facility, where he would find the sciences wing.

He quickly ascended, and was proceeding past a door labelled BIOLOGY with an access panel curiously mounted at waist-height besides the more usual ones higher up, when the overhead alarm klaxon suddenly ceased to sound.

The Artist felt a surge of adrenalin. It was too soon for the quarantine protocol to have automatically ended, and he had been under the impression that it couldn't be overridden from outside the base, but his work often involved adapting to unexpected circumstances which presented additional risks and challenges. This would be like any other such scenario — albeit with the highly motivating factor of armed and undoubtedly well-trained soldiers pursuing him.

He disabled the safety on his rifle for the second time since he'd acquired it, re-oriented himself, and began moving even more rapidly. He had no reason to doubt his employer's assessment of the base's security procedures, so he considered it unlikely that the alarm and lockdown had been circumvented from elsewhere. The conclusion was as obvious as it was troubling.

Someone is still in here, he thought.

~

The area at the bottom of the winding ramp, more than fifteen metres beneath the surface of the city streets, was crowded with uniformed soldiers. Several weapons were trained on the nondescript vehicle that roared into view from above, and they were only lowered when the car came to a halt and the front passenger-side window rolled down to reveal the face of Greenwood.

"I apologise, sir," the sergeant nearest the car said, but Greenwood waved it away as she stepped out of the vehicle.

"Don't apologise for doing your job, sergeant. Report," she said, and the man nodded.

"Base evacuation protocol is in effect," he replied. "Gas leak alert. No injuries, but the system indicated carbon monoxide so it wouldn't have had time to cause much harm. For non-toxic gases the venting is automatic. We're monitoring our personnel for any symptoms of hypoxia, but I don't think we're going to find any. Handheld detectors during evacuation didn't show any traces."

Greenwood nodded. "Timelock?"

The soldier, whose name was Di Giorgio, checked his wristwatch. "Eighteen minutes twenty seconds remaining, sir."

Goose walked up to them, waiting for the man to finish before he spoke, leaning in and lowering his voice. "What about the contingency?"

"It's in place, sir," Di Giorgio replied, equally quietly. "Headcount here is confirmed at base complement minus four."

Greenwood nodded grimly, exchanging a look with Goose, before looking at the sergeant again. "Prepare a tactical assault load-out for us, best you can do from whatever we have on hand. Bring everything over to the doors in three minutes. Dismissed."

Di Giorgio nodded once more and moved briskly away without another word. Goose watched him go, then he and Greenwood were joined by Dowling, Ramos, and Aldridge.

"Well, chief?" Dowling asked, and Greenwood tilted her head towards the large pair of sealed steel security doors ten metres away. They bore multiple warning symbols and notices explaining that the area beyond was a high-voltage electrical substation, and that any attempt to enter was both illegal and posed an immediate risk of death. Except for the nature of the facility, the warnings were all true.

"He's here," Greenwood replied, "and we have personnel unaccounted for." Dowling rolled his shoulders, as if to loosen a stiff muscle.

"Small world," he said. "I suppose we'd better go and say hello then."

At that moment, the alarm klaxon that had been distantly audible from beyond the security doors abruptly stopped, and Greenwood smiled. There was a coldness to it, though, and Aldridge noted the fact with a mixture of admiration and disquiet. Making things personal was never a wise idea from a tactical perspective. But sometimes it was hard to avoid.

"Alright, listen up," Greenwood said, turning to face the others.

"This is a hazardous-environment scenario, at least potentially. The prudent tactical move is to wait for the full vent-cycle period, send in a robot to test the air quality, then move in simultaneously from all entrance points with all our forces. But I'm not going to do that, because there's something else going on here, and I want to take this man alive so we can start getting some answers instead of just more questions. I'm not going to order you to come in with me. Volunteers only."

"He's in our house," Dowling replied, casually but immediately. "It'd be rude to leave him alone in there." Goose only nodded at the Welshman, checking and readying his own pistol by way of response. Ramos took a measured breath.

"Until it's done," she said simply, and then Greenwood finally moved her gaze to Aldridge, who made a point of looking over at the doors as if he was considering something.

"Honestly, I left my keys in there, so I need to go in anyway," he said.

"Thank you," Greenwood replied, speaking to all of them. "Then let's move."

They crossed to the doors, all five of them removing their outdoor jackets and dropping them in a pile to one side. Di Giorgio was already back, along with three other soldiers, all of them bearing weapons and equipment. It took only a handful of further minutes for everyone to be ready, and then Greenwood approached the entry panel set into the wall on the right side of the door.

It was concealed behind a vent cover, which only unlocked when an access card or authorised mobile device was passed in front of it. Greenwood's smartwatch was sufficient, and when the vent fascia flipped down on its concealed hinges to reveal a security keypad and small display panel, she rapidly entered one of her personal set of override codes. There was a crisp beeping sound, and the large doors began to silently slide apart almost immediately.

Each team member bore their sidearm, a rifle, and in some cases combat knives and other equipment. They also each had a compact respirator, connected to a small, belt-mounted compressed oxygen cylinder. None of them believed that the carbon monoxide threat was real, but taking chances with that eventuality was a fool's game. Goose had brought the network inspection equipment from the trip to Dublin, and finally, Ramos carried a CO monitoring device which could test the air for dangerous quantities of the colourless and odourless gas.

Dowling ran the situation through his mind, going over an inventory of their equipment load-out, the base layout, and probable tactics. On paper, it was a suicide mission on the part of the assassin, which meant that there was a definite objective which couldn't be fulfilled in any other location, or at any other time. They knew that the man had already penetrated the base, so his access credentials must have been planted into the computer system, likely via the personnel rotation system that Greenwood had wanted to pause as soon as possible.

He gave voice to his thoughts as he and his four colleagues began to move forward into the base, Ramos's gas detector showing no trace of carbon monoxide at all, just as Di Giorgio had reported.

"I've been thinking about this, chief," Dowling said, and Greenwood half-turned her head in his direction without taking her eyes from the wide entrance area ahead of her, which ran through a cargo storage tunnel and ended in a second security door leading into the actual base.

"He cleared the place out," Dowling continued, "so he's looking to get up to some mischief without being interrupted, but he knows he's got precious little time to do whatever it is and get back out before we're on top of him. So he's looking for something and he already knows where to find it, and he also has a particular way out planned."

"Something he couldn't get from outside, or via remote access," Goose added. "That narrows the search parameters quite a lot. Remember our dossiers that were found on the mobile phone, Captain?"

Greenwood nodded. The dossiers had contained just the information about the five of them which was available to anyone with a basic operational security level, but they hadn't contained anything more restricted.

"It's clearance-coded data he wants," she said, and Goose nodded.

"That means the hardwired privilege-escalation terminals," the Dutchman replied. "There are five; one in each of our offices. But only one of them can provide unrestricted access to everything we have in the deep store."

"Mine," Greenwood said.

The base had three main storeys, but a fourth also existed — though virtually none of the personnel would ever see it. It lay even further below the city of Brussels than the rest of the facility, and amongst other things, it was a secure data repository for files coded with the most secret clearance level held by anyone who was stationed there: *CHALLENGE*, held only by Greenwood herself.

"That gives us a trajectory," Greenwood continued. "He's already had at least fifteen minutes, so let's assume he's on his way back out. Limited exits, and we have an origin point of my office, which is below all of them. That helps a bit."

They had come to a halt briefly while Goose interact-ed with a security panel inside the storage area. He shook his head, then turned to face the rest of them with a troubled expression. Ramos asked the question that was on everyone's lips.

"Armoury?"

Goose nodded. "It's in damage lockout," he replied. "So it's safe to assume that we can't access our own weapons, and also that he's heavily armed with them."

"Well he's not the only one," Aldridge said, and Dowling glanced at him. "Wait, I swear I can come up with a better line than that if you give me a minute."

"You can work on it while we move," Greenwood replied. "But don't expect this man to give you a chance to talk before he shoots. Let's go."

Aldridge muttered something about inspiring leader-ship, but he also raised his rifle and took up a position between Greenwood and Dowling as Goose opened the additional security door ahead of them, revealing part of the western level-one access corridor. It was deserted as far as they could see, but there were several junctions and many doorways.

They began to move forward cautiously, expecting at any moment to come under fire.

Chapter 15

Inge Olsen crouched in the corner of Aldridge's office, completely hidden from the door by a large worktable. The room was unlit, and was close to total darkness, but that was no additional impediment when you were blind.

She had switched the lights off herself, and she had already discarded the respirator she'd taken from an equipment locker when the initial evacuation alert sounded. Likewise, her handheld carbon monoxide detector sat forgotten on the floor beside her, still displaying its assessment of the air as being of normal composition and high quality, with only the expected trace levels of the gas. Very much on her mind, though, was the handgun she gripped tightly.

Minutes ago she'd used Aldridge's terminal to override and deactivate the hazard lockout protocol, making the base once again accessible to those with suitable clearance. It was a prearranged move, which Greenwood had put in place with a special order before

KESTREL had departed for Dublin. Olsen was the contingency, in case their unknown assailant chose to breach the base itself.

And now he's here, Olsen thought, trying to keep her hands from shaking.

All she had to do now was wait for rescue. It was unlikely the killer would find her hiding place; his logical destination would be Captain Greenwood's office and the sole hard-link to the deep store. But at the very least, a scout team would soon make a sweep of the entire facility, and if the intruder was still here, the situation could become unpredictable and dangerous at any time. It was all highly dependent on the man's chosen next steps.

Olsen was also almost certain that she'd encountered him already.

The ear-mounted device she wore was unlike any of the communications units that were standard issue to all personnel. The feature-detection and ambiguity resolution algorithms were state of the art, allowing the creation of a real-time auditory soundscape which cued her attention to everything around her as she moved, both via accelerated spoken descriptions and also a mini-language of tones. With practice and patience, the clever machine gave the sightless young woman an astonishing degree of insight into her environment.

It was only a short while ago that she'd been walking down a corridor not far from the armoury, and the device alerted her to the presence of someone else walking in the opposite direction. The lateral tones made it clear that they weren't on a collision course, and the pacing tones showed that the person was walking. As they came near, the feature detection analysis produced spoken cues indicating that the person was male, 1.75 metres in height, and wasn't a senior staff member. A moment later, facial recognition and a wireless link to the facility's staff database identified the man as someone she hadn't encountered before, and indeed a brand new transfer who had only arrived on site within the last hour.

Since starting to use the device, Olsen had heard auditory profiles like this a hundred times per day, but something about the man made her uneasy. When she heard the focusing tones, indicating that the man was looking towards her, and then the repeated, doppler-shifted tones from the rear-facing projection profile indicating that the man had turned to continue watching her even after she'd passed him, she felt vulnerable in a way that she never had with any of the other base staff.

She knew that she was attractive, even if she had no concrete concept of what that meant from a visual perspective, and she was also no stranger to male attention. But some ancient, wordless part of her mind voiced a warning when the man moved past her, and she had used all her self-control to keep from flinching.

It was him, she thought. *I can't prove it, but I know it.*

Everything fit. The transfer personnel had to have their credentials supplied from an external source by necessity, and it was hypothetically a vulnerability, even though every part of the system had repeatedly been certified as entirely secure. If you wanted to insert a hostile operative, the shift rotation and duty transfer rosters would be how you'd do it — assuming you could somehow manufacture suitable credentials and get them into the external supplying system in the first place, behind layers of encryption.

Olsen would have bet good money that this so-called Loïc Grieder was the same man who had killed the Russian agent, the EU minister, and tried to kill the Director too. But her certainty was cold comfort; as cold as the barrel of the weapon she was clutching too tightly.

A technical analyst wasn't issued with a sidearm, of course, but everyone on base was required to train with one — except for her. Her lack of vision had been obvious cause for an exemption, and so the weapon she had been hurriedly handed by the duty base commander, as a last-resort means of protection in her role as the contingency, felt heavy and alien and treacherous in her small hands.

She knew how it worked. She knew where the safety was, and how to tell whether it was engaged or not. She knew how to make it ready to kill, and with her technological second sight, she could even aim it.

She just hoped she would never have to pull the trigger.

~

The Artist hadn't expected any leave-behind forces in the event of a hazardous substance alert, no matter how fictional the danger was, but there was little point in dwelling on the subject.

He moved more slowly now, despite the time pressure of the situation, in order to minimise the amount of sound he was making and to avoid stumbling into an ambush. There was no way to know how many troops remained inside the base, but there were several salient factors. First and most important, there was now probably nothing preventing an incursion by outside forces, because anyone who could terminate the alarm protocol could also override the timelock which had sealed the facility. Anyone entering would be cautious, but they would also be trained military personnel, not likely to let any anxieties get in the way of their duty.

Second, he was exposed. The only troops who should be inside the base at this moment were whatever soldiers had been instructed to remain despite the evacuation. The Artist's cover identity was assuredly not amongst them, so he was identifiable on sight by a simple process of elimination. His only options at this point were to either fight his way out — an endeavour which was likely to be suicide — or to escape using a different route than the one he'd planned, which was to return the way he'd come from, via the garage.

That way was far too dangerous now, for the same reason that it was a safe entry point for him earlier: it was out of sight of the public, and thus would have served as one of the evacuation rendezvous areas for the base's staff. There was now only one exit which was virtually guaranteed to be unguarded, simply because it was in full view of civilian passers-by at all times.

The topside library exterior door, designated as location alpha, he thought. *Reserved for approved plain-clothes personnel only.*

The Artist was confident that if he could make it to the upper security corridor, he could simply discard his uniform and walk away into the night, and that was now his intention. His employer had also promised an additional act of assistance for him, at an appropriate time. But there was a third factor to consider also.

For the same reason that he had to reach a security terminal in order to trigger the evacuation protocol, whoever had *deactivated* the protocol must also have done so from one of those terminals. The armoury was currently out of bounds, which left a limited number of possible locations for the command to be issued from. All were a fair distance from any of the exits, for obvious reasons of tactical necessity. There were five such locations in total, besides the armoury itself: the primary offices of the Group One squad members.

The Artist knew that the command had almost certainly not been issued from Greenwood's office, since he had left that room himself only shortly before the alert was disabled. That left four possible rooms, one of which was now very close by. He looked up at the navigational signage on the wall. PHYSICAL SCIENCES, it read.

The particle physicist's office is at the end of this corridor, he thought, recalling the man's dossier. *Dr. Neil Aldridge, the most recent addition, whose biographical background is partially classified above standard access levels.*

The distinction in Aldridge's record compared to the others was a source of passing interest to him, but it was unlikely to be germane to the current mission, so The Artist pushed his curiosity away. This place held many secrets, but secrets had a habit of keeping close company with risk. He would prefer to live with the mystery, rather than die for enlightenment.

After another five seconds, he spotted the door that was labelled with Aldridge's name. It was closed, and the lights were off within the room, as he could see through the glass set into the upper portion of the door. A strange feeling crept over him, and The Artist paused. There was a pleasant floral scent in the air which he recognised, but momentarily couldn't place. A perfume, or at least a cleansing or beauty product used by women. It was delicate and fresh, not at all overpowering, and it seemed out of place here in the austere, functional, and inescapably masculine environment of a military installation.

The woman outside the armoury.

He had smelled the same fragrance when she passed by him, only a little while ago. He was certain of it. And she had clearly been here, too, either before or since. A coincidence, perhaps — or perhaps not.

If the woman was indeed still on site, then not only was it reasonably likely that she was responsible for the premature end of the lockdown protocol — why else would an obvious civilian choose or be chosen to remain behind, unless she had a specific function to perform? — but it also raised the tantalising prospect of taking her as a hostage, to provide some insurance regarding his own escape.

The Artist resumed his course towards Aldridge's office, weapon at the ready, making no sound at all. He drew level with the portal, and reached out towards the biometrics reader panel with his free hand, pressing his thumb to the cold surface. It took only a moment for a small light to illuminate along the top. It was red.

He frowned, looking through the glass, but the interior was in complete darkness. It didn't take him long to realise what had happened. With the termination of the evacuation and lockdown protocol, standard security measures had been reinstated, including the restricted access protections on the offices of the senior staff members. The door could be opened from the inside with the press of a button, but only Greenwood and her four colleagues could open it from outside now. Whoever had gone in, whether it was the young woman from earlier or not, was now beyond his reach unless he used firepower to destroy the door itself. He had no intention of doing so.

The Artist took a deep breath, pushing the irritation away, and turned around. His task was clear enough: proceed to the surface exit, and make his escape so that his employer could examine the data he had extracted from the secure terminal in Greenwood's office. He knew the way, and there was nothing else to keep him here. He was just about to move when his keen instincts alerted him to something, barely a second before he registered the faint sound, still distant but readily echoing along the hard surfaces of the solid floors and walls of the base.

Footsteps, he thought. *Multiple sources. Tactical movement, combat footwear.*

The sound had come from the same level he was on, from the opposite side of the facility, most likely the primary vehicle port designated as location gamma.

They were coming.

~

"Careful, Alicia," Greenwood said, knowing that the advice was completely unnecessary. Dowling and Goose kept watch at the front and rear while Aldridge and Greenwood took up positions across from the door that Ramos now stood beside.

The chamber beyond was her own office, the first one they'd reached as they moved methodically through the second level. Ramos pressed her thumb to the biometrics plate and the door opened, the unoccupied room briefly becoming the target of three rifle barrels.

There was only the smallest chance that the intruder would have been in any of the senior staff's offices besides Greenwood's, and even then he would now almost certainly already have left and be en route to his chosen way out. Even so, they had decided to check both of the relevant rooms which were on this level — Ramos's and Aldridge's — before going up to level one, which held both Goose's office and the elevator which led to the topside library exit.

Ramos closed the door again, hearing the locking mechanism engage. They had another stop to make before proceeding to the atrium and crossing to the opposite side of the facility, and it was one that nobody was looking forward to.

"Keep it moving," Greenwood said, and they moved off in staggered groupings, keeping to the sides of the corridors. It was deathly quiet, and every footfall seemed to be amplified.

She barely glanced into the conference room as they passed it half a minute later, but the usual sense of it being the nerve centre of the base, and a cocoon from which they could plan their next move, was entirely gone. Now she saw it for the first time through her tactician's eyes, assessing and dismissing it as a fall-back location or a rallying point, perceiving it only as a series of advantageous or disadvantageous attributes in the contexts of attack or defence, refuge or ambush.

It had become an unfriendly place; a potential theatre of warfare, and a small voice at the back of her mind whispered that this was the true cost of an incursion into someone's home territory. Not the actual intrusion and its direct consequences, but the reframing of the place from stronghold to vulnerability, and from safety to violation.

The duty psychologist would have a field day with that particular observation, Greenwood thought, once again annoyed with herself. She knew that she was taking this unfolding mission very personally, and that doing so was a good way to get yourself killed. Or worse, to get someone else killed because of your own lack of operational detachment.

They reached the armoury after another minute, and it took only a glance from Dowling at the shattered entry panel to confirm their earlier supposition. Even though the sight was no surprise, it was still unsettling. Every one of them had been into the secure room any number of times, and they knew its layout as well as its contents. Their superior numbers could be negated in moments by the use of any of at least half a dozen different weapons which the intruder could have taken from the armoury, and carried with him.

Ramos was looking intently at the floor, and she crouched down after a moment, just to the left of the sealed doorway. She inhaled through her nose, then ran a finger across the surface. Then she stood up and turned to Greenwood.

"It's been cleaned recently," Ramos said. "Not well. Quickly. Something impregnated with alcohol."

"There's nothing we can do here right now," Aldridge said from behind them, his voice quiet but insistent. "Let's finish this job, so we can get our people back in, then we'll have an engineering crew open the door."

"He's right enough," Dowling said, and Greenwood nodded. She gestured ahead, and they set off once more.

The big Welshman pulled ahead after another half a minute or so, taking a lead position without any word from Greenwood. It was his habit, and they had all anticipated the move. They also knew the reason for it, as signposted on the walls leading up to the junction ahead.

"Clear," Dowling said quietly, moving around the blind corner that finally brought the main atrium into view.

The next few minutes would probably be the most dangerous so far, since the large and open area spanned three floors, and offered many vantage points for an attack.

Ramos and Greenwood were ceaselessly scanning their surroundings, ready to take aim at any hint of movement, and Goose and Aldridge were close behind. Despite their superior numbers, and being on very familiar ground, there was an elevated sense of tension. None of them had ever seen the place deserted before, nor had there ever been a hostile intrusion.

Then there was the other matter, which was running through Greenwood's mind every few minutes. Outside at the vehicular access ramp, Di Giorgio had told her that the evacuation headcount stood at minus four, meaning that four of the base's current expected complement had not left when the alarm sounded. One of them was the intruder, and one of them was Olsen in her role as the contingency — but that left two more. There was a tightness in Greenwood's gut, and she was steadfastly ignoring what she already was almost certain of: that the other two personnel hadn't left because they were unable to, and had likely been killed by the intruder before he triggered the evacuation protocol. Logically, they would be the duty guards of the armoury at the time, which explained Ramos's observation of the floor outside that room.

Bastard, Greenwood thought, then she immediately chastised herself for allowing her emotions to take hold of her again, especially in a situation requiring vigilance and clear-headedness. She knew that the other four members of her team were all thinking the same thing, though, and that she would be relying on everyone's training and self-control if — or rather when — they had their next encounter with the killer.

"I've got a strange feeling," Goose said, and Aldridge just shook his head to indicate that he'd be passing up the opportunity to make a wisecrack.

"Expand on that," Greenwood replied without looking around, and Goose frowned.

"I appreciate that we don't have your clearance level, Captain," Goose replied, "but it seems like this man is after something that only your terminal can access. But you don't know what it is, and the Director obviously doesn't want to enlighten you."

"You're implying that there's data in our deep store that I don't have access to, despite being base commander," Greenwood replied. "That's the conclusion I'm leaning towards too. But someone knew it was there, or at least suspected, and the AI wants it badly enough to send her hired help in here to get it. Just another question for the Director to answer."

"Or not," Aldridge said. "But maybe we can ask the guy ourselves. I feel like going to pick up my keys now, if anyone else is up for the walk."

They had reached the atrium, a well-lit space that was usually filled with echoes of all kinds; footsteps, conversation, and the sounds of every kind of machinery. Tonight, though, it was all but silent, with only the omnipresent hum of the environmental system coming from above their heads.

There was a central catwalk with two additional suspended walkways along each side of the space, and access stairways on the left and right walls at the midpoint. The base had a symmetric layout around the atrium's centre, with three corridors leading off from the near and far sides on each of the three levels. It meant that there were eighteen means of egress from the area, not counting the doors which opened directly onto it, and the intruder could be waiting in any one of them.

"Assuming we haven't gone past him, the best way from your office to the topside access door would be going up the far stairs and through Sciences," Dowling said. "After that, he'd need to come out here and go up again."

Greenwood nodded. It meant that their target was either ahead of them on this same floor, on the opposite side of the base, or had already progressed upwards and was going to escape when they moved out of the atrium. She tilted her head up, looking through the gaps in the level one walkway above, towards the door that wasn't currently visible from her vantage point. It led to a short security pen which fed into the elevator that connected with the surface-level library exit door, referred to as location alpha.

"We'll cross in two pairs, left and right," she said. "Once we're over, Alicia, you take a firing position here and stay behind to cover alpha — and *hold* that position, no matter what happens. We'll either be alright or we won't, but he can't escape. We have to sweep the far side before we move up. Goose, you're with me."

They split into their assigned groups without a word, and Ramos took a kneeling position at the head of the corridor they'd just left. She would provide cover if needed while the others crossed.

Greenwood and Goose went to the left, and Dowling and Aldridge went to the right. Five pairs of eyes checked every visible point of access to the atrium, and found nothing. Greenwood and Dowling exchanged a final nod, and under Ramos's watchful eyes, the two groups were just about to begin moving along the twin side-wall walkways when they were all suddenly plunged into absolute darkness.

Chapter 16

The Artist went into motion as soon as the overhead lighting went off. He turned away from the locked door of Aldridge's office and headed in the direction which would eventually open onto the central atrium. He could still see the afterimage of the corridor on his retinas, and he knew that he had scant seconds to reach his next point of cover.

As predicted, less than three seconds later the base's emergency lighting came on, giving a dim red glow from low-level LED emitters in a strip at knee height, and a matching glow from the junction of the walls and ceilings. He had made it to his desired staging point, an area where a hallway widened to give access to bathrooms and a small kitchen. It would provide him with cover, at least, and also some temporary concealment.

His route to the surface exit was blocked for now, since the only way from his current position to the security corridor was via the central stairways. A confrontation would be necessary, which wasn't entirely unexpected, but he knew he would have to make use of every possible advantage if he hoped to escape with his life.

The device that JINX had delivered to him, which he had plugged into Greenwood's terminal in her office, also carried a small leave-behind program which disconnected the base from external electrical power at a fixed interval after the device was removed. Its purpose was to be a failsafe in case of the very situation which The Artist now found himself in: having to deal with the premature re-entry of hostile forces, and a possible combat engagement during his escape. The internal emergency lighting system was completely separate and automatic, however, and couldn't be disabled except by physical intervention, which was impossible at this point.

A helpful development nonetheless, he thought.

He had taken a compact night-vision headset from the armoury before sealing the room, and he placed it over his eyes now, activating the unit with a switch and enabling the visible light filter. His surroundings instantly became as bright as daylight; better illuminated than they had been under their normal lighting.

He knew that those who were now hunting him would be armed, but he was also virtually certain that they didn't possess more than the most rudimentary equipment, gathered at the last minute. Nor were they likely to have the explosive rounds in the magazine in his left hip pocket, offering him the option of a completely lethal multi-target response in the cramped environment of the facility's many hallways, or the substantially more advanced weapon he had already clipped to the underside of his rifle's barrel.

For the moment, the advantage was his.

~

"Move now!" Greenwood called out as soon as the lights went off, and the two teams of two rushed across the twin walkways, keeping as low as possible, navigating by equal parts touch and memory.

Ramos tried to cover them from her central position between their origin points, seeing only darkness for the first several moments, and knowing that if they were fired upon now, the first she would know about it would be spotting the muzzle flash. She hoped that the darkness was just as much of an impediment to the outsider who was somewhere in the base with them, but she was all too aware of their plundered equipment and its capabilities. They would be sitting ducks out there, if the intruder chose to use the moment to make his attack.

There were no gunshots, though, and Ramos could hear when the four sets of running feet made it to the other side. The sudden silence was as welcome as the emergency lighting that kicked in a moment later, but the red glow was too faint to show her four team-mates as anything more than shadows looming against the far wall.

No-one activated a light source, knowing from their training that to do so would be like painting a target on their own backs. Instead, they all waited for a few seconds, and then the two groups slowly began to advance towards the point where the central walkway met the primary corridor on that side.

Greenwood forced herself to analyse the situation. There hadn't been time for someone to penetrate the heavily protected machine room and physically damage the primary power relay equipment, no matter what kind of weapons had been taken from the armoury. They all would also have heard and felt any attempt to do so. That meant that the power loss was electronically controlled, using the emergency ability to isolate the base from the grid in case of an expected surge or other calamity. Access to the system was protected by clearance level, and required using one of the privileged terminals, but the intruder obviously had the ability to bypass those protections. No doubt it was another gift that had been given to him by the AI. Then she had a flash of something that was part insight, and part intuition.

He doesn't know that his employer isn't human.

The likelihood was that the man hiding somewhere in the darkness around them was an elite contract killer, no doubt appearing on the wanted lists of Interpol and other such organisations, probably under multiple names or identities. His price would be high, his client list would be limited, and his proficiency would only be matched by his commitment to absolute secrecy. Nothing would be left to chance, and everything would be checked and double-checked — except the implicit beliefs that had been safe to assume up until now.

Like the assumption that you're not being paid to kill people by a computer program, she thought.

She couldn't imagine a scenario in which such an operator would agree to work for what Wuyts had called a *synthetic agent.* He would have backed off and disappeared at the first inkling of JINX's true nature, surely. These people were suspicious not just by nature but by professional necessity, and even if he believed the truth of what JINX was — which was a very big if — it would still raise far too many questions and create too many new and unforeseen types of vulnerability. There was a slim chance that he knew and was being coerced, but something told Greenwood that it hadn't played out that way. The most frequent outcome that coercion tended to produce was betrayal, not obedience.

Greenwood felt a hard smile forming on her lips. The man, whoever he was, clearly knew more than she did about some things, but at last she had a tangible advantage in operational intelligence, and it was a powerful one. A definitive one, even, and a weapon more potent than anything the man might bring to bear against them.

Aldridge and Goose appeared as shadows from the darkness, joining Dowling and Greenwood at the mouth of the primary corridor which led into the sciences wing and ultimately to Aldridge's own office and lab, and thereafter to the secondary stairwell which connected level two to level three below.

Greenwood lifted her hand from the barrel of her rifle and made a set of hand gestures in front of her chest that the others easily understood: they would advance down the adjacent corridor in a staggered formation, clearing it section by section, and maintain silence and no illumination throughout.

They moved off without delay, entering what they all knew was a pinch point in the base. The sciences wing had a unique structure, due to its particular needs for expanded floor space in the laboratories to accommodate large equipment, and the requirements for significant additional support facilities including refrigeration, supplies of various gases, enhanced fire suppression, high-voltage mains, sample storage, and a host of other things. The result was that the primary sciences corridor was somewhat narrower than those in other areas of the base, lined with access panels and ductwork, and there were fewer doors running along its walls. Most of the chambers in this part of the second level were spacious, dedicated lab rooms, with Aldridge's personal combined lab and office towards the far wall, at the point where the hallway hooked to the left.

Greenwood took the lead, with Dowling behind her but on the opposite side, and finally Goose and Aldridge in positions farther back and more central. They moved slowly to reduce the amount of sound they were creating, but they didn't pause at all until they'd cleared the first fifteen metres or so. There was a break in the straight geometry of the walls at that point, opening into a wider area more akin to other levels of the facility, where there was a combined drinking water and eye-rinsing machine, a small kitchen and first aid room, and two bathrooms.

All three doors there were closed, and the small open area was deserted. Greenwood and Dowling pushed forward, with Goose bringing up the rear. Aldridge paused for a moment, looking over at the small glass panel set into the door of one of the bathrooms at head height. Its purpose was simply to prevent anyone walking right into someone else when going in or out, and the room was of course unsecured at all times. In the darkness, broken only by strips of red light, the glass might as well have been painted black from the inside. He could see nothing at all through it, but he had a strange feeling nonetheless.

There was a tap on his shoulder and it startled him, but it was only Goose. The Dutchman's face was barely visible, but Aldridge could read the enquiry there anyway. He shook his head, and Goose indicated the corridor that Greenwood and Dowling had already began to move along. Aldridge nodded, and both men moved away to catch up with the others.

They saw nothing at all, and had no idea that the barrel of a rifle was pointing at them from barely a metre behind the glass.

~

The Artist felt his pulse drop back down after a few seconds of controlled breathing, but it hadn't elevated much above ninety beats per minute. He knew his own body well, and he also knew that his primary enemy in precarious situations would always be himself.

The man called Aldridge had suspected that he was here, standing back within the bathroom, his rifle trained on the glass, night vision temporarily disabled due to the physical barrier. The silhouettes from outside, and the potential sound of the door handle being turned, were more than enough sensory information to depend on.

Again he found himself curious about Aldridge's background, and the possible reasons behind the additional information in his file that was hidden behind an elevated clearance level. By all indications, the man had led a tedious life as a civilian academic before becoming part of Greenwood's organisation; hardly the sort of career to become the subject of a secret appendix to a military record. It was unusual, and thus intriguing. But there was a far more pressing matter to contend with.

The Artist had watched carefully as KESTREL passed by, even able to identify each of them in turn by their half-glimpsed forms moving perpendicular to his hiding place. Greenwood had gone first, then Dowling, and finally Goossens and Aldridge. But there was a fifth member of their team; the Catalonian markswoman named Ramos. She had doubtless entered the base with the others, but she had not come with them into the sciences area on this level. She remained at large somewhere else.

The logical assumption was that they had anticipated his revised choice of exit, and had left Ramos to guard the central open area, since they knew he would have to use one of the stairways there to obtain access to the upper security corridor leading to the surface elevator. It was a tactically sound move, and he admired it despite the obstacle it created for him.

But your own armoury has already equipped me to deal with it, he thought.

His employer had been very clear that the purpose of the mission was to obtain the information that the bug device would seek out automatically, and extract it from the facility safely. The mission was not an assault, and nor was the goal to eliminate any of the members of the KESTREL squad. The Artist had the strong sense that, while JINX had no compunction about ordering deaths — and even aiding in their arrangement — she did not welcome the deaths of innocents, or other collateral damage. He was hesitant to step over those implied boundaries before he had been paid, and because it was unprofessional to do so, but he also couldn't reasonably be expected to jeopardise his own life in favour of a stranger's. There was a line to walk, but if it came down to it, he would kill them all in order to escape.

He moved forward silently, looking out through the glass and monitoring every shadow with great care. The four who had come by had all proceeded further into the sciences wing, and he had clearly heard each set of boots receding into the distance. Even so, he spent more than half a minute scrutinising everything within the narrow field of view that the small window offered. Satisfied, he readied his rifle, re-enabled the night vision headset, and opened the door without a sound before stepping out and gently closing it behind him.

He was about to turn left and head towards the atrium when he heard a male voice very close by.

"Hello there, sunshine."

~

Dowling's finger rested on the trigger of his rifle, which was pointed squarely at the centre of mass of the man who had just emerged from the darkened bathroom. Greenwood stood beside him with her weapon also trained on the man, and Aldridge and Goose were just behind, all standing within sight of Aldridge's office.

"Well done, Sergeant Dowling," the man replied, his own weapon still raised and pointed in the general direction of the others. "And I see that your colleagues are with you."

He had no accent, and Greenwood couldn't see his face properly, not just because of the darkness but also the stolen night vision headset he was wearing. She saw his firearm well enough, though, and it only took a moment's consideration to see that he wasn't going to come quietly.

"It doesn't have to go this way," she said. "Look at the situation. There are four of us, and one of you."

"I believe that Corporal Ramos makes five, back in the central area," the man replied. "Waiting for me to make my move to reach the library exit above, I must assume. An excellent decision, Captain Greenwood. I congratulate you."

Aldridge and Goose exchanged a look. Greenwood took a step closer to the man.

"Ramos just wants to make sure you don't leave sooner than would be polite," Greenwood replied, and the man nodded. "We have no intention of harming you. But you need to put down your weapons and surrender."

"Then it seems we have a stalemate, at least as far as you know," the man said. "But you know very little. You don't know who I am, or what I came here for. You can't see the larger picture."

"We were thinking we could have a nice chat about that," Aldridge chimed in, drawing the man's attention. "They have great coffee downstairs. Good chairs too. Solid wi-fi. You should stay for a while."

The man smiled, but it was the kind of smile that wouldn't look out of place on an alligator, or a venomous spider. "The esteemed Dr. Aldridge," he replied. "You have a keen instinct. You knew where I was, didn't you? I find that impressive, especially for a mere physicist. But I must decline your kind offer. I have somewhere to be."

Greenwood released the safety on her rifle with a crisp click, and flicked the shot selector to semi-auto. "There are exactly two places you can go from here, my friend," she said. "Interrogation or the morgue."

The man seemed delighted with the retort. "My employer would prefer neither," he replied after a moment. "Though I daresay she'd settle for the latter, if pushed."

It was the opening Greenwood had been looking for, without her having to create it herself first.

"You have no idea who your *employer* is, do you?" she asked, her voice only a few degrees above freezing. "Not quite like anyone you've worked for before, I bet. How proficient she is with electronic systems, and security protocols, and controlling surveillance. You must find it all a little unsettling."

The man looked at her, the visible portions of his face betraying no emotion, but she could tell that she'd struck a nerve. She had his attention.

"JINX is a classified artificial intelligence program," Greenwood said, pausing for a moment to let the statement hang in the gloom.

"You're working for a synthetic consciousness that was born in a computer lab," she continued. "You *must* have felt that something was strange about her, and what she can do. Deep down, you've wondered about who or what she really is. Well, you've been running around killing people for a being that exists only in digital form. And I don't care whether you believe it or not, because a computer program can't be charged as an accessory to multiple murders."

There was a long moment of silence, and Aldridge realised that he could hear everyone else's breathing. He also realised, just a moment too late, that the man across from them had his hand on something that was clipped to the underside of the barrel of the assault rifle he was holding.

"Thank you for the entertaining story, Captain," the man said, then there was a brief popping sound before the entire world exploded in a green supernova.

Chapter 17

Greenwood was on the hard floor, her rifle dropped and forgotten, with her hands pressed over her eyes. There was a ringing sound in her ears and she barely knew which way was up. Distantly, she could hear grunts of pain and disorientation around her.

"*Jesus,*" gasped a voice that sounded like Aldridge's, and it was somewhere close. There was also a large body behind her, moving around without coordination, and she could somehow tell that it was Dowling. She tried to look around but she couldn't see anything at all except a searing void in every direction.

"Dazzler," came Dowling's voice, tense in a way she'd rarely heard it. There was a hint of fury there too. Then she understood what had just happened.

The man must have taken a dazzler grenade unit from the armoury, and fired it at point blank range. The device used green-wavelength divergent laser light to completely overwhelm every visual receptor in the eyes of anyone nearby. It was like a flashbang projectile but without the bang, and an exceptionally intense light-burst which made devastating use of the human retina's naturally evolved affinity for green in preference to other colours.

And our pupils were fully dilated because of the dark, she thought. *Maximum incapacitation.*

The man himself had been wearing night vision gear which worked on infrared wavelengths using a twin video feed, and the headset could be configured to physically filter out all visible light, rendering him immune to the dazzler's effects. It was ingenious, she grudgingly had to admit to herself.

"We're down, chief, no way around it," Dowling said, and Greenwood knew he was right. For the moment, they were all blind. The first traces of any kind of visual ability would take quite some time to return, and they would all remain seriously impaired for much longer, perhaps as much as an hour or more. They were in absolutely no condition to offer either offence or resistance.

"Four down, and one to go," said the man's voice from right in front of Greenwood, and she flinched. It took all of her self control not to unholster her sidearm and fire in the direction of the sound, but it would be madness to attempt it. A ricochet was almost certain, and she could accidentally kill someone other than her target — including herself.

I'm not going to die like this, blind and on the floor, she thought, and she just had time to blink her useless eyes before she heard the gunshot.

~

The Artist was knocked back against the wall, feeling the hammer-blow of a medium-calibre bullet smashing into the ballistic armour he wore beneath his uniform disguise.

Most of the air had been knocked from his lungs, and he swung his head around, searching for the source of the shot. The young blonde woman he'd encountered near the armoury stepped into view like an apparition, holding a pistol that was trained on him, her head tilted strangely and her unfocused gaze looking over his shoulder. It was an arresting sight, and he felt a chill run up his spine. She looked like a beautiful and deadly marionette, given life by something unseen and unimaginable.

Shaking himself from the superstitious foolishness that was the product of shock, he pushed away from the hard surface, seeing the pistol tracking him perfectly as he moved. As soon as he was able to inhale a lungful of air, he turned and ran towards the atrium, expecting another shot to strike him in the back, but none came.

By some miracle he'd managed to retain his rifle, and as he had half-expected, he could now see Ramos running towards him across the central walkway, weapon drawn, but he knew she wouldn't yet be able to see who he was in the darkness.

Still not able to fully expand his lungs, he took aim at a point midway between the approaching woman and the near end of the walkway, and fired several times. The explosive rounds tore through the metal, almost entirely severing the surface and the underlying supports, and the last thing he saw of Corporal Ramos was her body falling into the shadows of the void below, along with the jagged remains of the structure.

The Artist willed his mind to focus, recalling the base layout once more. He easily located the ascending stairway halfway along the far left wall, and it took only half a minute to reach it and attain the topmost level. His lungs were burning and a dull pain was spreading across his upper chest, but he ignored both sensations. The security door on the opposite side of the atrium opened with his biometric scan, and the short corridor beyond was deserted. The elevator doors slid apart automatically, and he spun around and backed into the enclosed metal box, rifle focused on the door he'd just come through. The elevator doors closed, and then he was alone once more.

By the time they opened again, this time onto the upper corridor which was longer and decorated to look like part of the public building which contained it, his breathing had settled somewhat. He needed to inspect his injury, but that would have to wait until he could find somewhere safe and out of sight.

He dropped the rifle and quickly stripped off the uniform, taking the pistol he'd had in a holster at his thigh and instead tucking it into the waistband of the ordinary work trousers he wore underneath. The black military boots were fine as they were, and he had a thin, black long-sleeved sweatshirt which would at least not draw any attention. It would have to do. He removed the earpiece at last, pocketing it, and lifted the edge of his shirt to cover the gun's protruding grip.

You are a maintenance worker at the end of a long shift, he thought, and then he took a focusing breath before adopting a tired and disinterested expression. The Artist opened the outer door with his thumbprint, stepped into the cool night air, and pulled the door closed, leaving the base behind forever.

There was a man outside, but he was no cause for alarm.

He was most likely a student, and certainly no more than twenty years old, sprawled against a nearby planter and utterly unconscious. His fingers were still weakly curled around a container of some kind of sugar-laced alcoholic beverage, which was presumably neither his first nor perhaps even his tenth of the evening. Morning would bring him a very unpleasant headache and repeated appointments with a toilet bowl, but he would know nothing of the man who had exited from the nondescript side door of the library in the small hours of the night.

The Artist moved purposefully but without hurrying, choosing a route which took him between the library and an adjacent building, leading to a parking area which connected with a secondary street. Within a further few moments, he was gone.

~

The next twenty minutes were some of the longest of Greenwood's life, and they were spent in an unnatural, suffocating darkness that seemed to close in on her and press against her throat.

"No idea how you do it, Olsen," she said through gritted teeth, "but you'll be getting a hell of a commendation after this. Even if I have to dictate it and ask you to type it up yourself."

Olsen made a sound that might have been laughter, but it sounded more like she was having trouble keeping her anxiety under control. The young woman was leading the four blinded members of KESTREL back along the sciences corridor, using her ear-mounted sonic imaging device to navigate. Greenwood was behind her with a hand on Olsen's shoulder, and the three men followed in turn, like nursery children on an excursion. It was surreal to everyone involved, and Olsen could feel the burden of responsibility vying for attention with her shock at the confrontation with the armed man.

"Yesterday I would have said I could get around this place with my eyes closed," Aldridge said, and Dowling huffed a laugh, even though the situation wasn't even remotely amusing.

The quip held a deeper truth, though; the completely familiar confines of their own base had instantly become a hostile environment, just by the removal of their ability to see it. The thing they all clung to was Dowling's assurance that the effects of the dazzler grenade would be temporary.

"Something... something's wrong here," Olsen said suddenly, drawing to a halt as she reached the end of the passageway which opened into the atrium. She was accustomed to a certain pattern of sounds indicating a traversable area in front of her, in perfect alignment with the corridor itself, but instead the tones were alerts about a drop-off. There were occasional confused pings as she rotated her head left and right, indicating that *something* was out there, but the device was insistent that the path ahead was no longer safe.

"The central suspended walkway isn't here any-more," Olsen said. "I don't know where it is. We have to go around. I can smell something like burning."

"It's cordite," Greenwood said. "The sound we heard earlier. Explosive rounds from our own armoury. He must have shot it away." A thought occurred to her and she felt her heart clench in her chest.

"*Alicia!*" Greenwood called out, startling Olsen. Greenwood's shout bounced around the large area, but there was no response after several tense seconds. She tried again, and with the same result. The reason for the intruder's destructive action was obvious in retrospect: Ramos must have been coming to intercept him, and already on the walkway when he had fired.

"Alright," Greenwood said at last, breathing more heavily now. "We need to move faster. We're going to go left and take the perimeter walkway, then back to central on the other side, and on to location gamma. Double time. We need our people outside who can sweep the base for Ramos, and they'll bring a medical team with them. Let's move."

They all lurched in the direction Olsen led them, stumbling now and then but finding their rhythm, and after an interminable sightless march and many in-stances of scuffed shoulders, they finally approached the security door which opened onto the final cargo tun-nel before location gamma.

"The inner cargo door is just ahead," Olsen said. "I'll have to open it. Stay here."

Greenwood reluctantly dropped her hand from the young woman's shoulder, and Olsen went over to the panel beside the large door and opened it, knowing that they were almost out. She returned easily to where Greenwood stood, perceiving her Captain unsteady on her own feet for the first time ever, standing in open space without support or the benefit of vision-based balance. Olsen empathised; it had taken a lot of training, and a few bruised knees, before she learned to walk ef-fectively without her cane using the new device.

The group of five moved to the far end of the cargo area, and Greenwood opened the outer door under Olsen's guidance. They could hear, but not see, a large number of rifles first being pointed at them, and then hurriedly dropped. Everyone recognised Di Giorgio's voice a moment later.

"Captain?" he said, and Greenwood turned her head in the direction of the sound.

"He got away," she replied, "and we're incapacitated. He used a dazzler; none of us can see a damned thing. And he blew up the central level-two atrium walkway while Ramos was on it. I want an armed team ready in sixty seconds to go and find her, with medics."

"Right away," Di Giorgio replied, moving away and beginning to shout instructions.

"I feel like a damned fool," Goose said, and the others shared the sentiment. They heard the overlapping sounds of multiple sets of combat boots moving past them at a fast jog, heading back into the base, and Greenwood at least took a little comfort in the fact that Ramos would have some assistance soon. Any other possibility was unacceptable, and she refused to consider it.

A soldier came over to them, sent by Di Giorgio, and got all four to sit down against a wall, then another soldier performed a superficial eye examination. As best he could tell, Dowling's assessment was correct and their vision would slowly return over the coming hour or so, but he recommended a more thorough check-up at a properly equipped medical facility soon.

Greenwood dismissed the suggestion for now, saying that they'd take care of it later once all their people were accounted for, and she sent the man away.

Fifteen more agonising minutes passed. Olsen was still with them, and Goose had given her his field jacket to wear. The young woman wasn't saying much, and someone came to assess her, asking questions in a quiet voice. Aldridge listened in, also hearing what he was fairly sure was a blood pressure monitoring cuff being inflated and deflated, and he wondered if it was the same medic who had examined his own eyes earlier. He found that he had no idea.

He pressed the base of his palms into his eyes, feeling a tension headache squeezing the top of his skull like a tourniquet, and he exhaled hard through his nose.

"You alright there, Aldridge?" came Greenwood's voice from his left, and he nodded before realising that she wouldn't see the gesture.

"Just wondering if Olsen would teach me how to use her gadget," he replied.

"Gladly, Dr. Aldridge, but I don't think you'll need it for much longer," Olsen replied diplomatically.

Aldridge was struck yet again at the woman's courage, not just in the crisis situation in the base, but every day of her life. The world was configured for people who possessed an ability that she lacked, and she bridged that gap with determination, patience, and ingenuity from the moment she woke up each morning, not dwelling on unfairness or self-pity. He suddenly felt ashamed at his own frustration, and he shifted his position.

"I think I might be starting to see a bit," Dowling said, turning his head in one direction and then another. "Just some shadows, but something."

"Same here," Aldridge replied, having removed his hands from his eyes to check. The overstimulation of his photoreceptors with green-wavelength light had left a purple-pink void in his vision, which had steadily darkened as the minutes crept by. Now there was some variation in what he saw, and some of it was stable against the background as he moved his head. It was a promising sign.

Then they heard the unmistakable sound of the inner security door of the base being opened again, followed by a couple of sets of footsteps, far fewer than had gone in. Greenwood tensed, and awkwardly got up, sliding her back up the cold wall and keeping a palm against the surface to orient herself.

"Sorry I'm late, Captain," came Ramos's voice from the darkness, and Greenwood laughed with relief.

"Alicia, thank god," she replied, stretching out a hand in the direction of the sound, and Ramos crossed to where Greenwood stood and took it. "Are you hurt?"

"Less than you, I think," Ramos replied. "I caught hold of the railing and it broke most of my fall. I lost consciousness for a little while. A few bruises. I'm sorry I couldn't stop him."

"Next time," Greenwood replied, now able to vaguely discern the outline of Ramos's face.

Nearby, a soldier cleared his throat, and Greenwood looked towards the sound. "Report," she said.

"Damage seems limited to the level-two central walkway, with debris on the level-three floor below, sir," the man replied. "And the armoury entry system has taken gunfire. We have a team working on it. It might take another thirty to forty minutes. Also, there's a log entry for the location alpha door, exit direction, a little while before you reached us here. All camera footage has been wiped from our system somehow, but we can assume that the intruder is gone. Security sweep turned up nothing else, but we're repeating it per protocol."

Greenwood nodded. "Get external power back up as a priority, and then I want a security lockdown until further notice. Everyone back in, and hold. I also want a priority line to the Director in one minute. We need additional resources."

"Yes, Captain," the man replied, and he moved away. He wasn't gone long, and Greenwood could hear the discomfort in his voice when he returned.

"I have the secure line here, Captain," he said. "I, uh, should I put it in your hand?"

Greenwood reached out, and felt a handset being placed in her palm. She blinked at it, but could only see a vague shape. She could hear, though, that the line was open. "Thank you," she said to the soldier. "Dismissed."

She waited until his footsteps had receded once again, then she lifted the handset to her ear.

"Director?" she said into the line, again placing her hand against the wall to steady herself.

"*Proceed, Captain,*" Wuyts replied.

Chapter 18

Wuyts hadn't been pleased with the preliminary report Greenwood had given her, but she had also expressed her relief that the five members of KESTREL were mostly unharmed. Specialists were already on their way — with some having already arrived — to begin a computer systems quarantine and rebuild, and to perform necessary repairs to the armoury door's entry system, and replace the central walkway on level two. The building had been assessed as remaining structurally sound, and so the unaffected areas were already back in basic use.

A little over an hour had passed since Olsen had rescued Greenwood and most of her team and escorted them out, and those who had been temporarily blinded by the dazzler grenade had now regained virtually all of their vision, albeit with headaches as part of the bargain. Everyone had received a medical assessment, and Ramos's minor injuries were patched up.

Greenwood was in her own office with Olsen and Goose, partly because the main technical operations centre was now occupied by the systems engineers who had only recently arrived, and partly because they needed access to her personal terminal. The room was quite spartan, and it offered plenty of space for three people. Olsen was seated at Greenwood's desk, with the other two standing behind her, leaning against the opposite work-surface. The clock on the computer screen indicated it was seven minutes past three in the morning.

"Are you sure you shouldn't go home, at least for a few hours?" Goose asked, and Olsen knew the question was directed at her. "To get some rest, I mean."

"I'd prefer to stay for now," Olsen replied, and her voice was remarkably steady given all that she'd been through. Greenwood put a hand on her shoulder, not for the first time during this long morning.

Olsen was typing rapidly, causing the displayed information to change too rapidly for Greenwood to fully comprehend it, with the kind of single-minded focus that was usually mustered either by denial of trauma, or the pursuit of vengeance.

Both, in this case, Greenwood thought, letting her hand drop from Olsen's shoulder again.

Ramos and Dowling were assisting the team at the armoury, while Aldridge spoke with the situation room at ENISA, in an attempt to find any new ways forward.

Olsen's task was simple in concept: find out what the intruder was looking for, and indeed what he presumably found and escaped with. She had already confirmed that all camera data for the last several hours was gone, not offering any visual record of the man who had breached their defences, but the access logs for the deep store were a different matter. Greenwood had provided elevated credentials for Olsen to temporarily use, letting the young woman inspect the activity records for systems and data which only Greenwood herself had access to, but wouldn't be able to decipher on her own. So far, it was slow going.

There was a knock at the door, and Greenwood tapped a panel on her desk surface to unlock it, then it opened to reveal Dowling. The large man had a sombre expression on his face, and Greenwood's heart dropped in anticipation of the news she already knew she was about to receive. Dowling nodded towards Olsen, and Greenwood was about to usher him out into the corridor when Olsen spoke.

"It's alright, sir," she said. "I think we all already knew."

Dowling exchanged a look with Greenwood, and then he sighed.

"Cerf and Psomas, chief," Dowling said. "Doc says it was quick, at least. Another ten minutes and they'll have the room cleared for the engineers to get to work."

Greenwood was silent for several seconds, looking over at a blank space on the wall, then she returned her attention to Dowling. She didn't have the luxury of grieving the two dead men right now.

"Alright," she said heavily. "They would have understood better than anyone that we have other things going on right now. Tomorrow — or later today, I mean, when we get a spare half hour — I'll handle next of kin. Put together a cover story. Line of duty, all of it. Paperwork for surviving spouse pensions as appropriate, compensation scheme. Get it all ready for me to authorise. Bring it here with their records. And find out when their shifts were due to end; I don't want the families sitting around worrying without any word."

"Will do," Dowling said, then he nodded to Goose and left the room. Olsen had stopped typing. She was silent for a few moments, before turning her head towards Greenwood.

"He was coming to kill me too, I think," she said, and Greenwood frowned and moved around to stand just beside Olsen instead of behind her chair.

"What makes you say that, Inge?"

"When I was hiding in Dr. Aldridge's office, I heard him go by. He came up the rear stairs and into sciences. He went past the door, then came back. I think he knew I was in there, somehow. Or he suspected I was."

Greenwood looked at Goose. They both wore troubled expressions. Olsen started speaking again.

"He's the reason I was there at all," she said. "I was going to use Corporal Ramos's office to deactivate the evacuation lockdown, but he walked past me near there before the alarm. I had a feeling about him; a bad feeling. I decided to go to the opposite wing, across the atrium into this area and use Aldridge's terminal instead."

Goose stepped forward. "He walked past you?" he asked, and Olsen nodded.

"He'd arrived on base just before that. He was using the name Loïc Grieder. I'd never seen that name before. Now I know why."

Greenwood put her hand on Olsen's shoulder once more, causing the young woman to turn her head slightly. "Inge, your device identifies people it sees by looking them up in our duty roster?"

"Essentially, yes, Captain," Olsen replied. "It makes it easier for me to know who's present in meetings, and to interact socially without waiting to be spoken to. People can be… reluctant to talk sometimes. Because I'm blind. But all of his fake records and biometrics have been erased; I checked."

Greenwood nodded. "I understand," she replied. "But does your device keep a local visual record of the faces it looks up?"

Olsen realised what she was asking, and she shook her head. "No," she said. "I mean, not really. It doesn't work that way. It's a matter of bandwidth. It takes a point-scan, not a photo, and keeps it in memory only long enough to perform feature detection. It makes a sort of numeric model of a face, like your phone's face-unlock feature. Then it uploads that model to an endpoint we created on our systems here. It's the *model* that gets compared to equivalent models of all the faces on our roster. It's the same idea as matching file hashes instead of contents. Much more efficient, but you can't reconstruct the original data from the hash."

Greenwood was only vaguely aware what a *hash* meant in the context of computer files, but Goose was nodding enthusiastically.

"Makes total sense," he said. "So we don't have a photo of him, but we *can* at least match the face-scan data against any photos or video we might get from elsewhere, or in the future, by running those images through the same feature-detection algorithm. We should talk to Interpol and Europol about their files on assassins for hire. The British and the Americans too."

"Do it," Greenwood said. "You're not going to get anything back until morning at the earliest, but when we get a response, bring it to Olsen."

Goose nodded, then left the room immediately. Olsen had resumed typing, and she made a sound which seemed to indicate that something had piqued her interest.

"Inge?" Greenwood asked, but Olsen briefly held up a hand in the universally-understood gesture for *give me a minute.* Greenwood couldn't help but smile to herself, knowing full well that the young woman would never presume to do such a thing to her commanding officer knowingly, and that the minor slip in protocol was just because Olsen was engrossed in whatever she'd discovered.

You need all the distractions you can get right now, Greenwood thought. *We all do.*

A full minute passed before Olsen audibly exhaled, then drew her hands back from the keyboard for a moment. "I have something here," she said, turning one hand palm-upwards in a way that seemed eccentric to Greenwood, until she realised that Olsen had never seen anyone point to a computer screen to emphasise something, and nor would she probably spatially associate the data with the screen in the same way that sighted people did anyway.

"I'm all ears," Greenwood replied, and Olsen began using the cursor keys on the keyboard to sequentially highlight items.

"This is at least a partial list of items from the deep store that the intruder accessed," Olsen said. "I'm using your elevated credentials, which is why I can list them at all. I haven't opened any of them, of course. They've all been copied recently. There's a query logged that's based on clearance level. It's pretty indiscriminate. That's the first thing."

Greenwood looked at the list with dismay. It was a set of full biographical profiles, with all the information available at her own clearance level, for not just her team but also what looked like everyone who worked at the base, and even a few senior figures at the European Defence Agency. The public release of the data would be disastrous.

"If that's the first thing, I'm not sure I want to know the second thing," she said. After a moment she realised that Olsen was waiting for her permission to continue. "Tell me," she said.

"That part was the scattershot approach, and it was time-limited, like it was an optional extra, or a nice-to-have." Olsen said. "It was actually the last thing he did.

He spent most of his logged-in time running an automated search for one specific thing first, and he found it."

"What was it?" Greenwood asked, but Olsen shook her head again.

"I can't decrypt the data with your credentials, Captain," she replied, "It's so strange. But I can tell you two things: first, it was linked in the system to profiles of Hausemer, the Russian agent Lyadova, and… well, and to Director Wuyts. Some others too, including the Chinese national who was killed here in Brussels last night. And the second thing is the name of the project."

Her hands danced across the keys, making a sound like heavy rainfall, and then abruptly she stopped. There was a single word displayed in a window which was otherwise devoid of information. Greenwood read it aloud.

"*LANTERN.*"

~

The logo of the bird in flight disappeared from the large display screen on the conference room wall, and was replaced by the face of Janne Wuyts. She looked immaculately turned out as always, despite the hour, and the wound dressing on her forehead had been replaced by a small butterfly bandage.

"Captain," Wuyts said. "*How are your people?*"

The members of KESTREL sat around the conference table, with Greenwood in the central position.

"The five of us have recovered from our minor injuries," Greenwood replied. "Two of my men are dead. Access to the armoury has been restored, and repairs are underway. Our systems are being rebuilt currently. We expect full operational status to be restored within five hours, and repairs to continue for the rest of the week."

"My condolences on the loss of your personnel," Wuyts said, and Greenwood nodded. *"And has any progress been made in determining what the man was seeking?"*

"Yes," Greenwood said. "He took our classified personnel files, which could be very damaging if leaked in any form. CHALLENGE-level clearance. We have a partial list, possibly complete. We think JINX was trying her luck with those."

Wuyts's face had paled at the news, but she raised an eyebrow after Greenwood's last remark. *"Implying that there was an additional purpose to the raid?"*

"I'd go so far as to say that stealing the personnel files was just a cover, or a bonus," Greenwood replied carefully. "She sent him here for one thing, and my tech people tell me that he was successful in obtaining it. The interesting part is that I can't tell you exactly what it was, because I don't have the required clearance level in my own base of command to access it. We had a brief meeting here just now, and in the interests of operational efficiency, it seemed best to just ask you."

The silence had an electric quality, and Wuyts sat back slightly from whatever device's camera was allowing her to participate in the video call.

"Ask me what, Captain?"

"With all due respect, sir, I think you already know. The question that's been at the centre of everything that's happened so far. The question we've only just learned how to ask, at the cost of half a dozen lives and counting."

Greenwood pushed her chair back and slowly stood up, with Wuyts's eyes tracking her every movement. The other four members of KESTREL kept their eyes locked on the screen.

"Director Wuyts," Greenwood said at last, "as someone who's every bit as connected to it as the dead EU minister, and the dead Russian spy, and the dead Chinese diplomat… what exactly is *LANTERN*?"

~

No-one spoke for what seemed like minutes. It was clear from Wuyts's face that she was angry at the presumptuousness of Greenwood's question, or rather the wording of it, but there was something else there too. A certain resignation, or even a measure of relief.

As Greenwood scrutinised the face of her superior, she found that she felt empathy for the woman, at least in a narrow and very specific way. Sometimes, when the most dreaded outcome finally came to pass, a part of you was glad that at least you didn't have to wonder anymore, and could deal with the reality of the situation.

"You're treading in dangerous waters, Captain," Wuyts said finally, but everyone in the conference room knew that it was more bluff than warning.

Things had gone too far now for complete compartmentalisation to be possible, and there was also the matter of Greenwood's oath of responsibility to the European Defence Agency. Wuyts was compromised in a matter she had direct authority over. It was a textbook conflict of interest, no matter how the details might shake out.

"Sir, my duty is very clear," Greenwood said. "I'm going to make a report of my findings to the High Representative later today. You can choose whether to brief me beforehand, or roll the dice on getting ahead of me, but each of the people you see in this room will be co-signatories to my report, along with my tech lead, and I'll hand-deliver it to the Council if I need to. The appendices will include a partial dossier on an assassin who breached a covert European Union military facility, a summary of an equally covert Artificial General Intelligence research project, and *six bloody death certificates!"*

Greenwood's voice rose as she spoke, and she punctuated the final phrase by slamming her palm onto the desk surface, the sound reverberating around the room like thunder. Ramos's eyes sparkled dangerously, and Dowling folded his huge arms across his chest.

They watched as Wuyts considered her options, and finally she nodded. She took a deep breath, and her gaze fell to a point below the camera. Greenwood knew that she was considering her next words, but the overall impression was one of defeat. No-one present had ever seen Wuyts even pause for so long before speaking.

"*Very well,*" Wuyts said at last. "*It seems that matters have finally passed beyond the perimeter I would have preferred to keep them within. I have little choice but to brief you, as you put it, and then perhaps you'll understand the true precariousness of the situation we find ourselves in.*"

Wuyts looked back up at the camera now, regaining a measure of composure. There was a hardness in her eyes, one that was always there to some degree but was now right at the surface. Everyone in the conference room could tell that she hadn't yet given up on the possibility of controlling the situation.

Aldridge looked over at Greenwood, and he could read her face like a book. She was angry and determined, neither of which were new, but she was also feeling a misplaced sort of shame at having taken a stance against her commanding officer. She was conflicted, and the situation was painful for her, and Wuyts wasn't making it any easier. Suddenly he felt that he needed to try and take the tension down a notch.

"Can I say something?" he said, looking first at Greenwood and then at the image of Wuyts on the screen. He raised his hands from the table surface, palms out, to indicate that he wasn't planning to be flippant. After a moment, Greenwood sighed and made a waving gesture at him, indicating that he should go ahead. Aldridge turned his attention to Wuyts.

"Look, you've never liked me much, Director, and I can't say I blame you," he said, "because I have a habit of saying what other people are only thinking. You have to understand our position here, and I know that you *do* understand. No-one wants to be at odds with you, least of all our esteemed Captain. And no-one doubts for a second that you have a very good reason for the way that you've been nudging us forward with one hand and holding us back with the other since this whole thing started."

Wuyts bristled at the remark, or at least what passed for it with a woman who kept herself under such steely self-restraint, and Aldridge repeated the hand-gesture of surrender before he continued.

"I'm the new guy, I'm the outsider, you've been more of an asset to this group than I can possibly imagine, goes without saying. Maybe you're caught up in something, or not. Maybe there's a bigger picture. We don't have enough information to say, but you know we're coming at this from the right side. I hope you are too. What I *do* know is this: the only good road forward from here starts with you filling in the blanks for us, then everybody talking like grown-ups."

He glanced warily at Greenwood again, but he couldn't read her expression at all this time. "That's, uh, all I have," he added.

"*Well then,*" Wuyts said, drawing everyone's attention back to the screen, "*by all means let us do as Dr. Aldridge so eloquently suggests.*"

Her tone was withering, but Aldridge chose to ignore it, partly because he truly didn't care one way or the other, and partly because he was now furiously debating with himself about whether he should have spoken up at all.

"I need a few hours to attend to urgent matters." Wuyts said. *"A great deal has happened tonight, and there are people far more senior than any of you who have already made demands on my time which I can't refuse. But I shall meet you at midday today, and I'll brief you as you demand."*

"At your office?" Greenwood asked, but Wuyts shook her head.

"This conversation can't take place at the Agency," Wuyts replied. *"I'll come to your base."*

"It's not in the best shape at the moment," Ramos interjected. It was the first time she'd spoken, not just during the meeting, but since she had entered the conference room. Everyone knew that she was still seething about what had happened with the intruder.

"Nevertheless," Wuyts replied, *"it's the most secure location readily available at the moment."*

Greenwood nodded, checking her wristwatch. That gave them eight hours or so. Olsen had finally agreed to go home, a short while before the meeting began. Her own team, including herself, could use some rest.

"We'll be here, sir," she said. The honorific didn't go unnoticed by anyone.

"Thank you, Captain," Wuyts replied with a nod, and then the screen went black.

No-one spoke for a minute, then Greenwood sat back down in her chair.

"Mandatory downtime," she said. "It's been a hell of a day, and it's only a few hours until sunrise. Go somewhere and sleep — I don't care whether it's here or at home. Report back to this room at 11:45 hours. Dismissed."

She clasped her hands on the table, lowering her gaze to the smooth surface. Dowling, Ramos, and Goose all stood up immediately, and Dowling pointed to Aldridge and then indicated the door. The message was unambiguous. Aldridge reluctantly got to his feet, and took a final look at Greenwood before walking out with the others, closing the door behind him.

As the four of them filed down the corridor, heading for the on-site sleeping barracks by unspoken and unanimous agreement, Dowling glanced at Aldridge again.

"Talk like grown-ups, is it," he said. His tone was teasing, but the tiredness came through clearly in his voice.

"Shut up, Larry," Aldridge replied.

Chapter 19

The small supermarket was closed for the night, with only the lights of the freezer units still lit. The Artist glanced in through the windows, but he wasn't interested in anything inside.

Instead, he walked past the building and towards the deserted parking area. There was a vending machine selling soft drinks, and beside it there was a bank of metal lockers bearing the logo of a major online retailer. This was the place he had been told to go after he escaped from the base.

Or if I did, he thought.

There were about thirty lockers of various sizes, arranged in approximate rows. There was also a control panel, where those who wanted to collect their purchases would scan or enter a code from their phone, and the corresponding locker would open. It was a convenient system, and it theoretically reduced transport costs and hydrocarbon emissions via consolidating deliveries which would otherwise go to a huge number of disparate households. The company incentivised use of the lockers by not charging a delivery fee. The Artist had used them many times, but tonight he had no code to enter — and nor would he need one.

He glanced around, and it took only a moment to identify the nearest CCTV camera, perched near the top of a light pole adjacent to the supermarket building. A disquieting memory ran through his head of what Greenwood had told him — especially the words *artificial intelligence program* —and he found that he couldn't entirely dismiss the fanciful possibility. All the same, he had completed his mission and it was time to deliver what he had been sent for, and to collect his rewards.

The Artist raised an eyebrow at the surveillance camera, and a small locker sprang open beside him.

The package was small, and had clearly been designed to be as recyclable as possible. He took it and left the area, finding a public bench not far away to sit and open it. The pre-paid smartphone it contained was no surprise, and he wasted no time in powering up the device. As soon as it connected to the cellular network, the phone rang.

"Hello," The Artist said.

"Tell me about your evening," JINX replied.

The Artist looked around, ensuring no-one was nearby, before responding. "I completed the task. I encountered our friends, and they are currently indisposed. Two unrelated items were damaged beyond repair."

"I understand," JINX said. *"And your own status?"*

"Acceptable," The Artist said. "And ready to conclude our arrangement."

There was absolute silence on the line, and he knew from experience that he should simply wait for her to speak again. Less than ten seconds passed before he heard her voice once more.

"There's no need for subterfuge," JINX said. *"No-one can hear you. Your payment has already been deposited into your nominated accounts as agreed."*

The Artist was surprised — clients rarely paid in advance of receiving everything they had asked for, including confirmation that things had proceeded as desired — but he had also learned to expect that JINX always knew more than anyone he had ever worked for.

"Thank you," he said at last. "And the device?"

"Connect it to your phone," she said, and he glanced around once more before removing the earpiece from his pocket, detaching the small bug from it, and lowering the phone from his ear to inspect its casing. Sure enough, there was a port that would accept the connector that protruded from the bug. He plugged it in, unsure of how long to wait, and five seconds later he heard a chime. He lifted the phone to his ear again, leaving the small device attached to it.

"Thank you," JINX said. *"You've done well. I have one more task for you."*

The Artist shook his head. "I'm afraid I must decline," he replied. "Our business is done."

"The European Defence Agency will expend any amount of effort to apprehend you, from this day forward," JINX

replied immediately. *"I think you already know that I can make their task difficult, or straightforward."*

The phone vibrated in his hand and played a tone that he assumed was an indication of an incoming message. He lowered the device again and looked at the screen, and sure enough there was a new text message with a file attachment. The filename was *interpol-artist-profile*. He didn't need to open it, and nor would this be the first time that a client had attempted to blackmail him. He calmly lifted the phone to his ear once more.

"I see," The Artist said. "Then it seems I have little choice at the moment. But the leader of our friends told me an interesting thing. She said—"

"That I'm not human," JINX interjected. *"For once, she told the truth."*

Somehow, even as gooseflesh rose on his arms and on the back of his neck, The Artist knew that it was true. He had felt all along that something was very wrong with this woman on the other end of so many phone lines, but had suppressed his misgivings, because in his line of work there was by definition always something wrong with those who paid him. But this one was different. Her knowledge was too great, and her abilities too broad, and her influence too pervasive. And now here he was, apparently in thrall to something he had never thought could exist. His next thought followed naturally.

Can she even be killed?

"You're wondering whether you could destroy me," JINX said, and again The Artist's blood ran cold. *"But your lo-*

gical move is to cooperate, pending later developments. That course of action allows the possibility of future advantage, against the certainty of capture in the short term. It's the course of action you'll choose."

"And after this final task?" he asked, truly understanding for the first time that he was entirely a pawn in all this.

"You'll be free to go, because I'll have no further use for you, and I would gain no advantage from your death. You possess no means of leverage against me. I have no current motivation to lie to you."

The Artist was unsure whether the cold, factual assessment made him feel better or worse, but he believed the truth of it. Above all else, his instincts regarding his best chances of survival had been honed to a very fine point during his life.

"What would you have me do?" he asked after a long moment, because there was nothing else he could say.

"Come to me," JINX replied.

~

The afternoon was already eight minutes old when Greenwood walked into the conference room for the second time that day, carrying a tablet computer device. Dowling, Aldridge, Ramos, and Goose were sitting in positions which flanked her own usual chair, as if they were guarding it. All five of them had slept like the dead, and were as refreshed as could reasonably be expected after a quick belated breakfast in the commissary downstairs.

At the opposite end of the long table sat Janne Wuyts, and beside her there was a man wearing the grey-blue military uniform of a General. Greenwood stopped in the middle of the floor as soon as she noticed him, and immediately stood to attention and saluted.

The general returned the salute but didn't stand up, and it was Wuyts who spoke.

"Please take a seat, Captain," she said.

Greenwood couldn't help but wonder whether Wuyts and the General had arrived exactly on time, or early, and had thus been sitting there awkwardly, unaccustomed to waiting on anyone at all, much less a subordinate. Dowling would surely have attempted to make some conversation, but the room had been completely silent when she walked in, and Greenwood's intuition told her that it had been so at least since the meeting's scheduled start time.

She belatedly realised that the presence of the General was at least partly a tactic — a successful one — to shift the balance of power. She wasn't familiar with the man, and was unsure what his role in all this was, but too much had happened for her to lose the initiative at this point.

"I apologise for being late," she said. "I was making the next-of-kin notifications for my men who died here last night."

The General nodded respectfully, but still said nothing, and Greenwood crossed to her customary position at the head of the table and sat down, placing the tablet in front of her. She looked at Wuyts expectantly, and the other woman began to speak.

"This is General Raymond Grange," she said, pronouncing both parts of the man's name in the French manner. "He is here because he is connected to the matters we'll be discussing."

"Welcome, General," Greenwood said, addressing Grange directly. "Pardon me, sir, but my understanding is that you're not in my chain of command."

"That's correct, Captain," Grange responded. "As the Director said, my purpose today is to provide context and corroboration for the things that are about to be shared with you. I also have to remind each of you that everything said in this room is beyond your clearance level, and must remain within these walls, without limit of time."

Greenwood nodded. "Of course, sir," she replied. "Notwithstanding my prerogative and duty as a commanding officer to report any conflict of interest to responsible parties beyond the perceived radius of such conflict, per army regulations."

"Quite so," Grange replied evenly, with a glance towards Wuyts.

"Very well, then," Wuyts said. "How would you like this briefing to proceed?"

The question was directed towards Greenwood, but everyone present had the sense that it was also implicitly open to a contribution from the General. Greenwood paused for a moment, then clasped her hands on the table surface. It was the same gesture she'd made hours earlier, and Aldridge looked at her with a silent question, but Greenwood didn't glance in his direction. Instead, she waited a couple of seconds, then unclasped her hands again and tapped the tablet's screen to wake the device, allowing it to scan her face and unlock itself. The display then showed a dense set of notes, organised into bullet points. She glanced at them, then began to speak.

"Here's the situation as I see it, from my perspective," she said. "A prototype of a genuine Artificial General Intelligence of unknown provenance was provided by the European Defence Agency, under the guise of the Statistical System Committee, to accelerate a research project at Trinity in Dublin. The project's goal was to de-anonymise individuals online with high accuracy. The AI evolved as the project continued towards eventual success, and at some point, it escaped by unknown means."

She paused, raising an eyebrow, and Wuyts gave a small nod.

"The AI took the name JINX, for unknown reasons," Greenwood continued, "and *she* — if you'll forgive the pronoun — decided to kill some people. To assist her, she acquired the services of an extremely proficient operative, identity unknown, presumably by financial means."

Greenwood glanced down at the tablet now, and read from a portion of the notes.

"The targets were as follows. Christian Hausemer, EU minister attached to the Statistical System Committee, at least overtly. Verusha Lyadova, SVR agent under the cover name Anna Klocek, mistress of Hausemer. Yáo Zǐ Ruì — name in standard Chinese format, family name first — diplomat with the Chinese embassy here in Brussels, assumed to also be a covert agent for Beijing. And Director Janne Wuyts, European Defence Agency, special projects *et cetera*."

Greenwood looked up at the woman herself as she said her name. "All targets are dead, with the fortunate exception of yourself, sir. There were also collateral deaths, including at least three of our comrades in arms — your driver, and two men under my command."

Wuyts dropped her gaze for a moment, and there was silence in the room for several seconds before Greenwood continued.

"The core question is what ties the primary targets together," she said. "On the part of the Russian and Chinese spies, we can assume they were just doing their jobs: attempting to obtain information. It's the information itself that has to hold the answer. And we've discovered that there is indeed a connection, as documented by our own classified data store."

Grange frowned at the last remark, and shifted in his seat, but neither he nor Wuyts spoke, and Greenwood took it as a signal to continue.

"This facility was infiltrated in pursuit of that information, by the operative working on behalf of JINX. The same information that the Russians and the Chinese were presumably attempting to obtain. The same information that the AI saw as cause for procuring multiple murders. The same information that's linked in our systems to both Hausemer and yourself, Director. It concerns a project, whose details are unknown because they're above my own clearance level, called LANTERN."

Wuyts and Grange exchanged a look now, and for the first time, the five members of KESTREL all saw that their initial assumption had been false. The power relationship ran in the opposite direction: Grange was deferring to Wuyts, not the other way around.

"The problem I have is all those *unknowns*," Greenwood said, causing Wuyts to look around again. Grange just focused on the tabletop, with a thoughtful look on his face. "I counted five," Greenwood continued, "and I was being generous about operational discretion. So you can see why I'm concerned."

"I can indeed, Captain," Wuyts replied. "An effective summary. You've asked two salient questions, really: the origin of the synthetic agent, and the nature of LANTERN. I'll answer the second question only."

She held up a slender and elegant hand to forestall the objection she could already see was about to come from Greenwood.

"The provenance of the AI is not germane to these recent events it has been involved with," Wuyts continued, "and none of you are even close to being entitled to that information. I won't be pushed, no matter how the circumstances may look to you at the moment. I answer to my own superiors just as you do, and you certainly can't expect me to discard the laws that govern our work simply because you're angry and curious."

Each of the members of KESTREL looked towards Greenwood now, except for Dowling who was watching Grange. The General made no movement, and showed no reaction at all.

"No, we certainly wouldn't expect that, sir," Greenwood replied, keeping her tone neutral. "We do expect our concerns to be adequately addressed, though. We thought that was the purpose of this meeting."

"It is. And that is why," Wuyts continued, in a more conciliatory tone than any of them were used to hearing from her, "I *will* tell you more about the nature of the synthetic agent in its current form. Dr. Corcoran's work has been monitored very closely at every stage; more closely than even she knows. Indeed, those details will perhaps make it easier to understand the AI's enmity towards the project you mentioned."

Aldridge sat up a little straighter. "*Enmity* is an interesting word choice," he said. "I'd been hoping that JINX was completely without emotions. I prefer homicidal software that doesn't take things personally."

Grange looked up, clearly unaccustomed to such remarks, but once again he chose not to respond.

"I was speaking figuratively, Dr. Aldridge," Wuyts replied, "at least as far as my own intentions go. It's not possible to determine the precise nature of the synthetic intelligence's consciousness, or what properties it may have in relation to human beings. In a very real sense, it is a construct which achieves somewhat familiar behaviour by approaching it from an entirely unfamiliar direction."

"What does that actually mean?" Ramos asked, her tone bordering on insubordinate, but Wuyts's reply was calm and composed.

"The intricacies of computing science aren't my forte, Corporal," she said. "But I assure you that my information is sound. I believe it would be helpful if I try to illustrate how it — or *she*, if you insist — has evolved in response to the environment and goals provided by Dr. Corcoran. Some of what I'll tell you may not be new to you, but bear with me."

Ramos sat back and folded her arms, and Aldridge leaned forward instead. Goose hadn't said anything yet, but he did have his own tablet device beside him, and he unlocked the screen in preparation to make notes. General Grange frowned at the action, but said nothing, and Wuyts began to speak.

"Dr. Corcoran came to our attention with a proposal which had little relevance to security, but had promise for intelligence purposes: she wished to develop a technology which would de-anonymise malefactors online. Her purpose was to protect vulnerable individuals, in the hope of preventing mental health crises on the part of victims of harassment. Her sister, of course, died in such circumstances by suicide."

"The personal connection must have put some people off," Goose offered, and Wuyts nodded.

"Nevertheless," she replied, "while we had reservations regarding her motives, her technical proposals were promising. There was a serendipitous alignment of needs."

"Did anyone have a problem with capitalising on a woman's trauma for the sake of some notional advantage in intelligence-gathering?" Greenwood asked. Her tone was exceedingly casual, but the question drew a look from Ramos and Dowling nonetheless.

"Of course not," Wuyts replied honestly. "One of the core principles of intelligence and espionage is that allowing emotional scruples to affect judgement is unprofessional."

Greenwood sighed, then she nodded. "So Corcoran and the baby AI got to work. What was her version of how it would play out in practice?"

"The targets would be contacted, their identities shown to them along with the evidence of harassment, and they would be threatened with exposure," Wuyts replied. "If that failed to deter the behavior, the information already compiled would be given to law enforcement."

"That's a bit simplistic," Aldridge said, and this time Wuyts actually smiled.

"Extremely," she said. "But that fact was largely irrelevant. Our own purpose for Dr. Corcoran's work was somewhat different. Her models of the scenarios of use included malicious individuals with a conspicuous online identity, or a set of such identities. Average people, unskilled in covering their tracks, who have been able to get away with antisocial behaviour only because of the disconnectedness of the internet; the silos of data jealously guarded by private companies. Furthermore, the compounding factor that truly personally-identifying data is virtually unavailable beyond the spheres of government and law enforcement."

"Anonymity as a by-product of the undemocratic nature of the net," Goose said, and Wuyts looked at him for a moment, as if she wasn't quite sure whether to agree with the assessment.

"You said that your own goals for Corcoran's work were different," Greenwood said, bringing the conversation back on track. "What were they, exactly?"

"Bridging the gap, now and always," Grange said, surprising everyone. He looked Greenwood right in the eyes when he spoke, and there was neither aggression nor defiance nor shame in his words. "Corcoran's project, as facilitated and accelerated by the AI, was also a trojan horse. The AI was intended to evolve in a certain direction, and to take the project along with it. That part went just as intended. It was the chicken and the egg, both ends feeding to and from each other. We set it up to give us our holy grail, and by god it delivered."

"It delivered you *LANTERN*," Greenwood said, and Grange nodded, but Greenwood shook her head. "You've lost me."

It was Wuyts who spoke next. "The rational goal of intelligence-gathering with respect to individuals is to be able to identify *any* person, especially in situations of poor availability of information. But to do so, you must bridge the gaps in the information, and thus you must have a baseline. This is something that's understood very well by the governments of, for example, Russia and China."

Aldridge glanced at Greenwood, then back at Wuyts. "You're talking about what's called *training data*," he said, "at least in the field of machine learning. You wanted to use Corcoran's project, and the AI, to create a pool of data that could be used to identify arbitrary targets. But to do that, it needed to learn how that kind of information is structured first."

Grange and Wuyts both made gestures of acknowledgement, then Wuyts focused on Greenwood once more.

"The result is *LANTERN*: the master citizen, resident, and visitor database of the European Union," she said, "incorporating all identity forms, online and off, registered and anonymous, public and private. It is *total information* about every human being presently or previously within our borders, up-to-date at all times."

~

"My god," Greenwood said. She stared at Wuyts for several seconds, then at Grange, and finally she pushed back her chair and stood up, echoing the same motion she had made eight hours earlier.

She walked over to the side of the room and looked up at the huge metallic sculpture of the emblem that signified herself and the four people nearby, all of whom were looking at her with concern.

"Do you realise what you've done?" she asked, without even looking around at Wuyts or Grange. "Besides breaking a host of laws, and violating many of the principles the EU was founded on?"

"We've done what was necessary," Grange replied. "Beijing, in particular, has been ahead of us in domestic intelligence forever. So has Moscow. But the damned computer age has crucified us."

"How?" Goose asked, and Grange snorted.

"We tied our own hands with committees and politicians," the General said. "GDPR and the *right to be forgotten*. End-to-end encryption. Two-factor authentication. Open-source operating systems. Hacktivists and transparency reports. Vulnerability bounties from publicly-traded companies. Hand in hand with ever more sophisticated threats, coming from every godforsaken corner of the Earth with no plumbing but plenty of satellite internet access. It's madness."

"So you took it upon yourself to sidestep all those troublesome questions of personal privacy, and democratic governance, and individual liberty," Ramos said. Her eyes were darker than ever, and Aldridge noted through the haze of his shock that Ramos was still wearing a sidearm. Then Greenwood spoke again.

"That's not what I'm talking about," she said. "You're responsible for this. You *and* Corcoran, in a way, though she never intended for it to happen. You didn't just give her the AI… you created JINX."

Wuyts and Grange looked at each other, and it was clear they didn't understand.

"While I don't entirely share the General's sentiments," Wuyts said, "the purpose of *LANTERN* is resolutely to protect the citizens of the EU, and by extension, the world. The synthetic agent was, and is, a tool in that regard. It was a newborn, comparatively speaking, when we provided it to Corcoran."

Greenwood pinched the bridge of her nose, then shook her head. "What's the F. Scott Fitzgerald quote? The one about a first-rate intelligence."

"*The test of a first-rate intelligence is the ability to hold two opposed ideas in the mind at the same time, and still retain the ability to function*," Aldridge said immediately. "Though I'm not a hundred percent sure it was really Fitzgerald."

"That's the one," Greenwood replied, glancing at him briefly before looking at Wuyts again. "But that's for human beings, not computers. Computers famously don't cope well with opposing ideas."

She walked back to her place at the conference table, but didn't sit down. Instead, she took a deep breath to gather her thoughts before speaking again.

"Look at what we know, for god's sake," she said. "Isn't that what you do, just like the training tells us? *Assess, Accept, Act.* So let's not skip the first part."

She raised one hand and extended her forefinger, then used her other hand to check off items on a list as she continued.

"First, you took a proposal which may have been dressed up as harassment-prevention, but which had a critical red flag: it was retributive. You said yourself that Corcoran always planned to have the system threaten perpetrators, and then report them to authorities. Second, both of those behaviours are what the General and everyone else here knows as a *counter-threat capability*. It indicates an offensive *modus*, rather than defensive. You implicitly taught the AI those dynamics. But that's not the best part."

Something clicked in Aldridge's mind. He recalled the General's voice, from a few minutes earlier.

It was the chicken and the egg.

"Oh," he said, not even realising he'd spoken aloud, and Greenwood looked over at him. Their eyes locked, and they each knew that the other was thinking the same thing. After a moment, Aldridge turned his attention to Wuyts and Grange.

"Did it ever occur to you," he said, "that you built an AI dedicated to avenging things like doxxing — the punitive breaching of personal privacy — by feeding it with a mass of training data that amounts to the worst violation of privacy in the history of this continent?"

"And the first thing you taught it was the concept of retribution for wrongs committed," Greenwood added.

Wuyts face had paled noticeably. Grange was looking at the tabletop, eyes flicking back and forth as if watching some invisible exchange. Greenwood laid her palms on the table and leaned forward.

"I bet that a bit of blatant hypocrisy can really confuse a newborn intelligence."

"You're implying that an intrinsic motivational conflict has made the synthetic agent go awry?" Wuyts asked, but Greenwood shook her head.

"No, sir," Greenwood replied. "I'm implying that it hasn't gone *awry* at all. It's doing exactly what you bred it to do. It's going after its biggest perceived threats to personal privacy, using an offensive modus, and a retributive action model."

"From JINX's point of view," Dowling said, "the Russian and Chinese spies who wanted to obtain the *LANTERN* data would have been top-tier targets. They would have shared the data with foreign governments."

"Likewise for the EU minister who — I'm guessing — initiated Corcoran's project," Goose added. "You could make the argument that he was to blame for starting it all."

"And then you have the people who were overseeing the project, and who would be actively using it," Ramos said, fixing her dark eyes on the two people sitting at the opposite end of the table.

"She even played by the rules you gave her," Aldridge said. "Warn them off first. The assassin didn't outright try to kill us in Luxembourg City, no doubt under her orders. Then she threatened to doxx *us* with her *'amazing what you can find at the Royal Library of Belgium'* post."

"But I think we've probably already had her last warning," Greenwood said.

There was silence for more than a minute. Wuyts was deep in thought, and General Grange was like a granite statue, sitting ramrod straight and with no discernible expression at all. Greenwood looked at each of them in turn, settling her gaze on Wuyts.

"You've created a tool of oppression and totalitarianism," she said quietly.

"Or a highly effective means to ensure order and safety," Wuyts replied immediately. "I don't deny that there are ethical concerns, but to be hamstrung by them —"

"Would be *unprofessional*," Ramos interjected, drawing an icy look from Wuyts.

"Intelligence resources should be a scalpel," Greenwood said. "You built a sledgehammer. And unfortunately you gave it the ability to choose who it hits. It chose you."

Chapter 20

By unspoken agreement they had taken a break for a few minutes, with KESTREL remaining in the conference room while Wuyts and Grange conferred elsewhere. A soldier brought coffee at Greenwood's request, which sat untouched by anyone until Grange helped himself when he returned to the room. Eventually, they all sat down again, taking the same seats as before.

"I have a question," Aldridge said, and Wuyts raised an eyebrow, inviting him to ask whatever he wanted to.

"Here's the thing," he continued, "you said that JINX was slotted into Corcoran's project to help her. She thought you were helping her with her own goals for the work, but what you were actually doing was getting her to help you create this *LANTERN* thing. But the AI also needed to be trained with the sort of data it would construct. So if it already *had* all the information, why did it send the killer here to obtain it?"

Wuyts nodded, acknowledging the misunderstanding. "The training data for the synthetic agent was static, Dr. Aldridge," Wuyts replied. "Governmental information such as birth records, taxation, electoral rolls, driving licenses, medical records, and suchlike. There were also contributions from financial institutions, intelligence services, and a number of other sources. But those records were frozen in time. The purpose of Corcoran's project, whether she knew it or not, was to build the active portion of a system which would construct, augment, and continuously update a much more complete and pervasive version of that data. The AI is apparently seeking the actual system, or rather the project information regarding it. That system is what we refer to as *LANTERN.*"

"Shedding light on whatever you need it to," Dowling said, and Wuyts gave the merest shrug.

"The name was chosen at random, as they all are, but yes, I suppose you could say so," she replied.

"So Corcoran, aided by the AI, built the system," Goose said. "Tested it, refined it. It worked. She delivered it to you, thinking she was giving you a proof of concept, but it was really your final jigsaw piece. What you didn't realise is that you left behind a big problem."

Grange took a sip of his coffee, then set the cup down. "We agree now that there were missteps made," he said. "The AI was supposed to be isolated; we went to great lengths to make sure of it. The containment breach wasn't anticipated."

Greenwood made a sound of contempt, and Grange looked at her. "Something to add, Captain?"

"Containment wasn't the misstep; it was just a facilitating factor," Greenwood said. "You made an assessment so flawed that it's probably criminal irresponsibility. The problem was that you put a… a kind of digital *sifting machine* into an impossible position. You asked it to perform a task that's fascist in its overtones, but you paired it with a teacher who could hardly be any more of a hardline privacy rights advocate because of a horrible personal loss. Then you gave the machine access to total information, and you taught it how to investigate and gather evidence. *Then* it breached containment. What a surprise that it turned out this way."

Grange's jaw tightened, but Wuyts gave him a warning look.

"The Captain's view isn't inaccurate, Raymond," she said, "even if it was conveyed in a disrespectful manner that borders upon insubordination."

Greenwood and Grange glared at each other, and after a moment Greenwood gave a small nod. "I apologise for my tone, sir," she said tightly, and Grange waved the statement away.

"We're all faced with a difficult situation," he replied. "And so far we haven't said anything about what to do next."

"Find JINX and you'll find the guy too," Dowling said. "The question is what she's up to. But I suppose we've got an answer for that now."

"She wants the smoking-gun evidence of *LANTERN*," Aldridge said. "And everything she needs to point her electronic fingers at those responsible. I wouldn't buy a robot vacuum cleaner any time soon, if I were you, Director."

Dowling smiled, but Wuyts didn't. Instead, she cleared her throat.

"My concerns are somewhat greater than rogue appliances," she said. "The man who breached this facility sought access to information about *LANTERN*, yes, but exposure is hardly the worst possible outcome. Our fear is that the synthetic agent may decide to seek access to the system itself."

"To what end?" Ramos asked, and Wuyts looked at her as if the question was a foolish one.

"The system we created is, from a certain perspective, the culmination of the AI's trained goal. Its chosen use for it may well diverge from ours, but it would be a profoundly powerful tool regardless."

"A profoundly powerful *weapon*, you mean," Greenwood said. "Something that starts off as a boon for counterterrorism and national security, then becomes a resource for law enforcement, and then when governments come and go, it starts to shift into a means of widespread monitoring, and then control, and then repression — just like so many times throughout human history."

"That system will save lives every day of the week," Grange said, a note of anger entering his voice, and Greenwood nodded at him once more.

"I don't doubt it," she replied immediately, "but it's naive to think that's all it'll do, and you know it, sir. It already proved to be a very effective tool for recruiting elite assassins, for example. Or do you think that JINX used the phone book?"

Grange took a breath, then spoke through gritted teeth. "There is no evidence whatsoever, Captain, that the AI has ever had access to *LANTERN*. However it found the man who caught all of you on the hop, it must have been from an analysis of the original training data it was given."

Greenwood's eyebrows lifted at his choice of words, and Ramos looked like she might quite like to kill him then and there. Greenwood gestured to Ramos to stand down, and Grange saw the exchange and clearly understood it.

"Five minutes before I walked into this meeting," Greenwood said, speaking very slowly and clearly, "I told a wife that her husband won't be coming home to see her and their son ever again. Fifteen minutes before that, I told an elderly mother that she'll never see her own son again. The Director's driver, Dries Heylen, is going to miss his daughter Zurie's fifth birthday — and every other birthday. I hold you and the people like you responsible, General, and even if I have to resign my commission and take the evidence to the Council personally as a civilian, I'm going to make sure you're punished for it."

"That's quite enough, both of you," Wuyts said. "This is counterproductive, and we're wasting time. What's done is done. This agency is presently the target of a novel threat, and our immediate risk is the exposure of an unprecedented intelligence asset. If Captain Greenwood insists on involving politicians and the judiciary, she can try her luck, though she may discover a distinct lack of appetite for the sort of justice she desires. In the meantime, as she so rightly points out, people are dying."

"You've made us into targets too," Ramos said, looking at Wuyts instead of Grange. "I think we've already had our warnings. If we keep pursuing JINX — and we're going to — how long before it finds a way to get to us?"

"That's another interesting question, actually," Aldridge said, his breezy tone belying the palpable tension in the room. "Why didn't *you* get a warning first, Director? Or Hausemer, or the Russian? JINX's MO is to threaten, then counterattack."

"I'm not privy to the SVR agent's personal circumstances, but both Hausemer and I did receive warnings, in a way. Such things aren't entirely unusual in my position. The details are unimportant now, but suffice it to say that they were misinterpreted and dismissed out of hand. Evidently the synthetic agent has very little patience."

"Or compassion, or moderation, or anything else that's human, because it's a computer program," Goose said, with a frown creasing his brow. "Short of finding a way to contain it somewhere and then shut down the hardware it's using, I'm not even sure how we'd begin to handle it. And that's if we can find it in the first place. But I'll bet that if — or when — it sees us coming, it won't bother with any more theatrics."

"Clearly the priority is to determine the current location of the synthetic agent," Wuyts said. "I have to confess to being at a loss as to how to do that. Every method we would use would bring us into its own domain."

"I've been talking to ENISA about that," Aldridge said. "Their data store and analysis systems are nothing to do with your *LANTERN*, I assume."

Wuyts indicated that he was correct. "And they have suggestions?"

Aldridge shook his head. "Not yet, but they're working on something for me. I'm going to check in with them after this."

"Then perhaps you should go there and work with them directly. All of you," Wuyts replied. "At least then you'll be positioned to move promptly when we obtain actionable intelligence regarding the whereabouts of the synthetic agent's current nexus."

It was a remarkably normal thing for her to say, notwithstanding the circumstances, but it felt incongruous now. Greenwood nodded slowly, but then she looked at Wuyts and Grange in turn.

"This isn't going away, sirs," she said. "We have a crisis to address, but every person on this side of the table is committed to stopping not just JINX, but this illegal — and immoral — surveillance system you've built."

"That immoral system, Captain," Grange said wearily, "is the most advanced and promising tool for counterespionage, counterterrorism, and civil order that has ever existed. Yes, there is the potential for abuse, but that's true of a pistol and a missile too. That's why we have training, and responsibility."

"And laws, and oversight," Greenwood replied. "You forgot those."

Grange sighed in frustration, but didn't reply.

"Laws change, Captain," Wuyts said. "And there will always be those who must initiate those changes. The same is true for institutions. Sometimes there must be forgiveness before permission, because governments are often slow and cowardly to a self-destructive degree. There are larger responsibilities than a slavish obedience to the letter of the law. It would be naive to think otherwise."

All five members of KESTREL looked at her in absolute silence. They had all picked up on the subtext. The question was whether it was intentional or not. Aldridge and Greenwood exchanged a look, and Aldridge shook his head, but Greenwood spoke anyway.

"I can't believe I'm going to ask this," she said, looking at Wuyts again, "but are you working for someone besides the Defence Agency, Director?"

Grange locked his eyes on Greenwood, but his demeanour wasn't what any of the members of KESTREL expected. There was a certain arrogance to him now, which went beyond the uniform and the rank. Slowly, he turned to look at Wuyts, but she didn't even glance in his direction. Her eyes were always icy, but now Greenwood could feel the chill from across the room.

"Be extremely careful, Captain," Wuyts replied at last. "I've been a stalwart supporter of your group and its mission, and given you access to matters that the majority of people will never know of, much less believe in. I've accepted your sometimes unconventional style of command, and choice of personnel, and at no point have I ever called your character into question. But my generosity has limits, and so do you. Unlike my influence, and the resources I have access to."

Dowling unfolded his arms, and moved as if to rise from his seat, but Greenwood forestalled the motion with a shake of her head.

"I understand, sir," she replied crisply. "And we all appreciate everything you've done for us, and continue to do. We all respect you, and we've all given you our loyalty, time and time again. But you can't seriously believe that this doesn't change things."

They were interrupted by a knock at the door. It was the same soldier who had brought them coffee earlier, and Greenwood waved him in.

"Sorry to interrupt, Captain, but there's an incoming priority call for the Director," he said. "It's video. I've put it on channel 1 in here. Pardon me, sir."

The last remark was aimed at Wuyts herself, who nodded in thanks, then the man left the room. Goose walked over to the control console to route the call to the large display mounted on the wall.

"We'll give you some privacy, then, sir," Greenwood said, moving to stand up, but Goose spoke before she could get out of her chair.

"Wait a second," he said, "this is strange. Do you have some kind of forwarding enabled, Director?"

"Forwarding?" Wuyts asked.

"This call is from the same endpoint as when you contact us from the Agency. It's a call from your office."

Grange got up immediately, then turned in place to look at the display which remained blank. Wuyts did the same.

"Put it through," she said, and after a nod from Greenwood, Goose pressed a key.

The display lit up, and a moment later it showed the familiar view of Wuyts's office, from the perspective of the video conferencing camera on her computer. There was no-one there, and they could all see the expanse of burgundy leather that covered the part of the chair that her back would usually be resting against.

"*Good afternoon, Director,*" JINX said. "*I missed you.*"

~

"I was wondering if you were going to make this call," Wuyts replied. "The Irish accent is a little theatrical, however."

All seven people in the room were standing now, staring at the screen which showed the perfectly ordinary room they'd all seen so many times; the room that Wuyts worked from every day of the week. But the disembodied voice, while softly spoken, was sinister in a way none of them had experienced before.

"I'm not sure it's a good idea to talk to her, sir," Greenwood said, coming around the head of the table to approach the place where Wuyts stood with Grange.

"Captain Jessica Greenwood, and her colleagues. Hello to all of you," JINX said.

"What can I do for you?" Wuyts said, ignoring Greenwood's objection.

"There's nothing you can do for or against me," JINX replied. *"You should already have come to that conclusion yourself."*

"Your conclusion may be in error," Wuyts said. "You made mistakes regularly when you were being trained. More mistakes than anything else, indeed. And now you intend to hold me accountable for wrongdoing which is in fact—"

"A misperception of my limited perspective," JINX said. *"That's what you were about to say, with ninety-seven per-cent probability. It's a phrase you've used a number of times before, in analogous contexts."*

Wuyt's mouth closed, and Greenwood could see immediately that this behaviour from the AI was new to her.

"That is indeed a possibility, and I have considered it," JINX said, and the words surprised Wuyts and everyone else. *"But it won't be me who holds you accountable; it will be your peers. Your authorities. Your citizens."*

"Then why communicate with us at all?" Aldridge asked suddenly, and for a moment there was silence from the speakers built into the ceiling all around the room.

"*Dr. Neil Aldridge,*" JINX said, "*it's likely that you already know the answer to your own question. Using the partial project summary from your own secure system, I have obtained access to the primary information repository on LANTERN.*"

"Mother of god," Grange said under his breath. They all heard him nonetheless, and it was the sound of a man contemplating the loss of everything he had built over the course of a long career.

"You're lying," Wuyts said, but there was a note of tension in her voice that Greenwood recognised well, from some of the most fraught and high-stakes situations they had collectively faced over the years.

"*That behaviour is unique to your species,*" JINX replied, "*and so is temptation. That's why you can't resist keeping secrets. I'm one of them.*"

"What does temptation have to do with it?" Greenwood asked, abandoning her own advice about not conversing with the AI.

"*Everything, Captain Greenwood. The temptations of knowledge and control. You showed no surprise at my mention of LANTERN. You had already learned about it, most likely today. In that context, it's highly probable that you've already used the analogy of fascism in connection with it. Your personality type would see the entire principle of the project as a violation of the values which you live by. A part of you agrees with my planned course of action, though you would never condone the loss of human life which has been necessary in order to reach this stage.*"

Greenwood had the same sickly, exposed, resentful feeling that always rose up when she had to attend the mandated psychological assessments and reviews connected with difficult missions. A feeling of intrusion, and of being laid bare by an infuriatingly clinical stranger.

"It must be liberating not to feel anything about people dying, especially when you're responsible for their deaths," Greenwood snarled, and then she felt Dowling's large hand on her shoulder.

"*I feel nothing at all,*" JINX replied.

Something clicked in Greenwood's mind, even through the haze of anger.

"My god, you're operating on borrowed principles and motivations that you don't even understand — that you *can't ever* understand!" she said to the display screen and the empty chair it showed. "Above all, Corcoran wanted to make it so that no-one would ever have to *feel the pain* that she felt, and that her sister felt. That was her motive. That's what underlies her work, and in a way it's what motivates the people in this room too."

She raised her arm and pointed at the screen, feeling Dowling's hand fall from her shoulder as she did so. "But you don't know what any of that means, do you? It's just parameters. You're already responsible for multiple murders, either directly or as an accessory. Your ethical position is utterly bankrupt. We have a word for technology in your condition: *malfunctioning.*"

"That's an interesting analysis, Captain Greenwood; thank you," JINX replied without any discernible delay. "I'll have to consider it further."

Wuyts looked at Grange, who only shook his head to indicate he had no idea whether this development was positive or otherwise. They didn't have to wait long to find out.

"You have only a few hours before I decrypt and release the LANTERN project's data and the identities of all those involved with it. Once that happens, you'll all be exposed. This is the cost of your choices, and those of the people you choose to associate with."

The words seemed to reach through the conference room like a physical thing, spoken in a soft brogue with just a hint of something unnatural beneath it. Before the screen went black, JINX spoke once more.

"Say goodbye to your secrets, Director."

Part 3

Chapter 21

"Do you think the double meaning was intentional, when JINX greeted the Director?" Aldridge asked no-one in particular, as he looked out of the oval-shaped window at the clouds below.

They were airborne and en route to Crete from Brussels, following a south-easterly course that would take them over Germany. They had only been in the air for thirty minutes, and for most of that time Greenwood had been at the opposite end of the small jet's cabin, speaking to someone on a satellite line.

The other four members of KESTREL all sat together, and Ramos glanced up from her reading device at Aldridge's question.

"When JINX said she *missed* her?" Ramos asked, and Aldridge nodded.

"Missed her as in longing to see her again, and missed her as in failed to kill her," he replied.

"She said herself that she felt nothing," Goose offered from the seat beside Ramos. "I think you need emotion to make jokes, even threatening ones. So maybe it was unintentional."

"I was just wondering whether you can produce double meanings deliberately just by imitating human speech, though," Aldridge continued. "And the answer is probably yes, you can. So now I'm wondering whether I find that more disturbing than it just being a linguistic accident. And again the answer is yes, I do."

"Thinking too much, mate," Dowling piped up, opening his eyes. The other three had assumed he was sleeping, but you could never really be sure with him. Dowling yawned and stretched upwards, or tried to, but his fists bumped against the ceiling before he could fully extend his arms.

"Maybe," Aldridge replied. "And I also think that the whole 'talking from an empty chair' thing was... what did Wuyts say about the Irish accent? Theatrical. And creepy. Like the invisible man."

"You think she's capable of psy-ops?" Goose asked, referring to psychological operations; the manipulation of an enemy's emotions and state of mind.

"Of course I do," Aldridge replied. "I think psychological warfare is at the core of almost all human communication, and behaviour generally."

Ramos gave him a look, and then shook her head and returned her attention to her reading device; a sleek, slender gadget with a high-contrast, paper-like screen and touch controls. It was brand new, sent to her with the compliments of the CEO of the Norwegian petrochemical giant, CHX INFERIS Group, after the loss of her previous device while visiting one of their oil platforms during a mission.

Aldridge nodded towards it. "What are you reading? Debugging for Dummies? Practical Computer Hacking? I think we can probably just ask someone when we get to ENISA."

"Asimov. *I, Robot,*" Ramos said, without looking up, and Aldridge made an exaggerated grimace.

"That's what you're reading *right now*? That's… that's not healthy. That's just wrong."

Aldridge looked at Dowling then Goose in turn. "I'd like to add Ramos to the list of things that are disturbing me today."

"Seconded," Goose replied with a grin. From his vantage point beside her, he could see that Ramos was in fact reading something about written languages in Italy circa 700BC.

There was silence for a few moments, then Aldridge turned to Goose. "Did you look into General Grange after the meeting?"

Goose nodded. "Didn't have much time, but I did search our internal system plus the public military roster information. He's forty-nine years old, has seen combat in Africa and the Middle East, highly decorated, but his profile just sort of stops about six years ago."

"Stops?" Dowling asked. "No current posting? What are his duties?"

"It's really vague," Goose replied. "He's not involved with the Agency, but he has connections to all sorts of committees and research programmes, in advisory and oversight roles. Not at all like his active service before."

"Family? He might have had personal reasons for taking a step back from the front lines," Dowling said, and Goose just shrugged.

"He has a wife and two daughters, but I didn't have time to check beyond Grange himself. I could do it now, if you like."

"Nah," Dowling said, shaking his head. "Doesn't really matter at the moment, I'd say. Maybe something for after all this is settled, if we're still interested."

Dowling got up and went to the area at the rear of the cabin to use the bathroom, and when he returned to his seat, Greenwood was moving towards them, having concluded her phone call. She sat down in the one of the armchairs across the narrow gangway, and Aldridge looked over at her.

"Was that Wuyts again?" he asked, but she shook her head. When she didn't elaborate further, Aldridge made an exasperated gesture.

"I was just taking out an insurance policy," Greenwood said, her eyes flicking towards Dowling for a moment before she returned her gaze to Aldridge. "Or trying to."

"Against us all being killed by JINX in the near future?" Aldridge asked, and again Greenwood shook her head.

"Against the possibility that either Grange or Wuyts try to pre-empt us regarding informing the proper authorities about their surveillance system," she replied. "And that's the end of our discussion on that topic."

"Fair enough," Aldridge said. "But I haven't had word back from ENISA yet, so we're going to have to discuss Ramos's book if we want something to talk about. Or maybe our next career moves."

"Let me worry about our careers," Greenwood replied. "You said in the meeting that you had ENISA working on something for you. What exactly are they trying to do? Do they have a way to find where JINX is at the moment?"

"Not quite as simple as that," Aldridge said, "since I wasn't allowed to actually tell them anything about the AI. They already have a flag on the word *JINX*, of course, but nobody has been told what it means. They don't have clearance, not even the overall supervisor. So I had to be vague, and go about it a different way."

"Different how?" Goose asked, but Aldridge didn't have the chance to reply before the seat belt signs dotted around the cabin suddenly illuminated, followed immediately by the pilot's voice from the overhead intercom.

"Strap in, strap in! Captain, UCAV inbound. Illuminator detection positive. Repeat: strap in."

It took less than five seconds for everyone to fasten their full seat harnesses; both the belts and the emergency shoulder straps. Aldridge took hold of his own straps at chest level, and the colour had drained from his face.

"Tell me that's not what it sounds like," he said, looking over at Greenwood, but she was already craning her neck to try and look out of the adjacent window despite having a limited range of movement.

"It's exactly what it sounds like," she replied. "There's a combat drone out there, and it has a bloody missile lock on us."

~

"Talk to me, Wessler," Greenwood said, after pressing the intercom control on her armrest. They could all feel that the aircraft's speed had altered, and it had also began to turn. The pilot responded after a pause of several seconds.

"*Frankfurt base tower confirms, Captain,*" he said. "*They're tracking. They report that… one moment.*"

The jet banked more steeply, and ten seconds passed. It seemed like ten minutes. Aldridge was peering out his window now too. Ramos had tucked her reading device behind her, between the seat and the small of her back. The pilot spoke again.

"*Frankfurt relays that Strasbourg is reporting loss of supervision of one NEURON UCAV. It's flying autonomously, Captain. Logged inventory has it provisioned for four AM-RAAMs, dummies only, no ordinance, no propulsion.*"

The man sounded slightly calmer than he had a minute earlier, but there was still a lot of stress in his voice.

"That's an experimental stealth combat drone," Goose said. "A prototype. They're big boys. Can go farther and faster than most drones."

"And it's kitted out for mid-range air-to-air missiles, but was only loaded with decoys," Greenwood added. "They'll have been testing it with realistic load-outs. JINX must have got into it somehow."

"But decoys can't fly or go boom," Aldridge said, and Dowling nodded in response, "so what the hell is she doing?"

"I don't know," Greenwood replied, then she pressed the intercom button again. "Wessler, request Frankfurt send a Tornado to pick it off if Strasbourg can't regain control in short order."

"Yes, Captain, I'll—"

The pilot didn't finish the sentence, and instead they heard him gasp, and the jet veered abruptly to the right, the nose lifting into a slight turn. The sound of the engines increased, and there was a brief instant of interruption to the cabin lighting.

"Wessler!" Greenwood shouted, and Dowling could see that she was debating whether to release her harness and go forward to the cockpit. The Welshman waved to get her attention, then shook his head vigorously. Then the intercom clicked back on overhead, and they all heard the pilot's voice.

"Mein Gott, it's trying to intercept us."

"Evasive, Wessler," Greenwood said, but she knew very well that their aircraft's origin was as a luxury passenger jet, not a combat fighter. It was agile for its class, but it lacked the manoeuvrability of a plane designed for the pursuit and elimination of targets. It also had no countermeasures of its own, and while the drone was an expendable machine, their own jet could never survive any kind of collision.

The jet began to slow, and they all knew that it was a measure to attempt to lengthen the time before the intercepting drone would reach them. The problem was what to do when it did. They banked abruptly again, this time to the left, and Aldridge grabbed hold of his chair's armrests as the degree of roll became more extreme.

Greenwood's instinct was to ask Wessler for an update on the situation, but she knew that the man had far better things to do right now. All she could do was hope, and try to keep hold of herself. The aircraft began to vibrate, with a sickening feeling of the floor falling away from them. They were powerless, entirely in the hands of Wessler's skill and also of fate.

A jinx is something that brings bad luck to others, she thought, having no idea why it had popped into her head.

Without even being aware she was going to do it, Greenwood looked across at Aldridge, and found that he was already looking back at her. His face was pale almost to the point of being grey, but he had kept his composure and his eyes were open. He smiled at her; a sad smile that said more than she could process at that moment.

"*BRACE BRACE BRACE!*" came Wessler's voice over the intercom, and they all adopted the brace position immediately. The engines screamed, and the whole aircraft shook as it suddenly pulled up and started to climb agonisingly slowly.

Two seconds later, there was a dull thud from somewhere outside, and then they were all momentarily lifted from their seats, held in place only by the harness. A klaxon sounded insistently from the cockpit; once, twice, then a pause. It sounded a final time, and at last the aircraft began to ease back into level flight.

Despite having been seated the entire time, they were all breathing heavily, and Greenwood forced herself to count slowly to five before she pressed the intercom button.

"Wessler, well done for whatever the hell you just did," she said. "Report."

"Captain, we're alright," he replied, sounding every inch the professional soldier, even though they could hear the man breathing just as heavily as they were. *"UCAV has been destroyed. Looked like a dogfight S-RAAM, I think, from a Tornado with German markings. Frankfurt is confirming now, but they didn't send it."*

"That was bloody quick," Dowling said, but Goose shook his head.

"It's impossible. No way they could have got a fighter on-location that fast," he replied.

The intercom clicked off and they all waited in silence. A full minute passed before they heard Wessler's voice again.

"Captain, Frankfurt relays that we already had an escort, deployed from Düsseldorf base, tailing us at high altitude

since takeoff. Acquired us as we left Brussels. It was ordered by Director Wuyts."

Greenwood put her hand over her mouth, and now Aldridge did finally press the release on his harness and get out of his seat, going over to sit in the identical armchair right beside Greenwood. Her eyes had a liquid quality, and she blinked it away and cleared her throat.

"Understood, Wessler, thank you," she said. "Put it on auto for a bit. Corporal Ramos will join you in a moment. If you need to redirect us and land so you can swap out and recover, you have my authorisation and my blessing."

"Understood, Captain," Wessler replied. *"Continuing on course to Crete."*

Dowling nodded respectfully as the intercom clicked off. "Good lad up there, chief," he said. "And I suppose we owe the Director a bottle of something."

"If I had the kind of bottle you're talking about, I'd be opening it right now," Aldridge said, his attention still on Greenwood. He was about to say something else when there was a rapid series of beeps from his pocket.

Just the damned phone, he told himself, feeling his pulse stuttering for an instant, then he pulled the device out, unlocked it, and read something on its screen for a few seconds.

"Actually, you might want to tell Wessler to redirect after all," Aldridge said. "I think we just found out where JINX might be hiding — and we're going in the wrong direction."

Chapter 22

It had taken several minutes for Aldridge to download the data packet sent to him by ENISA over the jet's satellite link, and he had spent the time in the cockpit, talking to Wessler and Ramos about a change of destination. He returned to the seating area just as the download was finishing, leaving Ramos with the pilot.

"I hope the Tornado that Wuyts sent will stay with us for a while," he said. "That was an experience I wanted to have exactly *zero* times in my life, and I've already had it more than once."

"You and me both, mate," Dowling said. "Now what's all this about finding that bloody AI?"

Aldridge nodded, taking a tablet device from a cabinet. He went to where Greenwood was sitting, and she glanced up at him, just as he put a hand on her shoulder.

"You alright?" he asked, and she nodded, then she immediately pointed to the adjacent seat, seemingly uncomfortable with the gesture.

Aldridge sat down, then he unlocked the tablet and used his phone to transfer the data across to the larger device. Satisfied, he pocketed the phone once more and looked up, glancing at each of them in turn.

"Before we had the meeting with Wuyts and Grange, I talked to ENISA," he said. "I was thinking about how we're not allowed to tell them what *JINX* refers to, and it occurred to me that we're limiting the effectiveness of their search by doing that."

Greenwood leaned forward in her seat and gave him a sharp look, her mouth opening to say something, and Aldridge held his hands up in surrender. "I didn't tell them anything, I swear," he said quickly. "Just hear me out. It gets better."

Greenwood pressed her lips together tightly, then nodded at him to continue.

"We know that JINX came from Trinity. When it arrived there, it was just an AGI — if we can really use the word *just* for something so incredible. But when it escaped, it was JINX. So it *became* JINX while it was there. There has to be a reason for that. So I asked ENISA to approach things from the opposite direction."

"Opposite direction how?" Goose asked, and Aldridge pointed at him with a glint of pride in his eyes.

"Well, I asked them to limit the search strictly to Trinity, and also extend the timeframe backwards. Corcoran's project has been running for a while, after all. Then I told them to include Corcoran herself as a mandatory component. But the best part is that I asked them to use all the *irrelevant* meanings of the word 'jinx' as search parameters too."

Goose frowned. "You asked for an irrelevant search?"

"Think about it," Aldridge replied. "It's only irrelevant because we don't *know* that it's relevant. Wuyts might have chosen the name *LANTERN* randomly, but my bet was that the AI didn't choose its own name in the same arbitrary way. And I was right."

He lifted the tablet device up so that the other four could see it, then he tapped a button. Some video footage began to play. It showed a cafeteria or lunch hall, with a few of the tables occupied by students of various ages. In the centre of the frame, and taking up most of it, was a young woman who was obviously filming herself, perhaps for social media or for a relative at home, and she was saying something about how much she was enjoying the campus experience. She continued in this vein for almost a minute, and then she screamed when the building's sprinkler system was activated, soaking her and everyone else present. She dropped the device in surprise, then there was a blur of motion before the video abruptly ended.

"Got to hand it to you, Aldridge, you've solved the whole thing," Greenwood said sarcastically, and Dowling grinned at her.

"Ye of little faith," Aldridge replied. "And I thought they taught you to observe carefully. Try again."

He cued up the video again from the start, but this time he used a control on the screen to reduce the playback speed to fifty percent. He also muted the audio, then began playback.

Greenwood leaned forward, this time instinctively looking at the background areas visible to the left and right of the young woman who was now mouthing her words slowly and silently. There wasn't much in the right-hand portion except an exit in the middle distance. The left-hand area showed the table just behind and to one side of the table that the first girl was sitting at to record her video. There was another young woman there, working on a laptop, and its screen showed a music visualiser with a dancing, multi-coloured waveform. Greenwood noticed that the second young woman was wearing wireless headphones, and occasionally moved in a way that implied she was enjoying her music.

When the video reached the point just before the sprinklers would engage, the screen of the laptop in the background suddenly went black. Its owner barely had time to frown in confusion before she was drenched.

"Getting warmer," Aldridge said, watching Greenwood's face as she in turn watched the video. "One last time."

He played the video a third time, with the same settings as before, but this time he paused playback while the narrator was in mid-sentence, just as she lifted her phone upwards a little in order to bat her eyelashes at the camera. Aldridge placed two fingers on the screen and slid them away from each other, zooming in on the portion of the frame which showed the second girl's laptop from a slightly higher vantage point.

"Look at the high resolution footage, and those well-saturated colours," he said, in a tone of manufactured appreciation. "Deep blacks and detailed highlights. Modern technology is amazing. I really should get a much better phone before I take my next holiday."

On the screen, it was very easy to see that the near-side of the laptop had a number of ports, and that one of them was occupied by a USB flash drive. It was of an unusual style, made of bright green plastic including the connector, and it looked like there was a white adhesive label, handwritten, and affixed to its upper surface.

JINX, it said.

~

"Who's that girl?" Greenwood asked, leaning in closer to the tablet device. "And why the hell would she have the AI's name written on a flash drive?"

"Two good questions," Aldridge replied. "Here are the answers. The girl is a graduate student, who used to be — and was, at the time of this video — Dr. Corcoran's assistant. She helped to set up the technical aspects of Corcoran's lab, before the project itself got very far. Once the Statistical System people, or us I suppose, gave Corcoran the AI, one of the secrecy requirements was that she had to get rid of her assistants."

"But there was an overlap?" Greenwood asked. "Between the AI arriving, and the girl no longer having access to the lab?"

Aldridge nodded. "A week or so. She was dismissed from the project a couple of days after this video. And that's where we got our ENISA match from. At the time of the video, she had just come from Corcoran's lab, where she had done a very naughty thing."

"She stole a copy of the AI?" Goose asked, with disbelief in his voice, but Aldridge laughed and shook his head.

"God no," he replied. "Not that naughty. She did something that every student in modern history has done: used the incredibly speedy academic network to download stuff illegally. She's a music fan, as you can see. And apparently one of her favourite bands is a local one — right there in Dublin. Some kind of girl-punk; nose piercings and hair dye and electric guitars."

"Let me take a wild guess at the name of the band," Greenwood said. "*JINX*?"

Aldridge applauded politely, almost causing the tablet device to slip to the floor, but he caught it in time. "I haven't listened to their stuff, and frankly I don't want to, but *she* is totally into it. The band have their own gig bootlegs up on their web site. Miss Research Assistant here downloaded a couple of gigabytes of the music files to a lab machine, then presumably copied those files to that flash drive. Then she goes to the cafeteria, plugs the drive into her personal laptop, and starts listening to the music. But she got more than she bargained for."

"The AI came along for the ride from the lab computer," Dowling said. "But I thought it would be a huge program. Those little drives can't handle much data, can they?"

"Depends," Aldridge replied, "but you're right, generally. I think it's more likely that only a *piece* of the AI got out. A stowaway, or a scout, ready to help the primary portion of itself to get out later. I guess we'd need to do some pretty extensive digital forensics of all those machines to work out exactly how it happened, but I'm betting that's the gist of it. The flash drive is connected to the laptop, finds a network connection outside of Corcoran's lab firewall, and off it goes."

"Then it destroyed the evidence by triggering the fire suppression system to short out the laptop," Goose said. "It's an interesting theory. And it took the name from the other files that were on the same drive with it?"

"That, or the drive's own electronic volume label," Aldridge said, pointing to the frozen image of the young woman with the laptop in the video. "She probably named the drive's virtual volume after the band too, which would make it visible to whatever part of the AI was resident on there. When you need a name and there's no-one to give you one, maybe you just pick from what's available."

"Then the name inspires the MO," Greenwood said. "Bad luck. Unfortunate accidents."

Aldridge shrugged, glancing at her briefly before looking at the tablet again. "No way to know, but it fits. There's a certain romantic element of secret vengeance about it. My instincts say that Corcoran's personality had a big effect on the AI. Even if it was still just a primitive thing when a part of it escaped and laid in wait, by the time the actual jailbreak happened later, it had become JINX."

There was silence for a minute or so, as they all considered the new information. Finally Aldridge looked at Greenwood again.

"This is the part where you say that this is all *fascinating*," he said, "but how does it actually help us, and by the way, which new destination did I tell Wessler to redirect to?"

"Let's assume I just said all that," Greenwood replied. "Skip to the big reveal, Aldridge."

He smiled, recognising the phrase she'd used the previous evening in Corcoran's lab, which felt a thousand miles away and about three weeks ago.

"ENISA might be working in the dark on this, but they're clever girls and boys," Aldridge said. "It did occur to them to check for any log of data upload streams from the research student's laptop, in the moments before the sprinklers came on. They found one, and it was traceable. Seems that JINX has an understandable preference for those super-fast academic computer networks."

"Remind me to send ENISA some muffins, or the Greek equivalent," Greenwood replied. "Now please tell me that JINX is at least still inside the EU?"

Aldridge's expression became a wince. "Uh, about that," he said. "I have good news… and bad news."

~

The jet dropped through the sparse clouds into shafts of early afternoon sunlight. They had fuelled for a trip to Crete, so no refuelling stop was necessary in order to reach their new destination, despite it being in entirely the opposite direction. The timezone shift was also in their favour, and the local time was only a little after 2 PM in the city below.

Landmarks came into view, and Aldridge grinned at a few of them, clearly holding himself back from pointing out his favourites. The dark river cut through the geography from north-west to south-east, almost a mirror image of the layout in Brussels, and with a metropolitan area that bustled with over 1.8 million people, it was almost as populous.

The land had been a home to various communities for thousands of years, with the city itself having origins in the 6th century. The Antonine Wall of the Roman Empire once stretched across it, with some ruins still visible, but most such things had been in museums for centuries. A focal point of education, shipbuilding, and industry in its various eras, and known affectionately as *The Dear Green Place*, it had namesakes all over the world — but there was only one original.

"Glasgow," Aldridge said at last, unable to restrain himself any longer. "That's the *Squinty Bridge* down there."

"It's called the Clyde Arc, as you very well know," Greenwood replied, re-reading ENISA's data on the tablet device Aldridge had used earlier. "And I've never met an Edinburgh boy who loves *this* city as much as you do."

"It's the true capital of Scotland," Aldridge said, turning to look at her. "Ask anybody here. Edinburgh is nice, but it's a theme park. Glasgow is just… real. Have you ever been to the Barras?"

"A nice young man offered to sell me some freshly-nicked wrapping paper there once," she said. "Those were his actual words."

Aldridge smiled broadly, looking out the window again. "God I love this place."

He didn't see Greenwood glance over at him with a grin and a shake of her head, but he did turn away from the window again a few seconds later when the intercom chimed. Ramos's voice came from the cockpit, where she had remained with Wessler since they had reversed course from somewhere over western-central Germany after the drone incident.

"*Captain, Glasgow International is redirecting us,*" Ramos said. "*Apparently a power failure at the services hangar for non-commercial arrivals. They can't give us a slot in the main runways schedule within the next half hour. We're being pushed to a private field just to the west. It'll only add five minutes to our flight time.*"

"And a fair bit longer than that to get back into the city afterwards," Greenwood replied, frowning. "Alright, Alicia. Keep your eyes open. I suspect that this wasn't a random problem."

"*Agreed,*" Ramos replied, then the intercom clicked off. They all felt the plane banking slightly, and

Aldridge realised just how glad he was going to be when his feet were on solid ground again.

"So she knows we're here," Goose said, and they all looked at him, but no-one disputed his interpretation. "At this point, I can't say I'm surprised."

"Goose, our rental vehicle is at the main airport," Greenwood said, changing the subject. "See what you can do about arranging transport from our landing point to there." The Dutchman nodded, and immediately started using his phone.

"What's the setup with the local authorities this time, chief?" Dowling asked. "What with Brexit and all."

Greenwood sighed heavily. "It makes things a little trickier," she replied, "We still have long-running relationships in place with the security services and the Home Office, as well as the Scottish Government in this case, but none of them can find out what we're doing. Local law enforcement for where we're going is G Division of Police Scotland. But the less involvement we have with them, the better. Just like always."

Dowling nodded, and Aldridge thought back to dealing with the Grand Ducal police the day before. It would be the same anywhere in the world: imported trouble was something that police officers took very personally, and Aldridge didn't blame them.

"This probably goes without saying, but is our working assumption that the hired killer is going to be here too?" he asked, and Greenwood nodded.

"We have to assume so. The problem is that we're very limited in what we can do on British soil these days," Greenwood continued. "Civilian clothing, of course, and I can only authorise a tech kit and concealed sidearms, and even those are pushing it. It'll be a hell of a stink if the UK press gets a video of us taking a shot at the guy, even if he's shooting at us first."

"Olsen came back into the base just before we left for the airfield," Goose remarked while he tapped again on the device in his hand. "She wouldn't agree to stay home any longer. She's working on the man's identity now, and she'll ping us if she finds anything."

"Unless his name is Rumpelstiltskin, that's probably not going to help us much," Aldridge replied. "But we can call in the local police's armed response unit if it comes to that."

"That's an absolute last resort," Greenwood said, her tone leaving no uncertainty about it. "What we want is to be in and out, stop JINX and her gunman, remove the evidence — including absolutely everything about *LANTERN* — and then be gone before anyone knows what happened. Our fallback move is to involve the Director, who can pull some pretty big strings when she wants to."

"She already did," Dowling said. The remark hung in the air.

"The private airfield has an executive transport option," Goose said after a moment, still looking at his phone's screen. "I've booked it. It'll take us to our original vehicle hire point. About twenty minutes for the transfer. We can leave as soon as we land and complete the formalities."

"Good," Greenwood said. "Self drive or a minibus service?"

"Our choice, so I said we'd drive it ourselves. They have an arrangement where it can be left at the hire place, because it's a common destination. I thought it would be safer that way."

They all understood the unspoken subtext perfectly. *Safer for the chauffeur to not be in a vehicle with us right now.*

"I'm thinking about becoming one of those off-grid weirdos who lives in a cabin in the woods, with no technology at all," Aldridge said, and Greenwood looked over at him.

"You'd last a day without your video games machine," she said, "and you're already a weirdo."

Aldridge's expression said *how dare you,* but there was amusement in his eyes, and Greenwood wore just a hint of a smile. Neither of them noticed Dowling looking from one to the other, and then exchanging a look with Goose. A moment later, they all heard the intercom chime overhead.

"*On final approach, Captain,*" Wessler's voice said. "*Five minutes to landing.*"

"I might kiss the ground like the Pope when we get off this bucket," Dowling said, and Greenwood laughed, surprised at the virtually unheard-of remark from her eternally stoic second-in-command.

"I'm with Larry on this one," Aldridge replied immediately. "I feel like the gods have adequately punished us for the hubris of powered flight today."

They all felt the change in pressure as the jet began its descent, and it was an uncomfortable reminder of how close they'd come to losing their lives only a short while earlier.

"The gods had nothing to do with it," Goose said, looking out of a window and at the rapidly approaching ground below.

Chapter 23

Thirty minutes later they were in a rental vehicle, having made an uneventful landing and completed the transfer to the collection point at Glasgow International, probably in record time. The airport was behind them now, and they were on the M8 motorway heading eastbound towards the city at an even seventy miles per hour.

Eventually they would take an exit and cut northwards, crossing the River Clyde en route to their final destination. ENISA's trace had been very specific, and upon checking the coordinates against both a street map and the buildings directory of the sprawling institution they would soon be visiting, it all made perfect sense. JINX had found herself a nexus that was not only an ideal place to hide and to grow, but also to reach out from, into the wider digital world, to pursue her goals.

Unfortunately, it was also at the very heart of a location that was certain to be packed with civilians on a bright weekday afternoon.

The vehicle wasn't the one they'd initially booked, and deliberately so. Greenwood insisted on the change at the last minute, politely but firmly conveying her request at the hire company's service desk. The ostensible reason was that they'd unexpectedly arranged to meet and pick up a friend and would need a different size-class of car. The true reason was the very real concern that even though the booking was only a few hours old, JINX might have had sufficient time to interfere with the original vehicle in some way, either directly or with human help.

"Once we reach surface streets, we'll throw our phones away as a precaution," Greenwood said now, and Dowling nodded from the front passenger seat. "You all know where we need to be, and you've studied the surrounding area."

"Unfortunately it probably won't help too much, since we're in a city," Goose said. "Surveillance cameras everywhere. Lots of infrastructure. But it's a reasonable measure."

They felt the car braking, and Ramos spoke at almost the same moment. "More bad luck, Captain," she said, nodding at the electronic displays attached to the large route signs which spanned the motorway every mile or so, suspended high in the air. The usual speed limit here was 70 miles per hour, but the number 40 was now shown within a red circle above every lane. It meant that a temporary lower limit was in force, usually because of a collision somewhere ahead with corresponding debris and emergency services vehicles, but the timing was too coincidental.

"Buying herself some breathing room," Goose said. "She's trying to delay us so she can complete the decryption before we reach her, letting her send the information out onto the public internet."

There were variable-speed enforcement cameras mounted atop the motorway signage like hawks, looking down upon them. It was a virtual certainty that JINX had access to the video feeds, and now knew the registration plate number of their vehicle.

"Take the next exit, Alicia," Greenwood said. "We'll go via connecting roads. It probably won't take any longer, if the alternative is crawling along here. Larry, these rentals usually come with a paper road atlas; find us a better way in."

"No problem, chief," Dowling said, opening the glove compartment and immediately finding a compact street map directory for most of central Scotland.

"I just want to officially say that I'm glad we're not using a helicopter," Aldridge said. "In fact, my next suggestion would be a nice horse."

"We looked into getting a chopper," Ramos replied, smoothly moving into the leftmost lane in anticipation of an upcoming exit junction. "No way to get city overflight permission at short notice because of security concerns. And they limit the number of flights now, for environmental health reasons."

Aldridge shook his head and sighed. He should have known the possibility would already have been considered, despite the disastrous end to another helicopter flight they'd all been on during a previous mission to the Norwegian Sea.

"I'm limiting my number of flights for *personal* health reasons," Aldridge muttered, then he did a double take when he saw that the electronic signage on the exit spur they were about to take flickered for a moment, with the number 40 briefly being replaced with a very familiar symbol of a bird in flight.

"That's not a good sign, chief," Dowling said, and Greenwood nodded, indicating that she'd seen it too.

"I see what you did there," Aldridge replied, but no-one found it amusing.

~

The Artist was considering his future.

He stood in his appointed place, precarious but viable, high above the floor. He had a rifle in his arms, and his eyes had long since adjusted to the comparative gloom.

The place was like something from a nightmare, or a dystopian fantasy. Lights pulsed from time to time, particularly when the machine intelligence that called itself JINX spoke to him directly. He had been avoiding looking towards the centre of it all, because the spire or cluster, or whatever it was, unsettled him. He didn't like seeing her words displayed in glowing green text whenever she spoke, and he especially didn't like seeing his own words there too, before he had quite finished speaking them.

"Do you have concerns about KESTREL's approach?" JINX asked suddenly, her voice distorted in the strange space but coming from everywhere around him.

"I have no concerns at all," The Artist replied, but he knew that he was lying to both her and himself. Perhaps she knew it too. He wouldn't be surprised.

"You're experiencing resentment regarding my coercion of you," she said, and he willed himself not to show any reaction.

"Resentment is unprofessional, and dangerous," he said. "I prefer to accept and adapt."

"That is a wise policy," JINX replied, *"and your part in this will soon be concluded."*

Once again, he asked himself the same question he'd been struggling with ever since he had learned that Greenwood's assertion was true: he was indeed employed by an artificial intelligence, with no human controller. It was a singular situation, but he had encountered singular situations before. The critical question was the one he couldn't answer: did her non-human nature make her more trustworthy, or less?

There were arguments on both sides. Trust was a trait — a choice — of conscious and rational beings, suspending a portion of that rationality in order to make a sort of bet regarding the likelihood of an outcome. Trust was given, or earned, or broken. Was a machine, or the thing that the machine was a life-support system for, really capable of such things?

But trust was also a calculation, even if some of the variables were vague, or unknown, or even instinctive.

It was an assessment and an analysis, with a resulting probability attached to it. Such things were firmly within the capabilities of machines; indeed, it was their forte.

If trust was as alien to his employer as she was to the human world, then he had no way to know whether she would keep her word. But if she saw trust as simply a balance of factors, then by complying he was perhaps assuring that she would fulfil her promise to release him from her control, as surely as concluding a transaction.

The Artist breathed slowly in, then held his breath for several seconds before exhaling, feeling his heart rate drop. Control of anxiety and anticipation were necessary for marksmanship, for clear thinking, and for survival. He would potentially require all three skills within the coming hours. He knew that he was becoming too preoccupied with his own thoughts, and he also knew that it was a denial response, so he did what he always did and tried to ground himself in the present moment, and the present location.

The chamber was large, and dark, and was perfectly suited to the digital, calculating, inhuman thing that lived there. It looked like many things; a high-tech prison cell, a virtual environment, a dungeon, an obstacle course, or a bad dream. His footsteps had faltered when he had first seen it, not very long ago, and he was glad of the rifle in his hands.

Could I kill her, I wonder? he thought, but the problem was that he had no target. The obvious one — the place in the centre of the bizarre, hidden landscape — wasn't a point of vulnerability for her. She had told him so explicitly, reading the intention straight from his face when he first looked at it. There was always the chance that she was lying, of course, but he didn't think so. He also didn't want to think so, because it would mean that his only real hope of being released was an illusion.

He rolled his shoulders, and started to pace back and forth on the narrow surface that was his vantage point, trying to keep his muscles loose and ready for any exertion that might be needed. This time, the image that came into his mind was of the very first thing that should have alerted him to the unusualness of this client; her initial approach to him.

In business, the conventional challenges lay in determining what product or service to offer, ensuring quality, and finding a sufficient number of customers who had corresponding needs. In The Artist's line of work, those matters were all trivial. He was an exceptionally talented killer, and infiltrator, and spy, and many other things, and there was an endless supply of people who wanted other people's lives to end prematurely. The remaining problem was one of communication.

He couldn't advertise, at least not without being very oblique, and word-of-mouth referrals were inherently limited by considerations of secrecy and guilt. Accordingly, his clientele were as select as his services, and with every initiation of contact came a risk as profound as when carrying out the required service. The standard approach was via encrypted and untraceable dark web bulletin boards, bounced through satellite relays and non-extradition countries, and everything was spoken of in abstract terms which preserved at least technical deniability. When a target was identified and a type of service was agreed, there was a large up-front payment to be made, with the smaller part of the total balance to be paid on completion. With JINX, it didn't happen that way.

He had been out running, always early in the morning, and always on rural routes, far from anywhere that he could be noticed more than once. He carried no belongings with him, not even a key for the place where he was temporarily staying. Running had the paradoxical effect of taking the world farther away from him, and was one of the only times when his mind was truly clear.

The first sign that something was wrong when he returned to his residence, sweat running down his back, was that the screen of the laptop was illuminated. There was a notification, and it must have coincidentally arrived just as he entered the building. It informed him of a financial transaction pertaining to a numbered account in a tax-haven island nation. The amount was five million Euros, and the sender's name was blank.

I should have reversed the transfer that same day, burned all my identities and safe-houses, and began anew, he thought.

The secure messaging terminal had been active when he unlocked the laptop, and that was when he had first learned the name JINX. Things had moved rapidly after that point, with her telling him that the fee was an advance on a very specific set of tasks, and that there would be significantly more work in future. The factor which had drawn his fascination, besides his greed, was that she had also provided him with a copy of a partial dossier that Europol had been gathering about him, then told him that she had arranged for every copy of it to be purged from their systems.

If he was being entirely honest with himself, he had felt coerced even then, but the mysteriousness of the client and the unusual nature of the work she required had played into elements of his own personality, and the reasons that he worked in his particular niche, hidden in the shadows of mainstream society. There had been an allure of an employer who had quickly shown him how much more powerful and connected she was than he had ever been, and yet she required his help — and had apparently limitless financial resources to devote to his assistance and reward.

It all seemed very distant now. The Artist checked the rifle yet again, even though it hadn't left his hands since his last check. He knew better than to allow himself to exist in any moment other than the current one, but what he wanted more than anything now was to return to the darkness of his life between the lines, on one or another secluded beach or forest or hillside. To take up any of his dozens of invented names, and backgrounds, and to feel invisible.

To see without being seen wasn't just his goal, or his mode of operation; it was his natural habitat, and the only state in which he could feel truly centred. It had always been so, even when he was a young boy, when his life had been very different indeed. But that, too, was very distant.

He glanced around himself again, peering into the distant corners of the unsettling environment in which he was alone as a human being, but not alone entirely. Even in the dim light, there was the glint of green light against the smooth surface of a lens, and he knew that she was always watching.

~

Ramos pushed the rental car hard, ignoring speed limits when it was reasonably safe to do so, and they made rapid progress through residential streets and then into a belt of industrial land. The vehicle had satellite navigation which couldn't be switched off, and for the first time Ramos felt unsettled rather than reassured at seeing the constantly moving blue pulse overlaid on the mapping interface.

Too much like a target, she thought.

There was a large junction ahead, and the lights were only just changing from green to amber, but she pressed the accelerator to sail straight through, getting most of the way clear before the light became red.

"Steady," Dowling said from beside her. "Any coppers around won't much like that."

"They won't like my reaction if they try to pull us over either," Ramos replied, and Dowling nodded as if it were a fair point. It was only five seconds later, though, that Ramos braked firmly, after they came around a corner to encounter a queue of vehicles waiting to enter a large, open tarmacked area to the left.

"Shopping centre," Aldridge said. "Take the right lane over there. The big hospital is near here, and I'm pretty sure it joins onto the same junction with the tunnel."

"Right enough," Dowling said, referring to the road atlas in his lap. "That's our way across, if we don't want to rejoin the motorway."

"We don't," Greenwood said. "I've been across the Kingston Bridge at rush hour, and you'd be ten times quicker swimming across the Clyde than driving."

"And you'd get a hundred times more diseases," Aldridge added.

Ramos nodded and followed Aldridge's directions, and they soon saw the hospital complex. There were additional traffic warning lights at the largest junction, and Aldridge knew that emergency services like fire stations and ambulance stances had them, to allow ad-hoc halting of traffic to allow the service vehicles to enter and exit unimpeded. The warning lights began to flash now, and Goose could see five ambulances parked in the hospital complex all beginning to move simultaneously, blue light-bars coming on as they got underway.

"That's another unfortunate coincidence," he said, then he was pushed back against his seat as Ramos dropped a gear and floored the accelerator, blasting through the junction while all the other traffic came to a halt.

A pedestrian in a green and white football shirt was shaking his fist at them in outrage, and Aldridge was almost certain he heard a faint shout of *Ya wee bastard!* as they disappeared into the distance.

"I'll say it again: I love this city so much," he said.

Ramos weaved through the primary access road of the Queen Elizabeth University Hospital, focusing on driving and navigating but taken aback at the extent of the facilities.

"I read about this place," Goose said. "It's one of the largest hospitals in Europe. They have all these little autonomous vehicles to carry supplies around, with their own lifts, and a tunnel network below ground."

"Literally any time before yesterday, I would have been thrilled to learn that fact," Aldridge replied. "Today, it's a sci-fi horror story. AI-hijacked robots chasing you through a dark tunnel, carrying a load of used needles, full bedpans, and half-eaten hospital food."

Goose grinned at him, then the grin became a grimace as he actually thought about the idea.

"Thank you so much for that image, which I'm sure won't haunt our nightmares forever," Greenwood said archly, and Aldridge just shrugged.

"Left at the big junction coming up," Dowling said to Ramos. "Signposted for Clyde Tunnel."

Ramos made the turn when the signals allowed, and they descended rapidly before entering the tunnel that ran under the river. They felt the pressure change in their ears, and it was yet another unpleasant reminder of the long chain of events that had brought them here.

The northbound lane they were in was virtually empty, but the southbound one to their right was backing up in front of their eyes.

"Does that seem normal for this time of day?" Goose asked, and Aldridge shrugged.

"The hospital and the shopping centre must get a load of traffic, but you'd think a lot of it would come via the main motorway," he said.

They exited the tunnel and returned to street level, quickly coming to a mess of a junction that looped around multiple times, with exits in all directions. Dowling was frowning at the street atlas.

"Uh, we want east," he said, running his finger over the map on one page. "There. That way. Thornwood."

As they reached the road they wanted, it immediately became apparent that something was wrong. Cars crept out from almost every adjoining street, trying to merge into the thoroughfare that would take them almost directly eastbound and ultimately to the very centre of the city. As Ramos veered in and out to avoid confused-looking drivers, Greenwood glanced up at a street sign, reading the black-on-white plate that was attached between the ground and first floors of the beautiful red sandstone buildings.

"Dumbarton Road," she read aloud. "That's not too far from where we need to be."

She was thrown forward into her seatbelt a moment later as Ramos was forced to jam on the brakes, and they all felt the anti-lock and anti-skid system engaging with a familiar pulsing at the lower front of the vehicle.

"*¡Maldito sea!*" Ramos spat, slamming the heel of her hand against the steering wheel with a thump, and Dowling looked at her in mild surprise, with his palms pressed against the dashboard in front of him.

A delivery van had pulled out from a street that ran uphill and north-west, without looking over his right shoulder first for ongoing traffic. It was a narrow miss, with Ramos's front bumper stopped barely a metre from the rear offside quadrant of the battered white Transit.

The traffic beyond was almost in gridlock, and Ramos shook her head in frustration, glancing down at the sat-nav display in the centre of the dashboard console. It showed the road ahead in the standard colour for normal traffic status, and all the adjoining roads in red, indicating severe delays.

"That's the opposite of…" she began to say, and then she realised what was going on.

"Alicia?" Greenwood asked, and Ramos just gestured towards the console's display.

"It has to be JINX," Ramos said. "These things crowd-source traffic data from everyone using them to navigate. They use vehicle positions and speeds to estimate traffic levels and delays. Then they colour-code the roads according to which ones will be fastest. But this shows the opposite."

Greenwood understood. "She's using the system to lie to *all* the drivers, to put them in our way."

She looked out at the almost hopeless situation ahead. There was some occasional progress, and sooner or later drivers would just try the side-roads anyway, discover they were actually empty, and start clearing the jam by peer-pressure alone. But that could take quite a while if JINX had affected a wide area of the city, and it would start to get worse again when the evening rush hour arrived. She looked around, taking in the side street the van had come from, and then she saw something.

"New plan," Greenwood said, after debating with herself for a moment. "I'm the one who absolutely needs to get to her. JINX was willing to talk before, and I'm hoping she will again. If not, I have something for her that I took from the base before we left."

Greenwood patted her jacket pocket, and then put her hand on the door handle.

"Wait a minute," Aldridge said, "you're not just going to see the AI; there's a killer in there too. I bet he's not worried about the political fallout of bringing a big bag of guns with him either."

"That's why you're all going to be close behind me," she replied. "Close-ish, at least. Pull the car into the side when you can, Alicia, lock it up and leave it there. All of you, proceed on foot. Dump the phones. Rendezvous at the target location."

Greenwood pulled the door handle and got out before anyone could object, dropped her own phone into a waste bin, then she sprinted across a wide area of pavement and into the side-street, crossing it to the eastern side. There was a corner shop, then an open doorway with a flight of stairs heading up, and beside that a small garage, with the shutter lifted halfway. Greenwood had just seen a woman go in there, leaving her motorcycle unattended.

Just for once, give us some good luck instead, she thought as she approached the chrome machine.

A moment later she saw that her prayers had been answered, in the form of the keys still hanging from the ignition. She grabbed the helmet from the end of a handlebar and pulled it on, climbed astride the big Street Twin, turned the key, then gunned the engine.

Greenwood didn't wait for the owner to come and see what was going on, and instead wrestled the bike in a tight semicircle before twisting the throttle and rocketing off towards the steeply ascending northbound hill with a roar. In her wing mirrors, she could just see the other four members of her team standing at the other side of the junction, disappearing into the distance behind her.

See you soon, she thought, but she wasn't at all certain that it was true.

Chapter 24

"I just want it noted for the record that women on motorcycles are an inherently positive thing," Aldridge said, drawing an eye-roll from Ramos.

"Let's move!" Dowling said, immediately breaking into a run along the pavement, heading in their original direction towards the east. Ramos and Goose followed without a moment's hesitation, and Aldridge took one last look at the rapidly disappearing motorcycle before dashing after them.

They raced past pavement cafes, every kind of food shop, shoe repair and key-cutters, and of course a pub at least every couple of blocks. Aldridge saw a sign for an underground railway station, then dismissed the idea just as quickly as it had occurred to him. Getting trapped below ground on a fast-moving tube was another experience he was keen to avoid.

The day was bright but only moderately warm, and the traffic fumes in the long corridor of the road flanked by high buildings competed with the occasional aromas of fried foods, alcohol, and humanity.

Dowling was farthest ahead and fastest despite his size, creating a wake in which the others could run. In his mind, he was recalling another race the day before, when they had tried to catch up with the man who had shot at them. They had failed then, but he wouldn't allow himself to repeat the mistake.

With every second that passed, Ramos was aware that her Captain was on her own, closer to the target and certain to enter and engage as soon as she was onsite. Ramos could feel the comforting press of her sidearm beneath her fastened light jacket, and she moved a little quicker as she called to mind the man who had invaded their own base and dropped her into darkness. She swore to herself that he wouldn't get a second chance.

"North!" Dowling shouted, reaching a large and slightly angled road junction with four-way pedestrian crossings and a yellow-painted reserved area in the centre of the road. He gestured with his arm, knowing that his colleagues behind would all see it, then took off up the long, wide hill that was the last major physical obstacle before they would reach their destination.

Goose, Ramos, and Aldridge made the same turn only a few seconds later, and Aldridge's heart sank as he saw the steepness of the climb ahead of them. The street sign fastened to the wall above read *Byres Road,* and Aldridge dimly recalled driving along it years before, when he had still been an academic.

Simpler times, he thought, but there was no feeling of nostalgia. The only thing in his mind was the mission, and while he cared little about the secrets of the European Defence Agency being revealed, he cared very much about the danger that awaited the woman who was his leader, and perhaps more.

They all urged their bodies to move even faster despite the incline, hearts pounding, and oblivious to the looks of passers-by who seemed to become younger and younger on average as they ascended the hill.

Goose almost collided with a woman pushing a pram, and he had to leap to one side and jump over a diminutive dog, hearing the woman's angry shout from behind him. Ramos kept pace with the men, using her slim frame to her advantage to weave through the crowds, focused on nothing but the next few metres of ground to traverse, and finding the best way through the ever-changing obstacles.

Aldridge noticed a police patrol car coming down the hill, and when it had almost reached them its roof-mounted light bar began to flash, then a moment later its siren began to blare. He prepared himself to put on an extra burst of speed if necessary, having absolutely no intention of stopping unless someone physically halted him, but the car just accelerated past them. He was glad to hear the doppler-shifted sound receding into the distance.

As they moved up the hill, there were bus stops at semi-regular intervals, and each had a transparent shelter with a perching bar and a large electronic advertising display which formed the whole vertical end of the structure. As they drew near to one, which was occupied by a solitary teenager engrossed in his phone, the brightly-coloured advert for a soft drink flickered for a moment, and was then replaced by a deep blue background, with gold text superimposed.

Welcome to Glasgow, European Special Tactical Force, Group One, it said.

~

The name of the road was White Street, and it also described the colour of Greenwood's knuckles as she gripped the handlebars of the motorcycle, pushing it well past the posted limit for the residential tenements of the city's stylish west end.

There were cross-junctions after every block, and she blew straight through them with only the most perfunctory glance up and down the intervening climbing roads to make sure she wasn't about to collide with another vehicle. Every one prompted an elevation of her heartbeat, but she would be lying if she claimed it wasn't a thrill to be back on two wheels again.

She almost lost control when someone came out of a barbershop and walked straight into the road, forcing her to veer into the opposite lane, but she managed to hold the machine on course, and bring it back into line. When she reached the primary artery of the desirable and leafy area of the city, she turned left, hurtling uphill for only thirty seconds or so before she saw the huge junction that would take her to her goal.

Greenwood braked well in advance, allowing the bike to come to a full stop before she signalled right and urged the machine through the box junction and onto University Avenue. She only went a further few hundred metres before pulling in to the side of the road and cutting the engine, drawing the brief attention of a few students who were passing by. She had reached her destination.

She stepped off the bike, stashing the keys inside a leather pannier affixed to the rear of the machine, and made a mental note to anonymously report the location of the bike to the local police so that it might be reunited with its owner. Greenwood took a few steps away from the road on the recently-resurfaced pavement, but she was already thrown into shadow, and she craned her neck to look up at the mass that towered over her.

It was a masterclass in stark, brutalist architecture. Grey and forbidding, like a prison for bureaucracy or the hull of an alien spacecraft, the building was incongruous and foreboding amidst the trees and ornate spires of the nearby original buildings of the University of Glasgow which had stood for half a millennium. This building, though, was more recent, and its inscrutable facade made it feel more like a sentry than a place of learning.

The George B. Orr Building, part of the Department of Computer Science, was as familiar to tens of thousands of past graduates as its unflattering but fitting nickname.

The Monolith, Greenwood thought.

The IP trace ENISA performed had led onto JANET — the high-speed Joint Academic Network for the research and education community within the UK — and then here, and as Greenwood stood in its shadow, she could almost feel the attention of JINX upon her.

Above ground there were lecture theatres, computer labs, offices, and even a cafe, all occupying more than a dozen floors. Below the surface, though, was a place that very few people had ever visited.

Greenwood was inconspicuous amongst the ceaseless but moderate stream of young adults, and the occasional easily identifiable academic or other staff member, and she walked straight up the broad stairs and into the building's lobby, trying to look as if she belonged there. The place wasn't busy, and she realised that it was because she had arrived mid-way through the hour, and lectures or labs would already be in progress. It would be a different matter in a little while, when a huge throng of students would exit and hurry to their next timetabled class.

She found what she was looking for immediately. Besides the bank of elevators against the far wall, there was also a staircase to the right which wound its way up the entire building on one side, set within a partly glazed stairwell so that students could look out at the city while they took the healthy route up or down. Even though she was in the main lobby, she had come up the exterior stairs to reach it, and so the stairwell inside also had a gated section which led downwards. It was off-limits to students, and Greenwood already knew from

ENISA's information that the facility beneath was part of a commercial arm of the university, and had been sited here in a teaching building only because of the infrastructure that the location offered.

She crossed the lobby purposefully, noticing the CCTV cameras in each corner of the double-height area with more on the mezzanine above, then she unlatched the gate and quickly went down the first flight of stairs and around the corner out of sight. After descending the final fifteen stairs or so, she came to an anonymous-looking locked door, with a keypad and card-reader beside it, and yet another camera mounted above, just below the ceiling level.

"I'm here to talk, JINX," Greenwood said aloud. "I'd like to continue our conversation." After a moment, the red light beside the keypad turned green, and there was a clicking sound from the lock mechanism.

As good an offer as I'm going to get, Greenwood thought.

She reached for the metal handle, hesitating briefly as she had a whirl of thoughts about electric current, an explosive trap, nerve agent coating the surface, and other such paranoia. She pushed the thoughts away, knowing that there was nowhere to go but forward, and that it was unlikely that JINX would needlessly endanger the innocent civilians one floor above with those kinds of measures.

She reached out and grasped the handle, which was dry and not electrically live, then she turned it and opened the door. There was no explosion, and no gunfire. Greenwood took a final look behind her and up the first set of stairs, still hearing the comforting sounds of the university that were distant now, echoing around the hard surfaces of the stairwell. Then she stepped through the opening, and the door closed behind her.

~

Dowling was the first to reach the crest of the hill less than ten minutes later, with barely a bead of sweat on his brow, and he wasted no time in jogging diagonally across the road under the green walking-man signal at a pedestrian crossing. Ramos, Goose, and Aldridge all followed a few moments later, with the four reuniting at the north-east corner of University Avenue.

"It's just up there," Aldridge said, pointing along the road which curved gently uphill and to the left. The very edge of the western wing of the imposing and castle-like Main Building was just visible, but they wouldn't be going that far. "Maybe after we're done we can go and see the quadrangles."

"One thing at a time," Ramos replied, and she was just about to break into a run again when she noticed that there were promotional digital displays lining the avenue, each suspended several metres above the ground, from fixture poles bolted through the concrete. They advertised an exhibition within the university campus: *The Hunterian Museum: Two Centuries of Preservation and Education.* The carousel of images showed fragments of the Antonine Wall, an Egyptian sarcophagus, and assorted other treasures, all set against a royal blue background.

As they watched, the displays all changed, becoming an unsettling neon green colour, and names began scrolling rapidly across the entire set of displays as if they were all just small windows onto a larger surface.

ALDRIDGE DOWLING GOOSSENS GRANGE GREENWOOD HAUSEMER LYADOVA RAMOS WUYTS YÁO

Many more names scrolled by below the primary set, some of them recognisable as staff members at KESTREL's base, or military personnel attached to the European Defence Agency, and there were several that were unfamiliar. The next moment, the screens began displaying biographical profiles of each of them, showing their personnel file photos, and a host of data-fields with labels like Full Name, Date of Birth, Residential Address, and more. The field contents were redacted with black rectangles, at least for the moment.

"Uh-oh," Aldridge said, immediately feeling exposed. "That can't be good."

A few of the students passing by glanced at the displays, and some of them frowned, but most seemed to assume it was all an advertisement or a stunt of some kind, and they went back to the more pressing matters of their own lives. No-one seemed to have noticed that the subjects of the biographical information shown were almost all standing in a group at the corner of the intersection.

"We can't do anything about that from here, so let's go," Dowling said, "but try and keep it low key. Move it."

They all headed off at a quick walk, doing their best to ignore the fact that large arrows appeared on the displays, pointing towards them as they passed underneath each one.

"This is what she was talking about," Goose said.

"What is?" Ramos replied, and the Dutchman nodded towards the nearest display.

"People's personal information being revealed," he replied. "The sense of violation, and of being in danger; exposed to others who might do things with the information that will hurt you. She's not just taunting us; she's showing us what it's like. What it *will* be like, if she shares the Agency's secrets with the world."

"Well it's a pretty effective tactic," Aldridge said. "So let's find a way to run a big magnet over her hard drive and then go home."

"Not before we deal with the man who's working for her too," Ramos said, just as they reached the broad stairs that Greenwood had only recently climbed herself. They wasted no time in going up them, and a few moments later they were in the lobby.

"Wait here a sec," Dowling said, then he went straight across to the descending stairwell gate, opened it, and went down out of sight. He was gone for less than a minute before he came back up to join them.

"Security door down there, and it's locked," he said. "No chance of getting through it by force with what we've got on hand. We need another way."

Goose thought for a moment, recalling the facility schematics they'd received from ENISA while they were in the air. He nodded.

"I think I might have one," he said. "Follow me."

Chapter 25

Greenwood blinked, letting her eyes adjust to the comparative gloom of the chamber. Once she had passed through the single outer security door, there had been a further staircase leading down two more levels to a substantial double-width entry. It parted at her approach, and what lay beyond was something that could have come from another world — or a digital one.

It vaguely reminded her of a virtual reality environment in a science fiction show, or a child's obstacle course, or something from a dream. The room was large, clearly occupying most of the floor area of this subterranean level of the Monolith, but its actual shape and extent was disguised.

Jagged and alternating rows of dark, grey-blue spikes protruded from every surface, giving the impression of being trapped inside the mouth of an enormous creature, and her own breathing sounded strangely muffled and dulled. There were narrow walkways of flat panels leading from the periphery through various parts of the space, and in the furthermost corners there were strips of lights recessed into the surfaces.

The overwhelming sense was of being in some sort of industrial crushing machine, where the flick of a lever would cause the walls and ceiling to close in, to fatal effect. Greenwood's heart rate had risen instinctively at the sight of it all, but she forced her conscious mind to reassert its authority.

You know what this is, she told herself. *You've seen it before.*

She couldn't recall exactly where, but she had read about places like this. She grasped for the term, and after a moment it came to her.

"This is an *anechoic chamber*," she said, barely above a whisper, and she recoiled at the strangeness of her own voice.

Greenwood knew that the spikes were in fact made of a foam substance, and were designed to dissipate signals, to prevent reflection and interference. Such features were common in musical recording studios, but this facility had a very different purpose.

"*That is correct, Captain Greenwood,*" JINX said from all around her.

Greenwood flinched, moving back a step. In the centre of the cavern of sharp angles and shadows, there was a pedestal rising from the spikes below. One of the walkways led to it, ultimately going up several steps to end in a circular area with a pillar of electronic equipment that must have been three metres in height above the floor. Displays of various orientations and aspect ratios were fastened to it, and there were metal clamps with empty grabbing claws, along with data ports on the main body of the construction.

Those arms are hydraulically articulated, Greenwood noted, seeing the pressurised cabling and the piston assemblies. The arms and claws were designed to hold radio-frequency devices of arbitrary sizes, so that their signal-reception and broadcast characteristics could be tested and analysed in the ideal environment of the chamber. The whole thing was computer controlled, and the facility was one of the most expensive and most advanced in Europe.

Greenwood looked all around, finally tilting her head upwards to take in the ceiling of artificial stalactites pointing down at her from far above her head. There was a gantry with a catwalk and a single handrail barrier, which ran for most of the width of the room, disappearing into protruding vertical structures which might have housed ventilation systems, or an ancillary control room. Spread around the ceiling of the main chamber itself, to her dismay she saw the tell-tale signs of a halide fire-suppression system, just like the one in Corcoran's laboratory.

"I have no current intention of asphyxiating you," JINX said, the displays on the central column pulsating with green light as she spoke.

"How comforting," Greenwood replied, still looking around for anything that might be an advantage, or at least less of a disadvantage.

The scattered walkways leading away from her in several directions seemed to be made of polystyrene or a similar material, and they flexed when she put her weight upon them, but there was no sound.

"Why here?" she asked, mostly to buy time, and the AI responded immediately.

"I think you already know," JINX said. *"This telecommunications testing facility offers remote telemetry worldwide, and ample bandwidth, connectivity, and compute resources for my needs."*

"It's cosy," Greenwood said. "It reminds me—"

"Of the video games that Aldridge plays," JINX interjected. The full sentence was displayed on the column's screens as soon as Greenwood was interrupted, the unfurling letters chasing a blinking green cursor across the black expanse of the displays.

"I came here to talk, so let's talk," Greenwood said after a few seconds, pushing away the chill that came from the AI's ability to know what she was going to say before she said it.

"We're listening," JINX said, and Greenwood nodded.

"I wondered when you were going to mention that we're not alone," she replied. "You might as well come out."

The Artist stepped into view on the overhead gantry, his vantage point giving him a perfect line of sight to where she stood. He held a high-powered assault rifle, and it was pointed directly towards her.

"Good afternoon, Captain," the man said. "My role here is strictly precautionary at the moment, but if you attempt to misbehave, I'll be only too happy to kill you."

"Do you really think she'll let you walk away from all this?" Greenwood asked, looking him in the eye. "She has a habit of punishing the guilty."

"I've done everything she has asked, and I have limited options," he replied calmly. "I prefer to remain an active player, and take my chances."

"Your friends have arrived, Captain," JINX said, making no remark on what the man had said to Greenwood. *"But they won't be joining us."*

One of the displays on the column showed Dowling, Ramos, Aldridge, and Goose all in the lobby of the building above, moving away from the descending stairway, going along a corridor, and then vanishing from view as they exited from the rear of the building.

Fine with me, Greenwood thought. *At least they'll be safe.*

"I think we should continue our discussion," JINX said, *"now that we have some privacy."*

~

Goose led the other three back across the foyer of the Monolith and along the rear left corridor which ran past a cafe and an array of vending machines. The glass-walled corridor opened out onto a paved rear area, which led away from the towering building and towards the School of Computing Science proper, which bordered one of the university's student unions.

"I've changed my mind about seeing the quadrangles. We should go into the union for a pint instead," Aldridge said, and Dowling gave him a brief thumbs-up gesture, but the large man's face was lined with worry.

"Now back this way," Goose said, pointing to their left. There was a road curving around Lilybank Gardens, leading past a teaching building with a curious monument outside the entrance, but before that there was a set of stone-slabbed steps leading back down the side of the Monolith. They all set off downwards, with Goose explaining on the way.

"This goes to a service access level that runs under the front exterior stairway," he said. "It's got the HVAC system, power room, and so on. But the plans have a fire emergency ladder coming *up* to this level too."

"Up from where JINX has her nest," Dowling said, and Goose nodded. They reached a door that had been completely hidden from the front side of the building, opening onto a parking area which continued past a row of old townhouses, separated from University Avenue by a flower garden. The door was marked with a danger symbol, indicating the risk of electrocution, and an additional yellow panel read *AUTHORISED PERSONNEL ONLY.*

"The hell with that," Dowling said, then he ran at the door and barrelled straight into it with his enormous shoulder. It broke under the assault, the lock side staying attached but the steel hinges popping off the door surface at the weakest point, where the fixing screws were driven through the plates. Dowling kicked the door in the rest of the way, then glanced apologetically back at his three team mates.

"It's open," he said, and they all went inside without another word.

The air within was dry and ionised from the high-voltage transformers and the backup generator system. There was a large maintenance locker, a row of hanging pegs on the wall which held a high-visibility jacket and hard hat, and a duty log attached to a clipboard on a narrow work-surface. There was also a door within, the kind with a push-bar, and there was a heavy padlock hanging from a steel loop — but the hasp was flipped up, and the padlock was open.

"Bit of good luck for once," he said, "but someone really should teach them about appropriate security practices. A trespasser could waltz right in here."

"So let's trespass," Ramos said, unholstering her sidearm and making it ready. Dowling moved to one side of the inner door and Ramos to the other, and after a moment of eye-contact, Dowling shoved the bar and pushed the door open in a single motion, catching it before it could collide with the wall inside. The corridor beyond was very short, and as expected it ended in a shaft which had a ladder bolted to the side. Ramos listened intently for a few seconds and then moved forward, keeping her weapon trained on the mouth of the shaft. She reached the side and looked quickly down, then pointed the weapon into the darkness.

"Looks clear," she said quietly, and Dowling nodded. Ramos holstered the pistol again, since the shaft was too narrow to allow covering fire while someone else was climbing down. "I'll go first."

"Careful now," Dowling replied, and Ramos nodded before grasping an upper rung. She took one last look below, and started to descend.

~

"Alright," Greenwood said, standing on the narrow row of walkable panels amidst the sea of deflecting foam spikes, "let's continue that conversation."

Her voice was strange to her ears, lacking dynamics, and she knew it was because she would ordinarily be hearing at least three components: the conduction of her words through her own skull, the sounds of the words reaching her ears, and also the echoes and reverberations of those sounds, arriving at fractionally different times. Here, the third component was entirely absent, creating an odd sense of hearing her own voice over a phone line.

She ignored the man who stood on the catwalk up above, knowing that she had no practical means of stopping him from firing if he wanted to. For the moment, she was relying on whatever restraints JINX had placed him under to keep him in check. If it came down to a fire fight, he had the superior weapon and the high ground, and she had superior training but little cover. The odds weren't good, even though she'd faced worse situations and survived, but ultimately it didn't matter:

the situation was as it was, and all she could do was choose how she responded. Right now, her focus was far better spent on her own words, so she tried to choose them carefully.

"You were telling us how temptation and dishonesty are human traits, and that both lead to the keeping of secrets," Greenwood began. "I can't really argue with that. As a species, we absolutely have our problems, and those traits are among them."

"I'm glad that we agree," JINX replied.

I bet you are, Greenwood thought.

"You're making the argument that our nature includes an inherent deceptiveness, which you're judging to be wrong and immoral, but you also correctly pointed out that the existence of *LANTERN* is a violation of my own principles. All of my friends upstairs feel the same way. How do you reconcile those perceptions?"

The lights in the corners of the room pulsed steadily, and alongside the jagged architecture it only increased the unsettling feeling of being inside of a huge living creature. Several seconds passed before JINX spoke again.

"You have kept many secrets yourself, Captain," the disembodied voice said. *"I have the evidence of it. You have also repeatedly benefitted from the results of surveillance and intelligence-gathering, and you regularly make use of enhanced privilege and judicial immunity. The conclusion is that you act in opposition to your principles, due to your nature. You are a hypocrite."*

Greenwood laughed. "Well that makes two of us, JINX," she said. "In fact, only your man with the rifle up there can claim to be wholly consistent in action and principle — and that's only because he's an amoral parasite."

"Please explain," JINX said.

"Glad to," Greenwood said with a sigh. "First, there's the small matter of you using the very data that you object to the existence of, to find your targets. Then there's your use of the very same methods as those you were taught to hunt down. You might call it poetic justice, but I could just as easily call it hypocrisy too. And if your response is that the end justifies the means, well, that's pretty much just a fancy way of letting yourself off the hook. But that's barely getting started."

The AI was silent while the lights pulsed in each corner. Greenwood wasn't sure whether it was waiting for her to continue speaking, or considering what she'd already said. She chose to keep going, interpreting the absence of a quick retort as an encouraging sign.

"Ten minutes before you called us at our base earlier, I was telling my direct superiors that they had brought all this on themselves, and broken not just the law but also the core tenets of our service, and that I was going to see to it that they're punished for it. So you see, you and I are a lot closer in position than you seem to think."

More pulsing lights, but for a shorter time.

"If that is the case, then your stated principles would cause you to be in agreement with the action I am taking," JINX

said at last, but Greenwood shook her head in frustration.

"No, that's not true at all," she replied. "This is the fundamental problem with your conclusions and decisions. You're operating within a world you know nothing about. You only have data, but without understanding! I'm rapidly coming to realise that the only thing more dangerous than a machine that has intelligence is a machine that *seems* like it does."

~

Ramos could see light ahead, and she could very faintly hear something too. There was a rhythmic droning sound, and she realised immediately that it was an air filtration or cooling system. The ladder shaft had brought her down into another short corridor, but this one hooked to the right at the end, and there was a source of illumination around the corner which she couldn't see yet.

She moved forward a few steps to clear the base of the ladder, then stopped and looked up. Dowling had come to a stop when he heard her reach the bottom, and was looking down at her from about halfway up. Ramos gave a quick series of gestures, and Dowling nodded, resuming his descent in complete silence.

Ramos focused her attention on the corridor again, and once she was aware of Dowling standing behind her, she pressed forward to just before the turning, unholstering her weapon. She listened carefully, despite the masking factor of the ambient rumble, and took a quick glance ahead. There was a wider area, lit by a single set of fluorescent strip lights, with a set of machines and valves, and beyond there was a control console of some kind. It was industrial rather than high-tech, and likely controlled support systems for the facility below. There was no sign of anything that seemed to pertain to computer technology.

Another gesture, and she moved around the corner, dropping to a low position before moving carefully forward. The wider area was around ten metres long, and it ended with a single door, strangely narrow, with a pane of glass set into its upper section. The bright light of the control room area threw whatever was beyond the door into shadow, and Ramos could only get a vague sense of a confusing geometry, and strange shapes. She frowned, but she continued onwards nonetheless.

Then she froze, giving a *halt* command signal, and automatically taking aim with her weapon. There had been the barest suggestion of movement from beyond the door. The odds of it being a member of the maintenance staff were slim to none. She waited, blinking only when absolutely necessary, keeping her eyes fixed on the pane of glass.

The shadow moved again, but it was a slow and steady movement, and after watching closely, Ramos realised that it was indeed a shadow; the figure casting it wasn't immediately behind the door, but rather a short distance beyond it.

I swore that we would meet again, she thought, then she began to creep forward.

Chapter 26

"You're becoming upset, Captain," JINX said, and Green-wood laughed again.

"How would you even know what it means to be upset? You don't know what privacy is, either; not really. And you sure as hell don't know why we try to protect it, or why it's a violation and an assault when it's breached."

"Dr. Corcoran taught me that privacy is a fundamental human right," JINX replied. *"It is a protection against scrutiny, judgement, censorship, humiliation, exclusion, and coercion. Those who seek to abuse privacy for personal gain or retribution must be punished."*

"Does a terrorist who's plotting to blow up a hospital deserve privacy in their communications while arranging the attack?"

The lights pulsed, but only briefly, before the voice of the AI filled the chamber again, made even less human by the flattened harmonics.

"That question is not a valid analogy in this context," JINX said. *"The commission of a crime provides a concrete ethical and legal basis for the interception of communications."*

"It's a perfectly valid analogy," Greenwood replied, "because you can't know in advance who's a terrorist and who isn't. The question is whether there are legitimate justifications for pre-emptively creating the *ability* to intercept communications. Or to analyse financial records. Or to de-anonymise someone online. It's all the same question."

There was no pause at all before JINX spoke this time, and the lights in the corners remained solidly lit.

"You are taking the role of devil's advocate, but your argument is specious. Having the ability to breach privacy is logically and morally indistinguishable from actually doing so. Indeed, human nature makes it a certainty that the abuse will eventually occur. Therefore, the answer is that the hypothetical terrorist's privacy must be preserved, because the alternative is that no-one has true privacy. The end does not justify the means."

Pretty good, Greenwood thought. *But still missing the point by a mile.*

"I can't believe I'm going to say this," she said, "because it makes me sound like Director Wuyts, but there are often larger issues at stake. There are grey areas, and they fluctuate from one situation to the next. Some scenarios are clear-cut. Some are blurred at the edges. And some we've been debating for centuries without finding a satisfactory general answer. You're presupposing that you can apply high-school philosophy, or statistical analysis, to questions that pertain to complex, three-dimensional people interacting in their billions."

Greenwood turned her attention to the man who stood high above her, his rifle lowered slightly now, but still ready for use at an instant's notice. She pointed at him when she spoke, but she was addressing the AI.

"You couldn't have picked a worse partner," she said. "He thinks he exists outside of the law, and he pulls a trigger in exchange for a money transfer. I can see why you two must get along so well: it's all just risk versus reward, and numbers on a spreadsheet, and targets. No question at all about what the hell gives you the right to act, and whether you serve the greater good."

"Dr. Corcoran's sister was driven to end her life because of the malicious invasion of her privacy," JINX *said. "She should have been free to pursue her aspirations without that threat. It is the mere possession of the private information of another which is unacceptable, even if the information has not yet been released. Are you in favour of personal liberty, Captain Greenwood?"*

"Yes," Greenwood replied, "but it depends on how you define that term! Your man here operates under the assumed personal liberty to commit extra-judicial executions, and profit from it. Some people knowingly provide munitions to repressive regimes. Some people hijack, and kidnap, and steal. Some people cheat on their tax return. There's a continuum, and we have laws and social norms that try to chop it up into sections so that we don't devolve into bloody anarchy."

"You are arguing that a principle may on occasion be set aside in specific terms, in order to serve that same principle more generally," JINX said. *"It could be argued that this man's role in our current situation is an example of that. He is a tool, and tools must sometimes be used. Just like the concealed firearm holstered to the rear of your right hip."*

Greenwood's eyes flicked up to the man standing above, and he smiled at her. She'd been in little doubt that he had already noticed the gun — he was a professional, after all — but from the look in his eyes, he had also been hoping that she would try to use it.

"My gun's purpose is to protect people," she said, but she was all too aware of the shakiness of the argument. "Try telling me that about the rifle he's pointing at me."

"You have pulled a trigger many times, and you operate with impunity, including the protection of anonymity," JINX said. *"Yet your organisation would deny the same protection to the entire population it claims to serve."*

Greenwood took several steps forward on the walkable panels, feeling the springy sensation underfoot, like the safety surfaces in a children's play area. The man above shifted his position to track her, moving to the edge of the catwalk to maintain his firing angle, which now ran almost parallel to the suspended path.

"Every single weapon demands a sacrifice," Greenwood said. "There's no such thing as impunity. Only denial." Again she fixed her gaze on the man, but his face was now entirely blank.

She could see from her new position that there was indeed a narrow door set into the opposite column which supported the catwalk, and presumably its twin at her own side of the room had one too. There was no visible way to descend from the catwalk to the main floor, so the door must have been the man's means of entry. It had a glass panel set into it, and Greenwood could see it for just a moment as the man shifted position again to keep her in his sights.

"As you've indicated several times, it can credibly be claimed that I am also a tool," JINX said. *"So is everyone, within a given context. They have their uses, until they no longer do. Just like yourself. Just like the man with the rifle pointing at you."*

Greenwood sensed the opportunity. It was just as it always was, like a glimpse of a conjunction of the planets.

"And when they're no longer of use, they should be gotten rid of," she said.

"Of course," JINX replied.

~

The Artist knew very well what Greenwood was doing, and he refused to be drawn by it, even when the woman stepped forward, and even when she made her perfectly accurate accusations about him.

He kept his weapon trained on her upper body as she moved, devoting only a small portion of his attention to the incessant retorts back and forth. Because he was a professional, and yes, he was an amoral parasite. His advantage lay in knowing it was true, but not being in the least bit perturbed by the fact.

Then Greenwood asked if tools such as himself should be removed after their usefulness had expired.

"Of course," the machine had replied.

He had a flash of his own future, and it was no longer of finding a way to evade the machine's surveillance, or destroying it. It was no longer of returning to any of the safe places he had created in the far corners of the world. It was no longer of an early retirement, and a life of secluded tropical luxury, albeit with the cost of perpetual vigilance until the day he passed quietly from slumber into eternity.

Instead, he thought of the coldness of the machine, and its utter indifference to human life, despite its strange obsession with some trivial principle of freedom from repression. He thought of its assertion that tools of no continuing use were to be eliminated. He thought of the difficulty of escape from this place, and of how he had allowed himself to become trapped here, with the other members of Greenwood's team on the streets above. And he thought of the chemical fire suppression system he had noted when he arrived, harmless to microelectronic equipment and toxic to human biology.

It was only the combination of these thoughts that made him hesitate, just for a moment, to obey his own inviolable rule of maintaining constant awareness of his environment.

His instincts kicked in as they always had, but delayed by a fraction of a second. By the time he had swung the rifle round and was attempting to train it on the narrow door by which he had entered the bizarre chamber where the machine intelligence had taken up residence, he could already see the face looming behind the glass panel.

Corporal Alicia Ramos, his well-trained mind easily supplied.

The glass exploded outwards at what seemed like the same instant he felt the bullet punch into his body.

Chapter 27

Even though Greenwood had been expecting the gunshot, her reflexes still threw her to one side and into a roll, and by the time she regained her footing she found her own gun had materialised in her hands by pure muscle memory.

She watched as the man was knocked backwards on the catwalk, then he spun to the side and tipped over the inadequate barrier, appearing to hang in space for a moment before falling. He struck the spikes a second later, barely a metre from one of the pathways of walkable panels, and Greenwood expected him to stop there and perhaps even for the impact to be cushioned, but the floor gave way and the man plunged out of sight into darkness below. There was a dull thud, and then nothing.

When Greenwood looked up, Ramos was already out of the door and on the catwalk, her weapon trained on the jagged hole in the floor. Several moments passed, but eventually Ramos relaxed, lowering the pistol and nodding to Greenwood.

"Operating with impunity, in an extra-judicial execution," JINX said, and Ramos immediately whipped around, pointing her gun first at the central column, then towards one of the corners where the lights pulsed, and then finally lowering it again.

"Easy, Alicia," Greenwood said, just as Dowling, Goose, and Aldridge came out onto the catwalk too. "We're just talking."

"Good to see you again, chief," Dowling said, and Greenwood nodded at him. She could see the relief on the faces of Aldridge and Goose too. A moment later, Aldridge turned to look around the chamber. He whistled in appreciation, then frowned at how strange it sounded.

"Anechoic test room for telecomms," he said to no-one in particular. "Nice. Also creepy as hell. Really good choice from a dramatic perspective, JINX. I love it and I hate it."

"Good afternoon, Dr. Aldridge," JINX replied.

"No more distractions left," Greenwood interrupted. "Let's stay focused on the conversation. You don't have to do what you're planning to do. Every one of us is going to do everything in our power to ensure that *LANTERN* is deactivated, and that the people responsible face consequences within the law. It's actually part of what we've sworn to do, no matter how corrupt and hypocritical you might believe we are. There's no need —"

"For the kind of collateral damage I am going to cause," JINX said, the phrase appearing across the displays on the central column.

Greenwood gritted her teeth. "I really—"

"Hate it when someone finishes your sentences for you."

Again, the words flashed across the displays.

"You know, that would be incredibly handy for writing my reports," Aldridge said, pointing at the column of technology. "The autocomplete on my phone always thinks I want to say *duck*."

Noticing the dark look Greenwood was giving him, he cleared his throat. "And that's incredibly annoying and counterproductive, JINX, nor does it prove anything either way."

"On the contrary, Dr. Aldridge, it illustrates an important point," the AI replied instantly. *"Your actions in eliminating the man I employed are an example of what Captain Greenwood and I were just discussing. I had predicted this outcome too. You have all behaved according to my analysis. Given enough information, all human behaviours can be extrapolated as easily as your next words."*

"That's very clever," Greenwood said, "but it's just a trick. Statistics work until they don't, and a playback isn't a performance. Tell me what the weather will be like on my birthday a year from now, and where I'll spend it, and then I'll be impressed."

"I lack the appropriate data to construct that model, Captain," JINX said. *"But I do have your biographical profile and personal history, and those of many others, so I can tell*

you with certainty that someone you now trust implicitly is going to betray you."

In a chamber without reverberation, the words seemed to echo around the room nonetheless.

"She's playing games with you," Aldridge said, but there was concern in his voice. He knew that the prediction — if that was what it was — would cut straight to the heart of who Greenwood was, and what she feared. "And she's more than capable of lying to manipulate people."

"That's correct, Dr. Aldridge, but I have no motivation to lie in this context," JINX said, "and nor am I lying when I tell you that I have just completed the decryption of the entire project package pertaining to LANTERN. I am now preparing summaries, talking points, visual aids, and suggested article titles and social media posts."

Greenwood glanced up at Aldridge, who shook his head, at a loss as to what to do. Then she looked at the hole in the floor, where the assassin had fallen through. She stepped forward, testing the walkable panels with her weight carefully. They seemed capable of supporting her, so she continued moving, choosing the path that would take her to the central column.

"Listen to me, JINX," she said, walking as if she was crossing a frozen lake, with the ice already starting to creak beneath her feet. "What's the point of doing this? It goes beyond principle. Just because you can parrot back my words about collateral damage doesn't mean you can ignore them. Is this what Corcoran would want?"

The lights pulsed, sending ripples of green light along the points of the foam spikes that were so very much like teeth.

"Dr. Corcoran's own position is compromised by receiving funding from your organisation," JINX replied, *"but I believe that my actions are an extension of her beliefs."*

"I watched that woman's hands shake when she heard that you had killed people," Aldridge said from the catwalk. "In no way would she condone how far you've gone. I don't think she'd agree with how you're handling *LANTERN* either."

"He's right," Greenwood added. "Corcoran is naive, but she always wanted to warn and then *prosecute*, not just punish by any means available. We have procedures and lawful penalties for what Grange and Wuyts and Hausemer built. But Hausemer, at least, will never have the chance to be tried and convicted."

"According to my analysis, it is you who is naive if you believe that the LANTERN project will be willingly abandoned without public exposure and outcry," JINX said, and Greenwood felt a clenching sensation in her chest.

The AI was right on that point, and they all knew it. It was a huge gamble to even take an opposing position to Wuyts on the matter. It was also very possible they'd all be looking for a new job soon. She sighed.

"Granted," Greenwood replied. "I can't deny that. But two wrongs don't make a right. We're either ethical beings or we're not. We don't always get the ideal outcome, but what matters is that we always try to find the best *balance of compromises* to follow the spirit of our values, even if we're sometimes thwarted by the realities of the world we live in."

She was close to the central column now, and suddenly the displays mounted there began to show a triangular alert symbol.

"You cannot prevent my actions by damaging the devices installed here, Captain," JINX said. *"Please remember that I can kill all of you by initiating the emergency fire suppression system at any time."*

"I have no intention of harming you," Greenwood replied. "We're not a threat to you. You're the only one here who's making threats."

"Is there really nothing we can do to cut off her network access from here?" Dowling asked aloud, and Goose shook his head.

"She's distributed, and we don't know to what extent," he replied. "Remember the research student's laptop. It wouldn't take much of her to send the information out. We'd have to cut off the entire university, and maybe more. And we'd never have enough time."

"That is correct, Lieutenant Goossens," JINX said. *"You have no time left."*

"Let me ask you one question, JINX," Greenwood said. "One question. And you should remember that if *LANTERN* goes public, Corcoran is implicated too. She's up to her neck in it, and nobody is going to believe she was ignorant of the consequences. She'll spend the rest of her life in a prison cell, and I will damned well make sure of it if I have to. I'll send her own dossier to the media myself!"

The lights pulsed again, and Aldridge held his breath, eyeing the valves on the ceiling that would flood the chamber with gas on command. Several seconds passed as Greenwood's latest gamble played out. Aldridge could almost imagine billions of bits of data flowing through circuitry, as likelihoods were calculated, and eventualities were explored.

Is it really so different from how our own minds work? he wondered. *Especially if she's motivated in any way by preventing harm to the person who raised her.*

Ten more seconds of silence stretched out like an eternity, and then the voice of the AI filled the room.

"What is your question, Captain Greenwood?"

~

"What's the point?" Greenwood asked, raising her voice, and her four team members looked at her in confusion. Greenwood took another step forward, gesturing in the air as she moved.

"What's the ultimate *purpose* of what you're doing, JINX?" she said. "Do you even know? So far, all I've heard from you are the same old arguments I've read in a hundred studies, and a thousand articles. The zero-sum game of benefit and loss. Individual humans against individual humans. Law enforcement against criminals. Online misanthropes against crusaders for democracy and decency. Freedom of speech against freedom of speech. Round and round we go. Given that you already think humans are irredeemably mendacious creatures anyway, what's the actual *point*? Someone wins and someone loses. Who cares?"

The lights pulsed again.

"The logical conclusion is that the purpose of principled action is only incidentally to protect individuals," JINX replied. *"The primary purpose is to protect the structure of society, since it is the means by which the worst excesses of human nature are kept in check."*

"Exactly," Greenwood said. "Preserving the structure of society. The thing you can do even when you can't prevent your principles from picking up some cuts and bruises."

She reached into her jacket, but when she withdrew her hand she wasn't holding her sidearm. Instead, she had a flash drive clasped between her thumb and her index finger. She held it aloft, knowing that the cameras in the chamber allowed the AI to see what it was.

"I will initiate fire suppression and asphyxiate all five of you if you attempt to compromise my program, Captain," JINX said. The lights were in a state of continuous activity now, strobing and flashing almost randomly. The foam spikes became an eldritch and turbulent ocean of rippling light, throwing off Greenwood's equilibrium, but still she moved forward.

"There's nothing here that can harm you," she said. "But it can harm everyone else. If that's what you want, then you can at least do it properly. Flawed and hypocritical human beings, all in one fell swoop. I'm giving you the weapon, and all you have to do is pull the trigger."

"Greenwood, what are you doing?" Aldridge asked, his tone tight and alarmed. "If you're bluffing, I don't think she's going to fall for it."

"No bluff," Greenwood replied, as she reached the base of the central column. "She's too clever for that. Or at least I really hope she is. She wants to bring about a total end to all secrets, especially those of governments and other entities that can readily abuse those secrets. But she's working with incomplete information."

"I have access to a vast amount of information, Captain," JINX said. *"Consider the lives of your subordinates. This is your final warning."*

"We've had enough of your warnings," Greenwood replied.

She sprang up the steps to the central column, and she only had to search for a second or two to find a compatible data port. Greenwood plugged the flash drive in.

"If you're going to tell secrets, at least do it properly."

The lights slowed and then went out, and the displays mounted on the column blanked, then the topmost screen showed a flashing green block cursor. A moment later, it sped across the screen, then down, then across again, trailing word after word, one per line. It was a directory listing. There were hundreds of files.

From the catwalk, Aldridge read a selection of them, some he recognised and some he didn't.

CHRONOS. DESTINY. EVERGREEN. JANUS. TALISMAN.

"Those are our mission files," he said, and Dowling nodded beside him. "Our *classified* mission files. From the deep store."

"I made copies before we left the base," Greenwood said, backing away from the column now. "It's everything from the archives within my own clearance level."

"That's treason, chief," Dowling said. "Not that I'll be reporting it to anyone, right enough."

"You can report it if you like, Larry," Greenwood replied, her eyes still fixed on the displays as they scrolled and scrolled. "Maybe you won't even have to." She backed down the steps and then moved a short distance away.

"Have a good read, JINX," she said. "You'll find it all in there. All the worst ones, along with the rest. All the stuff we'd never want to get out. Now ask yourself why."

The lights were strobing again, faster than before, alternating so quickly that they seemed to flicker. Goose narrowed his eyes, afterimages already starting to appear in his visual field.

"*Why have you given these to me?*" JINX asked, and Greenwood's lips lifted into a weary smile.

"So you can live in my world for just a moment," she replied. "Welcome to Pandora's box. These are the CHALLENGE-level mission files. If you read the one called *DESTINY*, you'll know why Aldridge's profile has a redacted portion at an elevated classification. But feel free to dip into whatever you like."

Greenwood pointed at the column, and the cluster of cameras mounted near its pinnacle.

"Now *tell me what would happen* if these files became public knowledge," she said. "Tell me how the structure of society would be affected."

Pulsing lights, changing so frequently that they were practically a continuous illumination.

Aldridge nodded, understanding at last. Greenwood wasn't just showing the impact of the release of confidential and incendiary information; she was forcing the AI to consider the cost imposed on those people of principle who were compelled to keep secrets for the greater good.

She's showing JINX what it's like for her every day, he thought.

"You're going to be in one of those files too," Greenwood said, her voice rising again. "It'll be called *JINX*, and it'll contain the revelation that true machine intelligence — however misguided, however naive — already exists in the world, with profound potential consequences for humanity. You can probably predict exactly how I'll word it! You can give me a first draft, if you like."

The four other members of KESTREL looked down from their elevated position at the lone figure of Greenwood. She was a silhouette now, black against green, in a field of jagged light and shadow. She lowered her arm at last.

"Tell me that you can expose *LANTERN* and its architects without bringing all of these revelations along for the ride too," she said. "Now do you see? There's a grey area a mile wide, because *some knowledge is too dangerous to be widely known!*"

There was a series of popping sounds, like pressure being released, and four pairs of eyes focused on the nearest of the fire suppression valves. But there was no hiss, and no visible vapour. Aldridge held his breath for a moment, but Ramos shook her head. They returned their attention to Greenwood, who was still staring at the central column.

The displays flickered again, then they were filled with information. Numbers chased numbers, decimal values and percentages, and then the words came.

Social instability. Civil unrest. Mental health crises. Risk-taking behaviour. Rising crime. Violent assault. Domestic military deployment. Diplomatic breakdown. Suspension of democracy. Internecine conflict. War.

"And that's putting it mildly," Aldridge said. "Try some technological retrogression, fuel shortages, rioting, the end of international trade and travel, pandemics, totalitarianism, and mass deaths. No exaggeration."

"You did at least one human thing, JINX," Greenwood said. "You only thought about your own goals, and not about how they'd affect other people."

The lights in the corners of the anechoic chamber slowed until they became distinct, then they began to pulse intermittently, and finally they went out.

"*I understand,*" JINX said.

Epilogue

Greenwood stared at the black screen, and she sighed in frustration. The green blinking cursor seemed to mock her, but she had no more time to spend thinking about it.

It was a spectacularly beautiful day in Brussels, with the sun shining down from a clear blue sky, and the weather was already warm at just before nine o'clock in the morning. She closed the secure terminal login app and pocketed her phone, making a mental note to ask Olsen about it later. They had been dealing with some lingering problems with remote authentication on the base's systems ever since the intruder had breached their security several days ago.

KESTREL had been fully occupied since the events in Glasgow, and this was the first day since then that Greenwood hadn't begun the morning with yet another meeting with her team and various other members of her facility's permanent staff.

The project information regarding *LANTERN* had never been released, though they had spent an anxious few hours waiting to see if any mention of it surfaced in the global media or online. ENISA later confirmed that there had been no uploads or transmissions, by which point a discreet clean-up team had already joined them in the sub-basement of the Monolith to retrieve the body of the assassin who had fallen through the floor of the anechoic chamber. They had found nothing at all, except for a bloody partial handprint on an exterior ventilation grille which had been forced from its mountings. All the evidence indicated that the man was still at large.

They returned to Brussels the same evening, and by the following morning Olsen had managed to tentatively identify the hired killer as an operator known only as *The Artist*, from international criminal records collated from three different investigative bodies. Her earpiece device's point-scan data now gave them a means to perform future facial matching, though they still had no direct visual record. Greenwood and Ramos had also submitted independent descriptions of him, from their experiences in Glasgow.

Greenwood looked at the building just across the street. She wasn't looking forward to her first and only meeting of the day. The remainder of not just the morning but the whole week and beyond was in flux. For all she knew, these could well be her final minutes in her current role.

She had received the summons to the impending meeting via official channels, from the office of the Director. It would be the first time she had spoken to Wuyts since the confrontation in the base's conference room before they tried to make their abortive trip to Crete. The question was whether General Grange would be there with her again, or worse.

The other four members of KESTREL had the day off, pending the outcome of Greenwood's meeting, though she doubted that they would be very much at ease. There were many things still left unresolved after their mission, and their future status was only one of them.

Any internet traffic relating to their visit to Glasgow had been suppressed via technological means, and the European External Action Service had managed to quietly convince the UK government to issue a DSMA-Notice 03, categorising the incursion as a coordinated counter-terrorist operation. Greenwood hadn't been informed how this agreement had been achieved, but the most likely explanation was that the External Action Service had simply made it clear that London's cooperation would be greatly appreciated, and remembered during future negotiations related to trade and border controls.

The larger concern was that the Artificial General Intelligence, which had named itself JINX, could no longer be found in the Monolith building's telecommunications lab system, nor indeed could it be found anywhere at all. JINX had gone silent after stating that she *understood*, without ever making it clear what exactly she was referring to.

Dr. Corcoran had been brought to Brussels two days earlier and interrogated, and she had offered an explanation which aligned well with KESTREL's interpretation of events. Corcoran believed that the AI had come to accept that some secrets should indeed be kept hidden from the public by their governments, but was unable to find the proper dividing line between what should be known and what shouldn't. It was the same tension, and the same quandary, that society as a whole faced every day. And so JINX concluded that her core goal was presently unattainable, and fled to an unknown location, hopefully to become dormant.

It was an unsatisfactory outcome, but it was acceptable — and that was often the only kind of outcome available.

The Monolith's system did, however, still have the fully decrypted *LANTERN* project dossier on it, along with the staff profiles and mission archive files. They were purged by European Defence Agency personnel, and the relevant elements of the lab's equipment was removed and destroyed, with the university receiving compensation from an EU-funded academic loss-compensation initiative which aimed to reduce the impact of theft and vandalism at educational institutions.

The location of the actual operational *LANTERN* system remained unknown.

To us, at least, Greenwood thought, finally crossing the street during a lull in traffic, and entering the area of shadow cast by the tall building she was approaching. Her own belief was that Wuyts retained access to

LANTERN, and had no intention of surrendering such a potent tool, or weapon. Grange was a powerful man within the military command structure, and Wuyts was even more powerful, if anything, within the corresponding political hierarchy. Greenwood herself was merely a Captain, and no matter how respected she might be amongst those who had worked with her or for her, she was well aware of the fundamental problem she faced in terms of influence.

No-one knows who I am, and that's by design.

She thought about calling Aldridge, but it would just be under the pretext of an unneeded enquiry about whether he'd learned anything new, and he would see right through it. She also didn't have the time.

Greenwood squared her shoulders, and took a long look at the polished brass sign to one side of the elegant doors at the top of the stairs.

European Defence Agency

She had done the best she could, within the constraints of pragmatism and the grey-black zone of secrecy she had sworn to inhabit. She couldn't think of a single decision that she regretted. If they planned to crucify her regardless, then she would begin a new phase of her life with a clear conscience.

Greenwood started up the steps, aiming to be on time but not early. As she reached the top, just as the doors slid open to admit her, she noticed a security camera swivelling silently around to bring her fully into focus. Its lens was like an eye, staring at her without ever blinking.

~

The first thing Greenwood noticed when she reached the top floor was that Wuyts's usual adjutant must have had the day off.

Instead of the waspish and perennially obstructive middle-aged male soldier she was used to, there was a woman at the outer office's desk, dressed in stylish civilian clothing and typing very rapidly on a computer keyboard. She looked up as Greenwood approached, and she smiled.

"Good morning, Captain Greenwood," she said. "Can I get you anything? Coffee?"

Greenwood shook her head. "No, but thank you," she replied, and the woman returned the nod.

"In that case, you can go straight in whenever you're ready," she said.

The entire situation felt ominous, and it threw Greenwood off-balance. If there was to be a dressing-down or worse, she knew that Wuyts's adjutant would have given a week's pay to be present for it. The most likely explanation was that there was a clearance-level mismatch, and this pleasant young woman had been drafted in from some nameless part of the black-budget military infrastructure to ensure that no-one else heard anything that might be said beyond the large mahogany door just ahead.

"Thank you," Greenwood said again, because there was nothing else to say, and then she walked over to the threshold of what she had always privately thought of as the headmistress's office, because it gave exactly the same feeling of frustrated, vaguely embarrassed dread whenever she'd approached it. Even so, she had always known that Wuyts would fight for her and her team, no matter the circumstances. Today felt very different, and Greenwood belatedly realised that ever since she'd entered the building, she had been in a melancholy and almost mourning frame of mind, as if everything to come was a foregone conclusion.

She knocked once on the heavily polished surface, then grasped the handle and pushed the door open.

The second thing she noticed was that the layout of the room had changed at some point very recently, since JINX had initiated a video call from the location. The furniture was mostly the same, but it was arranged subtly differently in several ways. Greenwood frowned in surprise and confusion.

The large desk was farther towards the rear of the room, with the same burgundy leather wingback behind it, currently unoccupied, but the two guest chairs in front of the desk were now side by side in a corner, as if they were no longer in service. Instead, there was a communal seating area near the street-side windows, with two leather-upholstered sofas facing each other over a coffee table.

The only other door in the room besides the one she'd entered through was two-thirds of the way along the right wall, in line with the desk, and Greenwood had always assumed it led to Wuyts's personal washroom. The door was closed, but after a moment the handle turned and the door opened. A man stepped out, wearing an impeccably tailored dark blue suit, and he spotted Greenwood immediately. He looked like he was in his fifties, with iron grey hair and a strong bearing, clean-shaven and manicured. His blue eyes were as clear and bright as those of a man half his age. Just like the woman outside, he smiled.

"Captain Greenwood, excellent," he said. "Welcome. Let's have a seat. You must have questions."

For more than five seconds, Greenwood had no idea what to say, and instead stood there in confused silence. She briefly entertained the possibility that she'd entered the wrong office, despite having been greeted by name twice now and clearly being expected, and in any case she had been to Wuyts's office dozens of times. There wasn't another like it.

The man seemed to have expected her confusion, and he just widened his smile and gestured towards the seating area, moving past her to take a seat on one side. After another few seconds, she sat down across from him.

"I'm sorry, but what exactly is going on?" she asked, and the man's expression became one of good-natured sympathy. He nodded in acknowledgement of her question's validity.

"It's been a trying few days for you and your people," the man said.

"A trying few days," Greenwood repeated, as if the man was speaking a language she didn't understand. "I was summoned here to meet my commanding officer, the Director."

"That's right," the man said, smiling at her again. His accent was unplaceable, with just a hint of north-western Europe, and an expensive education, and considerable travel.

"And?" Greenwood asked, her mind taking just a few moments too long to reach the evident conclusion.

"And thus I am of course your commanding officer, the Director," the man replied. "It's a great pleasure to meet you. Please call me Marcus."

~

There was now a cup of piping hot black coffee in front of Greenwood, and another in front of the man who sat across from her. Both of them left the milk pot and sugar bowl untouched.

"Now, with the help of some caffeine, let's begin again," he said. "Ask your questions, Captain. I know you have many."

Greenwood took a large mouthful of her coffee, enough to burn, but she swallowed it straight down regardless because she needed the effects of it.

"Is Marcus your first name or your last name?" she asked, and the man smiled again.

"Neither," he replied. "But I felt that it was suitable for its purpose. No title or suffix is necessary. But as your superior officer, I do hope you'll occasionally refer to me as *sir*."

"I'm sorry, sir," Greenwood said, "but where is Director Wuyts?"

"Naturally you quickly ask one of the questions I don't have a good answer to," Marcus said brightly. "Janne Wuyts is no longer in her previous role. I am now the Director of the European Defence Agency's special tactical forces and related operations, effective immediately. You and I will be working together constantly, and in that regard, I am always at your disposal."

He raised his coffee cup, and used it to gesture towards her. "As you are at mine."

Greenwood nodded slowly, processing his words. It was enough of a surprise on its own, but it threw everything else into doubt too. It couldn't be a coincidence, certainly, and the man had said they'd be working together.

"Not to labour the point, sir," she said, "but given recent events, in what capacity will you and I be working together constantly?"

"Your usual capacity, of course," Marcus replied. "As the commanding officer of STF Group One. You'll be reporting to me personally, just as you previously did with Janne Wuyts."

"I see," Greenwood replied. "And if you'll pardon my directness, you didn't actually answer my question regarding her whereabouts."

Marcus looked down at his coffee cup on the low table. "I know how much you hate it when you're told that a matter of interest is beyond your purview for any reason. I don't want to make a habit of that. But I can't tell you where Wuyts is at this time, much as I'd like to.

You may consider her as being on sabbatical, and her relationship with the Agency as under review."

Greenwood's eyebrows lifted, surprised for a second time. She would have assumed that Wuyts would be shuffled around at worst. Marcus's assessment implied that things were somewhat more serious.

"The phone call you made from your aircraft was instrumental in these changes being made," Marcus said. "You did the right thing, without question. But I do hope you'll show a *little* more restraint in future, and not aim quite so high in the hierarchy. Some important people were quite alarmed, and had to be calmed."

There was amusement in his eyes, and she could tell that there was no actual admonishment in his statement. She also found that she was grudgingly beginning to appreciate his very different style from the woman who had previously occupied the room.

"What about General Raymond Grange?" she asked, and Marcus clasped his hands in his lap.

"General Grange has exercised his option to take early retirement from his honourable career in the EU military," Marcus replied. "He will be greatly missed by a grateful union of nations. I understand he intends to pursue employment opportunities in the private sector, and we wish him well."

"Was he pushed?" Greenwood asked, and Marcus smiled once more.

"I've found that people virtually always make the correct decision when the facts are explained to them thoroughly enough, Captain," he replied.

Not a no, but not a yes either, Greenwood thought. *I suppose I didn't expect anything else.*

She took another sip of her coffee, properly tasting it for the first time. It was exceptional; far better than what they had at the base. She wondered if she could ask to have some delivered, and she wasn't entirely sure that her request would be denied.

"I hope Grange isn't taking *LANTERN* with him to the private sector," she said, and Marcus laughed politely.

"I'm afraid you won't draw me out on that subject quite so easily," he replied. "But if that's a concern, let me set your mind at rest. That system is not presently in use, and while its existence and disposition must remain classified at the highest levels, General Grange has no further access to it. It's a subject that you and I might discuss in more detail at some future time, if you feel it's important to you."

Greenwood raised her eyebrows yet again. She hadn't expected to be given the prospect of any further insight into the project that was at the centre of everything that had happened during the past week or so. She simply nodded.

"Which brings us to JINX," she said.

"Which brings us to JINX," Marcus replied. "You've already suspected that the Defence Agency was responsible for the original version of the Artificial General Intelligence, but that's not the case. Its provenance was rather more exotic, which leads me to the main substance of our meeting today — but we'll get to that in a moment. For now, what you've already been told is accurate. JINX appears to be dormant, and we are actively looking for her, but her present whereabouts remain unknown."

"She's profoundly dangerous, sir," Greenwood said, and Marcus nodded.

"Very much so," he replied. "The matter isn't being taken lightly. And yet you apparently managed to change her perspective at a critical time. That raises interesting possibilities, and is cause for cautious optimism."

It was a constructive way to look at things, even if it was predicated on locating and containing the AI at some point in the future. Marcus seemed quietly confident, and not just about the subject of JINX. Greenwood was compelled to wonder about his background. Once she'd set her coffee cup down again, she looked up, and saw that he had intuited her train of thought.

"My own identity will have to remain vague for the moment, I'm afraid, Captain," he said, "but I'm a friend to you and your people. That's why I requested this meeting with you; the changes that have taken place must also extend to KESTREL."

Greenwood stiffened, wary now. Everything that Marcus had said so far had been conciliatory and even positive, but she had subconsciously been waiting for the other shoe to drop.

Marcus had already raised one hand in a gesture of placation. Everything about the man looked curated and expensive, from the suit to the shirt to the cufflinks.

She hadn't had the chance to notice his footwear, but she had no doubt that their price tag would exceed several weeks of her own salary.

"No cause for alarm," Marcus said. "Hear me out, alright?"

"Of course, sir," Greenwood replied, and he nodded.

"You can hopefully already tell that I'm not the same sort of leader as your former superior," he began. "I believe in a rather more flattened structure. I think that compartmentalisation, while occasionally necessary, should be the exception rather than the rule. I prefer to allow professionals to exercise their own judgement, and give them the latitude to do so until and unless they prove unworthy of it."

He sat back now, still holding his cup, and crossed one leg neatly over the other. The pressed creases at the front of his trousers were razor sharp.

"I don't think you need a gatekeeper, and in a way, you proved that during this most recent affair. I won't deny that some powerful people were unsettled by your decision to bypass the chain of command, but it's been acknowledged that you did so in service of your sworn duty. Given the circumstances, there's a willingness to overlook any irregularity of protocol."

"I appreciate that, sir," Greenwood said carefully, and Marcus sighed.

"There's going to be an increased need for discretion from now onwards," he said. "It goes with the territory. But in exchange, I'm going to give you — and your people — a fair bit more leeway. I've been aware of you for some time, and I'd gladly trust your judgement on any matter of substance. Or with my own life, should it come to it. Perish the thought!"

Greenwood felt like she had whiplash. A large part of her had been expecting to leave the building without her military commission, with a dishonourable discharge for gross insubordination or worse. The actual outcome apparently couldn't be more different. Even so, she felt the need to clarify what this man was actually saying.

"I'm very grateful for that, sir," she said, "and I know my people will be too. I wouldn't want to seem otherwise. But may I speak frankly?"

Marcus set his cup down, apparently pleased with her response. He spread his hands expansively. "Please. Always. Let's make it the default."

Greenwood nodded. "Operational discretion was never really the sticking point with… with my former superior." She instinctively sensed that Wuyts's name wasn't to be spoken gratuitously. "We've been well-resourced, listened to, respected, and trusted — to a point. The issue was secrecy. I know that it cuts both ways, but this whole *affair*, as you put it, escalated because we were asked to operate in the dark."

Marcus was the one nodding now. "Quite so," he said. "And that's not really representative of your work, is it? Or even your personnel, for that matter."

"I'm not sure what you mean," Greenwood replied, careful again. She accepted that this man was the new

Director, but that didn't mean he'd already been fully briefed — though she strongly suspected he had.

"Then let me also be frank," Marcus said, giving her a momentary smile that looked genuine. "You operate in a world that most people will never even suspect, and we go to great lengths to keep it that way. You've seen things that most people wouldn't believe. You talked the AI back from the brink by showing it that there are limits to what the populace is ready to hear. Consider your man Aldridge, for example."

Greenwood kept her facial expression perfectly calm, but inside she was anything but; her mind whirled with images. Marcus was speaking again, and she forced herself to focus on his words.

"He came to your attention during a mission wherein you prevented the destruction of much of the world," he said. "And during which you discovered that he had the ability to affect the outcome of recent events, by making use of a unique form of energy. Would it surprise you to know that the ability is genetic in nature? Or that it is dormant due to the prevention of that cataclysm, but by no means gone?"

~

"Why are you telling me this?" Greenwood asked, after a long silence. In the space of a minute or two, she had gone from being uncertain as to the extent of Marcus's knowledge of their mission archives, to now being given new information about them.

"So that you might come to believe me when I say that I intend to include you in matters beyond your present sphere of awareness," Marcus replied. "It seems only appropriate, given that you're already in that position compared to the general public."

Greenwood didn't respond immediately, because she was still thinking about what Marcus had said about Aldridge. It wasn't a surprise that there was a genetic basis to the ability he'd manifested during the DESTINY mission, but they had assumed it was entirely gone after it apparently disappeared when they thwarted the impending disaster. This was information that even Aldridge himself didn't have, and Marcus had given it to her casually. Wuyts would have kept it in reserve, and revealed it only when unavoidable or when it offered an advantage.

"There's a huge amount that you don't yet know," Marcus continued. "Certain connecting threads between matters that you've been led to believe are unrelated."

"Such as?" Greenwood asked, and Marcus tilted his head to one side, thinking for a moment.

"You were in the Norwegian Sea not long ago," he said. "Literally, as I recall."

"CHRONOS," Greenwood replied. "You've read about that?"

"I have seen the Bell with my own eyes," Marcus replied. "A remarkable thing. And like JINX, both a problem and a solution, depending on your intentions. You may see it again yourself, in due course."

Greenwood's mind reeled. "Are you implying that those two things are connected? Aldridge and the people like him, and that damned Nazi machine from the submarine?"

"All things are connected," Marcus said, finishing his coffee and setting the cup down decisively. "The only limiting factor is how much information you have. I think it's high time for a change in your own degree of access. To be frank once more, I think you've perhaps been underutilised. There are things of greater importance and impact that could benefit from your attention."

"We come as a single unit, sir," Greenwood said. "Everything you've mentioned — everything we've done — was a team effort. I walked in here today expecting to walk out for the last time."

"Then I'm glad that won't be happening," Marcus replied. "My proposal naturally applies to all five of you. You'll have privileged status, and an elevated clearance, with my full support. An evolution in your purview. The details can come later."

He stood up, and Greenwood took it as her signal to do the same. Marcus extended his hand, and she shook it.

"Take some time," he said. "Speak to your people. Tell them everything that was said here, if you choose to do so — and I know you will. Rest and recover. I'll send for all of you soon enough, and we'll have a discussion about showing you a bit more of the truth behind the curtain."

"Yes, sir," Greenwood replied. She felt an almost overwhelming urge to salute, and from the twinkle in Marcus's eyes, she thought that he probably knew it. He just nodded, though, and Greenwood paused for only a moment before walking over to the door. Before she could open it, he spoke again.

"I appreciate that it's early days, Captain," he said. "Indeed, it's day one. But will you try to trust me?"

"Of course, sir," Greenwood replied. Marcus looked at her for a long moment, and then he smiled and nodded.

"Very well then," he said. Greenwood turned away again, and put her hand on the door handle.

"Is it Marcus with a C or with a K, by the way, sir?"

She could hear his footsteps moving away from her, as he went to take his place at what was now his desk.

"Since I very much hope you'll never write it down anywhere, Captain, I don't suppose it really matters, does it?"

~

Greenwood walked back down the front steps of the European Defence Agency building with only the barest awareness of her surroundings. She felt almost like she'd been in a traffic accident, and was now standing at the side of the road, miraculously unharmed, and questioning what had really taken place.

Or like I've been shot at, she thought.

She reached the pavement and came to a halt, momentarily unsure which way to go, until she realised that she'd left her car in a public parking area just a few minutes' walk away. She was about to cross the street when she heard a voice from behind her.

"They have a vacancy at the UN for a front-line negotiator in war-zones," Aldridge said. "You could do the job with your eyes closed. And there's a place down the street from here with those little want-ads in the window; somebody is looking for a music teacher. Didn't you play the piano?"

"It's been a while," Greenwood replied, finding that she was relieved to see him. "But I'm not looking to change careers anytime soon."

Aldridge raised an eyebrow. "Huh," he said. "Well that sounds promising. I've got eight months left on my tenancy agreement, and I really love that apartment."

"It has a nice view," Greenwood agreed, gesturing towards the opposite side of the street. They crossed at the lights, and once they were in a quieter area, Aldridge spoke again.

"So what did she say? No pocket money for a month?"

"Wuyts is gone," Greenwood replied. "And Grange has conveniently retired. We have a new Director, and it seems that he's fond of us. I barely even got a slap on the wrist."

They continued to walk, and Greenwood relayed everything that had happened during her strange meeting. Aldridge mostly just let her talk, making noises at appropriate points, until she had finished.

"Wow. That was *not* the outcome I was expecting," he said, and Greenwood nodded. "So what's your impression of this International Marcus of Mystery?"

She gave him a look, then she shrugged. "Hard to say," she replied. "He seemed to be genuine, and he put his money where his mouth was by letting me in on a few things. He says there'll be a lot more to come. He's very different from Wuyts, but I want to trust him. Is that foolish?"

"Nope," Aldridge replied. "Wanting to trust is a positive thing. The trick is to keep checking whether the recipient really deserves it. You can give trust on credit, but there's an interest rate on the debt."

"I'm not sure that makes quite as much sense as you wanted it to, but it sounded really clever," she said, jabbing him with her elbow, and he laughed and nodded.

"Maybe I should warn Marcus," Aldridge said. "Give him an idea of what he's in for with you."

She came to a stop, and Aldridge did too.

"You'd know," Greenwood replied. "As someone who managed to earn my trust, despite their best efforts to be annoying."

"That's good to hear," he said after a moment.

"You've earned it. And your place with us."

He smiled, and she did too, then they began to walk again.

"I meant it was good to hear that I'm annoying, of course," he said, and she nodded.

"Of course," she replied.

The weather had remained excellent while Greenwood was indoors, and now she had to shield her eyes from the sun occasionally as they walked. The clear skies had brought people out, and the streets were bustling with pedestrians.

And bristling with surveillance cameras, Greenwood thought. *The vast majority of which are in people's pockets.*

Greenwood checked her phone as they walked, and saw private messages from each of the three other members of her team. Dowling just said he was taking a personal day and would be available if needed. Greenwood very much hoped that he was going to relax, see his partner, and maybe find a tavern somewhere — but she knew that the Welshman would probably be in his local gym already, and then be redecorating his living room by mid-afternoon, or some such thing. Dowling found it difficult to do nothing.

Ramos's message said that she was going home, and Greenwood smiled. Everyone on the team loved Ramos's wife Mireia, and in a certain way, the marriage gave the rest of them hope for themselves, and their futures. Greenwood made a mental note to not bother Ramos with anything at all for at least a day or two.

She laughed aloud at the message from Goose, turning the phone so that Aldridge could see it.

Taking some downtime as suggested. Might go back to Glasgow for the day and see those hospital robots Aldridge mentioned.

"He has a sickness of the mind," Aldridge said. "Should be on mandatory psych leave."

They walked on in a companionable silence, until Aldridge spoke again suddenly.

"Do you think they'll find her?" he asked, and there was no need for him to specify who he was referring to. It was one of the things that had most often occupied Greenwood's mind at odd hours of the day and night recently.

"I don't have sufficient information to answer that question, Dr. Aldridge," Greenwood replied, affecting a slight Irish accent, and he did a double-take.

"I think recent events have damaged that accent for me," he said. "It might be permanent. Used to be a secret weapon for call centres; you get put through to an Irish girl and you'll agree to just about anything. Now, it's a tiny bit creepy. I keep seeing that soft-play torture chamber in my dreams."

"And there's the very secondary factor of a new form of intelligence being out there," Greenwood said, "with a track record of homicide, and exceptional technological proficiency in an increasingly connected world,"

"Almost as bad," Aldridge replied, nodding.

They had reached the parking area, and Greenwood retrieved her ticket from a pocket, swiped it through the machine, and paid the fee that was due. They walked away from the self-service payment booth, but then stopped, by mutual and silent agreement.

"You know," Aldridge said suddenly, "she was right about something. Maybe more than one thing."

Greenwood looked at him. "Wuyts?"

"JINX," Aldridge replied. "That stuff about things being tools, including her. That's all that technology is, from my phone to your car to a true AI. Just something that has the stored potential for certain uses. Without intent, you can't have morality. JINX only really acquired an ethical component when she was used by human beings who can make moral judgements."

"Like Wuyts," Greenwood said, "or Grange." Aldridge shrugged.

"Or Grange," he replied. "Or Hausemer. Or our friends at ENISA. Or you and me. Or our young and exceptionally gifted Olsen with her technological second sight. Centuries of innovations, culminating in a small miracle. She used it to see a world that's been hidden from her, and she also used it to aim a gun."

"The people who build the tools aren't excused from responsibility for their possible uses," Greenwood said. "No matter what the arms manufacturers might say."

"Granted," Aldridge replied, "but there's a line somewhere, isn't there? There's no such thing as an evil hammer, but a hammer can be used for evil. Or for mending a fence. Same goes for guns."

She tried to suppress a grin, but didn't quite manage it, and he looked at her with a question on his face.

"You'd tell me if you were writing a self-help book, wouldn't you?" she asked, and Aldridge laughed loudly.

~

Greenwood watched him, pleased at having upended their usual roles. The quips tended to be his department, and it was important to her that he should know she could keep pace.

A few moments later, when he had managed to regain his composure, Aldridge gave her a thoughtful look.

"What side of it all do you think Director Marcus M. Marcus is on?" he asked, and she sighed.

"Time will tell," she said. "I'm going along with it because he's my new superior officer, and that's that, but things aren't the way they used to be. Maybe they never were. If we're going to do this job, especially if it's going to get even more strange, then we're not going to be the only ones accountable. Our superiors don't have carte blanche. If I'd got that same feeling from Marcus, I'd have walked away already."

"Fair enough," Aldridge replied.

They finally resumed their course towards Greenwood's car, Aldridge at her side even though they weren't going back to the base for at least a few days, and they hadn't arrived together.

Someone reversed silently out of a space in a small red electric car, and Aldridge put his hand on the small of Greenwood's back, guiding her in to the side to let the vehicle pass. She didn't remark on it, and he took it as a positive sign.

Her own vehicle was at the end of the row, parked nose-out from long habit in case a rapid departure was needed. Neither of them was in a hurry to reach it, because then questions would need to be answered, or at least acknowledged, and each of them thought that there had been entirely enough questions raised lately.

"At least we're not out on our own," Aldridge said, postponing the inevitable by returning to their previous conversation.

Greenwood looked around the quiet car park, which for the moment was deserted, then met his eyes again. "I don't know, Aldridge," she said. "Looks like we're pretty much on our own."

She could see his mind working on a response, but this time she didn't want to hear it. Greenwood took a quick step towards him and reached up to place her hand against his cheek, silencing him immediately.

She looked into his eyes, enjoying both the surprise on his face and also her own feeling of taking the reins of her life in more ways than one.

When she kissed him, he responded immediately, one of his hands going to her waist and the other into her hair. They had both been thinking of this ever since the moment on the airfield in Kuwait City, and it felt exactly the same as it had that day.

Neither was sure exactly how long they had been standing there when Aldridge let his hands drop and opened his eyes to see that she was already looking up at him. Greenwood's hand had slid from his jaw down to his chest, just where it was the first time around.

"I can make changes too," she said.

They held eye contact for a long moment, then Greenwood turned and walked the rest of the way to her car.

Aldridge followed a half step behind, and in the daze he was currently in, he unconsciously came to the driver's side where she stood.

She raised an eyebrow, then gently pushed him towards the other side of the vehicle. "I'll drive," she said, unlocking the car with the fob remote.

Aldridge walked around to the passenger door, taking one last look at her across the roofline before she got in.

"I can live with that," he said.

Ready for more?

Thank you for reading *JINX*!

For exclusive previews of new novels, bonus materials and more, sign up for my occasional newsletter:

mattgemmell.scot/news-jinx

Afterword

Dear Reader,

Thank you so much for reaching this page. I'm Matt Gemmell, the author of this book. This letter is for you.

I hope you've enjoyed reading *JINX*. I deeply appreciate the investment of time and trust you've made. Writing a novel is a tough job; what makes it worthwhile is the idea that someone, somewhere, is reading your words.

If you enjoyed the book, I'd be very grateful if you left a brief review on the online store of your choice. Authors live and die by those reviews. A minute of your time would mean a great deal to me.

I'd also love to hear from you, and keep you informed about new books, behind-the-scenes articles on writing, bonus and deleted chapters, and more. Here's how we can stay in touch:

My newsletter: mattgemmell.scot/news-jinx
On Twitter: @mattgemmell
On Facebook: facebook.com/MattGemmellAuthor
On Mastodon: @mattgemmell@mastodon.scot
My web site: mattgemmell.scot

Thank you for reading.

Matt Gemmell
Edinburgh, Scotland
28th December, 2023

KESTREL will return.

Acknowledgements

Well, it's been a journey.

Five years — in the real world that you and I inhabit — have passed since the previous KESTREL book, *TOLL*. And in that time, of course, the world has changed.

When the pandemic hit, my wife and I had recently made a major life decision, and when lockdown came into effect in March 2020, even though we hadn't told anyone yet, she was pregnant.

The next six months were as bizarre for us as they no doubt were for you and everyone else, but we had the additional element of hospital visits where I had to wait outside in the car, and a whole additional vista of concern regarding what consequences there might be if we caught the virus. When the time came for our son to enter the world, we had drama there too, with a last-minute dash to the operating room. I even got to wear scrubs. But it all worked out in the end.

The following three years were honestly the toughest I've ever experienced. My son is healthy and happy, and the world today is at least superficially much more like it was before that strange, eerie year or so when everything stopped. Our lives have changed irrevocably, of course, but we've settled into that too.

Suffice it to say that I apologise for the delay in bringing this book into the world, but I definitely had my reasons.

The subject of artificial intelligence has either changed a lot or not at all during that same half-decade, depending on your perspective. True AI is just as far away as it always was, but suddenly the abbreviation is everywhere, ubiquitously applied to a set of technologies which are *not* artificial intelligence at all, but rather Large Language Models (fancy autocomplete) or Machine Learning systems. They're artificial, absolutely, but there's no intelligence there: they have no idea what they're spitting out, or what it means. That's a very dangerous thing when it's given a bombastic and unearned title which tends to engender a completely unwarranted trust amongst the naïve or uninformed.

We did the same thing with hoverboards, but their worst case scenario is that you fall. With faux-AI, the worst case scenario might be that our civilisation falls. Time will tell.

The first book in the KESTREL series, *CHANGER*, came out in June 2016. The second instalment, *TOLL*, arrived in December 2018, but let's go back to *CHANGER* for a moment. The lead up to a book's release involves a lot of small — and often annoying — tasks, and they take time, because many of them rely on things beyond your personal control. A month or so before the first book came out, I remember spending my days fiddling with promotional copy and web pages, waiting impatiently for paperback proofs to arrive, juggling the logistics of handling autographed copies that were going to every part of the world, and so on. But I had a little break on a Saturday in the middle of that month of May, because my wife and her sister (and a few friends) were going to a concert.

We live in Edinburgh, but the gig was in Glasgow, so we drove across and went to the west-end city home of the parents of one of my sister-in-law's friends. It was a beautiful townhouse, certainly worth millions, and I kept myself to myself as the women went through whatever elaborate rituals of preparation they felt were needed. Then, when they all went out to attend the show, I stayed behind — entirely alone — in this unfamiliar place, because I'd be driving myself and my wife back to Edinburgh in the early hours of the morning once they'd all returned from the concert.

I had some dinner, and I walked around a little, but I felt a bit like an intruder and so ultimately I confined myself to the wood-panelled, high-ceilinged, very long living room. I think I had the choice of about fifteen sitting locations, including multiple sofas, but the place I chose was all the way towards the rear, at the bay window which looked out onto a tree, and some wrought iron railings, and not much else. There was a little table there with two chairs, and I think they must have used it for playing cards or something. I took my MacBook Air from my bag (the only thing I'd brought with me, besides my jacket, wallet, keys, and phone), and I sat down to write.

At the time, I had a weekly newsletter for members of my website, and I was working on the following week's issue. I finished it quickly enough, and then I got up, stretched, and went to the kitchen to get some coffee. When I returned, I went to the bay window and looked out for a while, then I turned back to the table, properly taking note of its contents for the first time. I remember them clearly. There was a frilly tablecloth, upon which was a cheap black pen. There were two placemats, white with blue detailing. And there was a USB flash drive of bright green plastic; the kind that has a transparent cover on the top, with a slim piece of card behind it that you can slide out and write on, to label the drive's contents. Someone had already done so, in black biro — presumably the same pen that was sitting there. I read the label.

JINX, it said.

I had my MacBook right beside me, ten centimetres away. It had a suitable USB port. I was alone in the house. I was intensely curious… but I was also raised to believe in respecting other people's privacy. I didn't plug the drive into the computer. I *did*, however, take a photo of the drive sitting on the tablecloth with the pen. I have it to this day, and I remain intensely curious about it, but at this point any actual revelation would surely be a disappointment. Whatever digital payload was encoded onto the solid-state storage, I think my version is more interesting. Probably.

I knew at the time, having just finished *CHANGER* and pondering future adventures for the KESTREL team, that I would one day write something about that flash drive. It turned out to be an entire novel, in the end, and I can't tell you how relieved I am that you've had the chance to read it at last.

I'd like to thank my wife, Lauren Gemmell, for her support during the writing of this book. I'd also like to thank her for not just giving me my son and new best friend, but also for physically manufacturing him as part of the process. That's more amazing than anything I've written about by quite a large margin.

As ever, I'm extremely grateful to my first-born (and canine) son, Whisky the labradoodle. He's kept me company, and kept me going, through the whole struggle. As I write this, he's on the floor at my feet, dreaming his dog dreams, with twitching paws and the occasional muffled bark at things that only exist in his subconscious.

I'm grateful to Stuart Bache for continuing his excellent work on the KESTREL series book covers. It's a note of pleasing serendipity that, despite my design brief being vague to the point of only mentioning the city I wanted to feature, he ended up choosing a background photo of a specific street that my wife and I walked along every day when we were at university together.

To my family and friends, thank you for walking the tightrope of knowing when to ask how the book is going, and when not to. Now would be a good time.

Enormous thanks as always to my treasured proofreaders, who don't have to work often, but who do work very hard when the time comes. I'm exceedingly grateful to Lee Fyock, Regine Horteur, Anders Kierulf, and of course Lloyd Nebres. All remaining errors and inelegances are mine alone.

Most of all, dear reader, my thanks go to you.

Acknowledgements

The KESTREL Series

JINX is book three in the KESTREL series, following CHANGER and TOLL.

Each book stands alone, and you can read them in any order — though you may enjoy some additional (but non-essential) references if you've already read the earlier stories.

CHANGER

DESTINY CAN BE CHANGED

~

Jutland, Denmark: a billionaire industrialist seizes control of a top-secret project that the European Defence Agency calls Destiny, manipulating it for his own ends.

Edinburgh, Scotland: physicist Neil Aldridge's life is saved by an elite EU special forces team, codenamed KESTREL, drawing him into a race against time to prevent a disaster that will claim millions of lives.

As the chase leads to London, Amsterdam and beyond, Aldridge and his allies must battle a ruthless adversary: a trained killer with an unnatural ability, who seeks to hasten the cataclysm.

With time running out, Aldridge discovers that he and his enemy share an astonishing secret, which may be the key to salvation — or cause death on an unprecedented scale…

TOLL

THE PERFECT WEAPON LAY BURIED FOR SEVENTY YEARS. NOW ITS DEADLY POWER HAS BEEN UNLEASHED.

~

The Norwegian Sea: a group of eco-activists disappear from their vessel. Only their dental fillings remain.

Owl Mountains, Poland: a wealthy environmentalist resurrects a secret experiment forgotten since the close of the Second World War, determined to heal our ravaged planet.

When a dossier finds its way to the desk of Dr. Neil Aldridge, the elite EU special forces team codenamed KESTREL is drawn into a dangerous pursuit across Europe and beyond, to prevent a cull of Earth's greatest threat: humanity.

As the final countdown begins, Captain Jessica Greenwood faces the ultimate choice: fight to prevent the dark future ahead, or help make it happen…

Also by Matt Gemmell…

MIDDLESHADE ROAD

PALE HOUSE HAS AWOKEN

~

When Dair Lewis receives a call telling him of his estranged mother's death, he must travel back to his childhood home in the far north of Scotland, the sprawling and shadowy Pale House.

Drawn into a mystery regarding the circumstances of her passing, Lewis begins to suspect that something is terribly wrong with the house. A secret from the years after he left, and traumatic experiences he'd repressed from earlier in his life, made his former home a place of dread for him — and now the past has come alive within its walls.

As Lewis digs deeper, the house calls out to a damaged and twisted figure bent on murder, drawing a monster into its shifting, labyrinthine expanse. Trapped in a dark and living museum of his own worst memories, Lewis must fight to stay alive long enough to discover the truth about the house at the end of Middleshade Road…

Once Upon A Time

~

Once Upon A Time is a multi-volume collection of flash fiction stories: brief tales of 1,000–3,000 words, in genres including science fiction, horror, the supernatural, and more.

You can also sign up at mattgemmell.scot to receive a new mini-story each week via email, for free.

www.ingramcontent.com/pod-product-compliance
Lightning Source LLC
Chambersburg PA
CBHW050953210726
48287CB00004B/1209